Praise for the nove[ls]
New York Times bestselling a[uthor]

"Meticulously sensual details and steamy interludes make th[is a...g] erotic read."

Flying

"Hart's beautiful [ ] experience elevate[ ] yearnings of the h[ ] in its many forms." *Apart*

"[Hart] writes ero[ ] book, but it packe[ ] and this is a stunning [ ] *rarian*

"*Naked* is a great s[ ] with her characters.... [ ] that brings them to lif[e] *eviews*

"*Deeper* is absolute[ ] ...the writing is fabulou[s] [s]tory line brought tears [ ] nd bittersweet...Meg[ ] [ ]p Pick

"*Stranger*, like Meg[ ] emotional romanc[ ] a touching love stor[y] [de]livers on fully." Bussel

"[*Broken*] is not a t[ ] [ ]ex woman caught in a difficult situation with no easy answers. Well-developed secondary characters and a compelling plot add depth to this absorbing and enticing novel."

—*Library Journal*

"An exceptional story and honest characters make *Dirty* a must-read."
—*Romance Reviews Today*

New York Times **Bestselling Author**

MEGAN HART

vanilla

MIRA

MIRA

Recycling programs for this product may not exist in your area.

ISBN-13: 978-0-7783-1804-0

Vanilla

Copyright © 2015 by Megan Hart

For questions and comments about the quality of this book, please contact us at CustomerService@Harlequin.com.

www.MIRABooks.com

Printed in U.S.A.

First printing: March 2015
10 9 8 7 6 5 4 3 2 1

This is for you

You know who you are

vanilla

prologue

The hum and the sting.

The artist bent over my wrist, tracing the outline of the simple design with the needle, the gun. Filling in the lines with ebony and shadows. My skin soaked up the ink in a way that made the girl murmur appreciatively.

"This is going to look great," she told me. "Super fucking cool."

It hurt. Of course it did. Tattoos always do—it's not like they're licked on by baby unicorns with tongues made of kittens for fuck's sake. I had two others, a small Jewish star on my right hip and a somewhat-but-not-entirely regretted tramp stamp of a flaming sun on my lower back. This one on my wrist burned worse than the others had. Ink always hurts, but it's a clean sort of pain. An on-purpose ache that lingers when the tattoo is finished and healing, and sometimes even long after, like your skin forever wants to remember how it felt to be so marked.

"What do you think?" She sat back and wiped my skin again of any excess color.

I didn't need a mirror to see the inside of my left wrist. I'd picked that place because I would always be able to see it, whether I wanted to or not. The design there, no bigger than a fifty-cent piece, was simple. Black and gray. Stylized lines and curves that nevertheless clearly made a picture. The skin around the edges of the design was still a little raised and red the first time I saw it. Still stinging. Looking at it would always sting.

"Why a rabbit?" she asked with a tilt of her head. "I don't usually ask, to be honest. I mean, it's personal, yeah?"

I nodded. "Yeah."

"And far be it from me to judge," she continued. "I mean if you'd wanted a butterfly or a fairy or a flower, I wouldn't even ask. But a rabbit's cool. What's the significance?"

"It's so I don't forget," I told her.

She grinned and didn't ask me what I needed to remember. "Fair enough. You're satisfied, then?"

Satisfaction wasn't exactly what I'd been going for. Pain and permanence, yes. An eternal reminder. But since I'd been given those things, and the design we'd worked up together was exactly as she'd drawn it, I had to nod.

"Yes," I told her. "It's perfect."

1

There's something so lovely in the curve of a man's spine when he is on his knees, head bowed, hands behind his back. The back of his neck, vulnerable and exposed. The splay of his toes pressed to the hotel carpet that rubbed at his knees and would scrub them briefly red. I would leave my own marks on him, careful to be sure they'd fade as fast as the rug burns. I couldn't leave anything permanent on him. We'd agreed on that from the first.

I didn't want to hurt him much anyway. That had never been my game. A little sting, here or there. The slap of leather on his bare skin. The press of my teeth or scrape of my fingernails—those were things to make him shudder and moan. I would always rather get what I wanted by promising pleasure instead of pain. That was what worked for us.

Esteban had been waiting for me in that position when I came into the hotel room. The lamps off, late-evening sunshine glimmering through the mostly drawn curtain providing the only illumination. He would've been willing to do the things we did with the curtains open wide, every piece of both of us exposed and nothing soft about it. I was the one who liked the lighting to be dim, unfocused. Dreamy. I found myself more easily that way.

"I brought you a present," I said as I shrugged my shoulder bag onto the desk. It clinked heavily, as I'd meant it to, so that he'd wonder what on earth I had for him inside it—and maybe be a little nervous.

Esteban was not facing me, and he didn't turn while I unpacked my bag, even though I could tell by the strain of his muscles that he wanted to. Desperately. I laid out all the presents I'd brought. Sometimes I had a plan for how things were going to go on our monthly dates. Carefully constructed scenes I worked out thoroughly in my head so I could be sure to get it all right. Not today, though. Today I felt ripe with possibilities I'd not yet even considered.

With a hand behind my back to hide what I held, I took a seat in the chair in front of him. I let my skirt ride up a tiny bit to tease him with the glimpse of stockings beneath. I put one high heel between his knees, my shin grazing his inner thigh.

He smiled, but didn't move. His mouth was a little wet from where he'd licked his lips. I leaned and cupped his cheek, and he nuzzled into my palm.

"My good boy," I murmured. I held out the small box that had once held a bracelet. "Open."

He took the box from me and sat back on his heels to pull off the lid. Inside, a coiled black ribbon. He shivered a little when he took the satin from the box, letting it trail over his hands and wrists. He looked at me, and I tugged the end of the ribbon to wrap it around his wrists, now crossed in front of him, not too snug. There was enough ribbon to go loosely around his neck, too, and to loop down around his already hard cock.

"I thought it would be something...tighter," he said in that delightful accent that never failed to trigger a shiver of my own. "So I couldn't get away."

"If I need more than this to bind you, then I might as well go home right now," I said.

Esteban shuddered, his eyes fluttering closed for a moment. When he opened them, his gaze had gone dreamy and dark. Several beads of sweat had gathered on his upper lip, and his tongue dipped out to taste them.

I loved seeing how my simple words affected him. I leaned to nuzzle the corner of his mouth, close enough for intimacy, though we never kissed each other on the lips. It was another of our rules, this one unspoken but never broken. I stroked a hand over his dark hair and let it linger on the back of his neck, feeling the muscles bunch and pull at my touch. I let my mouth travel along his jaw to his ear.

"Open," I said again, not meaning a box this time.

Esteban opened his mouth at once. Obedient. Willing. Delicious and beautiful and, for the moment, mine.

I slipped my first finger into his mouth. He bit playfully; I took him hard by the chin to make him go still. He gave a soft sigh-moan, so I gripped him a little harder. I pulled his face toward me, teasing him with the promise of a kiss we both knew would never come—but that was part of what worked for us. That promise, that denial.

I ran my wet finger down his chest and circled the head of his erection, which was tapping his belly. When he strained toward me with a small growl, I gripped him tight and said into his ear, "Hush."

He did at once, my good boy, his cock throbbing in my hand. I put my fingers in his mouth again, and this time he didn't bite but instead wet them eagerly for me. I stroked his ribbon-bound cock again with slick fingers, slowly, then moved my hand down to cup his balls.

"Tell me what you want." Sometimes I made him send me a list of things he fantasized about beforehand, though I hadn't this time. And I asked without any intention of giving him what he wanted, which we both knew. Yet today, without a plan, restless and feeling caged by work and family and life, I was curious to see if what he asked me for was something I would give.

"I want to kiss you," he told me, "there."

"Here," I replied, easing up my skirt to show him a hint of lace panties. I pressed my fingertips between my legs and raised an eyebrow.

"Please," he added.

"Maybe." I laughed at his frustrated expression. I leaned to take his face in my hands, looking into his eyes. "You are adorable."

He tilted his head, his eyes half closing for a moment. "I want to please you."

"I know you do. And I want your mouth on me—" I laughed softly again at his shudder. "But not just yet. Get on the bed."

Esteban blinked a few times, not responding immediately. I was ready for that, my hand already grabbing the ribbon tangled around his cock and tugging in sharp command. The tug wouldn't hurt him as much as my disapproval at how long it took him to get to his feet.

If you've ever tried to get up from your knees with your hands bound without pushing off from anything, you know how awkward and graceless it can be. Far from impossible, especially when the binding was mostly decorative. But still, he hated to be clumsy, which was part of the reason I yanked again, urging him to get up faster without taking the time to balance himself. We ended up standing face-to-face, my fingers still curled in the ribbon. In my heels I was an inch or so taller than he was, the perfect height to look down instead of straight on. I'd done that on purpose, too.

"Do you need me to repeat myself, Esteban?"

"No, miss."

"Tell me again what you want," I said.

"I want to please you."

Fuck, how I loved the shiver in his voice. Later, I would make him say it to me in Spanish. I would make him teach me how to reply, and we would both laugh at how I butchered the words. In this moment, though, there was no laughter.

Only anticipation.

I stepped away from him, and his body rocked forward as I pulled the ribbon free and let it fall to the floor. It had been a whim, something pretty to start off with. I'd seen it on sale at the craft supply store while on an errand for my mother and had thought of Esteban immediately. I'd caught myself thinking of him more and more often in the times between our dates. I didn't want to consider the reasons why.

"I want you on your back," I told him.

He took a step backward, then another, before turning to crawl up onto the bed. He'd stripped the comforter off before I arrived, and I took a moment to enjoy the view of a beautiful, obedient male sprawled out on crisp white sheets before going to the array of things I'd already set out on the desk.

I'd picked up the ribbon because it had been a little playful, and the thought of making a gift of him to myself had pleased me. The sleek, smooth object I had in my hand, however, had not been an impulse purchase. I'd taken a long time to research it, making sure I picked the right one. Molded of heavy tempered glass, the heft of it was enough to cause serious damage if you dropped it on your foot…or your balls. It didn't look like a sex toy as much as some sort of avant-garde sculpture, clear glass swirled with blue, red and orange. Cool to the touch, it would warm nicely to body temperature. You could wash it in the dishwasher, according to the product description, though the idea of that made me shake my head. I had a similar toy at home, longer and a little thicker, but the curve of this one had been designed to perfectly caress the prostate. This toy was not for me.

With the glass plug in one hand and a bottle of lube in the other, I knelt on the bed between Esteban's legs. "I brought you another present."

He pushed up on his elbows to look and grinned. "What is this?"

"You know what this is." I put the lube on the bed and ran my hand up the inside of his thigh. He shaved his chest and his balls, but here the fine black hairs tickled my knuckles. I stroked my fingertip along his cock, then lower.

His knees fell open at once, giving me access to his body. When I cupped his balls, Esteban gave another of those delicious, low gasps. His hips rolled.

"Look at your pretty cock, already leaking for me." I circled a finger around the head of it, drawing the slick precome onto my fingertip and holding it up. Locking his gaze to mine, I licked it away. It was a bit of a show for him, to trigger another of those noises, but no lie, the fact that he was so hard, so aroused that he dripped for me before I'd barely touched him, never failed to set me on fire.

"Tell me what you want," I demanded again, but soft and low, my voice a caress and not a slap.

Esteban shifted on the bed, his feet going flat on it as the space between his knees widened. His fists gripped the sheets, but he knew better than to reach for me. For a second I wished he'd try—I would never truly hurt him, but discipline him? Oh, yes. We could do that.

"I want to see you," he said.

I pretended to consider it, holding up the glass plug while I used the other hand to play with the buttons on my blouse. One, two, exposing a hint of nipple. The beauty of small breasts is being able to go without a bra, something which Esteban had once admitted to me drove him wild with lust. I stopped. He groaned. I laughed, and so did he. I put my free hand on his belly and the one holding the plug on the bed to support myself as I leaned over him, letting my mouth brush his chin before I nipped him.

"No," I told him. "You haven't earned it yet today."

He did reach for me then. His hands moved over my thighs and hips, bunching my skirt. He kissed my cheek then my jaw, and found my throat where he nibbled and sucked the way I loved it.

"I can convince you?" he asked into my ear, stroking his hand upward to cup my breasts. Thumbing my nipples through the thin fabric of my blouse, he moaned softly when they hardened at his caress. "So much easier to touch you…"

I slapped his face lightly and gripped his chin, digging the blunt tips of my nails into his flesh. Esteban's eyes closed immediately. His body tensed. His arms went over his head, fingers linking his hands.

I almost came, then and there, his reaction a better aphrodisiac than anything in the world.

"You will touch me when I say you may touch me." My voice low. Dangerous. Stern.

"Yes, my goddess."

"Fuck, I love it when you say that." My fingers loosed their grip, leaving a few marks I soothed quickly with my tongue. I sat back. "Look at me."

He did.

I shifted between his legs then straddled one of his thighs

to press my pussy against him. I was wet through the lace. I held up the lube and the glass toy.

His cock jumped. So did the muscles on his inner thighs. And, a moment later when I pressed a slick finger against his tight hole, so did the muscles there.

It wasn't the first time I'd ever played with his ass. One of the first things we'd talked about when we started this relationship was turn-ons and -offs. Limits, hard and soft. Expectations. Safe words. We'd been practical about it, making lists. Our agreement wasn't anything that would stand up in court, but it was one we'd worked on carefully to be sure it suited us both. Realistic, maybe to a fault.

This was not a love affair.

It was, however, the first time I'd ever used an object on him instead of only fingers or tongue. Esteban had told me his fantasies about being taken that way, and though on the surface what we had together might appear to be all about what I wanted, it was truly about satisfaction for both of us. He wanted to please me; I got off on being pleased. But more than that, I reveled in the way the smallest things I did to him got him hard. Made him ache. I loved making him come for me, his orgasms like a tribute. Something he owed me and I deserved.

I warmed the toy's chilly glass against my hot flesh while I ran my nails, scratching, up the insides of his thighs. Tickling over his balls and the shaft of his cock. I dripped lube on his prick and stroked him, though when he began to move into my closed fist, I laughed and stopped.

Esteban's laugh broke with a gasp. "Please."

"Not please." I pinched his nipple, not hard enough to hurt but definitely hard enough. "You know I shamelessly fetishize you speaking Spanish to me."

His hips had bucked when I pinched him, and he gasped again. *"Compláceme, por favor."*

Spread open for me, unbound but not moving because I hadn't given him permission, Esteban nevertheless gave me a wicked grin. He fucked upward, getting a few thrusts in before I gripped his cock tight at the base to keep him still. His eyes twinkled as he ran his tongue along his bottom lip and said something else in Spanish. I didn't know what it was. I didn't really have to. He could be reciting his grocery list or a poem. My Spanish was limited to ordering off the menu at a Mexican restaurant. It was the sound of him speaking his native language that worked me up, and he knew it.

In response to his naughty teasing, I pressed a slick finger to his asshole, making him gasp. "You want this?"

"Oh…yes. Please, please, please… *Por favor!*"

I tested the glass by pressing it to my lips. Still cool but not shockingly so. I held it up. "You want this?"

He tried to answer and only a soft and desperate noise came out. I grinned, running it along his leg, and let it rest on his belly for a moment so he could feel the weight of it. His smile grew lax, gaze distant.

I'd known women who prided themselves on making their pets cry or wail, but even as a little girl I'd never liked breaking my toys. I liked it so much better when the man beneath me writhed and begged for release not because I was hurting him, but because I was making him feel too impossibly good. Creating desire fed something inside me I'd never been able to fully explain or understand. All I knew was that I craved it and loved it, and Esteban gave it to me. Another few strokes of his cock and he would explode for me…but not until I let him.

That was power. That was control. In that moment, I owned him.

And really, what woman would not love being made a goddess?

Again the throb of desire pulsed between my legs, easing as I coated the toy in lube and pressed it slowly against him. He hissed in a breath, tensing, and I soothed a hand along his cock.

"Open," I whispered.

The plug was so perfectly designed that it practically seated itself, the curve pointing upward toward his belly so that it could press on his prostate. The flared base had a ring to keep it from slipping too deep inside, and also for gripping, so I could rock it back and forth. Esteban cried out when I did that, a low and guttural noise that mimicked pain. I knew him and all his sounds well enough, though. It might be a little uncomfortable, but he liked it more than he didn't.

I let go of the toy and ran my hands once more up the insides of his thighs. I didn't touch his cock, but I did draw a finger through the thick clear liquid that had puddled on his belly. I moved up his body to drag my fingertip over his lower lip then tucked it again into my own mouth and relished the taste of him.

"Tell me what you want," I murmured in his ear.

He turned his face toward me, his breath hot. "To please you."

I was already working my panties over my hips and thighs to kick them off. I inched my skirt up to show him my bareness and the stockings and garters framing it. His cock leaped, tapping his belly—if you'd told me even a few years before that erections did move on their own, that it wasn't something made up for sexy novels, I'd have laughed. But I knew very well now how a man's cock, aroused to the point of spilling without so much as another stroke, could throb and jerk.

"I want your mouth on me, Esteban."

He moaned, his hips rocking so that his cock thrust upward

into empty air. His ass would be clenching on that toy, too, I knew. A long string of precome clung to his prick, and I paused again to admire it. Then, facing his cock, I straddled his face so he could get his talented tongue and lips on my hard clit.

It was my turn to gasp and moan when Esteban's mouth moved on me. I ground onto his tongue, my hands braced on his hips as I leaned forward. I let my tongue swipe the head of his cock, but didn't take it in my mouth. I wanted to tease him, but also myself, and I knew the second I let myself take him inside my mouth, I'd be lost and out of control.

He put his hands on my hips, and I didn't deny him. I liked them there, gripping. He might leave a mark or two of his own.

Lower, I reached to curl a finger in the plug's handle. As I moved on his face, letting his lips and tongue urge me toward climax, I steadily rocked the plug—not thrusting in and out, like I was fucking him, but instead a gentle, steady pressure, on and off that internal pleasure spot. He pushed his cock upward, and I nuzzled the tip for a moment until he gave a muffled cry against me. Then I stopped. I slowed. I rolled my hips to push my clit against him in time to the steady pressure I was giving his prostate.

"Feel it," I said with a hitch in my breath. Words were hard to form, my voice nothing close to steady or stern. But I wanted him to hear me that way, breaking, so he knew how much he was pleasing me. "Do you feel it?"

"Yes," he said. "Oh…"

I pushed up with a hand on his hip, the bone hard beneath my palm. His dear cock was thick, straining for release, the color shading darker the harder it got. He was uncut, something that had been new to me with him, and I let my fingers tease the velvety foreskin that had retracted from his erection.

"I love your cock," I told him matter-of-factly. I raised myself just far enough that he'd have to strain to reach my flesh, but my body was clenching and pulsing, so close to the edge that I wanted to hold off for a moment longer. "This thick, beautiful cock."

"It's yours," he told me, and I let him lie to me because we both wanted to pretend that was true. "I'm yours. I belong... Oh..."

Another string of muttered Spanish, a few words I did recognize, eased out of him on a desperate, gasping sigh. The sound of it, his words, the edge of hungry, mindless pleasure in his voice, was at last enough. I gave him my pussy again and let him feast on me as I sat up, hands on his chest, to ride his mouth until I came.

My body shook with it, hard spasms of pleasure. Esteban's hands gripped me hard, fingers digging. His cock leaped. He cried out against me, and as my vision went blurry from the pleasure, I watched thick come jet out of him to splatter his belly. He came without me even touching his cock, and I went mindless myself at the sight. I came again, hard enough to feel faint, and as the surge of orgasm eased away, I rolled onto my back next to him and splayed, boneless and content, on the king-size bed.

We both lay still for a moment or so, the sound of our breathing the only noise—though the pounding of my heart had been loud in my ears, it was fading. His hand had moved to rest on my shin. My head was close enough to his leg that I could turn my face to kiss the side of his knee. I sat up, moving on numb legs to grab one of the hand towels he'd taken earlier from the bathroom and put on the bed.

"Slow," I said quietly as I eased the plug out of him and wrapped it in the towel to take care of in a bit. I used the edge of the other towel to gently clean him off, and when I was done, him naked and me still fully clothed except for my panties, I curled up next to him with my head on his shoulder to cuddle him.

We breathed together. I laid my hand on his belly, the skin still warm and a little sticky. He'd gone flaccid, but something in the intimacy of this moved me more than I expected, and I cupped him for a moment before pressing a kiss to his shoulder. My eyes closed. I took in his scent, knowing I would leave with it infused into my clothes. I would carry it with me for the rest of the night, until later when I would shower him away. But for now, I felt and smelled Esteban all over me, and for now, I didn't want to move.

He would shower before he left. He always did. Always careful to leave without any evidence that we'd been together, unlike the way I let myself stay covered in him for hours. I never asked him why. I didn't want him to tell me, because then I would know.

His phone buzzed from the nightstand. Neither of us looked at it. His hand came up to stroke my hair and pull me a little closer, something I noticed. Believe me, I did. He chose to cuddle me closer rather than to answer his call, and that might have meant nothing or everything.

A few seconds after the phone stopped buzzing, the trill of a voice mail tone sounded. He sighed. He kissed my temple.

"I need to go," he said.

I nuzzled against him, considering being stern again, but the truth was that I could order and command and demand, but in the end, he would only do for me what he wanted to do. I kissed his shoulder and gave it a small press of my teeth to make him hiss in a breath, then sat to let him get up. When he came out of the shower, his hair rubbed briskly dry and a towel wrapped around his lean hips, I held out the final gift to him in the palm of my hand. Esteban sat on the edge of the bed next to me and charmed me with the pink tinge on his cheeks and the tips of his ears, endearingly exposed by his short haircut.

He took the sleek silicone plug, similar to the one I'd used earlier but smaller and more lightweight, into his hand and curved his fingers over it. He didn't look at me at first, though he leaned into me. I put an arm around him as he pressed his face into the curve of my neck.

"You're so good to me," he said.

"I want you to think of me during the days when we aren't together."

He paused. "I think of you every night before I go to sleep."

"You do?" Pleased, I nuzzled his cheek. When I tried to pull away, Esteban held me close for a few seconds longer. I stroked his hair, petting him.

"I don't want to leave," he whispered.

So don't was the answer that rose to my lips, but I didn't say the words aloud. Briskly, I pushed away from him and cupped my hands around his. It wasn't the first time I'd given him a task to complete while we were apart, but it was the first time I'd added a prop.

"I want you to wear it for me." I squeezed his fingers around it. "At work. Not every day. But when I ask."

And then, as I'd known he would, Esteban nodded and gave me what I asked for.

He said yes.

2

My partner didn't want to work. I wanted to get paid. It was kind of an old argument.

"One of us is *not* independently wealthy," I told him sharply as I pushed his feet off my desk. "Unless you intend to fully support me in my old age, you'd better get working on that long, long list of things I told you needed to be signed off on before the weekend."

Alex Kennedy could've made a career out of being charming, and he knew it. "C'mon, Elise. It's Wednesday. Hump Day!"

"So hump yourself over to your desk and sign these files!"

"Yes, ma'am," Alex told me with a cheeky grin.

I rolled my eyes, refusing to give in to his relentless charisma. "Doesn't work on me."

"Sure it does."

"Not from *you*, it doesn't," I said and pushed a folder toward him.

"Damn it. It works on everyone else."

I lifted a brow. "I'm not everyone else."

Alex got up to pace in front of my desk. "Work is boring

and annoying, and we've been doing it all day. Let's go out for a late lunch. My treat."

"Far be it from me to turn down free lunch, but we have to get all of those clients squared away first. Paperwork." I held up a hand at his groan. "Yeah, yeah, I know. Bane of your existence. I get it. But you're the one who has to sign off on this stuff, or else none of it will go through."

Alex sighed. "Fuck my life. I thought starting my own business meant I got more time off."

"Sign this shit!" I waved the folder at him. "Then take all the time off you want! Buy me lunch, too, that's all good. But get this stuff done, so I don't have to deal with a bunch of pissy voice mails about transactions that didn't go through because you were too busy dancing around to sign anything."

He did dance then, wiggling his ass and giving me another grin. "Dance, dance, dance…"

A short rap at the door turned us both. Olivia, Alex's wife, poked her head around the door. She laughed at my expression.

"Is he giving you a hard time again?" she asked.

"Baby." Alex went to kiss her. "I'm *trying* to take her out to lunch. I'm trying to be *nice*."

"Lunch?" she asked. "At this hour?"

"We've been hard at work all day," he said.

"Well, one of us has. He's being lazy," I told her.

She gave me a face that told me she knew exactly what dealing with that was like. When Alex tried to dance over to her, she held him off with a hand on his chest, though when he dove in to kiss her neck, she giggled and gave in for a minute before pushing him away. Over his shoulder, she said, "I sent you a link to your album with the shots I worked on for the calendar project. I marked the ones I thought came out the best, but you let me know if there are any others you'd like me to work on."

I'd started modeling in college when a friend taking a photography class had needed someone to pose for a final project. The pictures hadn't been very good—my friend was no artist. But as it turned out, I was a very good model. Other people in the class asked for help with their projects, one thing led to another and before I knew it, I'd collected quite a portfolio. And, because I was up for anything, most of the pictures were what my mother considered "filthy." I've never considered being naked on camera porn, but I guess that's in the eye of the beholder.

A few years ago I'd been new to the D/S scene, just getting my feet wet, so to speak, when I'd attended a munch, a purely social meeting sponsored by a group of women and the men who liked to serve them. The munch had been held in a local art gallery, hung with Scott Church's work. He was looking for people willing to pose for a series of BDSM-themed portraits. I agreed. We'd done lots of shoots together since then, from sweetly provocative lingerie cheesecake to hardcore portraits. I liked working with Scott, never for the money even if sometimes there was some, but because I liked having my picture taken. In some ways, modeling, like the things I did with Esteban, was all about control, except that when I posed for pictures, I wasn't the one in charge. And there's power in that, too, sometimes, giving someone else what they want to take from you and make their own.

I'd met Olivia at one of Scott's photography seminars, where I'd been one of the models. Shortly after that, she'd been asked to participate in a local annual calendar project for a Harrisburg charity, and though it wasn't exactly the type of shoot I'd been doing before that, it was for a good cause. The pictures Olivia had taken had turned out to be so much fun and so well received that we were back for a third year.

"Hey, pictures. Can I see?" Alex came around my desk to

look over my shoulder, though I hadn't even opened the email from his wife, much less the online album.

"Since apparently you're not going to bother doing any real work," I told him as I found the link and clicked through, "I guess so."

Alex leaned closer as the screen populated with thumbnails of the shots Olivia had taken. He pointed. "I like that one."

I enlarged it. "Me, too."

Olivia grinned as she looked to see which we'd both picked. "I figured."

Together, we'd done a re-creation of a famous Vargas portrait, the artist known for his pinup paintings of women in various situations showing off their garters and stockings. This one was me in front of an apple-bobbing barrel, my hands tied behind me as I captured an apple in my teeth. Pretty vintage skirt, stockings, a lady with her hands tied. No innuendo about it, this picture was meant to be sexy.

"It's a little too bondagey for a charity calendar," I said. "But it's fun."

Alex looked at me. "It's sexy as all hell, that's what it is."

"You're right, my darling perv," Olivia said, scrutinizing it. "But so is Elise. It's too sexy for the project. The ones I marked would work better. Elise, let me know. I have to run now. I have a shoot scheduled with a set of newborn twins, and their mother tells me if we don't catch them at nap time, it will be impossible to get any good shots. I tried to tell her I could work with kids, but hey, she's the client."

She kissed her husband and gave me a wave before heading out. Alex was now clicking through the rest of the pictures she'd taken. All variations of some kind of pinup imagery, though all far tamer than the first he'd picked. He paused on one of me with my head tipped back and eyes squinted closed, laughing. It had been a good day in Olivia's studio.

"You could do this full-time, you know. Why are you crunching numbers and doing data analysis for me?"

"Because I'm more than just a pretty face?" I posed it as a question, adding an innocent blink and making dead doll eyes. "Because I like to pay my bills and do things like eat and buy stuff?"

"Bills, schmills," Alex said.

I rolled my eyes. "Says the bazillionaire."

"Pfft." Alex leaned over my shoulder again to scroll through the pictures then nudged me. "Seriously, I know my wife's a bloody genius with the camera, but you...look at you."

I looked over the photo he'd pulled up. Critically, I could see what he meant. False modesty is a worse sin than vanity, I've always thought. I was pretty. I'd been pretty my whole life.

"There's more to me than eyes and mouth and tits, Alex."

He stepped away as I swiveled in my chair, and though Alex could be counted on to make light of nearly anything, this time he looked solemn. "Yeah. You're right. I'm sorry."

"You don't have to be sorry." I shrugged, looking again at the pictures. "I like having my picture taken. I like working with Olivia. I like the idea that something we've done together goes to raising money for something useful. It seems to make it worthwhile."

"And if you hadn't met Olivia in Scott's workshop, you'd never have met me, and I'd never have been able to convince you my life would not be complete without you by my side." Alex put his fists under his chin and fluttered his eyelashes at me. "So, lucky me."

I was the lucky one. Alex had started his own investment-planning business a few years back, consulting mostly. He had the contacts and the skills to make people a lot of money if they let him. He'd brought me on as a partner, my job to take care of all the bits of the business he found boring, which was just about everything other than figuring out the best places to make money grow. I handled client accounts, paperwork, office filing, billing...and though there were days when working with him felt more like trying to wrestle a bag of kittens into a top hat worn by an eleven-armed octopus that hated cats, I wouldn't have given it up for any other job. Before agreeing to take on the responsibility of keeping this joker in line, I'd been drowning in the corporate world of human resources for Smith, Brown and Kavanagh, where going to work every day had been like feeling another small piece of my soul shrivel and die.

"Serendipity. If I'd never met Scott, I'd never have met Olivia, and then I'd never have met you while you were throwing a pity party about how starting your own business was so much more work than you wanted to do..."

"It wasn't a pity party," Alex interrupted. "I was just, you know."

"Whining," I told him with a grin and ducked his attempt to poke my upper arm. The truth was, he might like to slack off in the office during the boring bits of paperwork and filing stuff, but he was a genius with the clients. And he knew how to make money grow, no question about that.

He leaned over my shoulder again to look at the picture of me in front of the apple-bobbing barrel. "That picture is hot as fuck, Elise."

From another guy, in another office, this might've been grounds for sexual harassment. Instead I eyed it, then him, with another lift of my eyebrow. "You like the whole woman tied up on her knees with something in her mouth, huh?"

"Who doesn't?" Alex laughed.

It wasn't like Alex and I talked in detail about our sex lives. We'd become friends, but there are some things you don't talk about with the people you work with. Especially when he's a married man, and you're basically the only two people in the office. I had no idea if Alex had seen any of my other photos, the ones I did with Scott. Alex and I were linked on Connex, of course, because these days everybody collected *connexions* like kids used to collect baseball cards. I'd posted a few shots on there a long time ago, but I now avoided putting anything too private on that social networking site because I'd *connexed* with family members. My mother had a hard enough time accepting the fact I posed in my bra and panties. If she saw me in a black vinyl catsuit with a whip in my hand and a man at my feet, she'd have *plotzed*. I wasn't embarrassed or ashamed about any of it; it wasn't a secret, but it wasn't as if I went around introducing myself like "Hi, I'm Elise, and some-times I like to dominate men."

I laughed, too. "Lots of people like it the other way around, believe me."

"Both work," he said with a flash of a grin I suspected had wooed him into the pants of many a woman in his day. Alex Kennedy was just one of those guys who turned heads and made lashes flutter. It wasn't just his face, which was gorgeous. It was the way he looked at you, like what you said mattered, like in that moment, nobody else existed but you.

"You could be a model yourself, you know," I told him somewhat abruptly. "I'm surprised Olivia doesn't use you more often."

Something flashed in his eyes, and a secret sort of smile slipped across his mouth before he focused again on me. "I've let Olivia take pictures of me."

"Uh-huh," I said, but didn't ask. The look on his face told me everything I needed to know about *that*. "Tell you what, rock star, how about you sign off on all this stuff, you take me to lunch and then you can get home early to your gorgeous wife and make some more pictures together."

Alex grinned. "You got it. I'll even take you out for sushi, how's that?"

"Awesome." I pushed the folder toward him. "Sign."

Fifteen minutes later, I was teasing him about how painless it had been to actually finish some work, and we were walking to the closest sushi restaurant. Tucked in a small storefront on Front Street and directly across from the parking garage, it was a favorite lunch spot for a lot of the people who worked downtown. Fortunately for us, Alex's procrastination meant the lunch rush was over, and the dinner crowd hadn't yet arrived. We had our choice of tables in the restaurant's cozy back section, and we took a seat in the corner. The server brought us hot tea and bowls of miso soup. I dipped my porcelain spoon into the golden broth, stirring up the bits of scallion, then blew on it to cool it. I was suddenly starving.

We talked for a while about our favorite TV program. Alex had turned me on to the show about two monster-hunting brothers who drove around in a black Impala—sometimes in the office, we'd toss quotes from the show back and forth to each other, trying to stump the other. Because Alex was way more into the show and had been watching it for a lot longer, he was usually able to beat me at the game. Now, asking me which of the brothers I'd be if I could choose, he claimed he would always be Dean, the older brother, and I was stuck being the younger brother, Sam.

"Except shorter," he said.

I made a face. "And without a penis, don't forget that part. That's kind of important. Anyway, I'm totally Dean. Dean's way cooler."

"We can't both be Dean," Alex pointed out.

"You have Sam hair." I gestured at the raggedy mop of dark hair that spilled over his forehead.

"But you're the smart one, and you do all the computer stuff," Alex said. "You have to be Sam."

We both laughed at that. He pushed the platter of spicy salmon toward me then took some for himself. Alex waved his chopsticks at me.

"So…how was your…meeting…last Friday?"

I paused. My once-a-month dates with Esteban weren't a secret, exactly. Alex had no problem with me rearranging my schedule to accommodate appointments. Well, once a month, always on the second Friday, I had a "meeting." I'd never told Alex what it was for, nor had he asked, until just now, though I could tell by his tone he suspected I hadn't been seeing a chiropractor.

"It was very productive," I told him.

He waited. I smiled. He shook his head.

"What's your story, Elise?"

I gave him a falsely innocent look. "I don't have a story."

"Everyone has a story," Alex said. "We all have secrets. What's yours?"

"If I tell you, it would hardly be a secret, would it?"

Alex grinned. "C'mon. You know you wanna."

All at once I did want to tell him, the sudden urge to share swelling up inside me with unexpected fervor. Why? I didn't know, other than I hadn't told anyone about the lover I'd been seeing once a month or so for the past year and a half, not even my best friend, Alicia. She'd moved to Texas two years ago, which had made it easier to keep Esteban a secret. If I hadn't shared our relationship with the girl I'd known since elementary school, it certainly wasn't something I should share with Alex.

My phone booped with my nephew William's ringtone and saved me. I swiped the screen to take the call. "Hey, kiddo. What's up?"

"Can you come get me from my lesson?"

I paused, dragging a piece of sushi through a puddle of wasabi-smeared soy sauce. "When are you finished?"

"I'm supposed to go until six-thirty but the rabbi had another meeting so he let me go now. I texted my mom a couple times, but she didn't answer me." William hesitated. "I texted my dad but he said he's in a meeting and asked if you could get me."

"Maybe she's stuck in traffic," I offered around a mouthful of rice and fish. "Can you give her a few more minutes?"

Another short pause came, then William said quietly, "Can you please come and get me, Auntie?"

He hadn't called me that in a while. Heading toward thirteen, William had taken to calling me Elise without even an aunt in front of it, a habit that made me sad but one I didn't denounce. Kids grew up. It's what happened.

"Sure, kid. Let me finish up my lunch, and I'll be right there. Another fifteen minutes or so, okay? If your mom gets there first, text me." I disconnected and gave Alex an apologetic look. "My nephew needs to be picked up from his Bar Mitzvah tutoring. I guess his mom's late. I'm only a few minutes from the synagogue. Mind if I run to get him?"

Alex shrugged. "Sure. Are we all done in the office?"

"*I* am." I gave him a significant look that he returned with a grin. "I guess you are, too. Thanks for the sushi. See you tomorrow."

It took me about ten minutes to get back to the parking lot in front of the office. Another ten to get to the synagogue, and only because I hit every red light on Second Street. I spotted William sitting on one of the benches at the shul's front doors. He was tapping away on his phone, head bent, still wearing his *kippah* as was required by the synagogue for males while in the building, though he didn't usually wear one outside it.

He looked up when I pulled into the half-circle drive, his expression wary. I hated to see that on the kiddo's face, not sure why he looked like that.

"Hey," I said through the passenger-side window. "Is your mom on the way or do you still need a ride?"

"Yeah, I need one." William slid into the passenger seat, backpack at his feet, and put on his seat belt without being reminded.

God, I loved that kid. I had a strange and winsome flashback to the smell of his head when he was a baby. My brother and Susan had gotten pregnant and married at age twenty, one year before we all graduated from college. I'd lived with them for the last four months of her pregnancy and the entire first year of William's life, both so we could all save money and to help them out with the baby so they could finish their degrees. I'd changed diapers and done midnight feedings, the whole bit. William would kill me if I leaned over to sniff him now, though, not to mention that I was sure the experience would not be the same as it had been when he weighed ten pounds and fit in my arms like a doll. Instead, I waited until he'd settled before pulling out of the synagogue driveway and onto Front Street.

"Your mom didn't get back to you?"

"She said it was okay if you took me home." William's phone hummed, and he looked at it. "She says she was running late at yoga and to tell you thanks for picking me up."

"No problem, kid. My pleasure." Traffic was still fairly light, though in another half an hour it might start to get heavier with rush hour commuters all trying to merge onto the highway. It was only late April, but one of the first days that promised summer after a bitter and seemingly endless winter. "Hey, you wanna go get some ice cream?"

William shifted to look at me. "Right now? Before dinner?"

"Yeah, of course, before dinner. That's the best time to eat ice cream." I shot him a grin that he returned.

Instead of turning right to head over the bridge to get him home, I kept going a little ways so I could head across town to our favorite ice cream shack. Every year I figured would be its last, that competition from chain frozen ice places would put it out of business, but so far the Lucky Rabbit was still around. My twin brother, Evan, and I had both worked in the Lancaster location during the summers in our long-ago teenage years, flipping burgers and scooping the homemade churned ice cream into waffle cones. Time had weathered the Lucky Rabbit sign and left huge potholes in the parking lot, but that was what Pennsylvania winters did to all the roads, left them pitted and rough.

I pulled into the gravel lot and avoided the ditches as best I could and found a spot near a splintery picnic table. We ordered not only sundaes but also onion rings. Not even a bare nod to providing a reasonable dinner, because aunties don't need to do that.

"So, how's it going?" I asked around a mouthful of hot fried onion dipped in chocolate ice cream.

William shrugged. He'd ordered mint chocolate chip with caramel sauce, a combination that made me shudder. "Okay, I guess. My Torah portion is really long."

"You have time. Another three months or so, right?" His Bar Mitzvah was scheduled for his birthday weekend in late July, which meant a sucky early summer of tutoring and attending services.

He shrugged again. We ate mostly in silence after that—William devouring most of the onion rings, all of his ice cream and the rest of mine that the late sushi lunch had left me incapable of finishing. We talked a little bit about the school year that was coming to a close. His new video game. His best friend, Nhat, who might be moving to another school district. William lingered over the last few bites, drawing it out until I finally asked him what was wrong.

"I don't want to go home," he said.

"How come?" I gathered the trash and watched him from the corner of my eye as I got up to toss it.

William shrugged again. It was becoming his favorite response. "Just don't."

"Is something going on at home?" I sat again on the picnic table bench, wincing at the scrape of the rough wood on the back of my thigh below my hem. I'd be lucky to get out of here without a bunch of splinters in my butt.

"No."

I knew he was lying, but I wasn't going to prod him. William looked like his mother, but he was his father's boy in personality. My brother had always held things close to the chest, and poking him to get him to talk never worked.

"You have to go home, kid. It's a school night. Your dad will be home soon, and I'm sure your mom is wondering where you are."

"I bet she's not."

I paused at this, but decided not to push. "C'mon, let's go. Hey, maybe you can come and spend the weekend with me. You haven't done that for a while."

"Can't," William said sourly. "I have to go to services."

I loved that kid, but there was no way I was going to volunteer to take him to the three-hour Saturday Sabbath service. I'd fallen off the religion wagon long ago, a fact that killed my mother on a daily basis. Her angst about it had probably contributed a lot to my lack of observance. Sometimes you twist a knife because you can't help it, even if you're ashamed to admit it.

"How about Saturday night? I could pick you up after services. We could go to the movies."

"I'll have to ask my mom," William said doubtfully.

"Like she'll say no?" I scoffed, but stopped myself from reaching to ruffle his hair. "I'll talk to her. But it's a plan. Okay?"

That earned a ghost of a smile from him, which relieved me. In the car, just before we pulled into his driveway, I said casually, "You know, you don't have to be perfect at this Bar Mitzvah thing. Nobody's going to be expecting you to nail it without any mistakes, the rabbi and the *gabbaim* are there to help you if you need it. You're not performing a play that you have to memorize. It's okay if you're not exactly perfect."

He shook his head. "Mom says she expects me to do my best."

"Your best," I said as I turned off the ignition. "Not perfection."

I went into the house with him, both to make sure there was someone home before I dumped him off and to talk to my brother if he was there. Evan wasn't, but Susan must've made it home right before we got there because when we came into the living room from the front door, she was coming down the stairs with her hair in a towel. Without missing a beat, she told William to put his stuff away and set the table for dinner. She barely looked at me.

"Thanks for getting him," she said, clearly distracted. "I ran late at yoga. It's this new class…"

"No problem." I waited a second or so, but my sister-in-law wasn't going to give me the time of day. I was used to that. We'd never been close, and I'd never been sure why, but it had stopped bothering me years ago. I took in her wet hair and the smudges of mascara under her eyes. The traces of lipstick in the corners of her mouth. She wore a pair of yoga pants and a loose T-shirt, but also a pair of pretty dangling silver earrings, along with a matching bracelet of hammered links. Not exactly the sort of accessories I'd have picked to exercise in, if I ever did such a thing.

"I was happy to do it," I added when she didn't answer me. "You know, the shul is only a few blocks from my office. I'd be happy to pick him up anytime if you need me to. Or he can walk down and hang out with me—"

That got her attention. Frowning, Susan shook her head. "Walk to your office? In downtown Harrisburg? He's not even thirteen yet, you want him to get mugged?"

I didn't point out that it was literally less than a mile walk along public streets in the middle of the afternoon, not a saunter through back alleys at two in the morning. "If you need me to, that's all."

"Thanks." Her chin went up, and she finally looked at me, though her gaze skated away from mine without holding it. "Yeah, that might be great. It's this new class. It runs—"

"Late, got it." Awkward silence hung between us, and I could've eased it but frankly, I'd long ago decided that whatever problems my brother's wife had with me were of her own making. However, since Evan wasn't home, she was the one I had to talk to about William. "I invited the kiddo to stay with me this weekend. I can pick him up from services on Saturday, if you want. I'll bring him back Sunday."

"He has religious school Sunday morning."

"So I'll take him to religious school," I told her easily. "I'll make sure he gets there on time. Anyway, it'll give you and Evan a date night. You can even sleep in."

A short, harsh bark of laughter rasped out of her before she swallowed it. She did meet my gaze then, for a second or so. "Sure. That sounds great. Thanks. I'll make sure he has a bag with him. Thanks, Elise."

"No problem," I said again. "I love having him."

Another few beats of awkward silence moved me toward the door. I shouted out a goodbye to William as I left, but he didn't answer. Susan shut the door so firmly behind me there was no question about how happy she was to see me go.

Some people love you. Some hate you. Some tolerate you for the sake of keeping the peace, and if everyone in the world managed to do even just that, we'd have a lot less woe in the world.

3

I want to see you tonight.

Not *may I*, or *I wish*, but *I want*. I hadn't been expecting the message, though as far as surprises went, it was definitely a pleasant one. With my phone tucked into the front pocket of my purse while I shopped for a quick cart of junk food for my nephew's sleepover, I'd missed the message when it came in twenty minutes before. I thumbed a reply as I waited in line to check out.

I can't tonight.

To my additional surprise, *JohnSmith is Typing* appeared at the top of the app. That meant Esteban had read and was replying immediately, which wasn't usual for a weekend. In the beginning, we had connected late at night in those dark hours between midnight and three, when smart people were asleep. Most of our conversations now happened during the workweek between two and four in the afternoon.

I really want to see you.

Before I could type an answer, my phone rang. Even more surprised now, because Esteban never called me without asking me first for permission, I thumbed the screen to answer. "What's wrong?"

The woman in front of me gave me a curious glance. I lowered my voice. "Are you okay?"

"I want to see you," he told me, which was not the answer to my question. "Can we meet tonight?"

"I have…" I hesitated. Esteban and I didn't talk about our lives, not in great detail. We talked about our jobs. We talked about sex. The rest of it, by unspoken agreement, was covered in vagueness and clouds. I had my reasons for keeping it that way and had always assumed Esteban did, too. "Plans. I can't change them. I'm sorry. If I'd known sooner—"

"I didn't know I would be able to see you tonight." He sounded disappointed.

We'd never had a last-minute sort of relationship, even before we'd settled into our regular monthly dates. This sudden urgency from him made me wary. "Sorry. I didn't know you'd want to."

"I miss you."

I glanced at the woman in front of me in line, who was clearly eavesdropping. "What's going on?"

"Nothing. You just feel very far away." His voice deepened for a moment, his impeccable English overlaid by that delicious accent that was as much about the spaces between his words as it was the way he pronounced them. Esteban sighed. "I *need* to see you."

Before Esteban, there'd been other men. More than I wanted to think about, not because I was ashamed but because most of them had not been worth the effort. When you lose something you love before you're ready to give it up, you look for it wherever else you can find it, and I'd looked for what

I wanted in a lot of places before Esteban's sweetly respectful message had showed up in my inbox at OnHisKnees.com.

I'm starving, he'd told me when we'd been talking for a few weeks. I'd asked him what he was looking for, why he was on the site. What he wanted. *I'm hungry all the time for something I can't seem to find.*

I understood what he meant. About hunger. About how you could glut yourself on something and yet still be empty.

I couldn't stop myself from liking Esteban. He was sweet and smart and funny; he made me laugh and challenged me mentally as well as gave me delicious orgasms. It wasn't something we talked about, the tenuous emotional connection between us that wasn't supposed to be there because what we had was meant to be only physical.

"I'm right here." I cradled the phone against my shoulder as I put my items on the conveyer belt. I'd kept my voice low, cautious of giving the people around me a free show. "I'm at the store now, though. I have to go. Can you call me in about an hour? I'll have some time to talk to you then."

He sighed. "An hour until I get to bathe in the melody of your voice? Okay."

I disconnected, bemused at his urgency. Flattered, a little. The melody of my voice? It was over the top and silly, but warmed me anyway.

I dropped off my groceries at home and got back in my car to head for the synagogue just as my phone rang again. I let the call ring through to my car speakers so I could drive while we talked.

"Are you driving?" Esteban asked. "I hear noise."

"Yep, I'm in the car."

"Drive to me," he said. "Meet me!"

I didn't answer immediately. It wasn't like him to be so demanding, and though desire is an aphrodisiac, this game had never been about Esteban telling me what to do. I wasn't about to start playing it that way now.

"Hush," I said sharply. "I told you, I can't. I have plans."

I'd heard that same soft intake of breath often enough to know his reaction. It was my tone of voice. The idea of my disapproval and of facing the consequences of it. He'd be hard as a rock right about now.

Damn, I loved that.

"I'm sorry," Esteban said, instantly apologetic.

I softened. "Hush, I said. I'm happy you want to see me. And normally, I'd love to see you tonight. But I can't, as I said."

"You have a date?"

"It's not your concern," I said, harsher than I wanted to be, but proving a point. "I told you I have plans. That's enough for you to know."

"Would he do for you the things I will?"

I didn't answer right away, turning over my own reaction in my head before letting it take control. Other men had tried to bully me into giving them what they wanted, whether it was a blow job or an endearment. I had to remind myself that Esteban was not other men and had proven it time and again.

When I tied him up, I was responsible for making sure he didn't get hurt beyond his limits. I was in charge of his body. I was also in charge, in some ways, of his heart.

"It's not a date, Esteban." His laugh sounded relieved, and I cut him off before he could speak. I believed I understood why he was acting this way, but that didn't change our dynamic. "But if it were, it would not be your business."

"I'm sorry. I should not have asked," he said after a moment. Did I hear a tremble in his voice?

"What's wrong, honey?" I relented. I was alone in the car, but my voice still dipped low. I imagined him, eyes closed, on his knees, leaning to press his cheek into my palm. Esteban's hair is soft and light as dandelion fluff, and his golden skin is always warm. "What's going on? Talk to me."

Another soft huff of indrawn breath. "I miss you, that's all. Wanted to see you. I know it's not our time, but I could make it work."

I looked up to see the synagogue doors opening, people coming into the parking lot. William would be out in a few minutes. I made an offer assuming Esteban would say no. "I have to go. I can't see you tonight, but I could meet you for coffee tomorrow morning…"

"Yes. Yes, I would like that very much. I just want to see you."

Something was going on with him, for sure. "Nine-thirty, Morningstar Mocha. You know it?"

"Yes. Thank you, miss."

It was odd to hear him call me that outside of a hotel room, but it still sent a shiver all through me. "I have to keep my boy happy, don't I?"

The instant the words were out of my mouth, a chill swept over me. Then heat, creeping up my throat and into my face. *Have to keep my girl happy, don't I?* George had often said that, and in the end he'd done anything but.

Not noticing my sudden silence, Esteban laughed and sounded more like his usual self when he replied. "Your boy is desperate for your touch, that's all."

"There won't be much touching in the coffee shop."

"It will be enough," he said.

I spotted another small surge of people exiting the synagogue, but my nephew was not among them. "I have to go. I'll see you tomorrow."

I disconnected, searching for signs of William. When the doors closed and he still hadn't appeared, I got out of the car to go in and find him. I'd forgotten about the Saturday kid-dush luncheon in the rec hall. Following the murmur of voices and the smell of toasted bagels, I spotted William talking to the rabbi at a table with plates of egg salad and tuna in front of them. William was nodding. The rabbi looked serious but then laughed and clapped him on the shoulder.

"Hey," I said, too aware of my jeans and tank top and the fact I hadn't covered my head, though in this Conserva-tive synagogue women weren't required to unless reading the Torah. I was glad I'd shrugged into a cardigan so at least my arms weren't bare. "Hi, Rabbi."

"I forgot you were coming," William said.

"Sit. Have some lunch." The rabbi gestured toward the buf-fet table still set with platters of food, though the custodian was starting to put it away. "We have plenty."

I'd only grabbed an apple on my way out the door this morning, so the thought of a bagel smeared with cream cheese and lox was tempting. Still, I didn't want to linger. I hadn't been to services in forever, so scarfing down a free lunch seemed inappropriate. And I didn't want to fend off any awk-ward questions about when I would be attending.

I shook my head. "I'm good, thanks."

"William tells me you're going to be reading Torah at his Bar Mitzvah," the rabbi said as William scraped his plate clean of the last bites of egg salad.

I nodded and tried to look excited. "Yep."

"That's great," the rabbi said enthusiastically. "We always need more people who can read Torah."

That was my cue to beat it out of there before he started hinting around about minyans or Friday night services or anything else. "Nice to see you, Rabbi. William, we have to get going."

In the car, William snorted soft laughter until I asked him

what was so funny. "You acted like he was gonna chase you around with a tallith until you read Torah for him."

I laughed, too. "Shut up."

"I wish I didn't have to go to services," he said after another minute. "It's so boring."

I couldn't really argue with him about that, not without being a total hypocrite. "A few more months, kiddo, and you'll be all done."

"Mom says she expects me to go to Hebrew High and get confirmed, that the Bar Mitzvah isn't the end of my Jewish education." William scowled.

"Your mom might change her mind, you never know. What does your dad say?"

William rolled his eyes. "He doesn't say anything."

Evan hadn't gone on to any further kind of Jewish education after his Bar Mitzvah, and he'd muddled through that, leaving me to take charge of most of the service we'd shared. If he went to services at all now, it was only because of William. Susan, however, had always been a little more observant.

I shrugged. "Well, kid, it's been my experience that moms are the ones who get to decide stuff like that. So I'd say talk to your mom about it. You never know. She might listen."

"Did yours listen to you?"

It sounded like a legitimate question, especially since I had to remind myself that to William, my mother was "grandma" and therefore, an entirely different entity. "Not usually."

He laughed. I did, too. I turned on the radio, and we both started rocking out to the Metallica song that came on.

It was a good day, but most of the ones I'd ever spent with that kid were.

4

Batting cages, junk food for dinner, an inappropriate movie I knew his mother would not have let him watch. That's how Auntie rolled. William had tried to convince me to let him stay up late watching old episodes of *The X-Files* from my DVD set—we were up to season four, and the kid was justifiably hooked. I made him go to bed, instead. Eight in the morning would come early, and I'd promised to get him to religious school on time. I wasn't totally irresponsible.

I didn't really need a three-bedroom town house since it was just me, but I'd bought it as an investment with an eye to having a room for William's visits. My nephew was likely the only child I would ever have. I liked that he felt as at home in my house as he did in his own. I checked on him about midnight and found him with the bed lamp still on, highlighting the paperback novel he'd been reading. He was sprawled on top of the sheets the way he'd always slept. When he was little I'd tuck him back under the covers and kiss his forehead, but now that he'd outgrown me by a few inches, he was too big for me to move around. I marked his spot in the book and put it on the nightstand and turned off the light then closed the bedroom door behind me.

Eight in the morning was still going to come early for me, too, but sleep ran away from me as fast as that annoying little fuck the Gingerbread Man from the story William had loved so much when he was a toddler. In my bed, I tried to read, but I'd finished the book I'd been working on for the past week so I stared up at the ceiling, instead.

I counted backward from one hundred, but that didn't work. I did it again. Still nothing.

I could've been with Esteban tonight, I thought unwillingly. Not resentfully—I loved spending time with William. But now, here, the idea of an unexpected night with my lover was definitely something I regretted not being able to take advantage of.

Idly, I pulled my phone from the charging dock and brought up my email account. I scrolled through a bunch of junk, deleting offers for "Hot! Live! Girls!" and penis enlargement and weight-loss pills. I also deleted a bunch of auto messages from Connex telling me I had notifications without bothering to open the Connex app. I did read several messages from OnHisKnees.com, though I didn't answer them. All of them were from men offering me homage, calling me Mistress or My Lady though I'd never met them, promising to worship and serve me in whatever way I wanted to use them. I hadn't updated my profile in a year other than to add that I was no longer looking for a boy to play with, but the messages still came in on a regular basis. Invariably, they curled my lip. All those promises stunk of desperation, not submission. Those men might claim they wanted to serve, but it almost always meant they wanted someone to fulfill their fantasies of a vinyl-clad woman—always beautiful, always a little cruel—who would never actually demand something of them they didn't want to give. She would maybe tie them up or tease and deny them for a while, but would always still let them come. Probably all over her tits or face. Whatever humiliations she offered would be really, when you got right down to it, orchestrated by him. *For* him. They had no idea who I was, what I wanted or even how to give it to me.

To me, that was not submission.

The question could sometimes be what *was* submission, but I guess like the old quote about pornography, I knew it when I saw it. Or felt it, rather. It was never something as simple as a guy getting on his knees, it was always far more complex than that. What had worked for me with one guy didn't with another, and I couldn't ever be certain why. Only that some men gave it to me and other men didn't, and sometimes their compliance was a deal breaker…but sometimes it wasn't.

And I didn't see a damn thing wrong with that.

The longer I'd been a part of the kink scene, the more people I'd met who seemed to think that somehow being kinky meant being rigid and strict and incapable of flexibility. Well, just because I loved steak didn't mean I also didn't want a salad now and again. Hell, I liked a steak salad with fries on top of it, and I liked my sex the same way. Sweetly variable and sometimes surprising. If I preferred to be in charge that didn't have to mean I'd been scorned as a kid and was bent on destroying all men or that I couldn't appreciate being bent over a chair now and again, either.

I liked what I liked and didn't need to explain it to anyone, even myself.

I'd never been a big fan of dating sites, but OnHisKnees. com was technically more like a Connex site than Match.com. You could join forums and have discussions and discover local munches, post pictures and blog-type entries and private message the other members. Still, it was also a place to meet partners, even if you had to wade through an ocean of crap to find a few decent prospects.

I had met Esteban on that site, so it *was* possible to find someone. From the start, he'd been properly respectful without being obsequious. Clever. Funny. Responsive. We'd had an online relationship for four months before he'd even approached the idea of meeting in person, and I'd been incredibly attracted to the idea that for him, this was more than casual play. That he'd been taking his time to make sure I was who he wanted to give himself to, that I was not some random woman starring in a recurring mental loop of porn clips.

That I was different.

That I was special.

I hadn't kept all of his early messages, but there were a few I'd saved. Nostalgic, I opened the email folder to look at some of our first conversations. I opened the first picture he'd sent me of his dear face. He was nothing like anything I ever would have said I wanted. Slight. Dark haired, big brown eyes. Physically, not at all my type. Yet willing to give up to me, to be my toy. His worship was sincere, and he got off on it as much as I did, which was more important to me than the lines and curves of his face.

Esteban had wanted to see me tonight because he missed me.

I didn't want to think too much about this. We'd never discussed turning our monthly dates into something more serious. His profile had, in fact, indicated he was only interested in a cyber connection, nothing in real time, while mine had stated specifically that I was into multiple partners and short-term arrangements. Both of us had changed our minds about what we wanted, I guess.

Esteban missed me, and I had to admit that the times between our dates had been getting longer and longer in feeling, if not the actual passing of hours. My sweet, submissive boy had settled into a place somewhere close to my heart. I wasn't sure I liked that. On the other hand, I wasn't sure I didn't.

Restless, bored, unable to sleep, I clicked through a few games on my phone I hadn't played in forever. I lost one round of Bubble Burst and quit. I sent a small poking "hi" Esteban's way, but as I'd expected, the small *S* next to my message meant he wasn't logged in to the texting app we favored.

It had been months since I'd logged in to my old instant message app, but insomnia breeds desperation. Seeing the list of screen names made me glad I'd logged on as invisible. I'd used this account a lot before meeting Esteban. Some of those people had been relentless in their pursuit of a mistress, and I'd been occasionally foolish enough to engage even when I knew I had no interest in continuing anything serious with them.

And then. There. Halfway down the list, another name stood out to me. Not a name, actually; I'd changed it a while back to a small picture of a bunny because looking at his name had made me feel sick to my stomach.

There it was now, standing out in the list of words, that one single emoticon. Seeing it forced my heart into my throat, and my fingers twitched so fiercely that I dropped my phone. It hit me in the face hard enough to send sparks flying in my vision, and that pain was enhanced by the fact I'd stupidly and reflexively also bitten my tongue.

"Fuck, shit, dammit," I cursed, struggling to sit up in the tangle of my sheets. I tasted blood. My phone had fallen into the mess of my blankets, the lighted screen dimming and going out before I could grab it. I swept the bed, but found only more soft fabric.

By the time I found the phone and sat up, opening my IM app again, the bunny had hopped away.

I clutched the phone to my heart, hating that I still cared enough to cry over simply seeing him online. I pressed my fingers to my eyelids, willing away the burning slide of tears, but all I managed to do was gasp out a strangled sob. *No*, I told myself. *Do not. Don't open that app, don't look for his profile, don't send him a message.*

Don't do it, Elise.

You'll be sorry.

And I *was* sorry, but I did it anyway.

Once you told me I was strong, but lately, the strongest thing I seem to do is not message you at three in morning when I can't catch my breath because of the weight crushing my chest that comes from missing you. And oh, shit, look, here I go, sending you this message when I know you will read it and not answer me. So I guess I'm not so strong, after all. Not when it comes to you.

5

The Morningstar Mocha was super busy. I dropped off William and circled the block twice before I found a spot a block up the street. The extra time I took parking meant I was a few minutes late, but I still paused to look through the front window before going in. I saw Esteban at a table in the corner, a mug in front of him. He wasn't looking my way, so I studied him for half a minute.

We had met once or twice for lunch. Every time had been before we'd ever met in a hotel room, when we were still deciding if we wanted to go to that next step. Since we'd begun that, we'd never met again in public.

He looked so different with his clothes on.

This wasn't what we were supposed to be. Coffee shop pals who chatted about muffins and maybe played footsie under the table or held hands? No. We were dim hotel rooms and commands and fantasies, not reality. Weren't we? I was on the verge of walking away when a man in a long black coat came up behind me wanting to go inside, and I let myself be swept up along with him as though I had no other choice.

Esteban stood up when I walked in.

Being greeted with a smile and a look almost of relief, as

though you are, in that moment, the most important sight in the world to the person who's been waiting for you…it's heady stuff. I wove through the crowded tables to him and slung my bag over the back of the empty chair. I wondered if he would embrace me, and if I would allow it. He didn't, though he ran a hand down from my shoulder to my wrist, squeezing gently before moving away.

"I was thinking you would not come," he said.

"I would've messaged you, honey. I wouldn't just stand you up." I had considered doing just that, but Esteban would never know it. I sat. "What are you drinking?"

"Coffee. Would you like?"

I twisted to look at the menu board. "I'll take a mocha latte. Oh, and a blueberry muffin."

He gave me another tiny, discreet squeeze as he passed me. It both amused and touched me emotionally. He touched me physically all the time, of course, but this had been different. Brief, but not hesitant. He was different outside the hotel room, but then, I guess so was I.

Esteban returned in a few minutes with my drink and food and took the seat across from me. He grinned, his gaze searching my face, though I wasn't sure what he was looking to find. He leaned forward.

"You look beautiful."

I didn't laugh. I had made an effort, of course, because who ever goes to meet a lover without looking their best? But unlike most of our meetings, which featured me in full makeup with carefully chosen outfits, this morning I'd pulled my dark curly hair into a messy bun and wore jeans with a tunic blouse suitable for taking my nephew to religious school. Put together? Sure. But beautiful?

"You do," he said, though I hadn't protested.

I leaned forward a little too, echoing his posture. "It's good to see you."

He beamed, eyes not leaving mine. "It's better to see you!"

"You're so good for my ego." I did laugh then, and broke off a piece of my muffin. I pushed the plate toward him. "Have some."

He broke off a piece. Together, we ate the muffin and drank our coffee while tables emptied and filled again. We didn't talk about anything that seemed important, which was the perfect sort of conversation to have on a bright, late-spring Sunday morning.

"This was nice," I told him when we'd stayed as long as we could before it would be time to order lunch.

Esteban nodded. "Yes. Very nice."

I thought for a second or so that he was going to ask me if we could do it again, but he only looked at me with an expression I couldn't read. Not quite sad. Reluctant. Resigned, maybe.

"Walk me to my car," I said. "I'm not ready to say good-bye just yet."

I could read that expression, at least. I'd made him happy. We didn't hold hands while we walked, and the distance between us was enough that nobody would ever have guessed how many times his mouth had been between my legs. I watched him from the corner of my eye as we navigated the buckled sidewalk.

At my car, I faced him. "What's going on?"

He might've been able to put me off on the phone, but not in person where I could see his face. He tried to cut his gaze, but I took his chin gently in my palm and turned him until he had no choice but to look at me. Still, he didn't answer me right away.

"Esteban," I said sternly.

His shoulders sagged. To my immense surprise, he hugged me. Hard. His face pressed to the side of my neck, his skin hot. His breath tickled me.

I hugged him back for a moment, before saying, "Get in the car."

Obediently, he went around to the passenger side. I got in my seat and twisted to face him. "Tell me what's going on."

"I'm wearing it," he said, which was not the answer to my question.

Despite this unusual disobedience, a shiver tiptoed up and down my spine at the thought. "My gift?"

He nodded. I swallowed, my gaze dropping to his lap for a moment before meeting his. He licked his mouth. Tension wove between us, fine and strong as a spider's filament. All I had to do was run a fingertip across the back of his hand, placed on his thigh, to make him shudder. His soft moan made me clench my jaw to keep my own inside.

"How does it feel?"

"I feel…full. Of wanting. It makes me think of you." His voice rasped, low.

"Good. I like you to think of me when we aren't together." I circled my fingertips on his skin, my eyes never leaving his. "But what? It makes you uncomfortable? You're worried about something? I want you to use my present to please me, but if it doesn't make you happy, too—"

He shook his head sharply. "No. No, it does. So much. Too much, maybe."

I thought I understood that, at least. How something could make you too happy. I leaned a little closer and let my hand slip down the inside of his thigh to press against the rising bulge of his cock. "Tell me how it feels, deep inside you."

"I thought it would be too much. A little too big," he whispered. "It hurt a little, at first."

"And now?"

He shook his head. "Not now. Now I feel it when I move. It hits the spot just right. And if I shift just right, if I clench…"

I smiled.

He shuddered. I didn't stroke his cock, though by now I could feel it was thick and hard, compressed against the front of his jeans. Esteban moaned again, a little brokenly.

"You want me to touch you," I said in a low voice.

His eyes, which had gone heavy-lidded, opened wider. "Oh, yes…please…"

"It makes me very happy to know that you're using my present," I told him as my hand pressed against him. Withdrew. Pressed again. To anyone looking at us, we'd appear to be having a conversation, nothing more. Leaning a little closer, maybe, but not even kissing. Nothing outrageous…except that my sweet boy was pushing his cock against my palm. I imagined the press and tug of the plug in his ass, hitting him in the perfect spot. "I want you to feel it inside you. Do you?"

He shuddered again. "Yes. It's so good."

"Fuck, I want your fingers inside me," I muttered, which sent another spasm through him. Urged another moan. My nipples had gone tight and hard. So had my clit. I clenched my own internal muscles, rocking a little, though I had no toy to help me out. "Look at me."

He did, though it took him an understandable few seconds to focus. A faint blush had painted his cheeks, and his brown eyes had gone darker from his dilated pupils. He licked his mouth again, and I thought of how good his tongue felt on my pussy, and I could not stop myself this time from moaning, too.

"You are so beautiful…" Esteban's words trailed off into a groan as he moved so slowly against me that he hardly seemed to move at all. Then he said other words I couldn't understand in Spanish, a language so fluid and sexy that every word sounded like part of a poem.

"How does it feel," I demanded in a broken voice.

Esteban looked at me again. "It fills me up the way I want you to..."

"Oh..."

I'd tied men up. Blindfolded them. Spanked some, beaten a few with floggers, dressed more than one in frilly panties. But I'd never yet fucked one in the ass with a strap-on. The thought of that sent another thrill of pleasure through me.

And why? Because Esteban wanted it so much. Because he'd approached me on the subject of pegging so casually hopeful, so obviously afraid I would recoil in horror, or maybe mock him, that I couldn't think about taking him that way without remembering how hard it had been for him to even ask me, and how beautifully grateful he'd been when my answer had been, "I would love to."

It could've been about the domination—what makes a man more submissive than being the one getting fucked instead of the one doing the fucking? It could've been about control and power, because those were things that turned me on. But really, it was because my sweet boy wanted it, craved it, yearned and ached and burned for it, and I was the only one who would give it to him.

Because it made me something to him that nobody else had ever been.

I wasn't touching myself, but it wouldn't take more than a stroke or two to send me toppling toward orgasm. I almost slipped a hand between my legs, but a couple walking a dog was due to pass us in about a minute and a half, so I took my hand off his crotch. They'd see only two people in conversation. Nothing more.

"I want that," I told him. "I want to be inside you. Fucking you. Taking you to the edge, over and over, until you beg me to let you come."

"Please," he breathed at once. His fingers had curled tight in the fabric of his pants, digging. He rocked his hips again, the tiniest amount. "Please, will you…?"

The dog-walking couple had just passed by, so I leaned close to nuzzle his neck and breathe into his ear as I pressed my hand to his cock again. "Yes, baby. I will. And I will love it."

Esteban let out a low, gruff gasp. Under my touch, his cock throbbed. Heat spread against my palm. His entire body quaked as he turned his face toward me to press his cheek against mine. We were both breathing hard. My nipples ached; my clit throbbed. I wanted to rub myself all over him.

I sat back, instead. He blinked rapidly before he could focus on me. I wanted to touch his face. I wanted to kiss his mouth. Instead, I pulled a package of tissues from my center console and handed them to him without a word.

He laughed, embarrassed. "I am like a boy."

"You're *my* boy," I told him. "And that was very sexy."

"But you didn't—"

"Next time," I told him.

That's when I finally understood why he was acting so strange. It took only a second or so to see the look on his face. To figure it out.

I should have known that his urgent desire to see me outside of our routine had to mean something bad. I should've guessed it, no matter how loving he'd been. I should've known better.

"Oh." I sat back, surprised. Stunned, actually. And stung. "There is no next time?"

"*Querida…*"

I knew that word, at least. "Darling." He'd called me that a couple times before. I'd always liked it, but this time it felt too much like an apology and not an endearment. I sat back.

"Don't call me that," I said in a cold, distant voice. I turned to face the windshield, my hands on the wheel.

Neither of us moved. I could hear his breathing quicken, but I didn't look at him. I caught sight of his hand, reaching as though he meant to touch me, but in the end he must've decided against it because he let it settle again on his thigh. After another few moments, I heard him unzip, the crinkle of the tissue package, some shuffling. He cleared his throat.

I knew he was waiting for me to say something, but I didn't know what. In the past, even before I'd learned him so well, I'd still never doubted what I wanted to say. How I wanted our scenes to go, the reactions I wanted to elicit. I'd been wrong a few times and missed the mark, but I'd adjusted. This time, I had no idea what Esteban needed from me.

"Please don't hate me," he said.

I swallowed a rush of emotion. "I don't hate you. But you should get out of my car now."

He didn't, not at first. I thought I would have to face him, and I didn't want to, not with my emotions printed all over my face the way I was sure they were. He was breaking up with me. I didn't need to know why. I didn't want to know. At the sound of him starting to speak, I cut him off.

"Out."

And, as he always had, Esteban gave me what I wanted.

6

"Put your hand on her hip. Lower." The camera whirred and clicked. Scott paused to shake his blond hair out of his face and look at the picture he'd taken. He frowned. "Jack, I want you on your knees."

Jack and I both laughed, and I said, "Woo!"

Scott, serious, smiled but put the camera back to his eye. "Head bent…okay, tell you what. Elise, you do whatever you'd…do."

I put my hand on Jack's dark hair. Thick and glossy, he wore it a bit longer in the front so it had a habit of falling over his eyes. I threaded my fingers through it from his forehead back, getting a good grip and tugging his face up to mine. The camera whirred.

I said in a low voice, "I won't hurt you, but I'll still need to know if you're uncomfortable, okay?"

"Go ahead and hurt him," Scott said.

My fingers tightened a little more, and Jack laughed. I glanced at Scott. "This is just for the pictures. I don't really think we need to get a safe word or anything for the sake of art, do we?"

"If you don't need a safe word for art," Scott said, "it ain't very good art."

I looked back to Jack, and I let my smile fade. My fingers tugged the tiniest bit. "I'm still not going to hurt you on purpose. You tell me if I do."

Jack grinned. "I'm good."

I tipped his head back harder, watching to see if he winced. I really didn't want to hurt him—even if this had been a real scene between us, I wasn't particularly into causing pain. I liked the reactions to it more than giving the pain itself. For the sake of a picture I could make it look like I was being totally sadistic, though, if that was what the photographer wanted to see. With Scott's murmured words of approval, I looked down at the man in front of me on his knees and waited to feel something. Anything. He was gorgeous, thick, dark hair, a killer smile, a lean athletic build and a very, very pretty half-hard cock that I wasn't going to stare at, because that just wouldn't be polite. I appreciated the package, but that was it. No spark of attraction.

Modeling is sometimes about acting as much as it is posing, so I put on my best resting bitch face and worked it. And I worked Jack, who was a good sport and an excellent partner. We didn't fuck or anything like that, not even simulated. There was lots of skin to skin, though. He was totally naked, and I wore lingerie that was too small, a fact I'd pointed out when I put it on and had been told by a grinning Scott that the size was perfect. When we paused for a break, Jack did apologize for getting hard.

"Honey, I'd be insulted if you didn't," I told him. I shrugged into the silk robe I'd brought along. Jack had wrapped a towel around his lean hips. We were both drinking sodas that Scott's assistant had brought up from the shop downstairs while the photographer himself pulled up the first set of shots onto his laptop to preview for editing.

Jack stretched out long legs on the chaise in one corner while I took a spot in a comfy armchair. We'd spent the past hour mostly naked and entangled. I'd met him only two hours ago. He felt like one of my oldest friends at this point.

"You work with Alex, right? Olivia's husband," Jack asked.

I sipped soda and rolled my head on my neck to crack it. "Yep."

"Yeah, my girlfriend is like, her best friend."

"Sarah?" I laughed. "Wow, small world."

"Yeah, tiny." Jack nodded.

"I don't know her," I added. "I mean, I've heard Olivia talking about her, but we haven't met."

Jack nodded. "You have a boyfriend? Or a girlfriend? I guess I should've asked that, sorry. Didn't mean to be whatever you call it, genderist."

"I don't. Never had a girlfriend, thought about trying it once or twice but I'm kind of hardwired for cock. The last boyfriend I had was a long time ago." I leaned back in the soft chair and forced away thoughts of Esteban. He'd never been a boyfriend.

"How come?" Jack leaned forward, elbows on his knees.

I shrugged. "It ended badly. Haven't really wanted to have another since."

"How long is a long time ago?"

I paused, sort of embarrassed to say it aloud. "Something like four years."

"Whoa." Jack shook his head. "That's too bad."

I laughed. "It's okay. Really. I haven't suffered for lack of a boyfriend, trust me."

"Come look at these," Scott said from the desk.

Jack and I got up to see what Scott had done. He'd pulled

up a black-and-white shot from earlier in the day. Jack on his knees, my fingers in his hair. Scott had captured a small, assessing smile on my face. Jack's eyes closed, his mouth slightly parted. His cock not yet erect but clearly getting there.

"Beautiful," I said, meaning Jack.

Jack snorted soft laughter. "Pretty hot, man."

Scott didn't look at either one of us. His fingers continued smoothing and shifting the image in tiny increments. Enhancing, not changing. I loved the way he made me look. I'd worked with a few other photographers who always tried to make my tits bigger, my belly flatter, my ass rounder. Scott always made me look just like I do, only a little…better.

He looked over his shoulder at us with a grin. "Pretty, huh?"

I hugged him from behind and pressed my cheek to his. "Gorgeous. And I look okay, too."

"Are you kidding?" Jack said. "You look fucking amazing."

I gave him a small smile. "Thanks."

"You guys need more of a break? I have a few more things I want to try." Scott twisted in his chair. "You up for it? I want to take you outside."

We were both up for it. And let me tell you, I've never really been an exhibitionist, but there is something awfully exhilarating about stripping down to bare skin out in the middle of the woods with a totally attractive guy wrapped all around you. We had fun, too. Splashing in a small waterfall, both of us with teeth chattering and goose bumps. Lying out in the sun to dry, our fingers linked companionably while we chatted, and Scott took picture after picture.

"Good," he said finally with another look at his camera. "That's it. We're done."

Back at the studio, Jack and I hugged goodbye. We exchanged numbers and promised to keep in touch. Scott made sure we both took postcards for his upcoming gallery show, which would, he promised, feature some of the pictures he'd taken today.

"I'll be there," I promised.

"You'd better," Scott said and kissed me firmly on the mouth, then the cheek, and hugged me close to whisper in my ear, "I don't see you often enough. You okay? What's going on?"

I shook my head. "Nothing."

He gave me a suspicious look. "Uh-huh."

I wasn't going to tell him about Esteban, especially now that I'd been so unceremoniously dumped. "Really. I promise. I'll see you at the gallery show."

"You'd better see me before that," he told me, and I said I would, though I think we both knew it wasn't likely.

He gestured to me just before I left. "Look at this before you go."

He showed me the rest of the shots he'd taken. Even without editing, they were stunning. Anyone who didn't know that Jack and I had been strangers at the start of the day would've thought we'd been lovers forever.

"You're beautiful," Scott said, slow-clicking through a series of images. "Look at you."

I looked.

I saw what he meant. Lines and curves and shadow. Tits and ass and lips and hair. There was beauty there, all right. But it was like looking at a picture of someone else. I was a stranger to myself. That woman in the photos was someone adored and cherished and worshipped, and that was no longer me.

7

Funny how best friends just know when something's wrong. I hadn't talked to Alicia in weeks beyond a few texts, but that didn't matter. The second I saw her number on my screen I answered, and within minutes we were laughing as much as we always had.

"So, what's new, what's going on with you? Feels like I haven't talked to you forever," she said finally. "I got a Connex invite to Scott's gallery show. I guess you're going to be in it? Sexy pictures. Woo woo."

"If you're into that sort of thing," I said archly, as though Alicia hadn't been my best friend forever and hadn't gone with me on a late-night run to the hardware store to pick up laundry rope and carabiner clips for a booty call. "Weird he invited you, though."

"He probably invited everyone in the area, one of those blanket invitations. I can't be there, unfortunately. I thought about it," Alicia said. "My mom would love it if I came home. Can't get the time off. Bummer."

"Well, shit," I said. "That sucks."

"I know, I miss youuuuu," she cooed. "When are you coming to Texas?"

"It's hot in Texas," I told her.

"The men are hot in Texas," Alicia said. "You totally need to move out here with me. We can be roomies!"

I'd lived with her already for a few months just after college. That our friendship had survived it was more a testimony to how nice and patient and forgiving Alicia is than anything else. Some people are not meant to live full-time with other human beings, and I'm one of them.

"You know I can't do that," I said. "Where would I find a job as good as the one I have?"

She sighed. "True. Lucky bitch. But you could come visit me, Elise. It would be fun. And I miss the hell out of your face. You get vacation time, don't you?"

"Sure. Oodles of it. Alex is a big fan of vacation."

We chatted a bit longer about when would be the best time for me to come out—not in the summer, I told her. Not until after William's Bar Mitzvah, anyway, and in the fall, the days in Texas wouldn't be so brutal. "I'm a wilting flower, you know."

"Oh, you," she said with a laugh. "It's not so bad. You stay inside, that's all. Yay! I can't wait! And neither can Jimmy."

I paused. "Who's Jimmy?"

"Guy I want you to meet." I pictured her blinking innocently. "You'll like him."

Alicia knew what I liked, so it was a good bet she was right. Still, the thought of it, of meeting some random dude she was trying to set me up with…hot cowboy or not, I wasn't into it. "Alicia…"

"It's been ages," she said immediately. That was the good and bad thing about besties. They always know what you're trying to say even when you don't say it. "Forget about him."

"I can't." I owned it at once. No sense in pretending otherwise, not with her. This girl had held my hair after too many shots of tequila. She'd given me her last tampon. She'd been there all through that delirious agony that had been my last real relationship, and she'd been there after, too.

"Then get over him," she said without hesitating. "He's not worth it, Elise."

"I know he's not."

"And you can't help it anyway." She sighed, sounding disgusted, but not with me. "Yeah, I know."

"I know you know."

Alicia'd had her own doomed love affair. She referred to him as Mr. Darcy the way I called mine George. Not their real names. Literary references, a code of sorts we'd invented in college to refer to boyfriends. Hers to *Pride and Prejudice.* Mine to *Of Mice and Men.*

"Have you heard from Darcy?" I asked.

Alicia snorted. "Yes. Of course. Every few months, like a herpes outbreak."

"Oh, gross."

She laughed. "We had a real go-around the last time, a couple weeks ago. He had the nerve to ask me if I wanted to Facetime with him—"

"No," I interrupted. "Seriously? What the fuck?"

"Right? He said he was, and I quote, 'curious,' about my life." Alicia was silent for a second then sounded both angry and sad. "I told him I had no desire to have any kind of conversation with him anymore. I said it hurt too much to talk to him like we were casual acquaintances who'd barely meant anything to each other. He told me he didn't mean to hurt me, but it wasn't fair of me to get angry with him for making, and I quote again, a 'good faith effort at reaching out.'"

I groaned. "Clueless."

"Moron," she agreed, sounding more sad than angry this time. "I told him that I was sure he didn't mean to hurt me, but neither does a door when it slams my fingers. And I don't put my fingers in a door on purpose."

"No kidding."

"Then I deleted and blocked him," Alicia said.

"You didn't! Oh, girl." I was impressed. Mr. Darcy had been in and out of Alicia's life for a long damn time.

She sighed. "I had to. I was just…done, you know? Finally done. I wish you could get there with George, Elise."

I did, too, but I suspected it wasn't going to happen. I'd let him slam that door on my fingers over and over again, if only he'd talk to me one more time. If only.

We changed the subject after that. We talked about her job, not so new anymore, but still worth the move. We caught up on some gossip about people we'd gone to school with. I filled her in on the increasing family drama surrounding William's Bar Mitzvah.

"Oh, your mom." Alicia sighed. She'd known me since the third grade. That was all she had to say.

I laughed and groaned at the same time. "Yeah. I know. I'm just waiting for the shit to hit the fan. So far it's been okay, other than the hissy fit she threw about the date."

"Oh, God, what was that?"

I told Alicia how Evan and Susan had tried to set the date for William's Bar Mitzvah a week later than it was now going to be for some reason I didn't know and didn't care about—a Bar Mitzvah could be held anytime after the kid's thirteenth birthday, so if they wanted to give him an extra week to study or so it didn't compete with something else, it was nothing to me. But apparently, my sister, Jill, had a schedule conflict, my mother threw a hissy and the date had been moved to accommodate it.

"You'd think that would be enough, right, one huge fucking showdown at the start." I shook my head. "But there's more coming, you'd better believe it."

"Come to Texas," Alicia teased. "Avoid it all."

"I can't do that to the kid. Or my brother. Someone here has to be sort of sane," I told her. "But after it's all over, I promise I'll visit. Not setting me up on any dates, though, you have to promise me that."

Alicia sighed. "You're no fun."

"How fun would it be for me to visit you and go out on some lame blind date?" I demanded.

She paused. "It could be a double date."

"Oh." That was a game changer. "You're seeing someone?"

"Yeah." She paused then said nothing though I waited.

"I would've thought you'd have told me that right away." I wasn't hurt, exactly, but I did wonder about the hesitation. It was true we didn't talk as often as we had in the past, but every time we did it was like no time had passed. Now her finally kicking Darcy to the curb made total sense.

"If you ever bothered to log in to Connex," she said lightly, "you'd have seen it."

"Wow. Wow," I repeated. "He's Connex relationship worthy?"

Alicia laughed. "Yeah. He is. His name's Jay."

We talked for the next forty minutes about Jay, until she had to go. She made me promise again to visit, and I agreed. I meant it, too.

"You could've just told me, you know," I said. "I'm happy for you."

"It felt weird, that's all. We were both kind of united in our despair for a while, you know? Shit. I'm sorry, that sounded terrible."

I laughed. "No. I get it. Misery loves company."

"I didn't think I'd meet someone I could really…you know."

Alicia sounded shy. "Love. Again. I didn't want to. And I know you don't want to, either, Elise, but…"

"Hey, look. It's good. I'm glad for you. I'm okay, really. I'm not a celibate old maid or anything, Alicia. I date. I've been dating someone, on and off." The words tripped off my tongue before I could call them back. More of a lie than I'd meant to tell her, but hell. If I exaggerated the type of relationship we'd had, it was out of pride, not deceit. "It's not serious, or it wasn't, but his name is Esteban."

"Ooh, Esteban?"

"He's Spanish. I mean he comes from Spain." Before she could get too excited, though, I added casually, "But we broke up recently. And it wasn't bad or anything, just didn't work out. So really, you don't have to worry about me. I'm back on the horse."

"It'll happen for you, too. I know it," Alicia said with the optimism only the newly in love can manage to muster.

I didn't try to dissuade her. We said our goodbyes and hung up, promising to keep in better touch. She had a new boyfriend, so I figured it was a promise meant to be broken. And that would be okay.

Showered, tucked into bed, I tried not to look at the clock. The later it got, the harder it would be for me to fall asleep. Not for the first time, I thought about taking pills, but if there was something I hated worse than insomnia it was the idea of being dependent on something to guide me into dreamland. A couple shots of Fireball whiskey would've done the trick, but I wasn't going to rely on booze, either.

I counted backward to no avail. I slipped a hand between my thighs, hoping an orgasm would ease me into sleep, but though I came within a few minutes, the climax left me melancholy and gasping against annoying tears rather than passion. I rolled onto my stomach and punched my pillow then buried my face in it to breathe in the scent of the lavender oil I'd sprinkled on it before I went to bed.

Who was I to fault Alicia for not telling me about Jay sooner? I should've told her months ago about Esteban. We could've giggled over him, swooned a little, even. She'd have been happy for me, even if my relationship with him had been solely based on sex and not emotion. Even if he hadn't been a boyfriend, I could've shared him with her, so that maybe now that it was over, we could've at least talked about him. Now, all I had was my own discontent to keep me awake.

Anyone who's had chronic trouble sleeping collects tricks to help them get to dreamland. I'd already tried my standbys, counting backward and orgasm. My mother would've advocated warm milk. Gross.

Led by my heart, my hands found my phone before my head could stop them. I opened the message app. My fingers typed. Erased. Typed again.

I told George about Esteban. Everything—how we'd met online. How we fucked, the things we'd done, the places he'd let me take him and where he'd taken me. How I'd found myself thinking of him in the odd moments of quiet when my mind turned to whatever it would, without my conscious effort. I told him how we broke up…and that I'd never loved Esteban. That I would never love anyone the way I loved him.

I hit Send.

He didn't answer.

8

Three days had passed since my conversation with Esteban in the front seat of my car. I hadn't blocked or deleted him from my contacts, but I was still surprised when my phone chirped at me as I was changing out of work clothes and into something more suitable for a pint of ice cream and some streaming episodes of *Queer as Folk* on Interflix. Five minutes later and I wouldn't even have noticed, because I'd already put my phone on the charger and hadn't planned on taking it downstairs with me.

I held it, looking at the notification but not reading the message just yet. I let my thumb hover over the screen. One swipe and I could delete the message, unread. But then I'd have no idea what he said, and while curiosity might've killed the cat, not giving in to it was more likely to haunt me forever.

I miss you.

Well. That was nice. No lie, it lifted my heart a little. Made it go *thump-thump*. It also set my jaw and narrowed my eyes.

I didn't answer him. Not at first. I let half an hour go by, though I knew he would see that I got his message and read it. I got myself some ice cream and settled on the couch, my phone with its unanswered message weighting my pocket. I turned on the TV. Chose my show. And finally, because I hated when my messages went unanswered, I took out my phone and typed in an answer.

Don't.

The fact the little *D* became an *R* immediately told me he'd been waiting for my answer, phone in hand. *JohnSmith is Typing* appeared at once, and that set my heart to thumping harder again. My throat closed a little, but I forced away any kind of emotion. No relief. Especially nothing so disgusting as gratitude.

I'm sorry. I want to see you. Tonight? At our place.

Our place. As if we'd ever had one, or anything, really, that could truly be called "ours." I was cranky about it, all at once, when I knew I should not be. My relationship with Esteban had come with rules right from the start, most of which I had written and none I hadn't negotiated or agreed upon. I was hurt and stung by his sudden ending of it, but that had been one of the rules—that either one of us, at any time, could decide to break it off. I'd simply assumed I would be the one to do it. I deserved the slap to my ego. A reminder that no matter how special you think someone thinks you are, it's never really true.

I'm busy, I typed.

A minute passed. Then another. He'd read my message, I could see that, but he wasn't typing a reply. I put my phone to the side, wishing I could feel justified in being a dick about all of this, but finding very little satisfaction. I tried to get lost in the TV show, one of my favorites and usually a guaranteed pleasure, but watching Brian refuse to admit he loved Justin, even though it was obvious throughout five seasons of hot sex and angst, only made me think about Esteban.

I was lifting the phone to answer him when his message came through. One phrase, written in Spanish. Again, one of the few I knew without having to use a translator.

Por favor.

9

I did not dress for him.

I brushed my hair and my teeth and changed out of my pajama pants and into a pair of formfitting skinny jeans, paired with a slim-fit T-shirt. No bra, because I didn't really need one. No garters, no stockings, no lace or satin. Plain cotton panties, bikini and not granny-sized but certainly not sexy. I slipped on a pair of rubber flip-flops that had seen better days, forgoing even sexy shoes.

When Esteban opened the hotel room door, the sight of his face made me want to cry. His eyes were a little red, as if maybe he'd been fighting his own tears, and at the sight of me his entire expression showed his relief. I wanted to hug him close to me and stroke his hair and *shh, shh* him. To make him understand it was all going to be all right.

Instead, I waited until he'd moved aside so I could go through the doorway without touching him. My heart again did that stupid *thump-thump* when I caught a whiff of him— soap and water, like he'd just finished a shower. I had to swallow hard. My fingers curled, fingernails pressing my palms. Facing away from him as I headed for the armchair, I closed my eyes for a moment to compose myself. Smooth my expression. This was all a game, but a serious game nonetheless, and I had to keep it that way or I would end up losing.

I'd brought the book I'd been reading, a spooky gothic tale called *Those Across the River*. I was only a chapter or two into it, and truthfully I didn't expect to get much farther into it tonight. I hadn't brought any cuffs or rope or even a ribbon, no whip or flogger. But I had brought a prop.

I settled into the chair and kicked off my flip-flops to tuck one foot beneath me. I opened my book and bent to read it, or at least to pretend I was. I said nothing to Esteban. I didn't look at him. I knew he was looking at me, though. The weight of his gaze sent a shiver down my spine that I kept hidden. Tightened my nipples, though, and I couldn't hide that. I ought to have worn a bra.

He made a small noise as though he meant to speak, and without looking up at him, I flicked a hand. "At my feet."

He didn't move at first. He made another low noise, this time more like a groan. I kept my eyes on my book, though the words were swimming. My breath came a little faster as I waited for him to obey me. I didn't really doubt that he would—but that was always the delicious bit, the anticipation. When he could refuse me, but would not.

After a few seconds, Esteban folded himself onto his knees in front of me. Many times I'd had him assume that position, usually with his arms crossed at the wrist behind him, but today I could see from the corner of my eye that he'd settled his hands on his thighs. He bent his head, shoulders rising and falling with a deep sigh.

We sat like that for a long time.

I turned the pages of my book, though later I would not remember a single word I'd looked at. I was too aware of the soft huff of his breathing and the heat of him against my bare foot, so close but not touching him. My hands began to tremble, and at last, I put the book aside and looked at him. I didn't say anything. I simply gestured.

Esteban leaned, his arms going around my hips. He pressed his face to my belly. He started to say something.

"Hush," I said, and he quieted. My hand stroked over his hair. Then again. I found the back of his neck, the strong muscles there, and let my hand rest against his bare skin. He heaved another sigh and settled against me.

We sat in more silence, more content this time. Every so often he would nudge against me as I petted his hair. The motion of it became hypnotic, and after a bit, we both fell asleep.

I woke with a start to find him gone from me. The foot tucked beneath me had fallen asleep, too, pins and needles making me wince. The toilet flushed, and a moment later Esteban came out of the bathroom. When he saw me rubbing at my foot, he came to me at once to again kneel and take it in his hands. His strong fingers worked my bare toes, helping the blood flow until I was wriggling not because of the sting, but from his tickling.

"Stop," I said with a gasping laugh. "Enough!"

He pressed my bare sole to his lips and kissed it then set it down gently. He pushed up on his knees to take my hands, and I let him. He looked into my eyes. "Thank you for coming to see me. I was sure you would not."

I could've kept playing at being stern and cruel, but it's more exhausting to fake emotion sometimes than to simply feel it. I tugged his hands until he leaned close enough to me that I could hug him. I kissed his cheek and then pressed mine to his for a few seconds, feeling his breath on me.

"I thought I would never see you again," he said into my ear. "And I could not do it."

I didn't ask him why he'd felt he had to. He would've answered me with honesty, and I simply did not want to hear it. Instead, I squeezed him and sat back.

"No more about it," I told him.

Esteban's expression turned a little sly. "You will punish me for disappointing you?"

I blinked for a second before sitting back harder, letting go of his hands. Disappointment was not what I'd felt. Rejection, yes. Surprise. And now, thinking that perhaps he'd done all of this for the sake of getting a spanking or something stupid like that, angry.

I pushed him away and stepped around him. I grabbed my book. By the time I turned around, Esteban was on his feet and blocking my way to the door.

He took me by the upper arms. "Wait. I'm sorry. I said something wrong."

"Did you do this on purpose? Break it off so I would be angry with you? So I'd punish you?" I tried to yank myself out of his grasp, but I'd forgotten that although Esteban had willingly allowed me all this time to be in charge, he was still physically stronger than I was.

He held me tight enough to hurt, though I knew he didn't mean to. I didn't struggle. I gave him a hard look, but he surprised me again. His grip softened, but he didn't let go.

"*Querida,*" he said quietly. "I'm sorry. I was doing what I felt I had to do, until I realized I couldn't do it."

I'd deliberately kept my gaze from him earlier as a way to punish him, but now I found I could not look at his face. This wasn't love, but it was all we had. "We agreed. Either of us could end this at any time."

"But I hurt you in the way I did it, and I'm sorry." He pulled me closer, step by reluctant step, until we were embracing.

No man that I'd ever been with had apologized to me that way, and there'd been one who'd hurt me a lot worse than

Esteban had. Repeatedly, and on purpose. I breathed in the soap-and-water scent of him as I tried to think of how to answer. Finally, there was really only one answer. I pulled away to look at him.

"Don't do it again."

10

I was never afraid to love you. No matter how deep I fell, how hard I loved, there was no question in my mind that when we were together, everything felt right. When I held out my hand, you took it.

I wish you hadn't let it go.

Three in the morning, another message I sent knowing I'd get no reply. I chose instead to bang myself against that wall again. To slam my fingers in the door, as Alicia said. And why? I could've spent a lifetime and a million dollars in therapy trying to figure out why I held on so tight to what no longer gave me anything but constant heartache. It was stupid; it was pointless; it was worthless.

I did it anyway.

11

"I can't believe you're still doing this." My mother's lip curled. "Pictures like that? And I had to find out from Connex of all places. Some stranger inviting me to a show that's got you hanging up there on the wall with your tuchus out for the entire world to see? What an embarrassment!"

"I didn't know he tagged me in the pictures. But I'm not embarrassed." I leaned to drag a pita chip through the bowl of hummus. I didn't love that Scott's invitation had sent my mother into a tizzy, but hell, I was an adult.

My mother's twisted mouth thinned. Her chin went up. "I don't understand you, Elise. I raised you so much better. I didn't think you were still doing all that…stuff. With all those men."

"Ma," I said with a sigh, pretending she was talking about the pictures and not anything else, "it's an art show. They're pictures, that's all. I could be doing a lot of worse things, couldn't I?"

She crossed her arms. "Why can't you just find a nice guy and settle down?"

"Don't come if you don't want to see them. Nobody's going

to force you to look." I ignored her question, which had been asked many times and never had an answer.

"They're all over your whatdoyoucallit. Your Connex page."

My brows went up. Those pictures were ancient. "So unfriend me."

"All my friends can see. Joan Simon told me she was invited, too. What's he doing, soliciting everyone to come see your naked pictures?"

I gave her a sideways look. I could not, off the top of my head, name any of her friends who'd been granted access to my Connex page, but that didn't mean anything. I'd accepted everyone who wanted to be my "friend" early on. Now I didn't friend anyone.

"Not just me. There are lots of naked pictures of lots of people."

My mother rolled her eyes. "Wonderful. Perfect."

"It's art."

"It's unnatural," she said finally and waited for me to reply. Probably for me to reassure her that they were only photos. That I didn't actually do "those things."

I couldn't. I'd never told my mother I was kinky, but I'd never denied it, either. I don't think there are many people who enjoy discussing their sex lives with their parents, and people who get off on things not considered "normal" probably have an even harder time. I'd gone to my mother when I was about fourteen with some questions about sex, positions in particular, that I'd read about in one of the books she tried to keep hidden in the back of the bookcase. The woman on top position had intrigued me, but I'd been unable to figure out how, exactly, that worked. At fourteen I'd seen a penis— my brother's, which hardly counted, but at least I was a little bit more informed than most of my friends about what one looked like. Alicia had shown me some pictures in her dad's nudie mags of people fucking, but they'd all been doing it with the guy on top. I wanted to know how it worked the other way around.

My mother had told me then what she'd just told me now. It's unnatural for a woman to want to be on top. She'd said it when I was fourteen and again at twenty-two, the first time she'd seen my "filthy" pictures, and several other times since. Yet, that was how I liked it, how I'd always liked it since I'd first discovered it was possible. It was how I would always like it.

"I'm just saying," my mother continued, because of course she had to get in the last word.

"It's also a little creepy that you keep harping on it," I said sharply and got up to get another glass of water. "I thought we were here to help Susan with some Bar Mitzvah stuff, not talk about my private life. Where's Jill anyway?"

This was way more my sister's type of gig than mine. I didn't care about the color scheme or types of napkins or any of that stuff, but I figured I'd better be there as a buffer. If Susan and I had a neutrally pleasant relationship, she and my mom had what I'd consider a "temporary cease-fire" sort. My sister, Jill, seemed to have no idea that Susan actively loathed her, but then Jill assumed the world revolved around her, and the idea that someone could actually not like her never entered her mind.

"Jill had a school board meeting, and Susan is *late*," my mother said.

I looked at the clock. It was already close to eight. I didn't really want to hang out here all night, not with a forty-five-minute drive back home. My mom would try to insist I stay over. I'd have to not-so-politely decline. She would pout. I would snap. Susan would roll her eyes.

"What time was she supposed—"

"I'm here. Sorry, sorry." Susan, eyes bright, cheeks a little flushed, bustled into my mother's kitchen with a brimming accordion folder.

They squared off like cowboys in an old Western, but neither of them drew. After a moment, my mother grudgingly offered coffee, which Susan politely declined. The pair of them looked at me like I had anything to say about it, but I only shrugged, and they both went into the dining room to lay out menus and brochures from different locations.

The first disagreement happened over kosher catering. Never mind I'd gone out to dinner with my mother plenty of times and watched her devour a Cobb salad like it wasn't riddled with pig, but Susan would send her order back if it arrived with unexpected bacon. Or that neither of them actually kept a kosher kitchen with separate pots and pans and the like. My mother wanted to be able to invite and impress her friends. My sister-in-law wanted a nice place to have a party and have some good food. We didn't live in an area where kosher catering was a common thing.

Under other circumstances I'd have popped some corn and settled back to watch the show, but tonight I was already tired because I'd been up at three in the morning being a dumbass and messaging a man who always read my messages but never answered me. I didn't have the patience to listen to them quibble over hors d'oeuvres. It wasn't my event, nor my money. My phone hummed from my pocket, and I drew it out, surprised to find a message from Esteban. I was also pleased, though. More than I wanted to admit.

"I won't be serving shrimp cocktail," Susan said stiffly. "There will be a pasta station and a mashed potato bar, which William requested. We'll have grilled chicken skewers, too. I don't see why this has to be an issue."

"I simply think that you should serve food your guests will be able to eat," my mother said with a sniff.

Susan's eyes narrowed. "Anyone *I* invite will be fine with the food."

"You're having it at William Penn Inn, right?" I asked absently, reading Esteban's short but descriptive list of things he wanted to do for and to me. He'd started off with "I humbly request the honor" and ended it with "If it pleases you," and though the wording was campy and silly, I had no doubts he was sincere in his offerings.

Both of them shut up and turned to me.

"There were so many other choices," my mother muttered.

Susan made a contemplative noise. "That's where Evan and I had our wedding reception. We discussed this already."

"I know," I said, looking up with a grin at what my lover had sent me, not for either of them. "I was there, remember? Bright yellow dress, puffy sleeves? Groomsman stepped on the hem and ripped it straight off the waist seam just before we walked down the aisle?"

I'd been trying to make light. Susan didn't laugh. My mother's mouth twisted again.

"It's a great location," I told them. "I just went to a thing there a few months ago. They had a huge vegetarian buffet with hummus and grilled portobellos and stuff. You can do vegetarian meals for people who really care about it being kosher, which honestly, won't be that many. Nobody has to eat the grilled chicken if they don't want to. Just make it at a different station."

"Well, maybe you don't care what people think of this family," my mother said, "but I do!"

Susan scribbled something on her notepad, then excused herself to use the bathroom. My mother glared at me. I dragged myself away from my increasingly dirty messages to shrug at her.

"What? It's not your event, Ma."

"I want to be able to invite my friends and not be embarrassed!"

"You can want what you want," I told her, repeating one of her most-often-used phrases from my childhood, "but you get what you get."

My phone tickled me through the pocket of my jeans again, and I bent back to it while my mother got up to putter around the kitchen.

"Is she going to invite your father?"

I pulled my attention away from Esteban's message, which had included a photograph that made the ones my mother complained about look like they belonged in a hymnal. "I don't know. I'd assume so."

My parents had been divorced, at this point, almost as long as they'd been married. My dad had moved to Florida, which had meant the every other weekend custody thing hadn't happened for us, something my mother loved to point out over and over. How she'd been a single mother, did it all on her own. By now it was old news, especially since whatever generous alimony arrangement they'd made had allowed her to work only at part-time retail jobs she cycled through whenever she decided she wanted the employee discount at some new place. My mom hadn't had it all peaches and cream, I'd never say that, but she hadn't exactly had to work in a labor camp to raise us, either.

"He's not even close to William!"

"William spends a week with Dad in Florida every year, Mom. Just like we did when we were kids."

"A week out of the year?" She sniffed. "That's hardly anything."

I shook my head in warning. "Not your party. Not your choice. If Evan and Susan want Dad there, he'll be invited."

My mother scowled. "The way you talk to me!"

"Someone has to," I said, kind of hating that it had to be me, but for fuck's sake, Jill was my mother times two, and Evan was Mr. Avoidance. I was already the perverted black sheep anyway. I might as well also bear the burden of being the ungrateful child.

Susan came back from the bathroom with suspiciously red eyes that made me feel bad that all of this had to be such a big freaking hassle. "It's settled. I'll replace the pasta bar with a vegetarian buffet. Will that be acceptable?"

Before my mother could answer, Susan picked up her purse. "I have to get going."

She'd fled within ten minutes, leaving nothing but a few crumpled catering menus in her place. My mother, scrubbing the counter so hard I feared she meant to slaughter her sponge, barely said goodbye to her. She turned her face from mine when I tried to hug her goodbye.

"You want to stay over? Your room is ready. I saved some Shirley Temple movies on the DVR." She turned off the water.

I snuck a peek at my phone, but to my disappointment, Esteban had signed off with a hurried GTG. I shoved my phone back in my pocket. "No. I have to work in the morning. I didn't bring a bag."

"You should've. I never get to see you since you moved so far away."

We talked on the phone several times a week and texted more than that. I sighed and hugged her. My mother had gotten so much smaller over the past few years. We used to be about the same height—not that we'd seen eye to eye very often. Now it seemed almost like I could rest my chin on top of her head.

"I'll call you." I paused. Then, though I prayed the answer would be negative, asked, "So, you're not coming to the gallery show on Friday night?"

My mother shook her head. "To what, see you in some more of those pictures? No, thank you!"

"I could email them to you," I offered with a blankly innocent expression that Evan and I had both perfected as teens to totally flip my mother's shit. "The pictures, I mean."

"No, thank you!"

I laughed, though part of me cringed at the way she categorized what I considered art. And honestly, how she categorized what I considered one of the most significant parts of me. I hugged her again anyway, though, because she was my mother. Then I got the hell out of that house and headed for home.

12

Alex and Olivia were not coming to the gallery show. They'd planned months ago to go out of town for the weekend. Alex had, however, told me it was okay if I wanted to take off early to go home and get ready. I knew that was so he could leave early himself without feeling guilty, if Alex Kennedy could ever be said to feel guilt. I suspected he rarely did, which was one of the reasons we'd become friends instead of only co-workers.

"I'm not sure you're the one who gets to decide what time I leave," I said, putting a few last minute bits of data into a client file and glancing to where he lounged in my doorway. "I mean, I'm the one who prints the paychecks. So."

"Yeah, well, we have direct deposit, so yeah, fuck your logic."

I laughed. "Wow. What a great workplace environment."

"You love it," he said and tossed a paper plane at me that I hadn't even noticed he held.

I caught it in midair. "Where you going for the weekend?"

"A nude beach," Alex said.

I swiveled again in my chair. "What?"

"Gotcha. Have you ever gone to one of those?"

"A nude beach." I shuddered. "No. Are you really going?"

"How about one of those all-inclusive sex resorts?"

Again, I shuddered. "Um, no. Seriously, is that where you're going?"

"No. Just to Miami."

"Close enough," I told him. "Are you gonna get a little nipped and tucked while you're there?"

"Nah. Just lie out on the beach in my man thong." Alex grinned and turned around to show me his butt, clad in tailored trousers I was sure had cost as much as one of my car payments. Man knew how to dress, I'd give him that.

"Don't send me any selfies, please."

Alex looked deadpan. "Oh, I'll tag you in every one of them."

"Sicko." I shook my head with a sigh. "Are you coming in on Monday?"

"Why? Are you planning on being late?"

"No. Just wondered."

"You don't have some big weekend planned?" Alex asked.

I shook my head again. "Nope. The gallery show. That's it. Nothing much else going on. Oh, I might head over to the sex dungeon for some hardcore pony play, maybe look for a new vinyl suction bed—" I stopped at the look on his face. "Gotcha."

"What the hell is a vinyl suction bed?"

"It's this bed you get in and they put a little breathing tube in your mouth, and then they suck out all the air," I told him. "Like vacuum packed. Like those bags you use to store sweaters, only for sex."

Alex winced. "Shit. I thought I'd seen some stuff, but that is really..."

"I am *not* looking for a vinyl suction bed," I told him. "As if I'd tell you, if I were."

"That's maybe a little too kinky, huh?"

"It's only too kinky if you're not into it," I said with a laugh.

"But the pony play," he said. "That's real?"

We both burst into laughter. Pony play is totally a real thing, but I'd never done anything like that. I hadn't even seen it done. Nobody I'd ever met had really done it.

"I think that's some serious kind of Anne Rice Sleeping Beauty series stuff," I told him. "I mean, yeah, I guess it's real, but no, I'm not planning on harnessing my lover up to a carriage with a horsetail up his ass and having him pull me around this weekend."

"Why not? It sounds like fun," Alex said, and paused for a beat before adding, "so you *do* have a lover!"

"Oh, my God," I cried. "You're obsessed with sex! Get out of here, you perv! Go take your wife to Miami and lie around on a beach getting drunk."

"Don't forget about the man thong," Alex added and ducked out of the office before I could throw something at him.

He had got me to thinking, though. Alicia had moved to Texas a little over two years ago, but you couldn't replace a best friend the way you could a fuck buddy or even a boyfriend. I'd left my old job and discovered that work friendships didn't necessarily last without the bond of hating your boss. I'd met up with that crowd for drinks a couple times, but not being able to keep up on the office gossip meant I was usually left out of the conversation. When I'd first started getting online to really explore finding a play partner, I had met a bunch of like-minded people and become friendly with them, but there'd been few with whom I'd had anything in common other than kink. I'd met Esteban and distanced myself from that crowd, unconsciously, I supposed.

I hadn't been to a munch in forever, but a quick search of OnHisKnees.com showed me there was one scheduled for tonight. I could go to the gallery show and then the meet up afterward, if I still felt like it. I typed a couple quick messages to a few familiar online friends, several of whom were planning to be there. We chatted for a few minutes before I logged off to finish my work so I really could leave early.

I'd teased Alex that he was obsessed with sex, and it was true that on the surface that's what stuff like fetish play was all about. But there was more to it than that, at least for me and anyone I'd ever met who was seriously into things that strayed outside the vanilla norm. Dominance and submission was about power exchange, sure. Getting off. But it was also about an emotional connection. Finding that person who fit you.

And that made me think of *him*.

But instead of messaging George, which I only did at stupid o'clock or drunk-thirty, I messaged Esteban. Call me.

He did about twenty minutes later as I was packing up to get out the door. "Hi."

"Hi. Do you want to go with me to a gallery show tonight? And a meet up, later?" I had never asked him to go out with me on anything resembling a real, official date before.

He didn't say anything at first, and knew right away his answer would be no. "I want to, yes. But…"

"Never mind." I tried to keep my voice light, not clipped or angry. I didn't have a right to be upset if I was breaking the rules I'd helped set in the beginning. Esteban and I were lovers with parameters. I'd been very clear about that from the start. I hadn't wanted to get into anything emotional. But that's the funny and terrible thing about fucking someone. If you do it right, the more you do it, the easier it is to like them. Something had changed since our reconciliation, but maybe only inside me.

"*Querida…*"

"It's fine." My voice softened. "You'll have to make it up to me."

"Gladly." His voice dropped low to match mine. "Name your price."

"Go into the bathroom," I told him, already closing my office door and locking it, though Alex should've been long gone already.

"I have a meeting in twenty minutes—"

"Then you'll have to be fast." My tone was as hard as his dick was going to be, if I knew him at all. "I want to hear you come for me."

He made a muffled, choking noise. I grinned and leaned back in my chair, already inching up my skirt. I ran a thumb over my panties, letting the pressure of my touch turn me on.

"Oh, I want to be touching you," Esteban said five minutes later, after he'd told me he'd gone into the private, single-stall bathroom on the third floor of his building. "My cock aches for you."

"Show me." I wet my fingers and slipped them beneath the lace to circle my clit.

A picture came through a moment later that took my breath away. That hard, thick cock, already turning red with arousal. His fist around it, the foreskin just barely covering the head.

"Beautiful," I breathed into the phone. "Fuck your fist for me. Imagine my mouth."

"I am."

It wasn't going to take me more than another minute to come, but I teased myself, listening to the sound of his breathing get faster. Sharper. I couldn't hear the slick noises of him stroking himself, but I could imagine them. I edged myself, teasing, and when he muttered my name, I let myself go over. Orgasm blasted through me, fierce and hot and wonderful.

With my pussy still pulsing, I sat up in the chair. "Are you close?"

"Yes, so close. I'm so hard for you. So close…"

"Stop, now." I smiled, leaning on the desk with my elbow, my other hand cupping myself through my panties. I could come again, if I wanted to, but I held off.

Esteban stuttered his reply. "S-st-top?"

"Yes," I said sternly. "Take your hand off your cock. Now."

He groaned. "Please…"

"No. Anyone can make you come, but I want to know that you'll stop yourself for me."

Esteban let out a heavy sigh. "You kill me."

I laughed. "Show me, baby."

Another picture came through of his deliciously hard cock. The glisten of precome made my mouth go dry. For a second or two I almost changed my mind, wanting to hear him get off, knowing it was for me.

Instead, I said quietly, "The next time you come, it had better be all over my tits."

He muttered something in Spanish, a curse or a prayer. Maybe both. I smiled.

"I mean it," I told him, warming to this new game. "Your orgasm is mine. Do you understand me, Esteban? You will not come until I tell you that you may."

"For how long?" He sounded agonized and also grateful.

"Weeks," I whispered, teasing. Not meaning it. "Maybe months."

Silence. "Yes, miss."

"Say it," I whispered, an eye on the clock. I didn't want him to be late for his meeting or to get in trouble at work. I was responsible for him, after all.

"My orgasm is yours. My cock is yours," he added, though I hadn't asked him for that. "I want to only come for you."

"Oh, sweetheart, that makes me feel so…" I sighed, calculating how close I was to another orgasm of my own. "So good."

"Are you going to come for me?" he asked.

"Yes. Again. Oh…yeah. Tell me again."

"I am yours," Esteban said. "Your toy. I do what you want, everything to please you, my queen, my goddess."

I came, less fiercely this time but no less enjoyably. My breath shuddered out of me, and I made sure to let him hear it. I laughed a little through the pleasure at the sound of his groan.

Still easing down from my orgasm, I said, "Go to your meeting now. Don't be late."

"I want to talk more to you. I want to hear you come again."

"I won't, not a third time, and you need to be someplace," I said. "Go."

Esteban chuckled. "I do love it when you are stern with me."

"I know you do." I laughed along with him and closed my eyes to picture his face. "I like it, too."

13

I'm not sure there's a woman in the universe who could look at her own face and body blown up to poster size without being critical of it. It's hard enough to look at snapshots without judging a double chin, an unevenly plucked brow. Pores that are too big, breasts that are too small. Yet when I looked at myself in the portraits hung on the wall in this gallery, I didn't let myself dwell on the imperfections. I focused on the beauty of each piece, and not just the physical loveliness of the people in the photos, nor the setting or the subject, but that unnameable quality that Scott had managed to find and bring out in every scene.

"You take pretty pictures," I told him as he came up behind me to put an arm around my waist. I lifted my glass of wine toward the biggest portrait, framed simply in black. It wasn't a new one; we'd done it a few years ago, but I hadn't seen it in a while. "That's still my favorite."

Scott gave me a familiar grin. "That's the one where you can't see your face."

"That's not the reason." I studied it. The shot was slightly out of focus, the edges of everything blurred. I'd never actually made love to the man in the picture with me, yet Scott had still found a way to capture that moment between two people when passion had exhausted them, and all that remained was tenderness. In the picture, my face half-turned, my hand on my partner's cheek as he knelt in front of me.

"It's beauty," I said. "It's art. It's real and lovely and honest. And not a whip or a chain in sight."

He laughed and squeezed me, pulling me closer to kiss my cheek. "Plenty of whips and chains in those other pictures."

"Those are the ones people will comment on. But this one," I said, still studying it. "This one is…"

Real, I meant to say. It wasn't quite what I meant. Of all the pictures on display, this was one of the few that had been totally staged, which should've made it somehow less real than the ones he'd taken in an actual BDSM dungeon or during a play party. Yet somehow, it *was* more real, because while I'd been to a dungeon twice and participated in a play party maybe a few more times than that, most of the time for me it wasn't about the toys or the scene but the emotions. Not so much what I did as how I felt doing it. That picture, staged or not, showed the truth.

"It's gorgeous. You're gorgeous," he told me and kissed me again before being tugged away by a girl in a full-length black vinyl ball gown who wanted to talk to him about…something that I didn't care about.

I turned back to the photo and sipped my wine. Behind me in the gallery, the DJ had started spinning dance music. The free wine was flowing. People might not actually dance, but they were certainly getting drunk.

A flash of blue caught my eye, and I turned. The woman next to me looking at the photo had gorgeous turquoise, blue and pale green hair twisted into a pretty updo ornamented with a pinup flower that matched her sleek, vintage-style dress. She pointed at the wall to the portrait next to the one I'd been studying.

"I'm Sarah. That's my boyfriend in the picture with you." She grinned.

I held out my hand. "Elise. So you're the infamous Sarah. I heard a lot about you."

"All bad, I'm sure." She laughed and stood on her tiptoes to see around me, scanning the crowd before settling back to look at me. "He's around here, somewhere. But I wanted to come over and say hi. Jack said this shoot was one of his favorites."

"Did he? I had a good time, too. We got some really great pictures. Well, Scott did. But doesn't he always?"

Sarah's smile widened. "Yeah, he's amazing. I've used a lot of his pieces for clients."

Olivia had told me that Sarah did interior design and decorating. I wasn't sure what sorts of people would hang pictures like the ones in this gallery tonight in their houses—Scott's work was art, yes, but not of the seascape or fruit basket variety.

"I have him do landscapes for me," she said, seeing what must've been a strange look pass over my face. "Have you seen the one he did with the woman in the field holding the red fabric up, blowing in the wind? I put that piece together with some really sweet red satin as a wall hanging in a client's home office. That sort of thing. Probably not any of these sorts of things."

She gestured at the one hanging next to the one I'd been looking at. Two men, both clad in leather, one in a biker cap. Chains. A ball gag. It was a lot more hardcore and explicit than any of the pictures Jack and I had taken during our shoot. It was raw and fierce, and its beauty was harsh. It told a story, yes, with the looks on the models' faces, but it didn't seem to be one with a happy ending.

"But yours," she continued then sighed with a small, bemused smile. "It's so…soft. I really love it. I loved all the ones you guys took together."

"People don't think it can be soft," I told her, not sure why I felt compelled to suddenly explain myself to her but spilling some truth tea anyway. "They don't think about the tenderness, the responsibility, the give and take. How it feels to take care of someone and to be taken care of. Mostly, they want to see images like those, or the ones over there."

"Not everyone," Sarah said. "Some people get it."

There was no good reason for my throat to close, or my eyes to prick with sudden tears. No need for emotion here or now. Yet something about Sarah's nonchalant answer moved me.

"Yeah," I said. "Some people do."

I recognized the face of the man who appeared behind her, though the last time I'd seen him, he'd been wearing a lot less clothes. Jack's grin, though, that was distinctive. He kissed Sarah on the cheek then reached for my hand.

"Hey, you. How's it going?"

"Good. Have you been getting a lot of compliments?" I waved a hand in the general direction of the crowd.

Jack laughed. "Oh, sure. Some people are even looking at my face."

Sarah bumped him with her hip. "Who'd want to look at that ugly thing when your dick's so much prettier?"

I spotted my brother from across the room and excused myself to greet him. He'd always known about my modeling, and though he preferred not to look at my more risqué pictures, he'd been to a number of shows featuring my photos and had always been supportive. Evan was looking over a triptych, three different women in lingerie, all the same pose, shot from above so that the viewer seemed to be looking down on them. None of them was me, which was why he was staring for so long. He had a glass of wine in one hand, a plate of cheese and crackers in the other, though how he expected to eat and drink at the same time, I didn't know.

We greeted each other, as always, not with a hug and kiss but a simple tip of the chin. My brother and I had shared a womb; hugging hadn't seemed particularly necessary to either one of us after that. Without preamble, he nodded toward the guy with him.

"This is Niall. He works with me. This is my sister, Elise. She's the one in the dirty pictures."

Niall shook my hand and gave Evan an adorable, embarrassed look. I laughed and squeezed his hand then snagged my brother's plate of cheese.

"Don't mind my brother. He thinks he's funny because our parents believed boys should be comedians and girls ought to be princesses. But I *am* Elise," I said. "And I *am* in some of these pictures. None of those three. Feel free to ogle without worry."

Niall's hand in mine was warm, his grip stronger than I'd anticipated. He looked over his shoulder at the pictures Evan had been looking over. "Yeah…hi. When Evan invited me to an art show, I guess I wasn't expecting this."

Evan, the turd, laughed. "I told you it was art, man. What's the best kind of art? Naked people."

Niall and I shared a look. I didn't know what it meant. I couldn't read him. But it lingered, until both of us smiled at the same time. He let my hand go, but slowly, and I was intrigued to notice that I was reluctant for him to release me. We stared at each other until Evan snorted.

"Dude. That's my *sister*," Evan said.

Niall didn't look away from me. "Yeah? What're you gonna do, beat me up?"

"No," my dumbass brother said. "But apparently, she might, if you're lucky."

"I've always been kind of lucky," Niall said.

Evan and I both looked at him. Niall smiled and shrugged. I punched my brother in the arm like we were still in the fourth grade. "Shut up."

Evan danced away from me, rubbing his arm. "Hey! I'm supposed to look out for you!"

"I can look out for myself." I looked back at Niall. "You work with this idiot?"

"Yeah, same office," Niall said.

"Poor you."

"Hey!" Evan frowned, while Niall and I grinned at each other. My brother's phone buzzed from his pocket in the next moment, and he pulled it free with a small grimace I hated to see. He didn't have to tell me it was his wife. He held up a finger as he took the call, walking away from us both to find a quiet place.

Niall looked at me. "So. Elise."

"Niall." I smiled. "My brother dragged you along for a night out, huh?"

"He said I needed some culture."

"Do you?"

The question made him laugh and shake his head. "I guess… so?"

"My brother wouldn't know culture if it had fangs and bit him in the ass," I told him. "But it was cool that he brought you along to support the event. Did you get some raffle tickets? It's for a good cause."

Niall dug into his pocket and pulled out a handful of red tickets. "Lady at the door got me, yep. I bought an arm's worth for five bucks."

"That's the way to do it. You want some cheese?" I held out my brother's plate. "He's going to be gone awhile."

Niall waved a hand to decline the cheese but glanced over his shoulder to where Evan had gone. "Yeah…she wasn't happy about him coming out tonight, I think."

"Then she ought to have told him to stay home, or come along with him, instead of interrupting him while he's out doing stuff," I said shortly and pushed a piece of cheese into my mouth to keep myself from saying more than that.

"Maybe she doesn't like art," Niall said so blandly that I knew he'd met my sister-in-law.

I shook my head with a small laugh and swallowed the cheese. "No. She probably doesn't."

I didn't think Susan liked much of anything these days, to be honest, but there wasn't much I could do about it. Niall turned to look at the portraits, and I followed him as he made his way along the wall. I finished the cheese and dumped the plate, along with my empty wineglass. I'd seen all of the pictures before, so I watched him look at them instead of looking at them myself.

Scott had hung them in no obvious groupings—there were full-color graphic shots of naked people next to black-and-white pictures shot off-center or slightly out of focus to take away the emphasis of *what* the people in them were doing and let the viewer absorb the emotional impact, instead. Niall didn't comment on any of them, though some caught his attention longer than others. Several times he shook his head and gave me a glance, though I couldn't quite read his expression. Turned on? Turned off? It was hard to say, but I was having a good time trying to figure it out. We got to the final picture hung on this wall, and I paused, wondering if I should warn him.

Unlike the one I'd been looking at earlier, this picture had nothing soft or hazy about it. Black-and-white, every edge of the image was clear and crisp. Sharp enough there could be no mistaking any of the action.

I was in this one, too. Jack was not my partner. To be honest, I didn't remember the name of the man in the photo with me. We'd been strangers before the session, and we remained strangers still, our moment captured forever in ink and paper, imprisoned behind glass.

"Huh," Niall said, staring.

I laughed, low at first, then a little louder and even more when he gave me a wry smile. He looked back at the picture and crossed an arm over his chest to rest the opposite elbow on it, his index finger stroking along his chin. He looked at that picture very hard.

I leaned close to say into his ear, "Stop it, you're making me blush."

"I find that hard to believe," he said without turning toward me.

I wasn't blushing, that was true enough. But his intense study of the picture was sending heat all through me. Not embarrassment. Curiosity, maybe. Or anticipation. An electric crackle of it between us, unexpected and yet somehow no surprise.

Niall stroked a line in the air just above the glass, following the curves of my figure in the picture. In it, I wore a vintage dress, seamed stockings, my hair in Victory rolls. I sat in a carved wooden chair upholstered in crimson velvet that matched my lipstick, though in the black-and-white portrait, both the chair and my lips looked black. The man with me wore nothing but a set of leather cuffs, his hands behind his back. Head bowed. Maybe part of the reason why I could barely remember him was because in the picture, his face was hidden while mine faced the camera. I remembered touching the top of his head gently, my fingertips so light on his hair I barely felt the tickle of it. I remembered the camera's click and Scott's murmured instructions to tip my head down, turn a little this way or that. I remembered the subtle thump of my heart as I concentrated on being still.

Niall looked at me. "What were you thinking when you were taking this picture?"

"I…" The question stumped me. I shook my head a little and gave him a smile, playing it off. "Who knows?"

"You look sad."

I meant to answer with something light, maybe flirty or sarcastic. What came out was the truth. "I was."

"Why?"

I have an unconscious habit of pressing my right thumb to the inside of my left wrist, covering the tattoo there, when I am struck with emotion. Usually I don't notice, but this time the press of my nail was sharp on my skin. I forced myself to drop both hands to my sides.

"It was a long time ago," I told him.

"Whatever it was, does it still make you sad?"

I kept myself from pressing my wrist by curling my fingers tight into my palm, but didn't answer him. Niall nodded and looked back at the picture. Then at the one next to it on the wall, that one much smaller. I was in that one, too. Same clothes, same hair, but this time in the shot alone. Scott had captured me laughing at something off camera. My head turned, the background a little blurry. It was actually what I'd have considered an outtake, but leave it to Scott to turn an imperfect shot into something lovely.

"I like this one better," Niall said. "Even though you still look sad."

"I'm laughing," I protested.

Niall gave me a solemn look. "Not in your eyes, you're not."

"You don't even know me." I frowned.

He shrugged and looked like he might be about to say something else, when the music stopped and Scott's assistant Laura tapped the mic to get everyone's attention. It took a few seconds for the buzz of conversation to die down, but most of us turned expectantly. Niall ended up slightly behind me, and I imagined the caress of his breath on the back of my neck, my bared shoulder. Or maybe it wasn't my imagination.

"I'm gonna draw the first winner! Anyone who bought red tickets, get them out. You get to choose any picture on the wall to take home tonight!" Laura giggled and swirled her hand around inside a fishbowl filled with red tickets. She pulled one out, reading the numbers carefully aloud.

There was a moment of silence before Niall said, "That's me."

"We have a winner!" Laura called out, pointing at him from across the room. "Which picture do you want?"

Everyone was looking at him, not just me, but it was my face he focused on briefly before pointing to the picture of me laughing. My heart skipped a beat, one, two. I could not stop myself from smiling.

"That one," he said. "I want to take that girl home."

14

Niall was, indeed, taking me home. At least the picture of
me, which had been carefully wrapped in paper secured with
twine and loaded into the back of his car. Evan had left to get
home, but Niall had stayed. Now the two of us were in the
parking lot under a late-May sky sparkling with stars, and I
was wondering what, exactly, was going to happen.

"So," he said, but nothing else.

I smiled. "So?"

"So…it's early. You maybe want to go somewhere and get
something to eat?" Niall put a hand on his belly. "Man cannot live on cheese cubes alone. Or woman, either."

"I have plans, actually."

He nodded. "Ah. Sure, right. Of course you do. It's Friday night."

"You could…come with me. If you wanted to." I thought
about the munch. A bunch of kinky people standing around
eating cocktail weenies and talking about *True Blood*. It was a
simple social gathering; there wouldn't be anyone strung up by
the heels or anything like that. He might think it was boring.
I didn't even know if Niall watched *True Blood*. "It's nothing

fancy. It's just a little meet up of some friends I haven't seen in a while. There will be food there. Drinks, too."

"Oh, I don't want to butt in if you already have plans with friends." His words said no, but the look on his face was all yes.

I laughed. "I told you, it's casual. And I'm not really sure who will be there. I could end up not knowing anyone. You should come with me. It'll be fun."

"If you're sure you don't mind?"

I smiled. "I'm not really that sort of girl."

Niall smiled, too. "What sort of girl would that be?"

"The sort who does things just to be polite. I don't ask for what I don't want."

"A woman who knows what she wants," Niall said. "Why am I not surprised."

I tipped my chin toward my car. "You can follow me. It's at The Slaughtered Lamb, downtown."

This gave him pause. "Uh-oh. Should I be worried I'll end up in a bathtub full of ice or something?"

"Why…?"

"It's a kidney harvesting thing," he said.

I frowned. "Should I be sort of insulted that you'd assume I have any desire to harvest your kidneys?"

Niall looked apologetic. "I'm sorry, I was making a bad joke."

"I'm sure they're great kidneys and all," I continued. "But I have two of my own."

We stared at each other, me deadpan. Him still a little embarrassed. Then slowly, slowly, I smiled. After a few seconds, so did he.

"C'mon," I said. "Follow me."

It did occur to me as we walked up to the back door of The Slaughtered Lamb that I should've warned Niall that the munch was for dominant women and submissive men. I didn't expect anything outrageous to be going on—the meet up was in a public space, after all, and there was an etiquette about stuff like that. After the art show, anything that happened at the munch would be totally tame. I hadn't been able to get a read on him about what he thought about all the stuff my brother sometimes referred to as "chips, dips and whips," but I was getting a definite interested vibe from him, and he obviously knew which way I bent. Still, it didn't seem fair to toss Niall into something without letting him know what, exactly, we were doing.

"So, listen," I began, but before I could finish, I'd been descended on by Cubby. Enveloped in his enormous embrace, I couldn't get out anything more than a muffled yeep.

"Elise! Baby doll! My God, it's been ages and ages. Where have you been hiding yourself? Come in, bring your... friend...?" Cubby paused for an introduction.

Niall stuck out a hand. "Niall Black."

Cubby, who stood six-five and weighed at least three hundred and fifty pounds, had been a former professional wrestler of the theatrical variety. He and his wife, Sonya, had been organizing meet ups for years, and had been one of the first couples I'd met once I started reaching out online. I adored him, even when he was squeezing me too hard.

"Niall, great to meet you. Cubby." Cubby pumped Niall's hand. "C'mon in, guys, we have a cash bar set up back here, and there are appetizers. Just dump a fiver in the bucket on the buffet table, if you can. If you want to order something off the menu, I think there are some on the tables."

Then he was off to greet some other new arrivals I didn't recognize. I let Niall lead the way to the bar, where he ordered us both whiskey sours, and then to a table where he dove on the menu. I looked around, hoping to see familiar faces, but other than Sonya at the other end of the room, I didn't see any.

"I'm starving," Niall said. "Are you going to have something?"

I peeked at the menu. "Yeah…I'm going to have the fish and chips. It's really good here."

"Shepherd's pie for me," he told the server when she came over. "Fish and chips for the lady."

I can't say I like it when a man presumes to order for me, but somehow the way Niall did it gave me a warm, dangerous tickle down low. He'd listened to me and remembered what I wanted. He'd paid attention. Some might've found that overbearing, but it flipped my switch.

Shit.

"So, how long have you been modeling?"

I shrugged. "A few years. It's not my job or anything like that. I do it for fun. For charity, or for friends. I…like it."

Niall gave me a look. First curious. Then assessing. He nodded after a moment, as though I'd explained something I wasn't sure I understood myself.

"Evan said you work for a private company? Financial planning, something like that?"

I paused, wondering what else my brother had seen fit to tell this stranger about me. "Yeah. Estate planning, financial planning, college planning. That sort of thing. My partner used to do a lot of financial stuff, trading, stuff like that, internationally. He started his own company to help people grow their money and plan for the future. I do most of the marketing and outreach, handle client concerns. I balance the books and make sure the lights stay on. Kind of whatever else needs doing aside from the actual investment recommendations."

"Interesting. Evan told me you were an accountant."

I rolled my eyes. "Not really. I used to work for an accounting firm, in HR. I was a math major. Now I do this. All he knows is that I work with numbers, I guess. My brother isn't that observant."

Niall paused to sip from his drink and give a quick glance around the room. "So…I haven't been here before. It's cool."

"It's fun. During the week it gets a lot of hot businessmen." I watched for his reaction. Some men would be jealous even without a right to be.

He laughed and tapped his glass to mine. "Nice. I swore I'd never work for a place where I had to wear a suit and tie."

"No?"

"Nope. Polos and khakis all the way." He grinned.

"But a man in a suit is so…"

"Uncomfortable," he said.

"You should try wearing panty hose and heels," I told him wryly, testing him a little. "No, really. You should try it."

"I did dress like Dr. Frank-N-Furter for Halloween once. That was the last time you'll see me in heels." Niall shook his head. "I could deal with the lipstick, but damn, the shoes just about broke my ankles."

I giggled, delighted and tingling at the thought of it. "I love *Rocky Horror.*"

"We should go sometime. They show it at the Allen Theater every few months. Props and everything. But I'm not dressing like Tim Curry again."

"How about like Rocky?" The whiskey sour was warming my insides. Loosening my tongue. Making me flirty.

Niall snorted laughter. "In a gold bikini bottom? Wow. No way. Nobody needs to see that."

"I bet you'd look great." I made a show of looking him up and down. "You're a swimmer."

"How…" He shook his head. "Not anymore, I mean, not

competitively. But in high school I was, yeah. How did you know?"

"You have the body for it." I sipped more drink and sat back so the server could put our plates in front of us. "Were you any good?"

"Never lost," Niall said.

I paused with a fry dipped in my ketchup. "Never? Not once?"

"Nope." He shook his head, looking both faintly proud and a little embarrassed. "Not once."

"Wow. That's impressive."

He shrugged. "Didn't do me a lot of good in the long-term, you know? I mean, what you do and who you are in high school only really matters in high school."

"In high school I was a cheerleader." I tucked the fry into my mouth, relishing the salty, greasy yumminess. "How about that."

"Rah, rah, rah," Niall said.

"Elise!"

I turned to see another familiar face. Eric was a local ER doc I'd dated once or twice before we figured out we weren't really suited for each other. He'd been stumbling through his search for a mistress, looking for one harsher than I ever wanted to be. He'd wanted something full-time and long-term, a whole lifestyle thing, which wasn't what I'd ever really been into, but I liked him a lot. I introduced him to Niall.

"Hi, good to meet you. You're new?" Eric asked.

Niall hesitated, looking to me for a second. "Yeah, I mean, Elise invited me. I'm kind of along for the ride."

"Right on." Eric nodded. "Gotta get your feet wet somewhere. This is a great group to do that in. And Elise is a great lady. Treat her right. You don't want to get Cubby on your bad side."

Niall looked at me, his smile a little twisty, a little secretive. A lot sexy. "No, I sure wouldn't."

Eric looked beyond us to a small cluster of people at another high-top table close to where the food had been laid out. He held up the glass of white wine he was carrying. "I should get this over to my lady. Take care, Elise. Nice to meet you, Niall."

I wanted to ask Eric who his lady was—the icy blonde in the black wrap dress? She looked like the sort of woman capable of beating the hell out of a guy who was into that sort of thing. To my surprise, though, he pressed the glass into the hand of the short, plump redhead sitting on one of the high stools next to her. The redhead wore a flowery caftan-type dress that clung to ample curves, and a pair of orthopedic sandals. She twisted to let Eric lean against her as she kissed him. Thanking him for the drink, probably. My expression must've showed the surprise, because Niall followed my gaze.

"You know her?"

I shook my head. "No. I just wouldn't have picked her out to be…well… I guess you never really know what people like about each other, huh?"

Niall gave her a curious look then turned back to me. "I guess you never do."

More of my friends showed up then, and the crowd got lively. Someone had set up a small speaker system playing music from an iPod. The appetizers disappeared. People danced a little or ordered food, but most of us stood around in small groups chatting about life, work, families. I was talking with Randi, a woman I'd met a few times previously but didn't know very well, when Niall excused himself to use the restroom. As soon as he'd gone, she leaned close to me.

"How did you two meet?"

"He works with my brother," I told her.

Randi gave me a look over the rim of her wineglass. "He's very cute."

I looked automatically toward where Niall had gone, though I couldn't see him. "Is he?"

"Oh, sure. And he clearly adores you." She nodded.

I laughed. "Oh…we're not…"

"No? You're kidding." Randi's brows arched upward. "I thought you'd been together forever, the way you talk to each other."

I had to think about that. Niall and I definitely had a pat-ter down, riffing back and forth. "No. We just met, tonight, actually."

"I've been looking forever to find someone. Online dating is hell for straight people. God help those of us who are a little crooked. Half the guys are looking to find a mistress, what-ever that means, and it's usually nothing like what I want." Randi rolled her eyes and lowered her voice. "I mean, look, I don't mind pouring myself into a corset now and again, but most of the time I want to be in lounge pants when I whip someone, you know?"

"I don't really—"

"They say they want to submit, but it's still all about them." Randi looked disgusted.

I'd had my share of that, for sure. I thought of Esteban, my delightful boy. Finding him had been lucky and rare, and even so, not without its problems. How different tonight would've been if he were here with me. "Niall and I aren't on a date."

"But he's a sub, yeah?"

I laughed again. "No, I don't think so. He's not mine, at any rate."

"I'd convince him," Randi said just as a nudge at my elbow showed me Niall, a glass of iced tea in his hand.

"I brought you a drink."

Randi gave me a look so significant I had to cover my mouth against a sudden burst of laughter. Niall gave us both the sort of look men give women when they suspect they're the butt of some joke they don't understand and don't want to know about.

"Thanks," I said. "Would you mind asking the bartender to put some lime in this, instead of lemon? Crushed ice if they have it, too. And a straw."

Niall nodded without looking even the tiniest bit put out. "Sure, no problem."

Randi waited until he'd gotten out of earshot. "If he's not yours, can I have him?"

"Umm." I laughed awkwardly. "Sure? I guess?"

In a few minutes Niall was back, handing me the glass of iced tea. One sip told me he'd had it prepared perfectly. "Thanks. I was thirsty."

Randi gave me another look. I didn't mean to giggle, but couldn't hold it back. When she excused herself, Niall watched her go then turned back to me with a shake of his head.

"Ooookay."

The crowd had thinned a lot, and amazingly we'd made it almost to last call. "You want to get out of here?"

"Sure. If you do."

"It's late." I barely held back a yawn. "This party's winding down anyway."

In the parking lot, standing next to my car, I wondered if Niall was going to kiss me, and what I would do if he tried. Suddenly, strangely, it was all I could think about, even if I couldn't decide whether or not I wanted him to. I unlocked my car with the remote key and tried without much luck to shake off that tingly sense of anticipation rapidly spreading to my fingertips.

"What was that woman making you laugh about?"

"Oh. Randi? She thought we were a couple." I laughed again, shaking my head. I'd unlocked but not yet opened my door.

Niall smiled. "Did she? Huh."

"Yeah. She thought you were my..." I hesitated. He'd been to the gallery show. He'd seen the pictures. Evan had even made a joke or two. Even so, that was different than coming right out with it. He hadn't seemed to think I was a demanding bitch about the iced tea, but men had a way of making other kinds of assumptions when they learned about my kinks.

"Your what? Boyfriend?"

"Sort of. More like my...boy." I bit the inside of my cheek lightly, trying not to giggle.

It took him a second, but when he got it, Niall's jaw dropped. "What? Why?"

I thought of how he'd ordered my food because he'd paid attention. How he'd brought me the iced tea, assessing my needs and trying to provide for me as naturally as if we'd known each other a lot longer than a few hours. How he'd accepted my request to change it. He'd been good at it, too. Better than a lot of "boyfriends" I'd had.

"Well, we were at a meet up for..." I hesitated, deciding then to come clean. "It was for dominant women and submissive guys. Kind of a...not a club, exactly, not one with membership dues or anything. More like hobbyists. Like people who are all into keeping bees or scrapbooking or who drive classic cars, that sort of thing."

"Except that group is for guys who like to be what... spanked and stuff?"

My smile faded at his tone. "Some do. It's not always like that."

"Is it like that for you?"

I shrugged, giving him a sideways glance. "It can be."

"Weird," Niall said. "Why do you do that?"

"It's not something I do," I said in a clipped, hard voice. "It's who I am."

Niall was quiet for a moment. "Why didn't you tell me?"

"I was going to, but I didn't think it mattered, really. I mean, haven't you gone to any sort of social thing with a bunch of people standing around eating and drinking? How much does what they like to do in the bedroom really play into it? It's just…people."

"People who thought I was your…" Niall shook his head with a frown. "Damn, Elise. I wish you'd told me."

I thought about reaching for him, smoothing my hands down the front of his shirt to calm him, but didn't. He was not, after all, my boy. I couldn't just pet him because I wanted to. And his comment, "weird," had annoyed me.

"I'm sorry. You're right. But you'd never have known if Randi hadn't been so obvious about it. Would you?"

"No. Which makes it all worse."

"It was just a meet up," I said. "Not a dungeon party or something like that."

Niall frowned. "I guess I'd have figured it out a lot sooner if you'd taken me to one of those."

"The manacles on the stone walls kind of give it away, yeah." I let him smile first, but he did.

"Man. I had no idea," Niall said.

I leaned against my car. The night was chilly, the metal no longer even holding any heat from the sun. I rubbed my arms against the rising gooseflesh.

"You wouldn't, would you?" I said, and paused as he shrugged out of his jacket to hand it to me without a word. I got warm then, all right. All over. "Like I said. Just people."

"I guess I figured it would be more like what was in those pictures tonight."

"It can be," I admitted. "But you know, most people don't go to the grocery store in full leather outfits leading their subs on a leash. In regular life, we're just…normal."

Something twisted in his expression. Not disgust, which would've put me off worse than him saying *weird*. Not arousal, either, unfortunately. He shook his head and then scrubbed a hand over the top of it, mussing his dark brown hair.

"I feel like an idiot now, that's all."

"You shouldn't. I'm sorry. I really ought to have told you. Would you still have come with me?" I looked him over.

"I don't think so."

I nodded. "Are you sorry you did?"

"No. I guess not. It was fun," he said, looking into my eyes. "Hanging out with you."

We looked at each other without saying much of anything. I could feel my grin growing. Heat, too, tingling in my cheeks and throat, and lower down.

Niall made a gruff noise and tipped his head to look up at the sky. "Supposed to be some shooting stars tonight."

"Good for wishes."

He gave me a sideways look. "What would you wish for?"

"You know, the usual. A unicorn. World peace. A really good sequel to *Bill and Ted's Excellent Adventure*."

Niall chuckled and turned to lean against my car beside me. We both looked up at the sky for a while. Most of the night was obscured by the rise of buildings and the ambient light, anyway, but I looked hard to see if I could find anything shooting across the darkness.

"It's getting late," I said finally, when a series of yawns threatened to cramp my jaw. I shrugged out of his jacket. "Thanks for that."

"No problem. I guess I'm a gentleman," Niall said.

That, yes, I thought. But also more than that.

He didn't kiss me, and we didn't shake hands. He did ask for my number, and I gave it to him, though I didn't expect him ever to call me.

I pondered on that while I drove home, where I took a shower and scrubbed my face clean.

Niall liked me. I was sure of it. And I was free to date whomever I wanted, even while seeing Esteban. But would I want to *date* Niall, if he asked me?

I put on comfy pajamas and tucked myself into bed, then stared at the ceiling and regretted drinking that iced tea so late. It would press on my bladder. At least that's what I could blame this wakefulness on, though the truth was, I would've found it difficult to fall asleep anyway.

Too much thinking.

You look sad, Niall had said. *Why?*

I closed my eyes, but dreams were far away.

Does it still make you sad?

Yes, I thought. *Oh, fuck me, yes, it does. Every fucking day.*

And then, because it was late and I was stupid, I pulled my phone from the charger and swiped to open the app I could never bring myself to delete. There he was. Profile picture and screen name the same, unchanged. I always held my breath for a second or so when I opened the app, waiting to see if he'd have a different face, a different name. If he'd be gone altogether. But no, he was still there. He was always there.

And in the dark and silence, through a blur of tears, I told him the truth.

I miss you.

I miss you so much.

The dark is too big without you beside me.

I waited, hating the tears slipping over my cheeks and into my mouth, but knowing it was useless to think I could stop them. I counted the seconds, giving him a minute. Another. It was late, and surely he wouldn't read the message. I should delete it before I could see if he did anyway so then I would never know. I could hide the app again in the folder of things on my phone I never used. I could pretend to myself in the morning I had not been weak.

The small *D* next to the message turned to an *R*.

But he did not answer me.

He didn't delete his account, and he always read what I sent him, but he never, ever replied.

And I, the stupid one, the weak one, heart aching, erased the messages I'd sent him and closed the app before I could be stupid again.

15

"It's a little creepy," my brother complained over a plate of eggs and potatoes.

He'd dropped William off at Sunday school and was avoiding going home. I was hungry with no food in the house. We'd agreed on the diner.

"People have naked pictures of me, Evan. Of all the pictures he could've picked, that's about the least creepy." I dug into my eggs over medium. "His ticket got pulled. He won. It's not like he bought it on purpose."

"But you went out with him, after?"

"Yeah. Just…nothing happened," I said, disgruntled to be getting the third degree. "We went to The Slaughtered Lamb for a bit to hang out with some friends I'd made plans to meet. It was chill. Stop being such an old lady about it."

My brother grumbled and poured sugar into his coffee. "He works with me. It just seems weird. You're my sister, for fuck's sake."

"Maybe he won't hang it up in his cubicle," I teased. "Jesus, Evan. You act like you're worried he's going to try to make a suit out of my skin."

That got him, finally, and he laughed. "Gross."

We both ate in silence for another few minutes. He polished off his whole plate and, typically, stole some of my potatoes.

"Hey, so, you want to talk about what's going on at home?" I asked when we'd both sat back with replete sighs, fresh cups of coffee on the table and the clock ticking its way toward noon.

"Nope."

"Fair enough." I sipped coffee. There was no point in badgering Evan about anything. My brother would tell me anything and everything, but only when he was ready to.

Our conversation turned to William's Bar Mitzvah and the headaches it was causing. This time from Jill, who'd apparently called Evan to have a talk about his wife's "lack of respect" for our mother. Jill had always been a bit of a diva, that deadly combination of self-absorbed and totally not self-aware. She was seven years older than Evan and I, and her nose had been out of joint about the pair of us since my parents had lugged us home from the hospital. Some people grew out of their sibling rivalries; some people grew up. Our sister had not. I figured it was only a matter of time before Jill and our mom went toe-to-toe with Susan, and I was sure Evan's wife was going to come out on top of that fight, no matter what Jill and Mom thought.

"Jill also cried about how if only Susan had waited for the planning meeting, she could've been there. Planning meeting. Like it's a fucking committee thing, like one of those boards she sits on."

"What did you tell her?" I asked.

Evan shrugged. "Nothing."

"What do you mean, nothing? Why didn't you tell her to back off?"

"It's a fucking hassle," my brother said. "You know how they are anyway. Just let them talk, and it blows over."

I frowned. "They're trying to steamroll Susan about all kinds of things."

"I told her to just ignore them. The way I do. It's not worth the argument, you know? Smile and nod and go on and do your thing, whatever you want to do, that's what I told Sue."

Somehow I doubted that was the answer his wife wanted to hear. "The shit storm, she has begun. Hopefully, it won't be a repeat of your wedding."

My brother didn't look amused. For a second, he looked drawn and weary, and I wanted to hug him across the table the way I used to when we were small, and he'd fallen down and scraped up both his knees. I settled for squeezing his hand for a second.

"I just want my kid to do well and have a good time at his party," Evan said. "I don't really care what Mom and Jill want."

"So maybe you should tell them that."

He shrugged. The waitress came with more coffee, but we both declined. I was already about to float away.

Evan hugged me hard in the parking lot, which surprised me. I let him as long as he needed to.

"I got your back," I said into his ear. His arms tightened for a moment before he let go and stepped away. "You know that, right?"

"Yeah. Get out of here." He punched my arm lightly, and for a moment his smile looked genuine and not strained.

"Oh, hey, by the way, can you ask Susan if she needs me to get William from Wednesday school?"

Evan looked confused. "Huh?"

"She has that yoga class or whatever it is on Wednesdays. I guess it runs late? I told her I'd help out…?" Clearly, my brother hadn't received the memo. I sighed. "I'll call her."

"Since when does Sue take yoga?"

"Dude, I don't know. She's your wife, not mine." Once, I'd

overheard my sister-in-law complaining to one of her friends on the phone that her husband never listened to her. Never paid attention. I'd been annoyed at the time, taking my brother's side, but now I thought maybe she had a point.

Evan frowned. I punched him on the arm. He tried to grab me around the neck and knuckle-rub my head, but a quick jab to the stomach with my elbow got him to release me, fast.

"Shit," he complained. "Where'd you learn that?"

"Self-defense class. I took a course." It had been offered by one of Cubby's friends especially for people in the BDSM community. Too many people assumed all women were submissive, or all sub guys liked getting beaten up. Stuff like that. After one of our friends had been severely beaten into a coma after some unsafe play with someone she'd met through a mutual friend, I'd opted to spend an afternoon in a stinky gym learning how to toss people around.

"Well, you're not supposed to use it on me!"

I laughed and poked at him. "You can dish it out, but you can't take it, baby bro."

"Whatever. Hey." Evan jerked a thumb at me. "Listen. About Niall…"

I gave him a wary glance. "What about him?"

"He's a nice guy, Elise."

"Yeah? And?"

"Just that he's a nice guy. That's it." Evan looked away.

I stepped back. "So…I shouldn't go out with him again? Is that what you're saying? Because he's too *nice* for me?"

"That's not what I meant." My brother squirmed a little, rubbing at his mouth, though he didn't have any food on his face.

I poked him. "So what did you mean?"

"He's maybe not your type, that's all."

"Uh-huh." Frowning, I crossed my arms. "Maybe that's

my business. Or maybe you should tell him that. I mean, he's the one who chose the picture of me, after all. Did you have this conversation with him?"

Evan looked at me. "Not yet, but I guess I'll have to."

"You're not the boss of me," I blurted. Ridiculous. Childish. Yet true.

One side of my brother's mouth quirked up. I didn't want to laugh but I did, though I still felt the sting of his words. Evan shook his head.

"It's just a picture," I told him. "He'll probably donate it to a thrift store, if he even bothers to take it out of the wrapping. I'll be in his garage until he has a yard sale, that's all."

"I shouldn't have taken him to that art show," Evan said sourly.

"Shoulda coulda woulda."

He sighed. "You're not even interested in him, are you? That way?"

"I don't know." I scuffed the gravel with my toe, eyeing him. Evan had met George, of course. We'd been together a year, after all. Evan knew it had ended badly. He'd also known, vaguely, about the other men who came after, the ones who let me tie them up and blindfold them. "Would you rather I date a guy who isn't nice?"

"I want you to be happy, how's that?"

I grinned. "Aww, garsh, how sweet."

My brother scowled. "Well, it's true."

This touched me. I'd have hugged him, if we hadn't already reached our annual hugging limit earlier. Instead, I settled for a fist bump. "I don't have any designs on Niall Black, Evan. Okay? Does that make you feel better?"

"Marginally."

I laughed. "And I doubt he has any on me."

"He'd better not," my brother grumbled.

16

George had made me fifteen again, yearning and desperate and lit up with the knowledge I was wanted; and like I was fifteen again, desperate and yearning, my light had dimmed when he'd stopped wanting.

I should've been over it by now. Nearly four years later, not a word from him in all that time. Not since the last time, when he'd said *good-night* and I'd said *goodbye*.

I was stupid with this love. Not so stupid that I didn't understand that he'd become something else to me. A symbol, maybe. An ideal. Something to yearn for but never have, in some twisted self-denial kind of thing I'd need years of therapy for to untangle my reasons for craving it.

But it wasn't like I thought about him every second of the day. I had the rabbit tattooed on the inside of my wrist to make sure I didn't forget him, but there were long stretches of time, sometimes days, when he barely crossed my mind. There were many times, too, when thinking of him felt like something I'd read in a book or had seen in a movie. Something that had happened to someone else. Something not real. It was only in the dark when I was alone and unable to sleep that the memories churned up like some kind of monster that normally stayed hidden in the bottom of a lake among the mateless tennis shoes and broken beer bottles from 1978.

Like a junkie trying to distract herself from needing a fix, I tried to stop myself from messaging him. I really did. I tossed and turned and punched my pillow, flipping it to find momentary coolness. I counted back from one hundred, then again, and still, sleep eluded me. Still, my mind turned to the memory of his touch and the taste of him.

My fingers slid between my legs. I was already wet. My hips rolled when I dipped my fingers inside my slickness and drew them up to circle on my clit.

I thought of his mouth. His tongue. The way he'd slide his hands under my ass to lift my pussy to his mouth, and how he'd feasted on me. How once he'd made me come three times in a row with barely a break between, until I'd had to beg him—me, beg!—to stop long enough for me to catch my breath.

I murmured his name, his real name, not George, and it caught on the emotions stuck in my throat, snagging out of me like it had been ripped by thorns. Stuttering, shuddering. I fucked my fingers inside myself, wishing they were his. Up again, over my clit, stroking, stroking, until finally my muscles tensed, and pleasure swept over me and into…

Staring at the ceiling as the thumping of my heart slowed, I became aware of the steady, annoying bleat of a car alarm a few blocks away. And then, of course, because in the aftermath of orgasm I was even less able to resist the constant and steady urgings of my heart, I took up my phone and typed in his name.

If I could go back to the beginning and change it all, if I knew then what I know now, would I? Would I turn away from you instead of toward? Would I let you take me by the hand and dance with me, or would I shake my head and smile, putting you off the way I did with all those other men who tried to make me want them?

I don't know.

There are days when the only thing I want in this world is to curl up beside you and listen to the sound of your breathing match the in and out of mine. Rain on the rooftop and in the leaves on the trees outside. Our fingers linked, saying nothing, no words to say because together we can be silent and still always know what the other is thinking.

And there are days when I cannot think of you without feeling the floor tip and tilt beneath me, so that I am put to my hands and knees with the great raw gasping of my breath so loud in my ears it blocks out everything else. Because I fight not to cry, and the tears come anyway, burning and bitter. Because I am sick with love and wanting you, but you're not there.

You know what loving you is like? Standing on the edge of an abyss, tossing in pieces of my heart. Sure, I know I'll never fill that pit, and eventually I'll use up all the pieces and have nothing left for myself. But I do it anyway because I'm a fucking idiot. Because I love you. And if I'm going to tear my heart into tiny shreds and throw them into the darkness, you're the one I want to do it for.

If there is one thing I would change, it would be the last words I said to you. Not the texts that I've sent since. Not the subtext in my Connex statuses or the not-so-subtle messages in the profile pictures or the screen names I shuffle through depending on my moods. The actual words that came from my mouth. Those, I would change. I would swallow them. Take them back.

I would say good-night, and not goodbye.

17

My instructions to Esteban had been specific. Find what he wanted, and send me the links. I would ultimately choose which gear we used, but I wanted him to show me the ones he liked best.

I'd been a little surprised at what he'd picked. There was a variety, but a theme. The harnesses were all invariably less utilitarian than I'd imagined, more lacy and feminine than the thick leather straps and buckles I'd expected. The dildos ranged in length and thickness, all colors, but none of them looked like a real cock. All of them were curved to hit the prostate, and seeing the choices he'd left up to me, a sudden rush of fondness for him had made me incapable for a few minutes of choosing anything at all.

Only a few minutes, though, because after that I'd focused on the pros and cons of the different combinations and how I'd feel while using them on him. Being fucked in the ass was his thing more than mine, something he'd talked about from the start, at first hesitantly, and then when I didn't recoil, with more longing. He told me how he'd discovered ass play while jerking off, and how he yearned to be taken like that both as what seemed to be for a lot of men an ultimate submission, and because, as he'd said, "It feels fucking delirious."

I wanted him to lose his mind when he was with me.

So much of what I'd discovered that I crave and love about dominance was based not on props or outfits, but the simple, immediate and grateful acquiescence of a man devoted to pleasing me. Of one who paid attention to what I wanted and made sure to give it to me. Of being known.

I had played with toys plenty of times. Cuffs, floggers, plugs. Some I really liked, others I did not. I liked making Esteban writhe and moan and come for me; I adored teasing him to get the biggest reaction. Yet while I'd cross-dressed in men's suits and took what society would often consider the male role in my sexual relationships, I'd never actually fucked a man with a cock of my own.

I couldn't wait.

That didn't mean I wasn't a little nervous. I'd finally, after a couple hours' deliberation, chosen a pretty purple-and-black-lace harness that looked more like a garter belt. The black, smooth dildo wasn't the biggest one he'd sent, but it wasn't the smallest, either. The description had guaranteed "mind-blowing prostate orgasms," which I took as catalog-copy hyperbole, but the reviews had been unfailingly five-star.

Wearing it at home in front of my bathroom mirror, no lie, I'd felt stupid. It looked porny, and the cut of the straps squeezed me a little harder in some soft places I'd rather not have drawn attention to. I'd given the cock part of it a few exploratory strokes and burst into embarrassed giggles, and that was when I was alone.

Standing in front of Esteban, though, all I felt was beautiful. Dominance is all about self-confidence, even if 90 percent of it has to sometimes be faked. I'd had to put my game face on in that hotel bathroom, staring myself down in the mirror, taking a few deep breaths. Reminding myself this was what he'd asked for and what he wanted, and that no matter how ridiculous it looked, if we couldn't laugh together about it, then we shouldn't be fucking each other at all.

He didn't laugh when I walked out. His eyes widened, and he put a hand over his heart, fingers curling into his bare skin. He drew in a breath. His cock actually twitched at the sight of me, and right then, I no longer had to fake any kind of confidence. I owned this, and him.

"Hello, honey."

"Goddess," he said and fell to his knees in front of me, and anyone who thinks that instant adoration would be overblown and awkward has never had an erect and shivering man in front of them, ready to serve.

"Do you like it?" I stroked down to grip myself at the base much like I'd watched every lover I'd ever had do with their own cocks.

"Yes. It's perfect." He sat back a little on his heels to look at me, his smile turning sly. "You'll go slow?"

I took him by the chin and tipped his face to me. "Yes. I'll go slow, so slow."

He groaned. I leaned a little closer to lick his lips. Not a kiss, just a teasing flick of my tongue that opened him for me, and then I tucked my thumb inside his mouth to tug his face to the side for a moment so I could whisper in his ear, "Until you're begging me to fuck you harder, harder, harder."

When I slapped him lightly on the cheek, it wasn't to hurt him, even though he did give a low, hoarse cry. I looked down. His cock, so hard it tapped his belly. His hands on his thighs.

"Get on the bed," I told him. "Hands and knees."

"Facedown," he murmured, "ass up."

We both laughed at that, and I loved that we could. It made me light up inside. I waited for him to do as I'd said. I admired his body, lean and tight all over. He shaved all over, too, which I was less fond of, though it was his choice and nothing I'd ever demanded he stop. The backs of his thighs were so thick with muscle I wanted to bite them, and his ass… damn, that ass.

Smooth golden skin, pale in the places that hadn't seen the sun. Tight, hard muscles. He jerked when I got on the bed behind him on my knees and ran my hands up the backs of his thighs and over his cheeks.

"Shhh," I soothed.

I'd already laid out the bottle of lube that I'd ordered from the same website as the rest of it. It was supposed to be special, meant for anal, but didn't have any kind of numbing stuff in it. Just thicker, I guess. Water based, so safe to use with any kind of toys. My hands were shaking when I uncapped it and let a long, thick stream of it coat the shaft. Esteban looked at me from over his shoulder when I fumbled a little, easing closer.

"Slow," I promised him.

He smiled. "I trust you."

Then I knew it was going to be okay. And suddenly, fiercely aroused, I pushed the head of my artificial cock against his tight entrance. I went slow, as promised, until I'd seated myself deep inside him.

"Are you okay?"

"Oh, God…yes. Please, more."

I laughed a little, breathless, and withdrew as slowly as I'd entered him. Then in again. In, out, the pace quickening when he began to push against me. I gripped his hips to keep myself steady, find my rhythm. With every thrust, the blunt end of the dildo rubbed my clit as it was designed to do, and though I hadn't expected to, I felt the rise of orgasm building inside me.

"Harder," he begged me, and I obliged.

There's such amazing fucking power in controlling someone with pleasure, more than I ever found when using pain. I fucked him that way for a while until his pleas were lost in muffled, gasping groans, and then I withdrew and told him to get on his back. I settled between his legs again to fuck him in that position.

"I want to see your face," I told him, "when you come."

I pushed inside him again, easier this time. His cock was so thick and hard that when I grabbed it at the base, the entire shaft pulsed against my palm. Sweet, clear precome glistened, and I drew my thumb across the head of him to taste it as I always did.

I'd seen him lose himself in ecstasy before, lots of times, but I never stopped loving the way his gaze went unfocused. Jaw sometimes slack, sometimes tight with concentration. Now his fingers gripped the white sheets, and his back arched a little, easing the way inside for me.

I fucked a little faster, letting the pressure on my clit build. Sweat beaded on my forehead, and I tasted it when I licked my mouth. I'd never appreciated what hard work it was to be the one doing all the thrusting, but holy fuck, was it getting me off. Not so much the actual stimulation, but the mental aspect of it. Watching him try to control himself from rolling his hips or stop himself from thrusting his cock into my lube-slick fist, and watching him fail…watching him lose himself in what I was doing to him, and hearing him cry out my name. The way he begged…there is nothing like it. Nothing.

I gave up to desire, rocking with it. Harder. Faster. The pounding of the dildo against me wasn't quite on spot enough to get me off, but I kept going, and teasing pleasure edged me closer and closer until I was lost in it. No longer in control myself. Letting my orgasm steal away my reason.

Fuck, how good it was. Over and over, thrusting, my hands

on his bent knees, occasionally reaching to stroke his cock from base to head. He cried out and shook when I did that, but a nice, firm grip on the base of his cock kept him from ejaculating. I wasn't done yet—I hadn't believed I'd come from this, but I was so close now, so fucking close, I wasn't about to stop.

"Beg me to let you come," I ordered in a low voice.

His gaze met mine and locked. "Please, Goddess, please fuck me harder and make me…oh…"

I shuddered with my own climax, my thrusts ragged. I didn't mean to keep stroking his cock, but caught up in my own pleasure, I forgot to tease and deny him his. At the searing wet spurt of him covering my hand, I came. He jetted all over his chest and my hand, once hitting his face, and we both tangled into that final roller coaster plunge of simultaneous orgasm where nobody knows what the hell is being shouted out of their mouths or what parts are whose because everything has become a last thirty seconds of pumping, grinding, clenching, pulsing oblivion.

There was silence.

Slowly now, gently, I withdrew and pulled free the ribbons at my hips that held the harness in place. I wriggled out of it and fell onto the bed next to Esteban, who hadn't moved, not even to wipe his cheek. I did it for him, tenderly, with the edge of the pillowcase, though the mess on his belly I left for the moment. I curled next to him, my lips pressed to his shoulder. I tasted the salt of his sweat and breathed in his scent.

"Wow," Esteban said after a while.

I'd started to fall asleep. I smiled against his skin. He shifted to have me settle on his chest, and his hand stroked, stroked over my hair. He kissed my forehead.

"Wow," he said again.

I shifted to look at him. He smiled at me, though his eyes

were more serious. He let a finger trace my brows, the line of my nose. Over my lips.

"I want to see you again, soon," he said then added, "May I?"

I thought about it. "Next Friday?"

Esteban sighed happily and pulled me close. "Yes. Next Friday."

We were quiet for a few minutes. I pushed up on my elbows to look at him. "What are you thinking?"

He shook his head. "Nothing."

"*Nothing* isn't an answer," I told him.

He opened his mouth but then closed it. "Nothing I want to say out loud. Words might break what I am thinking."

I knew the feeling. I didn't press him. There were things I'd been thinking that were best kept inside, too.

18

I didn't recognize the number that came up on my cell phone, which was why I let it go to voice mail and then promptly forgot about it until after I came back from lunch and checked my phone to see if Esteban had messaged me. I was still going over our amazing night together, over and over, unable to keep myself from grinning when I thought of it. We'd seen each other for three Fridays in a row, and I was planning on this Friday, too. Alex had tried to call me out about it, but I wasn't saying a word.

"Hey, um, Elise. This is Niall. Black," he added as though I knew half a dozen men named Niall. "I was wondering if you'd want to go check out a movie at the Allen Theater with me. It's supposed to be really good."

He named an indie movie that had been getting rave reviews. It wasn't showing in any of the multiplexes, though I figured if it really took off, some big distributor would eventually snatch it up. I had, however, been thinking about going to see it, probably alone, since there wasn't anyone I knew who was into that sort of thing.

"Hey." Alex stuck his head around my office door. That was all. Just his head.

I paused in listening to the voice mail. "Um…yeah? What?"

"What are you doing tonight?"

I gave him a wary, narrow-eyed look. "Why?"

"It wounds me," Alex said, "that you don't trust me. Not that I blame you. I'm fucking unreliable as fuck."

I had to laugh at that and shake my head. "Have I told you lately how lucky I am to work in a place where reliability is rated in terms of *fuck*? And for fuck's sake, come all the way into my office. Stop hovering…" I stopped when he came through. "What the…"

Alex was not wearing pants. I blinked and blinked again at the sight of him, shirttails hanging down over what looked like a pair of soft pink women's boy-cut panties. Then I covered my face.

"What the hell!"

"Sorry," he said. "I spilled coffee."

He'd been wearing white pants earlier, a bold fashion move that I'd thought couldn't be topped…until I saw the pink underwear. Embarrassed laughter choked me, and heat flooded my cheeks, because the last thing in the world I wanted was to get a crush on my married partner. "Good Lord, Alex."

"Hey, they're super comfortable."

"I don't disagree with you. I just don't need to see you in your wife's panties." I swiveled in my chair to avoid looking at him. Sweet Baby Elvis in a pompadour, do I love boys in lingerie.

Alex snorted. "They're not hers. They're mine. Why should women get all the cool underpants?"

"Aghhh!"

"Okay, hold on."

I heard shuffling as he ducked outside the door, then came back inside a minute or so later with a skirt made out of sheets of paper stapled together, clinging to him in a way that was definitely not going to keep him covered if he did more than stand very, very still. But it was an improvement over him flashing his junk at me, and so I turned to face him. I shook my head.

"Don't judge," he said. "You're the one who insisted I come inside."

"Fair enough. Now that we've lost half an hour of work time, what is it that you wanted?"

"I just wanted to know if you wanted to come out with me and Olivia tonight. Dinner. Show. We have extra tickets to see the Chinese Acrobats at the Hershey Theater."

I twisted in my chair, considering it. "Sounds fun."

"Nice. We have two tickets. Maybe you can invite your…" He paused to give me a look. "Your *lover*?"

"No." I shook my head. I'd already asked Esteban to come out with me once at the last minute and been turned down. It wasn't a trend I wanted to start. "But I might be able to scare up another date."

He pretended to stagger. "God. You're killing me. You have some other guy, too?"

"It's the life of a crazy single lady, yeah. I know. To an old married guy like yourself, it must be shocking. Two men at the same time!" I grabbed my pearls. The fact they were fake and from a thrift shop didn't keep them from being perfectly clutchable.

Something flickered across his expression, and his smile slipped a little bit. "Oh, the horror."

"Hmm," I said thoughtfully. "It kind of sounds awesome to me."

"Depends on the men, I guess," Alex said. "So, who's the other guy if he's not your lovah?"

"Oh, this other guy I met who works with my brother.

He came to the gallery show, and then we hung out a little, after. He just left me a voice mail asking me to the movies."

"See if he'll come along to the show, instead. You're down for a double date?"

"Let me call him, see what he thinks, okay? Maybe he didn't even mean tonight."

"If he's calling you right now for a date tonight," Alex said, "you should just say no anyway, on principle."

"There are so many reasons why I like you. You know that?"

He buffed his fingernails on his shirt front. "I *am* pretty fucking likable."

"Get out of here. Let me make this call in private. And get another pair of pants!" I waved him out and thumbed Niall's number on my phone screen. I had a moment's panicky anticipation before he answered, but the second I heard his voice, it went away. "Hi, it's Elise. I got your message."

"Elise, hi." He sounded pleased. "How are you?"

We passed the social civilities back and forth, that silliness that always happens when both people are really thinking about the real reason for the call. I wasn't going to bring it up, though. I'd called him back; he could be the one to ask me out. Call me old-fashioned.

"So," Niall said, "would you like to see that movie with me?"

"I would. It sounds great. When were you thinking?"

"Friday night? We could have dinner and hit the later show, if you wanted."

I smiled into the phone. "I have plans on Friday, but maybe Saturday?"

"Sure, that would work. Saturday it is." He sounded like he was smiling, too.

We chatted awhile longer about work, the weather. The

construction downtown. Alex stuck his head around the doorway again, making gestures until I excused myself and muted the call.

"You said if he wanted to go out tonight that I should say no!"

"That's only if he asked you," Alex said. "You asking him is totally okay."

"You…that's…" I narrowed my eyes. He shrugged. I unmuted the call. "Hi. Niall. This is really last minute, but would you have any interest in grabbing some dinner and seeing the Chinese Acrobats tonight at the Hershey Theater? My business partner and his wife have extra tickets."

"Oh, wow. I can't make dinner," Niall said, and my heart plunged harder than I'd expected it to. "But what time's the show? I could probably do that, yeah."

I got the details and exchanged them, agreeing to meet him at the theater. I disconnected. My phone buzzed with texts from William and some from Jill that I read and rolled my eyes over. I sat back in my chair and waited for Alex to crow about my call.

He didn't. He had, however, put his pants back on. They were damp in the front, and probably permanently coffee stained. "You can still come to dinner with us."

"Can't. I just got a text that I need to pick up my nephew from Hebrew school and take him home, and another from my sister telling me she and my mother need to talk to me about my sister-in-law, and let me tell you, that's not going to go the way they hope it will." I frowned, dreading returning that phone call.

"Family sucks," Alex said sincerely.

"No. Kidding."

We agreed I'd meet him and Olivia at the theater, and he ducked out of my office. I texted William to remind him that

I'd be there to get him at six-thirty, and I texted my mother to tell her that she and Jill needed to let Susan decide what kind of fucking napkins to have at the Bar Mitzvah party, though I didn't say fucking, not to my mother. I might be disrespectful, disreputable and unnatural, according to her, but even I couldn't bring myself to say the *F* word to her.

The texts were flying back and forth while I waited for William in the parking lot. My mother didn't quite grasp the group texting option, so a lot of what she was replying had to be forwarded by Jill, until finally, disgusted, I gave up and called my sister directly. She was already on a tear, but I stopped her by quietly repeating her name over and over again until finally, she stopped.

"What?"

"This is not your party."

"Well, I've just planned dozens of events, that's all. Forgive me if I happen to know a little something about it." My mom could be counted on, at least sometimes, to back the fuck down. Jill was a pit bull.

"You're getting all worked about paper napkins, okay? Why is this even a thing with you?"

"I have a place," Jill said. "Susan wants to order from some online place. Who knows about the shipping or the quality!"

I sighed, rubbing my eyes. "Why do you even care?"

She started up again, but all I said was "Jill, Jill, Jill" in a soft monotone until she screamed out "What!"

If I laughed, she really would lose her shit, so I bit it back. But damn, making my sister crazy was fun. "Why do you even care?"

"I just do," she said.

"If Susan wants to order her paper napkins embossed with baby butterfly wings and hand-crafted from regurgitated Mexican restaurant takeout menus filtered through a unicorn's anus, Jill, then she's going to do that. When are you and Mom going to get it? You don't get to decide for everyone what they do, okay?"

"She asked for advice," Jill muttered.

"You can give all the advice you want, but the way you act when someone doesn't take it is the problem. You're getting your blood pressure all out of whack over something people are going to wipe their mouths with. Maybe put boogers in."

"Why are you gross all the time?"

Why are you such a raging bitch, I wanted to say, but didn't. My sister had been on fire that way her entire life. Nothing I could say was going to change her. "Just…I'm not on your side on this one, okay? I'm not going to get involved with it, and no, I'm not going to have some kind of fucking 'heart-to-heart' with Susan to try and bully her into using your napkin place. Leave me out of it."

I hadn't noticed William at the passenger-side door, which was locked, so I opened it. He slid inside, taking off his *kippah* and putting it in the front pocket of his backpack. He looked stressed.

"Jill, I have to go, William just got in the car."

"Why are you picking up William?"

"To be helpful," I told her. "To do something genuinely helpful instead of…"

I caught myself with a glance at my nephew, not wanting to have him overhear anything. Jill mumbled something stupid and mean that I ignored. I hung up.

I turned to William. "You okay?"

He shrugged, not looking at me. That wasn't good. I didn't know if I should press or not, so instead I turned the car toward what was becoming our Wednesday tradition, the Lucky Rabbit. After downing a double cheeseburger and a chocolate sundae, a meal that could only have been more nonkosher if it had been topped with shrimp and bacon, William let out a long, rattling belch.

I laughed at him over my frosted mug of root beer. "Eight points, plus one for the vibrato. Feel better?"

"Yeah." Unexpectedly, William pointed at my wrist. "Is that because of this place?"

I laughed. "Um, no."

"Dad said you guys worked here in the summers."

"Yeah, I did, but at the one closer to Grandma's house." I eyed the sign, then my tattoo. Both rabbits, but not the same. "No, this isn't because of this place."

"What's it for, then?"

"I... It's..." I hesitated.

"Grandma says tattoos are bad decisions," William said. "But I think they're cool. I think when I get older I'm going to get one or two."

"Thanks, kid." Bad decisions, indeed. I didn't consider my ink a bad decision, just a reminder of how easy it was to make one.

William sighed. I waited for him to talk, but he didn't. I didn't push it.

"You ready to go home?"

He shrugged again, finally looking me in the eye. "I'm going to mess everything up."

"What? At the service?"

"Yeah."

I shook my head. "No, you're not. You're going to be great. I told you not to worry, kid. You'll get it."

"I don't have enough time. I'm never going to learn it all. And the whole thing is making Mom and Dad fight."

I hesitated. "About you?"

"About the whole thing. The party, all that stuff. Dad and Grandma and Aunt Jill and Mom are all arguing all the time. Nobody asks me what I want," Willam said fiercely and stabbed a fork into the almost empty paper tray of fries. "Nobody bothers to find out what I want to have for food or what the stupid napkins should say!"

"Have you told your mom and dad this?" Susan, the mother of a single son, had always been a little prone to anxiety about anything regarding him, but my brother, I'd thought, was a little more even-keeled.

"No."

"Want me to talk to them about it?" My stomach hurt a little already in advance at the thought of having to tell Susan anything remotely derogatory about her parenting skills, but for my nephew I was willing to do it. I'd had a lot more experience dealing with my mother and sister, but I could do that, too.

"No. Mom will get more upset." He looked up at me with my brother's eyes, which were by extension my own.

I wanted to hug this kid so tight, to squeeze the breath out of him. In a lot of ways, though I'd never dare say so to his mother, I thought of William as my own. The way things were looking, maybe the only one I'd ever have. The fact that all these adults in his life were supposed to be taking care of him and making this huge transition easier, not harder, made acid rise in my throat.

"Your mom loves you, William. She doesn't want this to be harder on you than it has to be. I mean…do you need some extra tutoring? Would that make you feel better about it? I know it would suck if you had to go for some extra hours, but if it makes you feel more confident about it, maybe you could meet with the rabbi another hour a week or something."

He looked at first hopeful then shook his head. "I don't know."

"Tell you what. I want you to stop worrying about the party

bullshit, okay?" I watched him grin at the curse word. Yeah, I knew how to connect with an almost thirteen-year-old boy, that was for sure. "You concentrate on your stuff. And if you really want something special at your party—"

"I don't want a baseball theme."

I studied him. "Okay. What kind of theme do you want?"

"Robots, I guess." William shrugged. "Can you tell my mom?"

"Sure, buddy. I'll tell her." I ruffled his hair before I could stop myself. William suffered my touch and even gave me a grin that seemed much more like his normal self. "It's all going to be okay."

19

The Chinese Acrobats were amazing. Alex and Olivia's tickets were Orchestra, three rows back. I'd never been to a show at the Hershey Theater before, but the art-deco architecture was beautiful, and they sold chocolate during intermission. You can't beat that.

"He's cute," Olivia told me in the bathroom during the break. "Alex says you guys met through your brother?"

I'd washed my hands and now touched up my makeup in the mirror. "Is this lipstick too much?"

She eyed me critically then shook her head. "No. It works on you. That red is great."

"I don't want it to look like, you know." I laughed, self-conscious. "Like I'm trying too hard. Like this is a date?"

"Isn't it?" She laughed and dried her hands.

I shrugged. "He asked me out for Saturday night. I asked him to go tonight, but…I don't know. I haven't been on a date in forever, not the kind where the guy calls you up and asks you out."

"Why not?" Olivia smoothed the front of her dress and looked to me for unspoken affirmation that she was put together all right before we both headed out of the ladies' room.

"Haven't met anyone. Haven't tried," I added. "At least not for the boyfriend-type thing."

She nodded. "Yeah. I get you."

When we got back to our seats, Niall had bought me a glass of wine. It made me laugh a little, because the theater rules stated you could take drinks into the theater, so long as the cup was covered. It was like drinking out of a toddler's sippy cup. But still, it was good wine, and he'd bought chocolate, too.

"My favorite," I said about the rich milk chocolate and almonds. "Thank you."

"Not everyone likes nuts," Niall said. "But you looked like you do."

Beside me, Alex started to laugh. Olivia, on his other side, punched him in the arm. I laughed, too, still channeling teenage boy, I guess, but I also got warm and tingly because he was right. I do like nuts in my chocolate. We were both still chortling when the lights flickered and dimmed, and as the theater got dark, Niall leaned close to me to murmur in my ear.

"You have the best laugh I've ever heard."

I found it very hard to concentrate on the show's second act. His knee brushed mine every so often. His pinky finger, splayed on his thigh, brushed mine, too. I waited, semi-breathless, for him to take my hand. He didn't. But I wanted him to.

Just before the end of the second act, my phone pinged. I scrambled for it, embarrassed that I'd forgotten to turn off the ringer. The music in the show was loud enough that I don't think anyone heard it, at least not enough to be severely annoyed. I thumbed the screen to see a notification from my message app.

New message from JohnSmith

I didn't read it, and I tucked my phone into the side pocket of my purse, but the blink, blink of it lighting up let me know he was sending me a lot of messages. The show ended, and the lights came up. While we waited our turn to exit, Niall gestured at my bag.

"Do you need to check that?"

"Not right now."

We let the crowd sweep us outside and into the parking lot, where we said goodbye to Alex and Olivia. Neither of us made a move to get into our cars. It was a repeat of the first night we'd hung out, though much warmer. I found myself wishing it was cold, so I'd have an excuse to borrow his jacket again.

"So," Niall began, his standard start to a conversation. His phone rang from his pocket. "Ah, hold on a second. It's my mother."

While he chatted with her, I pulled out my phone to check the messages from Esteban. Close to twenty of them, increasingly graphic, and though he had to have seen that I wasn't reading any of them, increasingly inquisitive, as well. The last one was the direct question:

R U there?

Sorry. Out right now, will catch you in a bit, I typed, hitting Send as Niall disconnected.

"I told her I was going out tonight, but she forgot." He shrugged. "Since my dad died, she's been a little...needy."

"But you're a good boy to take care of your mother," I said lightly.

He didn't look thrilled. "Good boy, nice one. Thanks."

"I was teasing you. Good man?"

"I'd rather be called a man," he said, and looked at the phone in my hand, which was merrily lighting up every time a new message came in. "Everything okay?"

"Oh. Yeah. That...is a friend."

"A pretty insistent friend, huh? One of the guys from the pictures?"

I shook my head. "No."

Weird, awkward silence. The parking lot had cleared out, and we were among the last people there. Security would probably kick us out soon.

"So…" I laughed at how I'd picked up his pet phrase. "Do you want to go somewhere else, or…?"

"It's kind of late. Work in the morning." Niall looked around the lot then back at me. "Unless you wanted to? I mean…"

"No, it's all right." I waited to see if he'd lean in for a kiss. A handshake. An awkward shoulder punch. Something, anything, but all he did was take a few backward steps toward his car.

"I'll call you about Saturday," he said.

I nodded. "Sure. Talk to you later."

Feeling a little disgruntled, a little put off, I watched him drive away. In the front seat of my car, I looked over my phone again to find another few messages from Esteban.

Where R U?

What R U doing?

There'd been plenty of times when I didn't hear back from Esteban immediately. For him to be so adamant about a reply from me was irritating. I thought about simply deleting the texts, but that was a thing with me. I hated not being answered so fiercely that it had become sort of sadly pathological for me to never ignore a message.

I was out.

He read it and replied at once. Where?

The problem with having a conversation via written messages on a tiny screen is that you can't judge the other person's tone of voice. Add the tiniest bit of a language barrier—Esteban's English was impeccable, but he didn't always get the idioms correct, for example—and I knew I should be careful about assuming he was grilling me versus merely being curious.

I went to see a show with some friends.

After that, he didn't message again until I was walking in my front door.

May I call you?

Before I even had time to type an answer, my phone was ringing. "Hello?"

"Hello," he said in a low voice. "I've been missing you."

There are things that men say to women that should be flattering, but sometimes are not, depending on how and where and when and who. "You have great tits" whispered in a whiskey-soaked voice late at night in bed can make a woman moan; that same "compliment" shouted at her by a bunch of strangers as she crosses the street, not so much. Esteban had told me that he missed me before, but tonight it sounded more like an accusation.

"I was out," I said.

"Was it a good show? What did you see?"

I described the show to him as I undressed, an eye on the clock, thinking that the morning was going to come too early. "Listen, it's late, and I'm tired."

"Who did you go with?"

"Some friends."

"Was it a date?" he asked.

We were more complicated than we were supposed to be, but I was not his girlfriend. He was not my boyfriend. We had an arrangement that had been carefully constructed and was still somewhat fragile in the aftermath of his abruptly breaking it off.

"Yes, it was," I said.

Silence, then a sharp sigh. "I see."

"You know, Esteban, I don't ask you where you go or who you go with when you're not with me."

"You could. If you wanted to know."

"Well," I said sharply, "I don't want to know."

"I want you now, so much. I'm so horny."

I was not in the mood for phone sex, nor in the mood to coddle Esteban through whatever shit he obviously had going on. However, a good, hard fucking was not something I'd ever be likely to turn down, especially not these few days before I was due to get my period, when my hormones were raging. If I couldn't eat everything in sight, an orgasm or three would suffice.

"Come over." I'd never invited him to my house before, but I didn't feel like going out again.

"I…can't."

"Well, then, I guess you're out of luck." Annoyed again, I took off my earrings and bracelets and put them away. Next step would be the bathroom to brush my teeth and shower. His time was rapidly running out.

"I'm on fire for you."

I frowned. "And? What do you want me to do, sweetheart, talk you through jerking off?"

"Oh, please! *Por favor…*" He lilted another long plea in

Spanish that normally would've melted me, but tonight I only felt manipulated.

That was it. We were going to have an honest-to-goodness argument. Part of me wanted it, in that twisted sort of way that happens in complicated relationships where too much goes unsaid until finally you end up exploding with it. Part of me wanted to remind him of his place, because he did have one, and it was meant to be at my feet.

"You seem to have forgotten something, sweetheart, and that is you exist for my pleasure. Not the other way around." In panties and bra, I stood in front of my bathroom mirror and ran a hand over my body, thinking of Esteban.

"Oh, yes," he muttered. "Yes, I know that. I exist to serve you."

"Words. Nice words, but really, you don't, do you? You exist to work and eat and shit and sleep. *Not* to serve me."

"No," he protested. "I do. I want to! I want to please you, I want to give you—"

"You want me to get you off," I told him coldly.

"Yes. I do."

I looked away from my reflection. "I'm tired now. I don't want you to beg me. I want to go to sleep."

"Take me into bed with you. Let me help you fall asleep, touch yourself, I want to hear you make yourself—"

"You are not listening to me," I said. "Do you remember what I told you in the beginning? At the very start?"

He sighed. "I remember many things you told me."

"I said I wanted a man who would listen to me," I said.

"And obey you. Yes, I remember." He coughed a little.

"I don't feel like getting you off right now. I don't feel like making the effort. I am tired, and I have cramps and what I really, really want is to just eat something really bad for me. Okay?" I put paste on my toothbrush, but had lost the energy for more than toothbrushing. "I know your cock is hard, but you'll have to take care of it yourself tonight, and the more you pester me about it, the more aggravated I'm going to get."

"I understand." He sounded angry.

I didn't care. "I'm going to sleep now."

"Thank you for letting me call you," Esteban said, and my heart panged.

The bitchy domme is a stereotype for a reason—because there are plenty of men who get off on being humiliated, and lots of women who like to assert their control with arrogance or cruelty. And hey, I'm all about whatever works. If a guy wants someone to put his balls in a vise and his cock in a cage or to get whipped by a riding crop, I'd never say it's wrong. But that's never been my style. I would never call myself particularly tenderhearted, and certainly never unselfish. I might not always be kind, but I'm never purposefully cruel. I fumbled, sometimes, with him.

"Good night," I told him. "I'll talk to you tomorrow."

"Will I still see you Friday?"

"Yes. Of course."

"I thought maybe no. If you were angry with me."

"No. I still want to see you. Even if I'm a little angry with you, I still want to see you."

He made a noise as though he meant to say more, and I waited, giving him the chance to speak. But all he did was disconnect, and all I heard was silence. I looked at myself again in the mirror. Tits and ass and belly, tired eyes and no smile. And I was alone.

In bed, beneath the weight of a sheet that was too heavy for the heat, I cradled my phone and wept until I had to flip my pillow. Then I stared with swollen eyes into the dark and tried to imagine the stars. I couldn't do it. All I saw was dark.

I miss you.

The message went out. Unread. Unanswered. I was too tired even to cry again, but one thing I decided before I at last let sleep overtake me.

I'd wanted to be alone for a long time, but I didn't want to be alone anymore.

20

Thursday passed in a flurry of work. Friday, Alex was out of the office, meeting with clients and working whatever magic he did to get people to invest their money with him. I'd seen him put on the charm. It was pretty impressive. His absence left the office too quiet, though, which I noticed during a welcome lull in the steady stream of phone calls and emails I'd been dealing with all day.

Niall had not called. I'd checked my phone several times, when I remembered, and checked it again now. Nothing. I had his number. I'd called him already; I could do it again. Yet something stopped me. He'd said he would call me about Saturday. Shouldn't I wait to let him?

The pseudo fight with Esteban had left me restless. We hadn't spoken since. My stupidly predictable late-night text to George had been less than cathartic, even if it had made me think about my life and what I wanted from it now. The idea of actually *dating* made my stomach twist, but…well, who really wants to be alone forever? Monthly and even weekly hot sex dates were great and all, but there was a lot of time left in the month when that was over. Love could keep its distance, but finding someone to go out with on a regular basis, someone to cuddle with while watching TV, that was suddenly looking a lot more appealing than it had in the past few years. I wasn't quite ready to sign up on a dating site, and besides, when a ready-made date slaps you in the face, you don't turn it down.

I called Niall.

"Hey," he said, sounding wary. "I was going to call you."

"I had a little break at work and thought I'd call you," I said, then paused. "Is that okay?"

"Yeah. Sure. I was just, um, hey, I'm pretty busy now. Can I call you back?"

"Of course. Later, then."

"Sure. Later," Niall said.

And that was it. The full extent of our conversation had taken oh, fifteen or twenty seconds, tops. And he had not sounded glad to hear from me; nope. I didn't need a degree in astrophysics or even interpersonal communications to figure that out. I put my phone flat on my desk and ignored the chiming from my computer of more emails coming in.

To Esteban I might be Goddess—benevolent, stern and fully at ease with the knowledge I deserved every bit of his worship, but that self-confidence was not always natural. Sometimes, all it takes is twenty seconds of blatant disinterest to make even a goddess feel unwanted. Nobody likes that.

I spent the rest of the morning working and texting my mother and Jill, who were now all caught up in some kerfuffle about hosting a brunch on the Sunday after William's Bar Mitzvah. Susan, as it turned out, had told them to do whatever they pleased, to invite whomever they chose, and both of them were somehow affronted that they were getting exactly what they wanted.

"I don't care what you do," I said finally to my mother, when I could no longer deal with typing on my phone and called her. "I'm busy at work. Susan said you and Jill should plan the brunch, so just do it."

"Well, we need to think about who to invite. This is supposed to be for our family."

I grimaced. "So you don't want to invite Susan's family, or what? They're all coming in from out of town, I'm sure."

"I don't even know them."

"Ma," I said. "You can't have some kind of brunch thing and not invite Susan's family. They're William's family, too. Either invite everyone who's staying at the hotel, or don't have it. Why is this such a thing? It's common courtesy!"

"Don't you take that tone of voice with me. I don't need a lecture from you on how to live my life," my mother said.

"Apparently, you do."

When I was small, my mother had taught me how to dance the Watusi and the Pony to old records she played on the record player she'd had since high school. A cigarette tucked in one corner of her mouth, she'd roll up the living room rug and take my hands to teach me the steps while she sang along with whatever song she'd put on. My mother had taught me how to put on lipstick, how to match my shoes to my belt. She'd once gone to the school to confront a teacher who'd given me a hard time about the books I'd chosen to read for my book reports, telling him that her daughter could read any damn book she pleased, even if technically it was from the reading list two grades higher.

In short, my mom has not always been a raging thunder-twat.

"I find your attitude disgusting!"

I sighed. "I find your consistent and utter lack of consideration for anyone but yourself to be really disappointing."

She was quiet, to my surprise. Then she said, "Fine, I'll invite everyone."

I needed a shot of liquor after that conversation, but I settled for a coffee from the Morningstar Mocha, where I went to grab some lunch. "Hey, Tesla. How's the panini today?"

The Mocha's manager sported an asymmetrical haircut, bleached blond, and today wore a T-shirt with a picture of a zombie Marilyn Monroe on the front. She turned to look at the menu board. "I'd go with the avocado, Portobello and… oh, I'll make it without bacon for you. I can add some sprouts or something, instead."

"And some macaroni salad." I looked in the glass case. "Oh, I'll take one of those giant frosted brownies, too."

My brother called me while I waited for my food. I didn't mention the brunch, and neither did he. He didn't actually say anything about my mother or our sister or the Bar Mitzvah at all. He'd just called to chat, and I was reminded how lucky I was to have a brother who I loved and considered a friend.

"Hey, so, what's up with you and Niall?"

I licked fudge frosting off my finger. "Nothing's up. Why?"

"You went out with him again, didn't you?"

I laughed. "Did he tell you that?"

"He mentioned it, yeah. Gave me kind of the third degree about you, to be honest. Wanted to know if you had a boyfriend, how often you still modeled, what you were into."

"Did you tell him basket weaving and underwater interpretive dance?" I asked, only a little sourly.

"He meant, you know."

"Gross, Evan. That's so gross. I don't want my brother discussing my…God!" I lowered my voice when heads turned.

My brother laughed. "Hey, believe me, I don't really want to think about it, much less talk about it."

"Why the hell is everyone so fucking obsessed with what I choose to do in the bedroom?" I hissed and stabbed my brownie with a fingertip.

"Because it's weird."

I knew he was trying to make light, but it hit me hard. "Fuck you, Evan."

"Hey. Hey, I'm sorry. I didn't mean that. I just meant that… shit. I'm sorry. It's the pictures, that's all. Nobody would even know if you hadn't ever done any of those pictures. Or if you'd maybe just said it was a thing for the pictures, not something you…do."

"Sorry if I refused to closet myself for the comfort of my family and friends," I told him. "You're married. I could assume that makes you a reasonably straight male who gets laid once every few weeks and maybe gets a blow job for your birthday. You don't see me going around speculating or trying to psychoanalyze you about it."

"Calm down."

"Fuck you," I said again, hating the way tears clogged my voice. "While you were blabbing away to a stranger about how I like to fuck, did it ever occur to you to tell him to fucking ask *me*?"

"I did tell him," my brother said. "I told him that you were my sister, and you were awesome and that if he wanted to take you out, he'd better be fucking prepared to handle you with care, or I would mess him up."

I sniffled, hoping nobody in the coffee shop could see me crying. "You didn't."

"I totally did."

"I thought you didn't want me to go out with him."

"You're going to do what you do. Doesn't matter what I want."

That was the truth. "Well, considering he totally blew me off, maybe he's not such a nice guy, after all. Or maybe what you told him scared him off. So I guess your evil plan to prevent us from finding true lurve worked."

"C'mon, Lise, I got your back. You know that." Evan paused. "You know I don't care what you do. Whatever. Some people like black licorice and some people don't."

"Thank you. I love you."

"Gross," my brother said. "Shut up."

In the bathroom before I left the coffee shop, I got a clue as to why I was in such a bad, weepy mood. In high school, Alicia's mom had still referred to periods as "the curse." I totally felt cursed just then, cramping and bleeding and bloated and emotional. As I washed my hands, I caught sight of the rabbit on the inside of my wrist, and I let myself touch it briefly, just once.

George had always brought me chocolate ice cream when I felt this way.

And then I was crying again, deep and gasping sobs I stifled with the back of my hand while I prayed nobody was waiting too long on the other side of the door.

21

I could've canceled my rendezvous with Esteban. Should have, maybe, considering how I felt, physically. But it was how I felt mentally that kept me from calling it off.

I did prepare him, though, when he called me the morning before our evening rendezvous. "Just to let you know, my lady garden is in full bloom."

We'd talked about it before—fucking during my period was nothing I'd ever wanted to try, though Esteban had said more than once he wouldn't mind. Ask it of him, and he would comply.

That was why I liked him, after all.

He laughed. "I'll come prepared for whatever you want. I'm already tingling with anticipation."

"Me, too. I'm looking forward to it." The words were out before I knew to stop them—once said, impossible to call back. I meant it. I just hadn't meant to say it aloud.

He sounded pleased. "Kisses, until later."

We said our goodbyes. I lay back on my bed, the heating pad not even coming close to doing what it was supposed to do. Ibuprofen didn't help, either. The curse of womanhood, I thought with a sour, bitter sigh and pressed ungentle hands to my belly, thinking if I could rip my uterus out with my bare hands, that might be a lesser agony than this.

Cranky, crampy, emotional. I blamed that for the reason I took up my phone to log in to the email account I hadn't used in years except to store all my saved messages from George. The pictures he'd sent—his socks, his sandwiches, his smiles. The buckle of the belt I'd bought him, a snapshot that should've meant nothing but had me fighting an indrawn breath that wanted to become a sob.

I'm no masochist, but there was no doubting that I took some sort of twisted pleasure from hurting myself this way. Over and over. So desperate to cling to the memories of how he'd made me feel that I would gladly suffer this pain if only to have a moment's bliss of remembering.

It was bad enough to look at the messages and pictures, the screenshots of our conversations, but it was the final photo of the two of us that tipped me over the edge. Us, together, smiling as though there was nothing in the world that could make either of us happier than to be with each other.

I'd looked at the photo a hundred times if I'd looked once. That and the one I'd taken the first night we met. How many people have a picture of both the very first and very last times they were together? I hadn't known in the first that I'd ever see him again; I hadn't known in the second photo that I never would.

And, because I was stupid and melancholy, because I was hurting and hormonal, because I was in love, I emailed him the picture along with a message.

This is a picture of two people who are ridiculously happy when they are together.

One of them thinks that state of ridiculous happiness would extend into the kitchen at dinnertime and in the morning bathroom routine and at the grocery store and on road trips and during thunderstorms and bill paying and laundry and arguments and watching TV and being sick and during holidays and making love on clean sheets and using the Crock-Pot and in the backseat of a taxi at four in the morning after pancakes, and even at an amusement park in August, although that is its own level of hell.

The other one is you.

I'd sent dozens, no, hundreds of messages, but in three, almost four, years, I had never emailed him. Unlike the agony and ecstasy of being able to see that he'd received and read my text message, I would have no way of knowing if he'd opened an email. But I knew he would read it, just as I knew he would not reply, just as I knew it might hurt him a little even though really, I wanted it to hurt him a lot.

I wanted him to ache and burn and mourn and yearn and grieve for me the way I was helpless to stop myself from doing for him, but I knew he never would.

22

Esteban and I pulled into the parking lot at the same time. Usually he texted me the hotel room number ahead of time and I met him there. Seeing him get out of his car, I didn't get out of mine. We wouldn't walk in together. It wasn't like that for us, and never had been. Instead, I sat in my car looking uselessly at my phone, pretending to wait for Esteban's message but really waiting to see if an email reply from George had somehow managed to sneak through while I was driving. Esteban rapped on the window a few minutes later.

His smile, oh, his smile.

"Here," he said and slipped a hotel key into my hand when I rolled down the window. "Meet you upstairs."

I could've said that unexpected meeting, that skew in our routine, or even my relentlessly awful period were what changed the tone of our rendezvous, and I wouldn't have been lying. It was all of those things, but it was also my stupid email, still unanswered, that made it hard for me to shrug off the outside world the way I'd done for all our other dates. I tried, though. Of course I did. It wasn't Esteban's fault that I was in a bad mood—if anything, seeing him lifted something inside me, even if only the tiniest bit.

"Leave it," I told him when we were in the room and he started to unpack his bag. I'd always made him lay out whatever it was he'd brought, and I knew that was why he hesitated, but that three seconds of hesitation before he nodded and complied clenched my jaw. "Take off your clothes."

His hands were already moving to the buttons of his shirt, though I saw the twist of his mouth and flash of something uncertain in his eyes. Esteban stripped out of his shirt and laid it neatly on the chair. He left the T-shirt beneath to work at his belt and zipper, but I stopped him.

"Shirt off." I sat in the armchair, one leg crossed high over the other to allow my skirt to ride up, showing off the gartered stockings I wore beneath.

I wanted to be in flannel jammies. But the clothes were part of this—part of it for him. Most of it for me. The heels that made me three inches taller than him, the stockings, the vintage-style garters, the sleek wrap dress that came undone with one single tug. The clothes gave me power, and tonight I needed that more than ever, so instead of comfy sweats and a carton of ice cream, here I was.

Esteban reached over his shoulder to pull off his T-shirt, folding that neatly, as well, and putting it on the chair. He stood in front of me, his jeans shifted low on his lean hips. He looked, as he always did, at the shadow between my thighs. I watched his throat work as he swallowed. I eyed the growing bulge in his pants, and waited for that answering tug inside me that began when I saw him getting turned on. His fingers curled slightly at his sides then relaxed. His tongue slid along his lower lip; his teeth dented it briefly. He met my eyes.

Waiting.

I did tingle, then, at the sight of his face. I could order him to his knees. Tell him to put his mouth on my pussy, right here in this chair. Through my panties or not. Period or not.

And he would do it, I knew he would, because Esteban, unlike that other man, always, always, always fucking gave me what I wanted.

I didn't want to think about Niall, who'd blown me off so casually. And I definitely didn't want to think about George any longer. That bridge was burned. Suddenly angry—at both of them, at myself for letting it still hurt, at the world, at everything—I lifted a foot and pressed the heel of it into Esteban's bare, muscled belly. Not hard enough to hurt, though it wouldn't take much pressure to bruise him with the stiletto.

He drew in a breath, blinking rapidly. "Oh…"

"Hush." Neither of us moved. I couldn't keep this position very long. It looked good, but stretched me in ways that would've been uncomfortable even without the exploding uterus. I pushed for a second, making him sigh, and took my foot away. "Come here."

He did at once. Obedient. Willing. Eager, in fact, for whatever I was going to do. I grabbed him by the hips, just above the denim, and held him still so I could lean forward and kiss the spot I'd poked. The flesh there was red, not broken. It wouldn't be permanently marked. Still, I kissed it then let the tip of my tongue stroke along that tiny spot. His muscles leaped under my mouth, his belly warm and smooth, his skin fragrant and smelling of soap and desire.

"Take off your pants." My voice hitched. Arousal. Emotion. It didn't matter. I gave the command, and he obeyed. That was how it worked with us. It was what I wanted.

Right then, it was what I needed.

Esteban stepped back to unbuckle his belt. His button, his zipper. He pushed the denim over his hips and thighs and stepped out of it. Without waiting for me to tell him, he took his socks off, too. But not the briefs. His fingers hooked in the elastic, but he didn't push them down. He looked at me, waiting, and oh, God, there was that moment when I knew finally I was going to lose myself in this and him. When everything inside me coiled, and the edges of the world went a little red, a little blurry. When I was in control.

"Let me see you," I said in a low voice.

I delighted in the ripple of gooseflesh that rose immediately on his arms when I said that, and in how he trembled, just slightly. Esteban eased the elastic of his briefs over his hips, releasing his cock inch by delicious inch, and I lost myself in admiration of it as I always did.

He stood naked in front of me as he'd done dozens of times before, and I was no less moved this time than any of the others. Esteban gave himself to me. Sometimes I took him with a little cruelty. Sometimes with humor and fondness and affection. Tonight was the first time I ever did with desperation.

He was already hard. I took him in my hand, using his cock as a lead to pull him closer. Still seated, I looked up at him as I stroked the shaft, easing close to the head but not actually touching it. Stroke, stroke. I'd watched him making himself come enough times to know how he liked it.

When his eyes fluttered closed, I gripped his cock hard at the base. "Look at me."

He did. "Yes, miss."

As almost always, a clear bead of precome was dripping. I used my thumb to swipe at it, then tucked my thumb in my mouth. I would never pass up the chance to taste him. He shuddered at that, and my insides clenched at how lovely he was when he was reacting to me.

"I like to taste you."

"Thank you, miss." His voice, raspy and low, sent a thrill through me.

"Would you like me to taste you again?"

He blinked, looking uncertain for a second. "Yes...?"

There'd been many times we'd laughed about the things we did. Let's face it, ass-in-the-air is a position that leads to laughter, if you're going to be anything but hardcore about it. It was part of what I enjoyed so much about being with Esteban, that playfulness even when we were doing strange and beautiful things.

I didn't laugh this time. Not looking away from his eyes, my fist still gripping him tight, I leaned to let my tongue stroke along the edge of his cock head, then up to catch the shining droplets of his arousal.

His hips bumped forward. A low cry eased out of his throat. His hands went behind his back, crossed at the wrists, though I hadn't told him to do that. It pleased me, though, that he knew just what I wanted, even if I hadn't said so. I licked him again then took him in my mouth, sucking gently even as my grip on the base of his cock kept him from thrusting.

I had never been on my knees for Esteban before. That was not how it worked. Yet somehow, suddenly, I found myself slipping from the chair to kneel. To take him in my mouth as far as I could, engulfing him before drawing back. Then again, sucking harder this time.

He gave a startled gasp that under other circumstances would've made me smile, but this was not about surprising or pleasing him. I didn't want to think what it was about. I didn't want to think at all.

I closed my eyes and sucked his cock and refused to think about another man. I filled my head with scent and taste and the sound of my lover. I forced away thoughts of anything but the drag of my teeth along his flesh, the slickness of my saliva, the pressure of my lips. I thought only of making him come.

He cried out my name, my real name, low and wondering, and that broke my concentration enough to pull away. I looked up at him as he looked down at me. I'd stopped sucking him, but my hand hadn't stopped moving, and however startled I was by the sound of my name, he must've been as confused.

His cock throbbed in my fist, one and then two more strokes, and his head fell back as he came. I was not expecting it. Wasn't prepared. It was not the first time Esteban had ever ejaculated all over me, but it was the first time I recoiled from it. Most hit my blouse, some my neck. If I'd been wearing my hair down, it would've ended up in my hair.

Neither of us moved or spoke for a few seconds. He was shaking, breathing hard. So was I, though for different reasons. Without a word I got up and went into the bathroom, where I stripped out of my blouse and ran it under cold water, then took a washcloth to clean the rest of me.

I couldn't meet my own gaze in the mirror. I could only rinse and rinse the cloth then scrub my skin. He'd stained my bra, and I took that off, too. All at once the stockings and garters were too much—my skirt was soft enough, the waistband smooth, but everything still had to go. I kicked my shoes beneath the counter and ripped off the stockings then the garter belt, and pushed my skirt down, everything in a pile on the floor. Half-aware that my breath was coming in sobbing gasps, wearing only my panties, I bent over the sink and splashed my face again and again with frigid water. I did not cry, but I wanted to.

Esteban came into the bathroom. Silently, still naked, he took a towel from the rack. He took me by the upper arm and pulled me gently away from the sink. He turned off the water. He dried me with the towel.

Then he hugged me.

Without the heels on, I was made small enough for him to tuck me against his neck. He stroked a hand up my back before anchoring me to him with his fingers curled around the back of my neck. He murmured something to me in Spanish. Something soothing.

He took me into the bedroom, where he'd already pulled down the comforter. He'd turned off the lights, the only illumination coming from the bathroom. He led me into the bed and tucked himself up behind me, spooning.

I didn't move. Didn't speak. After a minute or so, his hand moved down to rub in soothing circles on my belly. Not questing downward, not sexual. Comforting, easing the cramps I hadn't been complaining of but had been feeling so keenly. He nuzzled my shoulder, and at last I melted into his embrace.

I let him hold me.

We were quiet for a while before I said his name. He pressed against me a little more in silent response. I turned to face him, both our heads on the same pillow. He pressed his knee between my thighs so we could get belly to belly. The pressure felt good.

I wasn't expecting him to kiss my forehead. Nor the corners of my eyes. I didn't think he'd murmur to me again in Spanish, words I didn't know and yet somehow understood.

"I like these here," he whispered, again kissing my eyes at the corner. "The lines there. And this." He brushed his lips to my temple. "The silver threads."

"Another man who pointed out the things that make me look old would get a knee to the nuts, Esteban."

He laughed softly and snuggled me closer. "Not old. Those things are your beauty."

He'd told me I was beautiful before. Of course he had. But this was the first time I believed it, and the tears that had been threatening me for hours at last forced their way free. I fought them back, but even so, a couple slipped out.

Esteban kissed them away. Then my closed eyes. Then my cheeks. My chin.

And then my mouth.

I tried to turn my face, but he caught me anyway. His lips, soft on mine, didn't demand. His kiss soothed as much as his circling palm on my belly, as his embrace. As everything about him always had, and craving that solace, I opened for him.

The kiss got deeper, but not frantic. Slow and smooth and soft. His fingers tugged the pins from my hair and freed it. He moved his mouth over my jaw and chin and throat, never biting. Never hard, though often that was what I'd demanded of him. And he didn't turn the kiss into something else, nothing urgent. He didn't try to move his mouth down my body, or to get something from me I'd have had to reject. Esteban worshipped me with his mouth, never asking for anything for himself, even though he got hard again almost at once.

We kissed like that for a long time.

Then we stayed in the dark in silence, entangled. With my hand on his chest, I felt his heartbeat slow. His cock softened. He pressed his lips to my hair. I needed to get up and take care of bathroom business, but I didn't want to move and break the contentment.

There was no helping it, though. I needed to deal with biology, and beyond that, both of us needed to get home. I got out of bed and grabbed my bag. In the bathroom, I took care of things then gathered my discarded clothes and shoes and went back to the bedroom.

Esteban hadn't yet dressed…but then I hadn't told him to. He'd turned on a single light. When I came out with my armful of things, he took them from me without a word. He folded my garter belt and stockings and tucked them carefully into my bag, along with my bra and then my still-damp blouse. He took his T-shirt from the chair while I stood motionless. He tugged it over my head, making sure to pull my hair free. He smoothed the fabric over my body.

"It fits you," he said and put his hands just beneath my breasts for a moment to give me a smile I found utterly charming. "Very nice."

Then he took my skirt and knelt in front of me to help me step into it. But when he moved to slip one foot into my pump, I shook my head. "I have flats in my bag."

With a nod, he took them out and put them on me. Then he stood. He put his hands on my hips. Face-to-face, I looked into his eyes. There were words I knew I should say, but I couldn't find them.

"You kissed me" is what came out, instead. Too soft, too full of emotion I couldn't put a name to. Too open and raw.

"You needed me to kiss you," Esteban said. "When you're hungry, you should be fed."

I hugged him then, fiercely. I clung to him, thinking in that moment that I should love him more than I did. For the first time, thinking that maybe I could.

But I was still the one who broke the hug and stepped away from him. Chin up, shoulders squared, back straight. I touched his face, looking into his eyes, but I put distance between us even as I did so.

Distance, but not coldness. "Thank you," I told him.

Esteban looked pleased, a flush rising in his chest and throat. His cock thickened a little in those few seconds, and I looked down between us to cup him there as I'd cupped his chin a moment before. He shivered. Our faces turned, our cheeks brushed, but we did not kiss again.

I stepped away from him a second time. "Good night, sweetheart. Drive carefully."

He nodded. I gathered my things. He helped me into my coat. He kissed my cheek at the door, and then, as I always did, I left him behind in the hotel room and I went back home.

23

I knew Niall was going to back out of our date-that-wasn't-a-date on Saturday before he even called me that morning. I listened to him fumble his way through it, letting him talk without saying much of anything myself. I didn't have much to say.

"Another time?" he asked. "I know maybe not that movie, but something else."

"Sure." If he wanted me to tell him it was okay that he was canceling on me the same day we'd planned to meet, he was going to wait a long damn time. Truth was, I didn't really feel like going out tonight. The night before with Esteban had been lovely, but strange, and though my period was already lighter today, I'd been thinking fondly of a night with Interflix and a heating pad.

"Sorry about it being last-minute. I'm sure you won't have any trouble making new plans, though."

I actually took the phone away from my ear to look at it in disbelief before I answered. "I wouldn't, if I wanted to."

"Yeah, that's what I figured." He didn't sound like he was trying to be a dick about it, but I didn't know him well enough to tell.

I did know how to be subtle and tactful, mostly because I'd long ago decided that I wasn't going to be like my mother and sister. I knew how to bite my tongue. But I'd also decided long ago there was no point in being coy with people when they were fucking with me.

"Why would you figure that?" I asked.

"Because you're...because you have...lots of friends," Niall said. "I'm sure lots of guys would love to go out with you."

"Sure, I have a whole waiting list of dudes just sitting around waiting for me to call them up last-minute, see if they don't mind being second choice on a Saturday night. Nobody minds not being top tier, do they?"

"Hey," Niall said. "That's not what I meant. Don't put words in my mouth."

"Don't assume you know me," I said.

We were both quiet then.

"Sorry," he said. "Something came up, that's all."

"I'm in a bad mood. I'm sorry." I apologized with a little less grace than he had. "No worries. Things happen. I get it."

"Another time," Niall said. "Okay?"

"Okay." I sounded wary and knew it, but he didn't seem to notice.

Now it was hard to stay irritated with him, uncertain as I was about what the hell, exactly, he was trying to do. Blow me off, let me down easy? Maybe the movie thing hadn't been meant as a date at all in the first place. Maybe I'd jumped the gun inviting him along to the Hershey show. Shoulda, coulda, woulda.

I remembered now why I'd stayed away from dating.

"Great," Niall said.

24

One of the things I'd made clear from the start with Esteban was that I didn't mind if we didn't talk every day, but I could not abide having messages go repeatedly unanswered. He'd always been good about it, so I didn't worry too much at first when a day passed without getting a reply to my last message, a breezy little joke I thought would make him grin. Then two days. Then three, four, five and I found myself checking my app to make sure nothing had gone wrong with it. I sent myself a message from another device, and that came through all right, so it wasn't a glitch in the server or anything technical. He simply wasn't talking to me.

I did not message him again.

I thought about it, though. Whether I should drop a casual *Hey, how are you?* or an angry *Where the fuck are you?* Or a concerned *Is everything okay?* In the end I sent nothing, because then I did not have to risk getting nothing back. I'd had enough of that in my life, and though I'd managed to resist any late-night messages to George for the past few weeks, I couldn't forget how terrible sending them always made me feel.

I had enough to keep me busy anyway with work and helping to get William where he needed to be and doing my best to ignore my mother and sister. I also had to practice the Torah portion I'd be reading, and since it had been a long damn time since I'd done anything like that, it meant more than an hour of effort. I had to put the time in, and there wasn't much time left.

"I don't want to embarrass myself. Or William," I told Evan one night when I was dropping William at the house after his extra study session with the rabbi. "How's he doing, by the way?"

"Better. I think he feels more confident with the extra studying. He's his mother's kid, that's for sure." Evan shrugged.

I leaned against the counter and cracked the top of the can of cola he'd handed me. "Hey, how's it going with Mom and Jill?"

"What do you mean?" Evan looked at me over his shoulder from the stove, where he was mangling scrambled eggs. How anyone could ruin scrambled eggs, I didn't know, but my brother was.

"Are they all settled down, or what?" I shrugged.

Evan scraped the eggs onto a plate and put the pan in the sink, adding a squirt of soap and water. "I guess so. I tune it all out. Susan was on my case about some kind of napkins or something. Whatever the hell that's about. I told her to just do what she wanted. You want to stay and eat?"

I glanced at the clock. By the time I got home, it would be past dinnertime, and I'd still have to cook something. I tried to gauge the emptiness of my stomach against the likelihood that Evan's dinner would taste like shit.

"Where's Susan?"

"Book club."

"Step aside, brother dear, and let me make something a little bit better than that mess you've got there. I mean, dude, you burned them. Who burns eggs?"

It didn't take long to put together a spaghetti dinner with some jarred sauce and garlic bread from the freezer. We were just sitting down when Susan came in through the garage. She had a tote bag slung over her shoulder, and the tips of her hair were wet.

"How was book club?" Evan asked. "Elise made dinner. I messed up the eggs."

"It was yoga," she told him, exasperated. "If you'd been paying attention, you'd have known that. And I met some friends after for coffee and had a sandwich, so I don't need dinner. Hi, Elise, thanks for getting William. How was the rabbi's lesson?"

"Fine," William mumbled, mouth already full.

Susan gave us all another round of blank, distant looks. "I'm going to go put my stuff away."

Evan waited until she'd left the room before saying, "I thought it was book club, excuse me."

I turned the subject away from potential domestic discord and got my brother and nephew talking about the latest Galaxy Vision game I'd bought the kid for his birthday and given to him early so he didn't have to wait months to play it. William invited me to hang out for a while to play, but it was already late enough that I wanted to get home where laundry and bill paying took up my time.

I checked my phone, but nothing from Esteban.

Online, I logged in to my OnHisKnees account, suspicious suddenly that I'd somehow been replaced. I looked up Esteban's profile, but couldn't find it using the search box. I opened some old, saved messages to click through that way, but got an error message. He'd deleted it.

I sat back, concerned. The worst I'd expected was to see him online, or at least that he'd been online recently, playing around instead of talking to me. But he'd disappeared.

I scrolled through the unread messages in my mailbox and searched also through the list of profiles that had viewed me. I had about ten different private photos I'd been granted access for, even though I hadn't been logged in in forever and hadn't requested any. Close-up, slightly blurred cock shots, men in restraints, some with leather zipper masks. One bold gentleman had sent me an artistically framed photo of his asshole with the caption "Use Me, Mistress."

"Fuck's sake," I muttered and flagged it as spam.

The site clearly showed the time of last log-in, which meant that all these desperately horny men were either not paying attention, or they simply didn't care that I hadn't been on the site in weeks. Probably both, since anyone who'd bothered to look at my profile would've seen that I'd checked off "not interested in acquiring." But that was the problem with a site like this—it might cater to people looking for specific kinks in a way that vanilla social sites did not, but that didn't mean anyone who used it was any less an idiot. Especially when it came to their hard dicks, I thought with a sigh. Submissive? Only when it suited them.

"Do not address me as Mistress. I'm not yours. Don't solicit me to fuck you in the ass or spank you or tie you up. Don't send me pictures of your naked cock until and unless I've asked you for them. Most of all, do not assume you know me." I replaced my former profile, which had been much blander, with that new one, and laughed. It wouldn't do any good, and was probably going to solicit even more unwanted attention from the sorts of men who would then want me to punish them for disobeying.

Randi was right; it was insanely hard to find someone you clicked with. I'd met Esteban here, and I'd thought we had made a connection, imperfect as it might've been. Then again, what was ever perfect anyway?

I let my cursor hover over the delete my account button, considering it. I scrolled again through the messages and so- licitations and deleted all of them, even the ones that had made the effort to be reasonably polite or clever. I deleted all the dick pictures. And finally, I went into my saved messages and deleted all of my original correspondence with Esteban.

If he wanted to be gone, I would make sure he was.

25

William was amazing. I hadn't done too bad a job with my reading, either. There'd been no fisticuffs on the bimah, nobody had lost their shit, nobody had even flubbed anything too badly. William had flown through the entire service like a champ, stumbling even less than the rabbi. He'd given his speech without faltering and good-naturedly ducked from the flying candy the congregation had showered on him when he finished.

Now he was suffering the reception line of hand shaking and mazel tovs from everyone who'd come to the party at the hotel, which, despite my mother's worries about her friends who wouldn't drive on the Sabbath, turned out to be almost everyone except my father, as predicted.

All that worry for nothing, but wasn't that how it went? You worried and fretted and then it all turned out all right. If only all of life could go as well, I thought, but then pushed that from my mind.

Now it was party time.

I made it through the hora and one line dance and then a bunch of speeches, and a truly awful candle-lighting ceremony before I managed to escape to the bar just outside the ballroom. There wasn't any booze being served at the party, but the bar was close enough to make it feel like I wasn't bagging out of the party to get lit. Not that I was the only one—the entire area, open to the lobby, was filled with Bar Mitzvah guests grabbing a drink.

And oh, there was Niall Black.

"Ms. Klein," he said from behind me, and I turned. He'd taken off his tie and had his jacket in one hand. "Fancy meeting you here."

I gave him just a touch of side-eye, thinking I'd have to holler at my brother later for not giving me a heads-up. "Hey."

Niall gestured toward the bar. "Can I get you a drink?"

"When a free glass of wine slaps you in the face," I began.

"You don't say no," Niall finished.

I gave him an assessing look and took a seat at one of the chairs at the bar. "White, please."

He ordered a bottle of beer and settled next to me. "So…"

"So," I repeated.

"So, it's good to see you."

I laughed and shook my head. "You are…really…"

"Intriguing? Talented? Clever? Handsome?"

"Confusing, is what I was going to say." I took the glass of wine from the bartender and sipped with an appreciative murmur. I could drink as much as I wanted; we'd all rented rooms here to visit with out-of-town guests and attend the brunch tomorrow morning.

"Confusing. Huh." He grinned, and damn it, he had a smile I found really hard to resist. "Do I want to ask you why you think I'm confusing?"

"Probably not."

"You're really not going to tell me?"

I looked him over. "If I say no, I don't want to, will you keep asking?"

"Yeah, probably." He grinned.

I frowned. "Figures."

Niall's grin faded a bit. "What does that mean?"

"It means," I said, "that like most men, you want what you want."

"Doesn't everyone?"

I thought about that for a second. "Yes. I guess we all do."

"And you probably always get what you want," Niall said.

"When I can. Sure." I lifted my wine toward him. "Cheers."

"So, tell me how it all works," Niall said after we'd sat in slightly awkward silence for a few minutes. He took a long pull from his bottle of beer.

I'd been waiting for the question. Under other circumstances, I'd have given him a cool smile and answered with a roll of my eyes, but what can I say? The wine was going to my head. Bar Mitzvahs made me emotional. And he was very, very cute.

But he had blown me off, and that wasn't something I could just ignore. I sipped from my glass and eyed him. "How what all works, exactly?"

"The her on top stuff."

If I'd had any sense that he was asking for some sense of skeevy voyeurism I'd have shut him down immediately. Not that I had an issue with voyeurism—after all, far be it from me to judge anyone's kinks. But I'd had my share of gross "wink wink nudge nudge" conversations with men who were secretly getting off on what I was telling them, and that was never okay with me, being the subject of some sort of underhanded beat-off material. I liked to be more in control than that.

"You've never been with a woman who liked to be on top?"

"Well…" Niall looked as though he were considering the idea. "Literally, sure. But not with the whips and leather and whatever."

I laughed, loud and long, turning heads.

"What?" he said.

"It's not like that." I shook my head and took a sip, letting the flavor of the good wine coat my tongue before I continued. "I mean, it can be like that, I guess. For people who like it that way."

"And you don't?"

I gave him a serious look. He seemed genuinely curious, so I gave him an honest answer. "No. Not really. I can play with the toys, sure, and the clothes can be fun. But overall? No. That's not really what it's about."

"So…what is it about? I just don't get it." He made a face. "What guy wants to be dominated?"

"Lots of guys. Believe me."

He smiled, looking into my eyes. "Oh, you could make me believe it."

"Don't flirt with me if you're not ready to deal with the consequences," I told him, putting the tiniest bit of edge in my voice, just to see what he'd do.

Esteban's gaze would've gone dark and shadowed; he likely would've shuddered a little, just enough for me to see. He would've made a small, low noise of arousal. His cock would've gotten hard, and I'd have known that, too.

But Niall was not Esteban. He leaned closer, just enough to let his knee brush mine and his breath caress my cheek as he said into my ear, "Who says I'm not ready?"

We were close enough to kiss, if I were the sort of woman to make out with a man I barely knew on a bar stool at a hotel bar during a Bar Mitzvah party. Instead, I let my cheek barely graze his before I pulled away and gestured at the bartender for two more drinks. Niall watched me for a second before sitting back.

He watched me sign the tab with my room number before he said, "You didn't have to do that."

"You can pay for them, if it really rubs you wrong. Or you could let that free beer slap you in the face," I told him serenely and crossed my legs.

His gaze flickered to the glimpse of thigh and stockings I'd given him, albeit not quite on purpose. "You're not going to insist?"

"You really do have it all wrong." The wine I'd just finished was working to loosen my tongue.

"You said that, but you haven't told me what it *is* like." Niall turned his bottle around and around on top of the bar. "So, tell me."

"You want to know why I think you're confusing?"

He blinked at the change of direction but said, "I do. Yeah."

I leaned toward him. "You took my picture home. You asked me out. We went out. Then you blew me off. Said you'd call and didn't. Said you wanted to take me out. Didn't."

"I…something came up," he said lamely.

I raised a brow.

Niall looked shamefaced but didn't say anything else. Around us, people laughed and chattered. On the dance floor not so far away in the ballroom, couples were getting down to The Electric Slide. Niall gestured toward the dance floor, a question in his eyes, but I shook my head.

"But you could go out there. Find yourself some cute young thing as a partner." I looked past him to the crowd beyond then met his eyes again. "Don't let me keep you."

"You're not keeping me from anything. I want to talk to you."

I laughed, and an uncommon flush of heat rose in my cheeks. I toyed with my wineglass and gave him a sideways glance, not certain why I found it suddenly difficult to meet his eyes. "Why?"

"Because you're beautiful," Niall said simply. "And fascinating. And there's nobody else in this place that I'd rather be sitting next to."

My stomach dropped like I'd crested the highest hill of a roller coaster and begun that throat-clogging plummet. I swallowed wine to keep myself from saying something stupid like "no, I'm not," or "I'm sure there could be." I gave my head the faintest shake, though. Not so much in denial or disbelief as a warning. I'd meant what I said about consequences, though he'd clearly disregarded me.

"You want to know what it's like, for me?"

"Being a dominatrix? Yeah."

I didn't laugh, though a small and somewhat indulgent smile tugged the corners of my mouth. "I'm not a dominatrix. That sounds like someone who does it professionally. Like a job. I am a dominant woman, but I don't like the labels, and I don't charge my lovers for my services, either."

"Lovers," Niall said in a low voice, leaning close again. "I've never met a woman who called them that."

"Well. They weren't boyfriends. What would I call them? What do you call women you slept with, but didn't date?"

Niall's eyes went wide for a second before he laughed, startled. "I don't… I guess I never… Flings? One-night stands?"

"I've never had a one-night stand."

"Don't tell me it's because you're too shy. Or reserved."

"No," I told him, leaning closer to be sure he could feel the gust of my breath on his neck and ear. "No man I've ever taken to bed has been satisfied with just one time."

Again, we were close enough to kiss. This time, I didn't pull back. Not right away. I breathed him in.

"You smell delicious," I said.

"Don't flirt with me unless you're ready to deal with the consequences," Niall said.

There, right there, was when he had me.

"Clever boy," I murmured. "Who says I'm not ready?"

Niall eased back on the bar stool and looked over his shoulder toward the lobby elevators. Then back at me. His smile, an invitation I discovered I wanted to take.

I slipped off the bar stool and put my hand out. He took it automatically, which was what I'd expected. He might not be submissive, but he was a gentleman, I'd seen that already. I squeezed his fingers then leaned in once more to say into his ear, "Come dance with me."

There's a part of every wedding reception or Bar Mitzvah party where things start to go sideways. Sometimes it's when Grandma gets a little out of control after too many gin and tonics, or that couple on the verge of breaking up decides now's the time and place, or the bride's brand-new mother-in-law loses her shit about that whore her son married. Most of the time, it's just toward the end of the night when jackets and shoes have been tossed and people start getting down to the Chicken Dance because they've lost all sense of what constitutes appropriate dance-floor behavior.

I love that part of the night.

"C'mon," I told Niall with my hand out for him to take. "Show me what you've got."

A lot, as it turned out. The DJ had started playing "Wobble" by V.I.C. just as we entered the ballroom, hard on the heels of "You Shook Me All Night Long," so anyone who was going to dance was already on the parquet dance floor. The paid dancers who'd been showing everyone how to do the latest group dance now started putting people in lines to do the steps to this song. I already knew them, but seeing Niall jump in without hesitation, adding his own flair to the drops and turns, totally made my night. It wasn't only that he knew how to do the dance, but also that he did it unapologetically, with enthusiasm. And style.

Oh, I was a goner.

The song ended with us both laughing. He pulled me into his arms as the music slowed a little. Not a slow song, thank goodness. This DJ knew what he was doing to keep the party hopping even as it was winding down. But slow enough that it felt okay for Niall to ease me a little closer.

"Your grandma's watching us," he said into my ear before twirling me out and then in again.

He dipped me, and I let him. "That's not my grandma."

"She's clearly someone's grandma," Niall whispered into my ear.

"Then you'd better behave."

"If that's what you really want. I thought maybe," Niall said as he twirled me again, this time so that I ended up with my back against his chest, "you'd want me to be naughty so you could give me a spanking."

I turned to face him as the music ended so the DJ could make some announcements neither of us cared about. "If I thought you'd like it, I totally would."

"Who says I wouldn't?"

"Your eyes," I told him.

Niall looked faintly surprised. "Really?"

"Yes." As the DJ kept talking about wrapping up the party, Niall and I inched our way off the dance floor. "I might not always be able to tell when a man's into it, but I sure can tell when he's not. It's all in the eyes."

"What do my eyes say?"

I studied him. The lights were coming on, the party dispersing. My brother and sister-in-law, both looking exhausted, were standing near the gifts table. I knew I should offer to help them gather and clean, but frankly, that's what they should be paying someone to do for them. I didn't schlep boxes or bag up trash on my own account, and I wasn't about to do it here.

"You want to get out of here?" I asked him, pretending not to see Susan's mother trying to catch my attention. No good could come from whatever *that* woman wanted. She made my mom seem like Mary Poppins. "We could go next door. Have a couple more drinks. Do a little more dancing."

Niall grinned. "Sure."

Before I could get roped into helping with anything more to do with my nephew's grand event, I grabbed Niall by the hand, and we escaped the ballroom. The bar attached to the hotel had a reputation as being a little on the skeezy side—the hunting ground of businessmen and cougars. But the drinks were reasonably priced and on a Saturday night, there was a nice mix of live music and a DJ who played in between sets. Tonight's band was a local favorite that played covers of everything from AC/DC to the Rolling Stones.

"Can I get you a drink?" Niall asked. "Or do you want to dance?"

The truth was, my feet were starting to hurt. I did love my high heels, but damn if they didn't start to pinch a girl's toes after a bit. I waved at one of the high-top tables that had opened up. "Can we sit for a bit?"

"Drinks, then. Wine for you? Or something else?"

I sat with a sigh at the relief of pressure on my toes. "Surprise me."

"Uh-oh. That's never a good thing," Niall said mocksolemnly. "When a woman says she wants to be surprised, it's usually a test."

"Let's see if you pass it, then."

Oh, the banter. It was like putting a match to a pile of dry leaves. I've always been a sucker for a man who can keep up with me, and so far, Niall Black had been doing an admirable job.

He brought me back something in a squat glass, his drink matching. "Whiskey sour."

"On top of the wine? Are you trying to compromise me?" I took it, though.

"Something tells me you're not a woman who's so easily compromised."

"You're probably right." We lifted our glasses to clink them.

"You didn't tell me what you meant. About the eyes."

I sipped the drink cautiously then licked my lips and enjoyed watching how his eyes followed the stroke of my tongue. "Mmm. Good choice."

"I passed?"

"You passed," I told him. I let my shoe dangle off my toe as I nudged his calf with my foot. Classic flirting move, no subtlety in it, even though I wasn't sure if I wanted to fuck him or just fuck *with* him. The line was there, and I hadn't yet crossed it. "As far as the thing about the eyes goes, it's something I'm not sure I can really describe, especially after a couple glasses of wine and now this."

"I really want to know," Niall said.

I gave him a curious look. "Why?"

"Because I find you fascinating."

I didn't have an answer for that right away—it seemed like a genuine comment, meant as a compliment, yet I couldn't help feeling the tiniest bit like a museum display. "Kinky girl, circa 2014." I should've been used to questions. People who don't play the way I do seem to forget that sex is still private even when to them it seems as though what I like and do is exotic and somehow therefore open to examination. *Be the light*, I had to remind myself often enough. *Educate people*. Still, I am who I am in all ways, in all times, and I couldn't help but give him an arched brow and a lift of my chin.

"Complex equations are fascinating. So is art made by monkeys splashing dung. *Fascinating* is a word people use to describe things they're not sure they like or understand but feel compelled to explore anyway." I took another sip of my drink.

Niall shook his head. "Wrong. I'm sure I like you."

"You barely know me, Niall."

He leaned a little closer. "I'm trying to get to know you, Elise. But you're making it kind of hard."

We stared at each other across the small table while all around us the crowd laughed and danced and drank and flirted. At least I assumed that's what everyone else was doing in that bar. All I could see, just then, was Niall.

"You have this idea about me. About leather and latex and whips and chains. You probably got it from watching movies, not even necessarily porn, or from the media coverage of that popular book trend. You think that men who like to bend to the will of a woman are pussies or weak," I told him. "So you make jokes to me about getting a spanking because that's what you think you know, but here's the thing. I've had lots of men joke with me about getting spanked, and the ones who really like it and want it, all of them, every single one of them, can't stop from showing the truth in their eyes. It's something really subtle, the faintest look, sometimes the way their pupils dilate or even how they might cut their gaze away, if they're somehow ashamed of wanting it. But the eyes always give it away."

"And mine didn't?"

I shook my head. Warm from the alcohol and the dancing and the banter, I also leaned a little closer. Definitely flirting now, though still uncertain where I wanted to take this. "Nope."

"Huh." Niall didn't move away. "Is that a deal breaker?"

I laughed. "I don't know."

"I didn't mean to offend you," he said seriously. "I'm sorry if I did."

I appreciated the unexpected apology and shook my head. "You didn't. I'm used to it. But think of how you'd feel if someone started grilling you on what you like to do in the bedroom and then saying something like 'weird' or 'why would you do that?'"

"I guess I wouldn't like it very much." He frowned. "Shit, Elise. I'm sorry. I didn't think of it that way."

"I know you didn't. Most people don't." I shrugged then looked at him. "If we'd met another way, not through Evan, and if you didn't know up front about my proclivities, would you still find me so fascinating?"

He didn't answer for a moment. The music swelled and throbbed as the DJ took over for the band taking a break. Niall turned his glass around then drank.

"I think so. Yeah." He nodded. "But it's hard to say, since I *do* know. And…like you said that first night, it's not something you do. It's who you are."

I barely remembered saying that to him. The words struck me hard now, in the tender spot between my ribs. Hard enough to set me back a little.

"Yes. That's true," I told him. "I am the sum of many parts."

"We all are."

I smiled. "True."

"Some of my parts would like to get to know some of yours a lot better," Niall said.

I laughed again, shaking my head. "Bad, bad, bad. So bad."

"You like a bad boy, though," he told me.

"No," I said, leaning closer. "I like a very good boy."

I finished my drink, which left me feeling slow and sultry

and definitely in the mood to dance. I held out my hand. I didn't say anything. I looked at the dance floor then at Niall. I let my eyes do the talking for me, and I waited to see if he'd pass this test, too.

Without a word, needing none, he got up. He pulled me onto the dance floor. And we moved together as though we'd been born for it, as though our parents had met and fallen in love or lust and come together for the sole purpose of making each of us so that we could find one another, right there, right now, on the dance floor where he put his hands on me like he owned me…and I let him, because right then, just then, I wanted to be owned.

I should not have let him kiss me. I knew it could lead to nothing but trouble and heartbreak at the worst, embarrassment at the least. But that's the funny thing about lust. It makes you stupid, not caring what might happen in the future when all you can think of is what is happening in the moment. I shouldn't have let him put his mouth on me, or his tongue to stroke mine. I should not have done a lot of things.

But I did anyway.

26

Niall had also rented a room at the hotel. He was smart enough to know that he'd be drinking just enough to make it inappropriate to drive home. He didn't ask me to go upstairs with him. I didn't promise him I would. We simply found ourselves in the elevator sometime after the bar closed, and when he asked me for what floor he ought to push the button, I smiled and leaned in to kiss him as my answer.

We didn't say anything as I followed him down the hallway to his room at the very end. We didn't touch. I don't know if Niall was thinking about what we would do if we passed friends or relatives, but I was. Fortunately, the hallway was deserted and quiet, because I wasn't sure what I'd have done or said if we had passed anyone.

He opened the door but stepped back to let me go through first. We'd both booked king rooms, though mine had a view overlooking the river, and his didn't. Both rooms had the same decor, though; his was a mirror image of mine. It made everything feel a little surreal.

I'd put my shoes back on to come upstairs, but kicked them off now as I turned to face him. He tossed his jacket onto the chair. With the heels on, I was an inch or so taller than he was, but in my stockinged feet I found I could kiss him very nicely without doing more than pushing up a little bit on my toes. My arms went naturally around his neck. His, around my waist.

I thought he might kiss me, but he looked into my eyes, instead. "Hey."

"Hey," I answered. My fingers toyed with the fringy edges of his hair in the back.

Slowly moving in a circle, Niall danced with me there in front of the enormous hotel room bed. He'd taken off his shoes, too, and the soft *shush-shush* of our feet on the carpet was our only music, but we didn't need more than that. He eased me closer, right up against him. My cheek found a natural spot to rest in the curve of his neck.

I wanted him to kiss me. Morning would be here in a few hours, but it still felt as though the night stretched on in front of us, endless and full of possibility. I was fine with waiting.

His hands moved from my hips to my ass, pulling me a little closer. Heat curled in my belly. I nuzzled his skin and let my tongue creep out to taste him.

He shivered, and I smiled.

"I want to kiss you again," he said against my hair.

I looked at him. "So kiss me."

"I didn't know if I needed to ask permission or something."

I laughed, though I wasn't sure if he was joking. "Why would you have to ask permission?"

"Isn't that how you do it?"

Ah, we were back to that again. He was fascinated; I was horny. I stepped back.

"This," I said, fisting a handful of the front of his shirt, "is how I do it."

I turned him, and he let himself be turned. I pushed him, and he let himself be pushed. Backward onto the bed, he fell a little harder than I think he expected, but I was already climbing up to straddle him. My fingers tugged open his buttons, one by one, and spread open his shirt so I could run my hands up the smoothly muscled plane of his belly and chest. Beneath me, his cock was hard, but I didn't touch him there with my hands. The pressure of my body was enough for now, the squeeze of my thighs on his hips.

I put my hands flat on his chest and leaned to offer him my mouth, which I held above his just far enough that he'd have to strain a little to reach it. "Kiss me."

In those last few seconds, I wondered if he'd refuse. A flash of something in his eyes, a small twist in his smile. But then he was kissing me, hard, his hands all over me. Mine all over him.

Mouths open, tongues searching. He hissed when I raked my nails down his chest, though I did it lightly, nowhere near as fiercely as I'd have done with someone else. I pinched his nipples next, and he growled.

Yes. Growled. Low and raspy in his throat, a wolf-like noise. Both his hands came up to grip my wrists and stop me from moving my hands.

Both of us were breathing hard, staring into each other's eyes. Slowly, never looking away from me, Niall rolled his hips to nudge his hard cock against me. Then again. When I tried to shift, he held me so tight there was no way I could, not without truly fighting him, and I didn't want to do that.

The third time he rocked me against his erection, I moaned. His grip loosened a little on my wrists. I kissed him, nipping gently at his lower lip. Then licking it.

Niall dug his fingers into my hair, pulling my head back. I gasped a little. His look of smug triumph, that gleam of satisfaction, shot a bolt of electric heat straight to my center. I might like being on top, but that never meant I couldn't enjoy a little good old-fashioned hair pulling.

He rolled us both until I was under him. Dress around my hips. I hadn't dressed for seduction tonight, leaving behind my fancy garter belt in favor of one with more vintage styling. It doubled as a foundation garment to keep all the lumps and bumps of ladyhood in place. My stockings, plain nude with a utilitarian band at the top instead of pretty lace, were also not what I'd have considered sexy, but at the sight of them, Niall paused.

"Damn." He pushed up on his knees to get a better look.

Pleased, I stroked a fingertip down one garter strap. "You like this?"

"Yeah." He ran his hands up my calves, over my knees. He stopped at the stocking tops to let his fingers touch the metal clips. "Very sexy."

I had a dozen far sexier bits of lingerie in my drawer at home, but I didn't try to dissuade him. I sat up and pulled my dress off over my head then tossed it onto the chair. I almost never wore a bra, but in honor of going to synagogue I'd put on a silky, clinging bralette that did nothing to hide the fact my nipples had gone diamond-hard. Propped on my elbows, I watched Niall's hazel eyes go dark with desire as he took me all in.

"So fucking sexy." He undid his belt then his trousers and shucked them off. He wore dark boxer briefs, already tenting.

I grinned with delight. "More, more, more."

"Greedy." Niall crawled up the bed to cover me with his body. Settling between my legs, several layers of clothing still a barrier, he rocked against me as he found my mouth again. Then my throat, nibbling.

It had been a long, long time since I'd just made out with someone this way. Dry humping. It made me laugh, and he pulled away to look at me.

"What?"

I shook my head. "Nothing. Just…this is unexpected."

He ran a hand over my breasts then my belly, which jumped under his touch. "Are you okay with it?"

It was the right question. He'd been confident to this point. Leading me, as I allowed myself to be led. But in that moment he proved himself to be a gentleman, as well, even if he was doing things to me that someone's grandma wouldn't approve of.

I took his face in my hands. "Yes. Are you?"

"Yeah." He turned his face to kiss my palm. Then the inside of my wrist, just over the rabbit inked there. "What does this mean?"

"It's to remind me of something important."

He rolled off me to look more closely at the tattoo. I thought he'd ask me what was simultaneously so important yet so forgettable that I'd felt the need to permanently ink it into my skin, but he asked a different question. "Why a bunny?"

"Because," I said, rolling him onto his back so I could straddle him once more.

He accepted my nonanswer. He did not accept when I slid my hands up his arms to pin his wrists. Laughing, he twisted to break my grasp.

"Maybe you want to tie me up," he said.

I sat up, not fighting to keep him held. With my hands on his chest, I leaned to whisper in his ear, "You should stop assuming you know me."

Then we were kissing again, and there was no room for words with Niall's tongue in my mouth. With his hand sliding between us to stroke me through my panties, and then inside them, his fingers finding me already wet. He groaned at that. His gaze went unfocused, and I drank in that look as I always did, gorging myself on that moment when need began to overpower rationality.

"Slower," I said into his ear when his fingers worked too fast. He slowed. "Better?"

I shivered, closing my eyes and resting my face against his shoulder. "Yes. Like that. Oh…"

"I want to be inside you, Elise."

Laughter shuddered out of me, breathless and full of need. "Yes. That, too."

"I don't have anything with me."

His slowly stroking fingers had eased me to the edge of orgasm, but I shifted now to look into his eyes. "Hmm. That could be a problem, huh?"

Niall rolled us again so that we lay side by side. He kept his hand in place, though he stopped moving. "I want to…"

"Fuck me," I breathed, watching his face for a reaction, which, oh, yes, he gave me.

His eyes half closed for a moment before he focused on mine. "Yes. I want to fuck you."

I reached between us to cup his cock. "Good."

He pushed into my touch and kissed me again. We wriggled around for another few minutes until he broke the kiss with a gasp. "Shit! I want you."

"I want you, too." I laughed. "Why do you not have condoms with you at all times, Niall Black? How is it that you've managed to get through life without learning that at any time you might want to be putting your penis inside a vagina?"

He blinked, looking taken aback for a second before grinning. "What the…"

I kissed him, long and hard. I slid my thigh between his to rock against him. "Don't act like it's never happened before."

"Oh, sure," he said. "All the time. Last week in the grocery store, some chick stopped me and wanted to bang me right there in the frozen foods aisle."

"Let me guess. You didn't have a condom."

His fingers shifted, easing inside me again so that my head fell back. "Nope. But let's be fair here. You don't have any, either."

"This is true," I breathed, unable to say much more than that because he was once again teasing me closer and closer to coming. "So whatever shall we do, instead?"

Before I could move or stop him, Niall rolled me onto my back to kneel between my legs. In the next moment, he'd hooked his fingers in the waist of my girdle, tugging but unable to get it more than a fraction of an inch down my hips. I burst into laughter at his efforts. He joined me, and we wrestled for a bit, but there was no getting that thing off without a struggle. He gave up and fell back, panting.

"Cock blocked by lingerie," he said.

I pushed up on my elbow to look at him. "I dressed for utility, not seduction."

He groaned and tickled his fingertips up my thigh. I wanted him to touch me higher. Give me more. But there'd been too much to drink, too long a day. A yawn slipped out of me, big enough to make my jaws crack. He tried to fight it; I saw the struggle. But he lost to his own yawn. With his head pillowed on my belly, Niall closed his eyes.

I stroked his hair, surprised at my own tenderness and at how quickly this had turned from frenetic lust to something simpler. I'd been with men who, in place of the sex we'd both been aiming for, would've demanded a blow job and some who'd have begged for one, and I was usually inclined to deny both approaches. Niall didn't demand, and he didn't beg. I waited for him to move or speak, but the minutes ticked past, and his breathing slowed.

"Niall," I murmured.

He snuggled closer, his fingers pushing beneath my thighs.

I let my fingers drift through his hair, then to trace his ear. He shifted a little, though not in protest.

"Feels good," he said.

It did feel good. Not just the kissing and touching and stroking, but…this. All of it. The way my fingers felt in his hair, the soft rise and fall of his breathing. The way he hugged me closer. Everything about being with Niall just now felt…right.

We weren't fucking, and I felt all right.

I didn't mean to fall asleep. Not fully clothed, cuddling, my face unwashed and my hair tangling around my shoulders. The lights still on. I only meant to close my eyes for a minute or so, not to drift into dreams with a stranger tucked up against me as though we'd known each other our whole lives. Considering how hard it was for me to fall asleep in my own bed with an arsenal of tricks, I didn't think I'd be able to at all.

I did, though. I fell fast and deep and didn't dream. I woke sometime later, disoriented. Niall had turned off the lights, and we'd both shifted on the bed to spoon, him behind me. His arm over my hip, his hand on my belly. My garters were cutting into my thighs, and my stomach churned from not enough sleep, a little too much wine, uncompleted arousal.

I didn't move, slowly becoming aware of the huff of Niall's breath against the back of my neck. Light came through the curtains, but I had no idea what time it was. Shit, had I slept through brunch?

I slid away from him, expecting him to wake, but he didn't. I used his bathroom to rinse my mouth and smooth my hair. I wiped away the smears of liner from beneath my eyes. I'd have to run and change in my room before heading downstairs, but at least for now I didn't look like I'd slept under a bridge.

Back in the bedroom, I found my shoes and didn't bother

putting them on. I leaned over him, but he hadn't moved. I stroked his shoulder, and he still didn't stir.

I did not kiss him on the cheek before I left.

27

"Really, Elise, if you're that hungover, maybe you should've just stayed in your room." Jill held out a mimosa in my direction, but took it back when I reached for it.

"I'm not hungover. Just tired."

"Well, you look it. Go put some lipstick on." She shook her head in disapproval.

"Jill, nobody really cares what I look like. It's all good. You and Mom did a great job with all of this stuff, relax." I snagged a mimosa from a passing waiter and tried to pretend I was not looking for Niall. I was starving.

"We just wanted it to be nice." My sister pinned me with a stare. "We wanted to make sure William had a nice party, that's all."

"He had a great party. And this is a nice brunch, okay?" In that moment I was trying hard to like my sister. "Look, Mom's in her glory."

She was meeting and greeting, directing people toward the buffet table laden with eggs, bagels, cream cheese and lox. I heard one confused guest asking if there was any bacon and prayed they wouldn't ask my mother, who could not be counted on not to be snide. All in all, though, it really was a nice brunch. Mom and Jill were good at planning things. Nobody would know how they dithered over stuff, and in the end, did it matter how long it had taken them to decide if they should have vegetable cream cheese alongside the plain?

"You look hungover." Evan shoved a plate of eggs and bagels at me. "You want this?"

I took it right out of his hand. "Joke's on you, butt wad, I'm not hungover, and I'm starving. So yeah. Thanks for the plate, buddy, looks like you need to get to the back of the line again."

"Nice. Butt wad. Good one. What are you, ten?" My brother tried to snag his plate back. Since I couldn't eat anything from it anyway with a glass in my other hand, I let him have it. He looked around the room. "Lot of people here."

"Yeah, well, there were more here last night. And in a few hours, it'll all be over. You can go home and never have to do it again." I grinned at him and slugged back the mimosa, put the glass on an empty table and headed for the buffet.

I made small talk with the people in line, but my eyes scanned the crowd for Niall. I could've texted him, I thought. He might've forgotten about the brunch. Or, I thought suddenly as I caught sight of my mother, who was still queening over everything, he hadn't actually been invited. Well, shit. That made sense. Niall wasn't family. My mother wouldn't have included him unless Evan had made sure to put him on the list, and really, I knew my brother well enough to know he wouldn't have thought to do that.

It was an excuse to text him, and I was nowhere near too proud to take it. I spelled out the details, the room location and timing, and hit Send right as I got up to the food. Tucking my phone into my purse, I loaded my plate with goodies. My stomach rumbled. As I got to the end of the buffet line and reached the spot where my mother was standing, still directing people toward the coffee and the dessert table, Susan approached.

"What a nice brunch," she said graciously, and, I thought, sincerely. "Thank you so much to you and Jill for putting this all together. Everything looks lovely. Thank you."

Watching my mother beam and my sister-in-law making an effort to reach out to her, I thought something of a miracle might be taking place. It was short-lived. Plate in hand, I eased by them on my way to an empty seat so I could check my phone for an answer from Niall, and that's when I heard my sister say, "I'm really so glad we decided to invite your family, as well. Mom and I really felt that it was the right thing to do, to include them."

Oh, no, Jill, I thought. *Don't. Just…for fuck's sake. No.*

"Why would you have excluded them?" Susan asked, a little too quickly. A little too loud.

My sister was still clueless, though the shift in Susan's tone should have alerted her that she'd misspoken, if her own social graces didn't. "Well…not exclude them, it's just that this brunch was going to be for family only. For William, of course."

"My family *is* William's family," Susan said through tight jaws. "Why on earth would you not invite them to a party to celebrate my son's Bar Mitzvah?"

My mother might like to battle, but she only ever caused a scene when she thought it would benefit her. She snagged Jill's sleeve to pull her back a step. "Lower your voices!"

"Why? You don't want any of the guests here to know that you didn't want to invite them?"

Oh, boy. I saw Evan on his way over to try and head off the showdown, but it was too late. My sister-in-law, who'd definitely put up with her share of hassles from my mother and Jill, had finally and spectacularly lost her shit.

The screaming started, and I'll give it to her, Susan had way more colorful vocabulary than I ever would've given her credit for. She suggested Jill perform a few actions that I'm sure were anatomically impossible, and when my mother tried in her wavering "I can't believe how I'm being maligned" whine to defend my sister, Susan flayed her alive.

It was kind of awesome to behold.

Not that I disagreed that my mom and sister deserved to be taken down, but this wasn't the time or the place. Nobody seemed to remember that William was there as those three women waged war on each other over who'd done the better job for him, but when I looked across the room at my nephew, he'd gone pale and looked shaky. I dumped my plate and went to him, tugging him out a back door into a service hallway, where he burst into horrified, mortified sobs.

"Hey, hey," I soothed. "Shhh."

"They're ruining it all!"

"They're all dicks," I said. "Don't…William, don't let it upset you. Shit. Yeah. Let it upset you. They're jerks. I'm sorry, kid."

He swiped at his face. "Why doesn't Grandma like my mom?"

"I don't know. Because your mom isn't like Auntie Jill, I guess." I put an arm around him, squeezing.

"You're not like Auntie Jill."

I laughed, painfully. "No, but I'd say that Grandma doesn't like me much, either."

"No, but she loves you, at least." That was a lot of wisdom from a kid.

"Yeah…well. She loves you, too, buddy. So does your mom. So don't let this ruin your time. When we go back in there, it'll all have blown over, and everyone will be pretending nothing's wrong."

"How do you know?"

"Because that's what people do when something awk-ward happens," I told him as the service door opened and my brother shot through it.

He looked at us with relief. "Oh. Hey, buddy. There you are."

William gave his dad a wary look. "Are they still fighting?"

"No. Mom went to cool down, and Grandma and Aunt Jill are…sitting down. Being quiet," he said with a look at me.

"Well, better they shut up because they feel so affronted than keep on going," I said.

Evan sighed. "C'mon back inside, buddy. Okay? Elise, you coming?"

"In a minute."

My phone had buzzed while this was going on with a text from Niall saying he'd be right down to brunch. I tried to reply with at least a bare sketch of what had happened in case he was going to walk into a shitshow, but my signal bars had dropped. I moved along the corridor past stacked chairs and trays of glassware until I turned a corner, then down another corridor and through a set of double doors, where my phone got better reception. That was where everything really hit the fan.

There was Susan, shoulders shaking as she pressed herself against a man I recognized from being at the party the night before, but whose name I did not know. He was stroking her hair while she said, "…and he just stood there and let them fucking walk all over him, and me, while his mother insulted me and my family. And he did nothing! Not a damn thing, as usual!"

The guy wasn't her brother or an uncle or a conveniently affectionate male cousin, either. He might've been a gay best friend, but when they started kissing on the mouth, even I couldn't make that one fly. All I could do was stand there with my mouth open, phone in my hand bleating with an incoming text message that alerted the lovers to my presence so they both turned at the same time, and I could not pretend I hadn't seen them.

"Shit," the man said.

Susan looked remarkably put together considering how short a time had passed since she'd been screeching like a harpy. And considering her dirty secret had just been found out. She lifted her chin and murmured something to the guy that seemed to put him off, but she repeated it, harder this time. He nodded and moved past her, heading toward the swinging doors that led to the lobby. She looked at me.

"Are you going to tell Evan?"

I didn't know what to say, other than "He's my brother."

"Well, don't tell him today. Okay? Let's not make this day any worse than it's been already." She looked tired. And sad.

I shook my head. "You should be the one to tell him, not me."

Susan laughed without humor. "I'm not telling him anything. Are you crazy?"

"You can't... I mean, he'll find out." My phone slipped in my sweaty palm.

"How's he going to find out? He doesn't fucking pay attention." Susan sneered. "To anything. You really think he's going to just figure it out on his own? And even if he does, Elise, your brother is a fucking master at ignoring things he doesn't want to deal with."

She wasn't wrong, but he was still my brother, and she was a woman who'd never bothered to even try to be my friend. I didn't say anything. She shrugged and eyed me.

"What did I ever do to you," I asked finally, "to make you hate me?"

Susan answered quietly. "I don't hate you."

"Then what the hell, Sue?" I leaned against the wall.

"It was everything," she blurted. "Everything about you."

I frowned, not sure how to take that. "What about me is so awful? I mean, I get why you can't stand Jill, but..."

"Jill's jealous of me, that's all," Susan said. "She's jealous because she can't have kids because of the...because of what happened when she was in college. And she's always been jealous of you and Evan."

"What the hell happened to her in college?"

Susan gave me a long, steady look. "She got pregnant. The guy wouldn't marry her, the way Evan agreed to marry me."

"Jill got pregnant?" I shook my head and wished I had a chair to sit in.

"Yeah, and she's never gotten over the guy or gotten married or had kids, and she hates that I have what she wanted." Susan shrugged and crossed her arms over her stomach. She looked at the carpet. "I've tried to feel sorry for her, but really, she's just a bitch."

"Well. Yeah." I shrugged, too. "She kind of always was."

Susan gave me a sideways look. "I'm jealous of you, Elise. So that makes me a bitch, too, I guess."

"But...why?"

"Because Evan talks to you when he won't talk to me. Because you stand up to them, and I just let them walk all over me. Because," she said on a low rasp, "when William was a baby and I felt trapped into having him and getting married when I didn't want to, there you were. I was afraid to drop him. You changed his diapers with practically one hand. And here you are now, with a job you love and you're just... so fucking put together and confident, and you always have been, and I never have."

We stared at each other.

"Jesus, I wish I still smoked," she said.

I would gladly have lit up right along with her. "I won't tell Evan anything, for William's sake. But you should. Or you should end it. Or both."

"I can't end it," Susan said. "I love him."

I winced. We stared at each other some more. Finally, she squared her shoulders.

"I need to get back in there and, I guess, make nice."

"You don't really have to make that much nice. They're going to leave you alone. Oh, they'll snipe at each other and probably wear off Evan's ears later, but you…" I gave her a grin that hurt my mouth and a shrug. "You, they're going to leave alone."

For a moment, I thought she was going to break down into tears again. I couldn't in any way not judge her for cheating on my brother—what the fuck was I going to do about that anyway? Still, I didn't blame her for finally laying into my mom and Jill.

"Look, Susan…" I paused, thinking of her Wednesday afternoon yoga classes, and being late. "I'm not going to put any sort of ultimatums on you or anything like that. But if you ever again use me to be responsible for your kid while you're off fucking around, I will make sure Evan knows everything."

She looked guilty, I gave her that. She nodded. My phone buzzed, and I looked at it. Without another word between us, she left me, and I thumbed the screen to find a text from Niall.

Where are you?

I told him where to find me, and when he got there, I hugged him, hard. Squeezing. I pressed my face to the side of his neck, and said, "Get me out of here."

★ ★ ★

Niall took me to a diner and fed me eggs and pancakes and toast and coffee, and he listened to me rant about my stupid, crazy family without trying to offer any advice. I didn't tell him about Susan—some knowledge is more of a burden than ignorance would be, and he worked with my brother, after all. When he reached for my hand across the table, I let him take it. A simple touch, but it meant a lot.

"Want some?" I offered a piece of toast that I'd sprinkled liberally with cinnamon and sugar. I bit into it, crunching, savoring the sweetness. I sighed. "My favorite."

"I've never had it."

Surprised, I blinked. "What, never?"

"Nope. Butter and jelly for me, always." He leaned to take a bite of my toast. I wanted to jump across the table and kiss away the crumbs from the corner of his mouth.

In the car, I got my chance. And oh, his kiss was sweeter than sugar. Sweeter than anything.

"I should get back," I told him after a few minutes of the kind of kissing that could make a girl forget she was in the front seat of a car. "Make sure nobody killed anyone."

"It's not your job to play referee, Elise."

I smiled. "Is that just an excuse to get me to make out with you some more?"

"Maybe." He leaned close but just out of reach, and when I moved toward him, he teasingly moved back.

I didn't go after him again. I let him come to me, and he did, after a moment's pause, taking my mouth in a lingering but sweet kiss that nevertheless pushed up my heart rate. Niall traced the line of my jaw and sat back. We stared at each other for a moment or so.

"I'm not crazy, am I?" I asked him.

He raised a brow. "Umm…?"

"There's something here." I gestured to the space between us. "I'm not reading you wrong, am I? We really did almost have sex last night, right?"

Niall blinked and looked a little embarrassed. "Yes."

I wanted to kiss him again, but didn't. "Just wanted to be clear, that's all. Because you're confusing."

"C'mon, I'm as clear as day," he said.

We laughed together, and I leaned back in the passenger seat with a sigh. Without looking at him, I said, "Why did you cancel our movie date?"

Niall didn't answer me at first. When I finally looked over at him, he looked a little shamefaced. "Because I'm an idiot?"

"It's because of those pictures, isn't it? And the stuff you asked my brother about." I kept my voice light, though I felt sort of dark. "It's too *weird* for you."

Niall reached for my hand. He kissed each of my fingertips then curled my fingers against my palm and kissed the knuckles, too. "It was all those messages you kept getting while we were at the acrobats show. I knew they were from a guy."

"They were, but so what?"

"I thought maybe they were from a boyfriend," Niall said.

I frowned. "If I had a boyfriend, I wouldn't have gone out with you. Wow. What kind of person do you think I am?"

"Fascinating, intriguing, intimidating as hell," Niall said.

I narrowed my eyes, though in truth his answer flattered me. "I *don't* have a boyfriend."

"Right. You have lovers." It was his turn to frown.

I took my hand away from his and linked my fingers in my lap. Staring straight ahead, I said, "I *had* a lover. One. And I don't see him anymore. But even if I did, that's my business, isn't it?"

"A guy just likes to know where he stands, that's all."

I gave him the side eye. "So, you thought I had a boyfriend...or a lover...and yet you took me to bed anyway."

"I think you could argue that you're the one who took *me* to bed," he said.

I was quiet, thinking of lonely nights and desperation, of unrequited longing. Of rules that were supposed to keep my heart safe but had not. Niall took my hand again. His thumb stroked the back of it, and I shivered.

"You think I'm this badass. That it's all whips and chains and hot candle wax. You think I'm going to be hard and sharp, but I'm soft, Niall. That's what you don't understand. That really, I want to be soft." I shook my head and carefully took my hand away again. He ran a fingertip down my bare shoulder and arm, tickling. I looked at him again. "I'm tired of games, that's all."

"No games," he promised and made an X on his chest with his finger. "Cross my heart. Hate 'em."

I made a face. "That's what everyone says, and the next thing you know, you're not being honest about something, or you're trying to manipulate someone, or you're trying to change someone into what you want them to be. Or change into what they want you to be, only you never really can, can you? And all you have is disappointment and grief."

"He must've really jacked you up," Niall said. "Whoever he was, that boyfriend you didn't have."

I frowned. "Yeah, well, that's what happens, isn't it? Bad breakups leave you scarred."

"So you take a lover," he said. "Instead of having a boyfriend."

"Are you offering to be my *boyfriend*?" I asked, annoyed.

He shook his head and gave me that damned smile. "I wouldn't dare."

"If you ask me out on a date again, you'd better follow through this time," I warned. "No bullshit."

"None. Not a speck of it, I promise. So, what do you say? You want to give it a try? Can I have another chance?"

Mollified, but only a little, I let myself study his face, searching for any signs he was being insincere. "I mean it, Niall. I'm not interested in being jerked around. What happened last night was one thing. Taking me to the movies is another."

"Can't I have both?" He looked totally serious. "Does it have to be one or the other?"

"You want to date." I said it flatly. "Not just fuck?"

He was silent for a moment or so. "What do you want, Elise?"

"I told you what I wanted." I shrugged.

He took my hand again. We sat like that for another long minute, until finally I leaned to offer my mouth to him. He kissed me.

"You can be soft with me," he said.

28

Niall did ask me out on a real, honest-to-goodness date, and I did agree to go. He picked me up at my house and everything. Brought a bouquet of flowers, daisies and some kind of purple blooms I didn't recognize but loved at once. We had dinner and drinks and then saw a movie, and he took me home to drop me off with a kiss at the front door.

And oh, what a kiss. Open mouths, tongues dancing, his hands in my hair, on my hips, his body pushing mine against the front door until I pushed him back a little.

"People in this neighborhood are nosy. You want to come inside?" I asked, my mouth already filled with the memory of his flavor.

Niall gave me a solemn look, then a sly grin as he surreptitiously adjusted the front of his pants. "Not on the first date."

"You're kidding, right?" I took a step back at his expression. "You're serious!"

"I took you on a date, a real date. The rest of it will happen when it happens."

He sounded so serene about it that I had to stop and think. Hard. There was something incredibly appealing about the idea, of letting go and going with the flow. Appealing and scary.

"That's very philosophical," I said.

He grinned. "What can I say, I'm a deep thinker."

"You're really not going to come inside. For real."

He shook his head, the grin getting bigger. "Nope. Not unless you want to order me to."

He was testing me, and I knew it. Stubbornly, I put my hands on my hips and narrowed my eyes, trying to figure him out. "You do realize we've already seen each other like, almost naked."

Niall nodded. "Oh, yeah. I remember. Believe me. I couldn't forget if I tried."

"Why would you want to try?"

"Good point." Niall took a step back, off my concrete front porch. "I'll call you."

I laughed and shook my head. "Weirdo. Maybe I don't want you to call me again. You didn't even ask if I had a good time."

"You had a good time," Niall told me, and with a grin and a wave, went back to his car.

Damn him, he was right. The night had been fantastic. We'd discovered we liked the same television shows, music, books. We ordered the same dessert, until he decided at the last minute to go for what would've been my second choice also, so we could both share. As far as dates went, aside from not getting laid at the end of it, it had been the best I'd had in…well, honestly, maybe the best date I'd ever had.

When I got out of the shower, I found a missed call from him. In bed, snuggled into my pillows, I clutched the phone to my chest for a moment before calling him back. "Hi."

"I wanted to say good-night," Niall said. "What are you doing?"

"I just got into bed. What are you doing?"

"Same," he said. "What are you wearing?"

"A smile."

He groaned. "You're killing me."

"Don't ask if you don't want to know the answer."

He was silent for a few seconds. "So…"

"So," I answered.

"I had a really good time tonight," Niall said.

I smiled. "I know you did."

"We'll have to do it again soon." He paused. "What are you doing tomorrow?"

"Blissfully, I have no plans. How about you?"

"I have to run some errands in the morning. Then I thought I'd hit the gym. But later, if you want, we could go bowling," Niall said.

"Bowling?"

He laughed. "Yeah. Bowling. What, you don't bowl?"

"I haven't been bowling in…well. God. Since high school, maybe? Wow." I tried to remember the last time I'd been to a bowling alley and had a vague memory of stinky shoes and loud music.

"So, you wanna go?"

I hmmm'd. "Yes. Okay."

"Great. I'll pick you up at six," Niall said.

We disconnected, and I put my phone onto its charging dock. And though I lay awake for a long time, fighting my usual insomnia and counting backward from a hundred, I didn't pick it up again. I wasn't even tempted to send George a late-night text.

For the first time in a long time, I had nothing I wanted to tell him.

29

You know how it is when you first meet someone, and everything they do is amazing and wonderful, and you can't get enough? But eventually, something annoys you. The way they chew, maybe. Or that they're always late because they can't make up their mind what to wear, or they don't like your favorite perfume, or they tell you they don't see the point of tattoos when they know very well you have several. Slowly, little hurts here and there, over and over, until eventually you can barely remember why you ever liked each other in the first place.

I kept waiting for something like that to happen with Niall, but nothing did. Instead, the weeks passed, and we moved along as though we'd known each other forever, yet we were still brand-new to each other every time we talked. The butterflies didn't go away. My heart leaped every time my phone rang and his name showed up on the screen.

Being with him was easy. Talking to him was easy. I never had to repeat myself to explain what I meant. If he asked me a question, and he did, lots of them, he listened to the answer and actually retained the information for like, longer than a day. He took me out for dinner on my birthday and bought me

a card, and I didn't even have to hint around for the week beforehand that I would be turning thirty-four. I'd never known
a man who did that. Even my brother had been known to forget to wish me a happy birthday, and we freaking shared it.

A month isn't such a long time unless you're falling in love,
and then it can feel like four years instead of four weeks. I
wasn't sure what I felt for Niall was love. It wasn't the same
as I'd felt for anyone before, I knew that much. The more I
learned about him, the more I wanted to know. Being with
Niall was easy, but it was also strange because it was so effort-
less. It scared me shitless, you know, how simple it was to be
with him. It was good, enjoying his company.

That terrified me.

I couldn't ignore how casually he took my hand when we
walked, his fingers stroking the inside of my palm every now
and then to send shivers up and down and all through me.
How he let his toes nudge mine beneath the table, or his fingers trail along my shoulder blades and the back of my neck
when he got up to use the restroom and came back. And
how he kissed me, all the time. Hello, goodbye, randomly
at any time I found myself tucked up against him, his mouth
on mine. Sometimes quick, sometimes lingering, his kisses
never failed to make my heart beat faster. We spent hours on
his couch making out, like in high school, before I'd started
having sex, only not like in high school, I knew exactly what I
was missing out on. Hands roaming, hair getting mussed, he'd
kiss me until my mouth felt puffy, my lips a little chapped. I
kept my hands on the outside of his clothes, waiting for him
to beg me to touch him, but he didn't. And I let him drift his
fingers beneath my clothes without ever urging him to go
farther. Waiting, waiting to see what Niall would do all on
his own, to see which one of us could hold out the longest.
There were nights I left his house on legs so shaky it was a

trick getting upright to the car, my panties soaked with my arousal. I hadn't been so turned on without getting release in…well, ever.

I couldn't stand it, and I couldn't get enough, delirious with anticipation. Tease and denial, only which one of us was doing the teasing and which the denying? Four weeks of that and nothing more.

No wonder I was losing my mind, just a little.

I'd become accustomed to negotiation. Laying it all out—expectations, desires, safe words, hard lines. I'd forgotten what it was like to simply allow a relationship to grow naturally, without intervention or force or struggle.

I should've just taken him, right? Because that's what dommes do. They take what they want. Demand and command. Maybe that was what he was waiting for. Well, that can be fun, for sure, and I wouldn't even try to pretend I don't like getting what I want, how I want it and when. But I'd also meant what I'd said to Niall. That maybe in porn or for other people it was all about the sharp edges or being fierce. I wanted to be able to be soft.

And because he didn't beg me, because he didn't force, Niall was giving me that.

We'd spent the day wandering the farmers' markets and quilt shops of Southern Lancaster County. Amish Country. Why? Because I'd mentioned earlier in the week that although I'd lived in the area my entire life and that my mother still lived in Lancaster, I'd never done any of the touristy stuff.

Niall took me on a buggy ride driven by a young Amish man without a beard, who wore an awesome, flat-brimmed straw hat that Niall tried to buy off him. The kid laughed and shook his head at the foolishness of us "English" and directed us to his aunt's shop. She sold quilts and canned jars of pickles as well as hats. Niall bought me a bonnet, and because the sun was bright, I wore it. I took a picture of us in our hats and made it the background of my phone.

This was…maybe not love, but something close to it, all right. Ooey-gooey, mushy, gooshy more-than-like. And I was all up in it.

"Hey, you want a whoopie pie?" Niall was already plucking up a few of the local treats and putting them into the quaint straw shopping basket.

They looked homemade, which was great, except that I couldn't find any ingredients. I shook my head. "I'd better not."

He looked confused. "No? How come? They're delicious."

"Probably made with lard." At his even more confused look, I laughed and said, "I don't eat anything made from a pig."

"Oh. Right. Right?" He looked at the whoopie pies. "These have pig in them?"

"They might." I took a jar of pickled red beet eggs from the shelf and put that in his basket, instead. "But that doesn't mean you can't have one."

"Nah. Not if it has pig in it." Niall shook his head and kissed me right there in the middle of the aisle. Two little Amish girls in matching dresses, their hair in braids, giggled.

It was a great day, and I didn't want to ruin it, but I was ten minutes from my mother's house by the time we'd done everything Niall had planned for the day. When I asked him if he'd mind stopping by, he laughed and shook his head. I laughed, too, but without much humor.

"You're taking me home to meet Mom?" he asked.

"You've met her already. You know what you're getting into. I just thought it would be nice of me." I made a face. "She's kind of a pain in the ass, but…she's alone."

Niall reached across the center console to take my hand. "Yeah. I get it. My mom's alone, too, which is why I feel like

I have to spend so much time doing stuff for her. I keep trying to get her to move closer, but she says she's been in her
house for forty years, and she's not about to leave it. I know
she'd be fine, she's capable of doing stuff for herself, but since
I'm an only child and she lost my dad…"

"You like to make sure she's taken care of." He was talking about his mother. I was thinking of how he acted with
me. "There's nothing wrong with that. I like that about you."

He looked pleased. "Yeah?"

"Yeah." I leaned to kiss him. "You're a good man."

So we went to see my mother, who opened the door and
scolded me for not calling her first so she could put on something other than her housedress. Never mind that my mother's *housedress* came complete with matching earrings, bracelet
and shoes, or that she was expertly made up even for an afternoon alone at home. She offered us both coffee cake, though,
which meant she wasn't too pissed off. When my mother is
really mad, she withholds food.

"So, he's very nice," she said in a low voice when Niall excused himself to use the restroom. "He works with Evan, no?"

"Yep. He was at the Bar Mitzvah. You met him there."

"I thought he looked familiar. I knew it. He's the one who
forgot to wear a yarmulke."

I had no idea if that were true, but I sighed. "Could be."

"He's not Jewish," my mother said.

"No, Ma. He's not."

"Well," she said with a sigh and a wave of her hand as she
lit a cigarette. "I tried to set you up with Myra Goldberg's son
who's a doctor, but you're going to do what you do."

"You just said he was very nice!" I reached for one of her
cigarettes, but she slapped my hand. I didn't really want one.
I was just seeing what she'd do.

"He can be very nice all he wants."

I rolled my eyes. "We're just dating. We're not even serious."

"You brought him over to meet me," my mother said. "That's pretty serious."

"He's already met you. I figured you couldn't scare him off." I used my fingertip to press a few moist crumbs into my mouth then glanced at my mother, who had a weird expression. "What?"

"So, he's into…?"

I blinked. "Oh, Ma. Jesus. When are you going to just not ask me that stuff? You don't really want to know, and it's not your business, and it's really awkward!"

"Your father had a foot thing," she said suddenly, sitting up straight in her chair as if someone had shoved a broomstick up the back of her dress. "Painted toes. Peep-toe pumps."

"Ma. No. Please don't." I shook my head, laughing in horror, praying that Niall would not walk back into the kitchen and overhear any of this mess.

"I'm just saying that I think you get it from his side of the family."

"I didn't *get* anything. God." I face palmed. "Sexual preferences are not a disease. If you want to know, it started watching Wonder Woman, okay? She had those really cool lassos, and she always tied up the cute boys."

"So it's not something I did?"

I thought she was kidding. She had to be, right? But when I looked at her, I could see that my mother was totally serious.

"No, Ma," I said gently. "You screwed me up in a lot of other ways, but not that way."

"Thank God!"

Niall appeared in the doorway, pausing at the sound of my mother's heartfelt prayer. He gave me a look. I shook my head a little.

"But you're still taking those pictures," my mother began.

"That's our cue to get out of here," I told her and stood. "Thanks for the cake. We're going to get going."

"It was nice to see you again, Mrs. Klein. The cake was great."

My mother sniffed, but I could see his compliment made her happy. At the front door she suffered a hug from me and said into my ear, "If he likes cake, maybe he'd like being Jewish, no?"

"That has nothing to do with anything," I said through a clench-jawed smile into her ear so he wouldn't overhear.

"You could mention it to him."

I didn't answer that, and when we got into Niall's car, I groaned and buried my face in my hands for a moment while he laughed and squeezed my shoulder. I looked at him. He shrugged.

"Sorry," I said. "It could've been worse, I guess."

Niall turned on the radio and didn't say much after that. I tried a few times to start a conversation, but he seemed distracted. I contented myself with scrolling through my phone. I don't like it when I want to be quiet and someone tries to talk to me, so I let him be silent. The weather was so great I put the windows down, and it only took me two horrible singalongs with current pop tunes for me to understand something I hadn't before.

I was happy.

Really, for the first time since things ended with George, I was well and truly content. I had a good job. Good friends. And there was Niall, who'd come out of nowhere and made me laugh, made me think and who always, always seemed to know exactly what I needed.

I sent Alicia a quick text, just a hey, girl. She replied quickly, and we texted back and forth for a few minutes. She was with

Jay, she said. They'd been picking out throw pillows for their new couch.

My fingers flew over the phone's touch pad, getting all the news from her about their new apartment. Things were getting serious. I shot a glance toward Niall, wondering if I should tell her about him.

Were things with us getting serious, too?

In my driveway, still sitting in the car, he kissed me. Gently at first, but like a match on dry leaves, within seconds we were both openmouthed. Tongues sliding. Our teeth clashed, and he sat back.

"I should get going," he said.

I licked my lips, tasting him. "Yeah. If you want to."

"This is insane." He leaned to breathe against my lips. His other hand went behind my neck to cup the back of my skull. His fingers dug into me there. "You make me crazy. You know that?"

I opened my mouth, inviting him back in. I took his hand and slid it between my thighs, under the hem of my summer dress. His fingertips stroked my bare skin as I kissed him. Light touches. The scratch of his fingernails. I shifted, pressing his hand higher, higher.

"Touch me, Niall."

He kissed me hard enough to take my breath away. Then he pulled away enough to look into my eyes. I didn't know what he was looking for, but he didn't seem to find it because he sat back again in his seat.

Niall ran a hand through his hair. "What the hell am I supposed to do with you, Elise?"

"Anything you want," I whispered.

He gripped the steering wheel. Both hands. Tight enough to turn his knuckles white. He didn't say anything. The silence between us stretched and grew until it engulfed me.

Maybe, I thought, he *didn't* want me.

Not enough.

Paralyzed by the thought of that, of what I would do if he told me now that this was the last time we would see each other, that he'd grown tired of me, that he didn't like me "in that way," that we simply weren't working out, I could not move. I opened my mouth, words trapped and burning in my throat, but I could not make myself speak.

The last person to do that to me was Esteban, and that had been bad enough. With Niall, my feelings were heightened by about a hundred times. The pain would be that and more.

Anxious and uncertain, I backed off. Closed up tight. I couldn't make myself look at him or lean to kiss him. I put my hand on the door handle and made my voice light and neutral so it wouldn't shake.

"Goodbye, Niall."

"I'll call you tomorrow," Niall said.

I nodded and got out of the car. I thought about turning back, but in the end, I didn't. I just watched him drive away.

30

"Chin up," Olivia said. "To the left a little...there. Perfect. This is going to be great."

We were taking more pinup shots, this time for a local store that sold vintage dresses. Most of their business came from their website, so they'd hired Olivia for an ongoing gig to provide pictures of their dresses on models. The clothes sold better when people could see them on real people. I loved dressing up, and Olivia had told me she was happy about the steady income.

"Alex wants to stay home and be a househusband," she told me as I went behind a paper screen to get out of one dress and into another. "I told him no way. He'd drive me crazy if he were here all the time. I'd never be able to get any work done."

"No, really?" I laughed and peeked at her over the top of the screen. "He'd bug you all day? Can't imagine that."

Olivia shook her head fondly. "My life would suck without him, though."

"Yeah...you guys are pretty amazing together." I came out and twirled, the skirt of my dress belling out. "I like this one a lot."

"You think so? About me and Alex, I mean. The dress,

of course, is amazing." Olivia smiled as she fiddled with her camera.

I took my spot in front of the plain background. "Yeah. I do. Some people bicker so much all the time, it's like they can't stand each other. Some people are way too into each other, like they don't have lives without the other. It's rare when you meet a couple who are...just right."

"Like Goldilocks," Olivia murmured, focused on what she was viewing through her lens. "Not too much, not too little. Just right."

"Just right," I agreed. "Lucky you."

She looked up at me. "You okay?"

"Fine." I smiled and twirled again while her camera whirred and clicked.

Later in my own clothes, but still wearing the heavy black eyeliner and red lipstick I'd worn for the pictures, I declined her invitation to have dinner with her and Alex. I had plans with Niall.

Olivia grinned. "So, it's on with you two?"

"I don't know if it's...on. Exactly." I smoothed powder over my nose and ran a brush through my hair. I'd taken it out of the Victory rolls, but it was still now much wavier than I normally wore it. I eyed myself critically. "Should I go home first? Or do something different with my hair? Is this too much? We're just going for pizza and beer."

"You look fantastic. And what do you mean, you don't know if it's on? Either it's on," Olivia said, "or it's not."

"I guess it's on. Casually on. Slowly. Hesitantly, maybe?" At least I felt more hesitant about it than I'd been feeling before.

"Slow can be good. No need to rush into anything," she agreed as she put away her camera. "Not so sure about hesitantly."

"I guess I have a fucked-up viewpoint on relationships,

that's all." I'd tumbled headlong and headstrong into my thing with George, and look where it had gotten me. I'd put all kinds of brakes on my relationship with Esteban, and it hadn't worked out much better. Niall was so different from them both, and we still hadn't even crossed the possibly huge chasm before us—the fact that we might want different things in bed. "I want to sort of let go and see what happens, take it as it comes. But it's scary, you know? Taking a chance."

Olivia looked at me. "Yeah. No kidding. But you like him, huh?"

"I do. I wasn't sure about him at first. But yeah. I like him." I leaned on the desk for a moment, watching her slip her SD card into her laptop's slot so she could pull up the day's shots. "We have fun together."

"Fun's important." She glanced at me. "He has a good sense of humor?"

"Oh. Yeah. A goofy sense of humor, for sure. So…we'll see what happens. I like that one." I pointed out an image.

She looked at my choice and blew it up to start touching it up. "Good eye."

I watched her work for another minute or so before I had to get going. We scheduled another session for next month, which would be a nice couple hundred bucks in my pocket, and I'd never complain about that.

Niall greeted me at his front door with a glass of iced tea so cold it was sweating. Perfectly sweetened. A squeeze of lime, not lemon, that quirk of mine that nobody else ever seemed to get right, even when I ordered it in a restaurant and was very specific with the server. Crushed ice, not cubed. And the crowning touch—a straw, because I hated the way ice bumped against my lips.

"Hey, baby, wow, thank you." I kissed him on the mouth,

then the cheek, and drank thirstily. I caught a glimpse of his expression as he let me past him into the living room. "What?"

"Just glad to see you, that's all. You look…different." Niall swept me with his gaze. "Turn around."

I set down my glass on the coffee table and spun, showing off my cute summer frock. It wasn't one of the ones Olivia had taken pictures of me in, but it was from the same shop. Sleeveless gray-and-white-checked cotton with a scooped neckline and a cute matching belt. The dress made me feel feminine and powerful because, wearing it, I also felt pretty. Paired with black pointy-toed flats, I also felt like I wanted to twirl and dip, so I did with the weight of his gaze on me making me blush.

"I was doing some pictures with Olivia," I explained when he still looked quizzical.

Niall frowned, though he tried to hide it. "Ah. Alone, or…?"

Jealous, but not willing to admit it? Laughing, I pressed against him, my fingers linked behind his neck. I tipped my face for a kiss, which he gave me.

"Alone," I said. "Are you going to ask me to stop modeling?"

"You're an adult woman. It's not my place to tell you what you should do."

It was the right answer, but it rang a little false. I kissed him again, just a brush of our lips this time. "But you want to. Don't you?"

Niall's hands settled on my hips, and he inched me closer. "Yeah. Kind of."

I had to force myself to keep my voice light when I replied. "You know, I had a guy ask me to stop modeling once."

Niall's eyes narrowed. "I guess you didn't."

"No, I did. For the few weeks we went out, sure I did." I

shook my head. "I'm not a total bitch, Niall. And yes, there are things I like, but I've dated a few guys who weren't into the props and rituals, and that was okay, too. Not everything is my way or the highway. I might not like being told what to do, but that doesn't mean if I'm asked nicely that I won't at least consider it. I might be selfish, but I like to think I'm not completely self-absorbed."

"No, you're not."

We swayed, dancing in a slow circle without music to guide us. We didn't need any. We were perfectly in sync.

"I don't like to think of you doing that sort of thing with someone else, that's all." He shrugged.

We stopped moving. I pushed up on my toes to kiss him again then hug him. I whispered into his ear, "Pictures are pictures, Niall. Modeling is like acting. None of that is real."

"But it's real for you," he said. "I mean, it's still your thing. I guess I wouldn't like it, then, if you were doing your thing with someone else, for real or for pretend. If you're mine, you're mine. I don't want you with anyone else." He frowned briefly. His fingers tightened on my hips.

I swooned a little. Okay, a lot. "Am I, then? Yours?"

"Do you want to be?"

I kissed him again. Slower this time. Lingering. The swipe of his tongue sent a shiver all through me, and when I pulled back, I'm sure my eyes were as bright as his.

"What are we doing, exactly, Niall Black?"

"I'm tryin'," he said, "to court you."

A month of bowling and dinner and movies. Kisses on the front step and late-night phone calls. Goofy texts. Flowers and perfect iced tea. And, other than the night of William's Bar Mitzvah, we hadn't done anything more than make out.

"It's a big responsibility, you know. Keeping me happy," I said against his mouth. My fingers toyed with the length of his hair in the back, and when he shivered, I grinned. "I can be very particular."

"I know, I know," Niall said. "Lime in the iced tea, not lemon."

I'd been dreamy, teasing, but at this I pushed away from him then so I could turn and keep my face from him. Not because I was mad or sad, but because in all my life, there'd never been a man who'd bothered to pay attention to such a small detail...or who got it right.

And then he hit a home run.

"You were left-handed as a kid," he continued in a low voice from behind me. "But someone must've made you switch, huh?"

Slowly, I turned, my heart pounding so hard it's a wonder it didn't block out the sound of anything but its beating. "Yes. My mother. Evan was right-handed, and she thought I should be, too. The kindergarten teacher said nobody forced lefties to switch any longer, but my mom insisted anyway. I learned to write right-handed, but yeah...I'm a leftie. I've never told anyone that."

"You didn't have to tell me. You automatically reach with your left hand," he said. "I've watched you do it with just about everything. I figured."

That was it, then. The moment I knew. Despite how strangely it had begun, the time I'd so far spent with him still so short it was hardly time at all, when I stood in front of him and knew that Niall Black knew me, really fucking knew me, that was it. I was done.

I was in love.

I made him dinner. Nothing fancy, but it was cozy, the two of us at his tiny kitchen table. We laughed over veggie lasagna, and he cleared the dishes without being asked. I watched him rinse them at the sink before putting them in the dishwasher.

"A girl could get used to this," I said. "All you need is an apron. No pants, just the apron."

Niall looked at me over his shoulder. "You know, Elise, when you objectify me in that way, it makes me feel all tingly inside."

I grinned. "When you do the dishes, it gets me downright full-on horny."

"Just think," he said as he pulled me out of my chair to kiss me, "what would happen if I did your laundry?"

"You'd kill me! That's what would happen." I linked my fingers behind his neck and looked into his eyes as I stroked my fingers through his hair again, loving how silky it was. Thick and dark, a few glints of silver at the temples. "How old are you?"

"Isn't that supposed to be a rude question?" He frowned.

"Hey," I laughed, "I just had a birthday. You already know how old I am."

"I'm older than you." He nuzzled my throat for a moment. "Does it matter?"

"No. I guess not. Just curious." I pretended to scrutinize him. "Do you not want to tell me because you're ancient, or...?"

"Ancient, damn. You know how to stab a guy, don't you? I'm forty. I had my milestone birthday in March."

"Wow. Forty. That's..." I giggled when he poked me. "Sexy. Forty is sexy!"

He kissed me. I kissed him. Somehow my ass ended up on the table, and the rest of the dishes were forgotten for a few minutes.

"You're terrible, you know that?" he said into my ear.

Surprised, I pushed back. "What? Why?"

Shaking his head, Niall pulled me closer. "Oh, no, you can't play that game with me. I see it in your eyes. You're totally undressing me with them." I started laughing as he continued, "And listen, I'm not just a sex object, Elise."

"I never said…" I couldn't go on, choking on laughter.

"You didn't have to say. It's all over your face. The sheer, raw animal lust in your eyes!" Niall stood, his hand still in mine, tugging me off the table. "Frankly, I'm both affronted and taken aback."

Giggling, I tried to act chastened. "I'm sorry."

"It's okay," he told me and pulled me closer. "I am pretty sexy, even for some kind of ancient, grizzled grandpa. I know you can't help being overcome with the lust."

"You totally are, and I totally am." I pushed onto my tiptoes to kiss him gently. "Thank you for taking pity on me and stopping me before I do something crazy."

"Like rip my clothes off and have your wicked way with me?"

"Yes, like that." I laughed again at his expression. "I know. The horror."

For a moment, both of us smiled and looked into each other's eyes but said nothing. He linked his fingers in mine and tugged me into the living room, where he put on a streaming comedy from Interflix, and we settled on the couch to watch. Several minutes after it started, Niall gave an enormous fake yawn and stretched to put his arm around my shoulders. Laughing, I snuggled in.

"Smooth," I told him.

"Hey, I don't want you to get scared off if I move too fast." He shifted a little closer and put his feet up on the coffee table. "Got to keep my girl happy."

It's what George had always said, and I frowned at how

suddenly and viscerally I reacted to it. "Ugh…don't…don't call me that."

Niall looked at me. "No? Sorry. I should call you a woman? Or a lady, I'm never sure what's politically correct."

"It's not…ugh. I don't mind being referred to as a girl. Or I thought I didn't." I shifted to angle toward him. "The last real relationship I had, he always called me his *girl*."

"And you didn't like it when he called you that?" Niall took his arm from around my shoulders, which wasn't at all what I'd wanted him to do.

"I did. At the time. But you know how it is." I shrugged. "When you're hot and heavy with someone and you put up with things you don't normally like, or you do things you wouldn't normally do because somehow…with them…it's okay."

Neither of us had moved, but there was an abrupt and vast distance between us. Niall looked at the TV, but he wasn't laughing. I looked at him.

"Hey," I said. "I'm sorry. Would you rather I didn't tell you when I don't like something?"

He twisted to face me. "No. I just don't like that something I did made you think of someone else, that's all. When you're with me, I guess I want you to be thinking of me."

"Ah." I chewed the inside of my lip for a second. "That's fair."

"I guess I need to know if I'm being compared," Niall said.

This surprised me enough that I took his hand to squeeze it. "Wow. No. I mean, sure, but favorably."

"I guess that's better than not favorably." His smile was thin.

I sighed, thinking almost guiltily of all those late-night texts and how long I'd been holding on. I hadn't texted George since Niall and I had started dating, but he didn't need to know any of that. "It was a long time ago, and it didn't end well. Scars, remember? If I compare you at all, it's only because everyone compares. I'm sure you've had girlfriends you're comparing me to."

He looked caught then nodded. "Yeah, I guess so."

"Oh, do tell." I perked up, interested and curious but also fighting off a pang of jealousy.

"I had a few" was all he said, but I wasn't going to let him get off that easy.

Kneeling on the couch, I took his face in my hands as though I meant to kiss him, but when he moved to let his lips touch mine, I shifted just enough that he'd have to really reach for it. "That's it? Just a few? Nobody special?"

"Are you asking me if I have baggage?" His hands settled on my hips, holding me close in a way I wouldn't notice unless I tried to pull away again. But I noticed.

"Everyone has baggage. I'm just trying to figure out how many girls have broken your heart before." I tried to make it sound light. I meant it to. But my voice cracked and chipped a little on the words.

Niall kissed me. "They all did, in their own ways."

"That's terrible." I frowned and settled onto his lap to tuck my face against his neck. I put my hand on his chest, over his heart. "I'm sorry."

"It's what happens," he said against my hair. "How many broke yours?"

"Just the one," I said. "Believe me, that was enough."

We were quiet for a while. I timed my breathing to his. In, out.

He'd hung my picture on the wall in the living room, which alternatingly made me feel odd and exhilarated, though I'd never so much as pointed out that I saw where he'd put it.

"I don't want to break your heart," I whispered.

Niall was quiet for a few seconds before he said, "I'll try not to let you."

That was an answer that could've been taken a few different ways, but I didn't dig for an explanation. I kissed his throat, his jaw then his mouth. He ran his fingers through my hair to tug my head back, and I liked the little bit of pain, enough that it made me sigh.

"Was it the guy you were seeing when we first met?"

I didn't really want to talk to Niall about Esteban, either. That was still fresh and stung, not as fiercely as thoughts of George, but still somewhat. "No. He wasn't a boyfriend. We had sex, but we didn't date."

"Why not?"

"Because that wasn't in the rules. My thing with him was…" I paused, trying to think of a way to describe it. "Special. And sweet. And very sexy. It was something I'd been hoping to find for a long time but had only managed to get pieces of before, from a few different people. We stumbled through it a little bit, but I think we both also figured out how to get what we needed. He didn't break my heart."

I'd been too glowing about it, I saw that written all over Niall's face. But I wasn't going to denigrate or downplay what I'd shared with Esteban just to make some other guy feel better. Shit, I'd had lovers and bad breakups and casual sex. If Niall had a problem with any of that, I'd better find out now.

His brow furrowed. "So why'd you break it off?"

"I didn't. He did." I had to clear my throat when I said that, unable to keep the slight bitterness from my tone. "Just before the Bar Mitzvah."

"Is that why you went upstairs with me?"

I let go of Niall's hand. In the background, zany hijinks on the screen provided an ironic backdrop to our unexpectedly serious conversation. "I'm not sure what you mean."

"Because you'd been dumped. Or you broke up, whatever you want to call it. Did you go upstairs with me because you were trying to get over him?" Niall sounded more curious than angry, but I was still going to tread really, really carefully.

"No. I went upstairs with you because you knew how to dance. And because I find you very attractive. And because I wanted to." I stopped myself from chewing the inside of my cheek again. I was going to cut myself if I wasn't careful.

"And you were single."

"I was single when I was fucking him," I said sharply. "I was free to do whatever I wanted, and so was he. That was part of the agreement. No questions, no explanations. And I was still fucking him when I met you, and I agreed to go out with you then, so it had nothing to do with him breaking it off."

"Why'd *he* break it off?"

I hesitated, unsure if this was drifting into argument territory. "I don't know. He didn't actually break up with me. He just stopped messaging me."

"Shit bird," Niall said almost conversationally.

My chuckle surprised me. "Yeah. Not cool."

"And before him? What did those guys do that you didn't like? The one who hurt you so much. What did he do?"

I hesitated again. "Seriously, Niall, what the hell?"

"I want to know what you don't like," he told me, "so I don't do it."

This dried my mouth. I sipped iced tea, trying to find a way to reply to that. I couldn't, at first. I gave him a sideways smile, instead.

"I mean it," he said.

"And what about what I do like? You want me to tell you what I like, so you can do that?" I had to put the glass down because my shaking hands were going to give me away.

"Well…yeah," he said as though there could be no other answer.

Switch flipped. Bell rung. If my clit were wired with a Klaxon alarm, it would've started blaring.

Then I was on his lap, and his tongue was in my mouth, and his hands roamed all over me until with a couple of matching gasps, we broke apart. Niall had that look in his eyes, the one I craved and adored and got off on. Hazy desire tempered with what I thought was contemplation. He looked like a guy with a plan. I hoped it involved his mouth on other parts of me.

Self-confidence can so easily be eroded by the simplest of things. Dominant doesn't mean invulnerable. Thinking of the last time I'd pushed him to go a little faster and he'd refused, I didn't move. I waited. Crazy with tension and anticipation. I was dying from it, but oh, what a fucking beautiful way to go.

Finally, with a groan, Niall slid his hand between my legs. The pretty vintage dress slid up my thighs without resistance. Beneath I wore soft cotton panties that provided a teasing barrier to his touch. He stroked lightly. I sighed happily against his mouth.

"You like that?"

"Yes," I whispered.

Niall shifted my weight a little to cradle me more easily. His thumb moved slowly, firmly. When I arched, he laughed into the kiss. Beneath my ass, the press of his hardening cock added to my arousal. When I wriggled a little, he groaned.

We kissed like that for a while. He'd ease me to the edge, then expertly keep me there until I could no longer stop myself from moving, lifting my hips to press myself harder against his fingers. I wasn't expecting it when he slipped them inside my panties, or when he filled me with two fingers, his thumb still working on my clit.

"You're so wet for me," he said into my mouth. "Fuck, Elise."

"Feels so good…"

Niall let his head fall against the back of the couch. "Son of a bitch!"

Not the words I expected to come out of his mouth, that was for sure. "What's wrong?"

He looked at me, his fingers still inside me but not moving. "You're going to kill me."

"Uh-oh." I shifted so he could move his hand. "Why?"

"I don't have any condoms."

"What?" I punched his shoulder. "You got two knuckles deep inside me before you remembered that?"

He gave me a sheepish grin and stroked a hand down my thigh. "I wasn't expecting to get past second base tonight."

"Lame. Didn't you think at *some* point you would? Aren't you the one who said it would happen when it happened? We've been dating for weeks!" I let my forehead press his for a moment then kissed his mouth gently. "I *am* going to kill you."

"Do you…?"

I sat up, trying to think if I did, but they'd always been Esteban's responsibility. It had always given me a tingle to imagine him at the store, making his choice and facing the cashier, all the while with his cock half-hard because he was thinking of me. I wisely did not share this memory with Niall.

"I don't. Not with me anyway. I probably have some at home."

He gave me a solemn look. "Maybe I should kill *you*."

"No! Then we'd both be dead," I said, "and that's gross."

"I meant to. But somehow or another I kept never getting around to it. Shit." He groaned and fell back against the couch.

"See what happens when you let things happen as they're

meant to instead of having someone take charge?" I teased and leaned to brush my lips over his.

Niall shifted underneath me. "Are you mad?"

"I should say yes, just to teach you a lesson."

"Ugh, what kind of lesson is that?"

I wiggled against him. "The kind where you learn when I tell you to do something like be better prepared, I expect you to do it."

"Ouch."

I laughed. "I take it you were not a Boy Scout."

"No. I hated camping." He nipped at my throat, making me sigh.

"Condoms are nonnegotiable without a clean bill of health," I told him frankly. "I've had chlamydia twice, and that was enough. Never again."

He flinched. "Wow... I..."

"I'm tested monthly," I said.

Niall was silent for a moment. "You're very responsible."

"Well...yeah," I said. "Duh. When it comes to my health, I don't fuck around."

"I want to make love to you, Elise," he said sort of formally and so sweetly it made me emotional.

I drew a fingertip over his lower lip. "I want you to."

"So," he said hopefully.

"So," I answered as I got off his lap and took his hand. "You know there are other things we can do without a condom."

Niall grinned. "I was hoping you'd say that."

He took me upstairs. I made myself at home on his bed with a show of testing the mattress. The pillows. When he leaned to kiss me again, I laughed and held him off with a hand on his chest. Then I scooted back on the bed to rest against the headboard and inched up my skirt. I ran a finger up the inside of my thigh.

"We could play gin rummy," I said conversationally. "Or chess. I'm great at chess. I bet I could beat you."

"I bet you could, too." Niall moved closer to kiss me, his fingers following the path my own had made.

I stopped him an inch from my panties with a hand on his wrist. He stopped kissing me. He tried to move his hand again, but I didn't let him.

"You don't really want to play chess, do you?" he asked.

"I really want you to think about the fact you invited me over here and started to get me all excited without having any condoms." I kept my hand over his, though he was no longer trying to ease it upward. "There should be consequences for your actions."

I was serious. Stern. Esteban would've been properly downcast, ready to be disciplined. On the other hand, it was unlikely Esteban would not have remembered the rubbers.

"Are you sure you wouldn't rather think about me going down on you?" Niall, who was definitely not Esteban, asked.

I smiled, charmed, and didn't push the issue. "I *would* like to think about that."

"I could show you. Then you don't have to imagine it."

Niall kissed my knee. Then a little higher, the inside of my thigh. His mouth brushed my panties. I gave a small, gasping laugh, my back arching. When he slipped his fingers under the edges of the cotton and tugged them down, baring me to him, I closed my eyes. My fingers gripped the sheet as my body tensed, waiting for him to kiss me there.

I cried out when at last he did, with a slow, deliberate pressure on my clit that had my hips lifting. His hands slid beneath my ass, pressing me to his mouth. He sucked gently then used the flat of his tongue. One stroke, another, the pace steady and delicious and oh, fuck, so good.

My fingers dug into his hair. Niall made a small noise, and I opened my eyes. He wasn't looking at me, his attention solely on what he was doing, and I was able to drink in the sight of him without him noticing.

"God, you're beautiful," I said in a low, hoarse voice.

He blinked and pulled away a little, his breath teasing me when he answered. "Me?"

"Yes. Kissing me there." I loosened my grip to stroke his hair then cup his cheek. "Feels so good. Keep going."

He moved up my body instead to kiss my mouth. His hand went between my legs, his first two fingers circling on my clit. Then dipping lower, inside me. His tongue stroked mine. He fucked deeper inside me, fingers curling while his thumb pressed my clit.

The kiss got harder. So did his thrusting fingers. I wanted to get his belt unbuckled, to get my hands on him, but when I shifted, he nipped at my jaw and didn't move to let me. He stepped up the pace until I was so distracted by it I moaned. I rocked with his touch, letting him tumble me into orgasm, hard and surprisingly fast.

Gasping, my body still tensing, I blinked and looked at him. I put a hand over his to stop him from going on. "Wow."

He looked pleased. "Hmm."

I fell back onto the pillows as Niall slid his fingers out of me and propped himself on his elbow to look down at me. I stretched a little, rolling to face him. Offering my mouth for a kiss.

"Yummy," I whispered against his mouth.

Niall ran a hand up my calf and hooked it behind my knee. "I'm so hard right now, I think my dick might break off."

"I don't want your dick to fall off. That would be a real shame."

"I *am* kind of attached to it, even if it gets me into trouble sometimes." Niall shook his head.

I slid on top of him, my knees pressing his hips, to kiss his mouth. Still kissing, I rocked against him. "You are pretty hard. Let's see what we can do about that."

When his mouth opened, I took his tongue. I slid my hands up his arms, taking his wrists to pin them above his head. Not thinking about it, simply moving and doing what felt natural.

"That's how you like it, huh?" Niall said into my ear.

I ran my mouth along his throat then pressed his skin with my teeth before answering. "Yes. I do."

He rolled us both before I could stop him, so that he ended up between my legs. He kissed me hard, his hand going between us to work at his belt buckle. I helped him with the zipper. Then helped to shove his khakis over his hips, until there he was, kneeling in front of me with his cock tenting his briefs. He hooked his fingers in the waistband and eased them lower, lower, lower, until I sat up to help him with that, too.

"Oh," I said. "Oh, wow."

He stroked a hand down the length of his erection, which was fucking perfect. Amazing. Not so big I recoiled, not so small I was disappointed. I looked at him then slowly, deliberately, I opened my mouth and pointed inside it without a word.

Niall burst into laughter. "Wow?"

I did, too, after a second, but then reached for him, delighted by the way he stuttered into a small groan. "Bring that gorgeous thing over here and let me get a taste."

He hesitated then moved a little closer. My hand closed over his. Together, we stroked until he let go. I didn't stop.

I brushed my lips over the head as I stroked. I took him in slowly, an inch at a time, then slid out as slowly while he made a low, guttural noise. When I looked up at him, he was looking down at me with that glaze-eyed stare that told me I was doing something right.

Niall pulled his shirt off over his head and tossed it to the side. I hadn't taken off my dress, but there's a kink called CFNM, clothed female, naked man, and while I wouldn't have said it was a fetish of mine, I definitely enjoyed the power play of remaining fully dressed with a bare-assed man in front of me.

I also love sucking cock.

With my own orgasm out of the way, I had no urgency to be anything but tantalizingly, teasingly slow. And since I've always enjoyed torturing with pleasure rather than pain, every single moan and groan I eased out of him was a treat for me. Every time he seemed close, I eased off, until at last he was making a series of low, mindless and pleading noises that I could no longer resist. I kept going until he exploded with a hoarse shout, and with a satisfied grin, I sat back to watch him coming down off the high.

"Mmm," I said. "Super yummy."

We lay quietly for a few minutes after that, entwined. He put his head on my chest, a hand on my belly. I toyed with his hair.

We kissed a little bit after that. Nothing out of control. Slow and sweet and sexy and deliciously frustrating.

I sat up finally with a heavy sigh. "I should go. Work in the morning, and I didn't bring anything with me."

"I have a toothbrush you can borrow."

I reached to tweak his belly, but he held me off easily with one hand. "I need more than a toothbrush. Contrary to what Beyoncé says, I do *not* wake up like this."

"Like what?" Niall said, deadpan. "Breathtakingly beautiful?"

His words stopped me solid, not because I didn't believe he meant them. But because I believed he did. Overcome but trying to hide it, I leaned to kiss him again.

He nodded then smiled. His hands on my hips, he eased me closer. "I'll call you tomorrow, okay?"

Neither of us moved.

I was going to tell him I'd changed my mind, that I'd stay, when finally, Niall took a step back from me. Our hands still linked, our arms stretched between us until the distance was too great and we had to let go.

"I'll see you," I said.

"Wait a minute. Not just yet. You stay right there. Just like that." He gestured at me, an up-and-down sweep, though I had no idea what he was talking about. "The light behind you, turning everything sheer and golden. I want to remember you just like that."

His words, dipping low and a little raspy, flooded me with heat. I wanted to cover myself; I wanted him to see all of me. My nipples hardened, and there was no hiding them. I couldn't move. I could only wait while Niall's gaze swept over me. All over.

"I want to remember you like this," he told me again.

Then he walked me to the front door, kissing me solidly before closing the door behind him, and trembling, I had to sit for a minute behind the wheel before I could get myself together enough to drive. At the sound of my car, I saw him twitch the curtain. I was glad for the darkness that hid me from him just then.

I wanted him to remember me all sheer and golden, too.

31

William didn't have to go to religious school anymore. His mother had tried to insist he continue on through Confirmation, but William had adamantly refused. I thought Susan felt guilty about what had happened at the brunch, and probably about lots of other things, which may be part of the reason she'd agreed. Still, Wednesday afternoons had become something of a tradition for us, and Alex never minded if I left a little early, so I'd picked the kid up from home and drove him to The Lucky Rabbit for a burger, fries and shake.

"Any big plans for the year? It's your last year of middle school. Are you going to tear it up or what?" I asked over the platter of junk food.

William shrugged. "I don't think so. I'll just be hanging with my friends."

I dipped a fry in ketchup. "Where do you hang out?"

"The park mostly." He shrugged.

"What are you, a pack of hooligans?" I teased and earned a roll of his eyes. We ate in silence for a minute or so before I added, casually, "So, how are things at home?"

I hadn't seen or heard from my sister-in-law since the confrontation after the brunch. I'd called my brother a few times, but he'd been busy. Or at least said he was busy. And I was being a shitty sister and letting him avoid me because I didn't want to get involved with his marital issues. It was cowardly, and I knew it, but I hadn't yet been able to convince myself that telling him was the best choice.

There was William, see. William, whom I'd held mere hours after his birth, the fourth person to ever hold him. Mom, Dad, nurse and Auntie Elise. I'd rocked him to sleep and helped to potty train him and taught him to read before he went to kindergarten.

I loved this kid like my own, and I did not want to be the one to blow up his family.

"They're okay," William said, seemingly without any hidden fretting. He was too busy digging into his Hollywood burger.

"Are you glad to be all finished with the Bar Mitzvah?"

He gave me a look so much like the ones I'd been used to getting from his dad that I was torn between laughing out loud and nostalgically getting choked up. I settled for taking a long slurp of my milk shake. We ate in companionable silence after that, occasionally breaking it to point out something funny in the parking lot, like the teen boy and girl who were having some kind of dramatic fight in almost total silence, or the little kid in the backseat of a car who gave William the finger, making us both burst into laughter.

"You would never have done that," I told him. "You were a perfect kid."

He laughed at that, but looked pleased.

"I'm so proud of you, William," I told him abruptly. "I don't know if I told you that, but I am."

He looked pleased, but also embarrassed. "For what?"

"For being a great all-around kid. For kicking ass at your

Bar Mitzvah. For just generally being someone I'm glad to know." I punched him lightly in the arm.

I dropped him off at home afterward. When he used the outdoor keypad to let himself into the garage, however, I saw that neither of his parents were home yet. Frowning, I waved at him from my car and then called out the window, "Hey!"

William turned. At thirteen he was definitely old enough to be left by himself, but the question was, did he really want to be? He turned to face me, looking surprised.

"Come here."

Dutifully, he came back to the car and leaned in the driver's side window. "Yeah?"

"What time do your mom and dad get home?"

His shrug and uncomfortable expression gave me more answers than I'd asked for. I sighed, tallying the chores I had waiting for me at home. Screw it, laundry could wait.

"Let's go to the movies," I said.

"Now?"

"Yes. Now. We can go see that new giant robot movie." I grinned.

William looked uncertain. "But you already took me out to dinner. And it's a school night."

"Get in the car, kid," I told him. "I want to see a movie, and you don't really want to sit around at home by yourself, do you?"

"No. I guess not." He came around the car again and slid into the passenger seat, good kid that he was, buckling his seat belt without being asked. "Can I see if some of my friends want to come along? They're not old enough to get in without a parent."

I waved a magnanimous hand. "Sure. If they can meet us there, I'll be happy to chaperone."

"You're the best," William enthused, and bent to his phone to start typing and making plans.

I didn't know about being the best, but I adored that kid, and while I wasn't about to track down Susan to find out where the hell she was, in case it was someplace I didn't want to know about, I also didn't want him to be at home by himself until who knew when. I typed in a quick text to my brother to let him know where his son was, and got back a vague thanks, working late. That wasn't terribly unusual, since Evan had to do server maintenance at least a couple times a month, which meant odd, late hours. Still, just because their son was technically old enough not to need a babysitter, that didn't mean that his parents should just fuck off doing whatever.

My phone buzzed with a message just as we pulled into the parking lot of the theater. Seeing it was from Niall, I waved William on ahead and told him to get in line. With a happy, giddy grin, I read Niall's message.

What are you up to?

Getting ready to see the new giant robot movie, I typed. What are you doing?

Wishing I was seeing the new giant robot movie.

I didn't think twice about it. Come see it with me. I'll save you a seat, movie starts in half an hour.

As soon as I sent it, I wished I hadn't. George had never been spontaneous that way. Oh, sure, he'd call or text and expect me to drop whatever I was doing to accommodate him, but anything I wanted him to do had to be planned in advance. Hell, he'd nearly needed forms filled out in triplicate with a full itinerary if I wanted him to meet me halfway between us for an impromptu midweek dinner; and even then he only said yes just often enough that the next time, when he said no, I was twice as disappointed.

I shouldn't have asked Niall to come with me, I told myself, preparing for his answer to come back with a "no." I got no answer at all, and I shook my head as I got out of the car, reminding myself not to let it bother me.

"Want popcorn?" I asked William, who grinned. I handed him a twenty-dollar bill and waved him ahead. "Get me some Junior Mints and a Coke."

Junk food procured, we made our way to the theater, one of the bigger ones in the multiplex. Almost full, too. *Well, that's what you get for being late*, I heard my mother say, and laughed to myself. Inside, William spotted a group of his friends who had an extra seat with them.

"Go ahead," I told him. "I'll sit up here. It's cool."

"You sure?"

"Definitely." I took one of the few empty seats. The row on the floor between the stadium seating sections had seats in groups of two with spaces between for wheelchairs, and I found one two-seat section empty. I settled in, checking my phone and forcing myself not to be disappointed when I found Niall still hadn't answered me.

It didn't matter, I told myself. It was only a movie. We were only hesitantly dating, I thought, refusing to contemplate how deep I'd already fallen. I turned off the ringer and tucked my phone into my purse as the lights dimmed for the previews.

Just as the movie itself started, a shadow slipped into the seat beside me. Creeped out, annoyed, knowing there were probably no other empty seats in the whole theater, I turned my body slightly away as I gave the intruder a fake smile. Then a real one, along with a gasp of surprise that was fortunately covered up by the giant robot's first appearance in a crash of cinematic thunder that rumbled the theater's speaker system.

Niall leaned into my ear. "I made it."

We took William and his friends to the food court after the movie for whatever kind of food they wanted, an offer from Niall that amused me so much I could only laugh and shake my head as the four boys took off to four separate places. Niall laughed with me. He pointed in the direction of the food court.

"You, too," he said. "Whatever you want."

"Oh, hey, fancy."

"Hey, when you go out with me, you get the full royal treatment." We followed the path of the boys so that Niall could pick up the tab for each of them. When he turned to me, though, I shook my head again.

"I'm not hungry. I had dinner before the movie then candy." I laughed at his expression. "But you eat, if you want to. I have to wait for William to finish anyway."

Niall ordered from the Indian place, and we sat at a small table across from each other and next to the boys. I didn't make a big deal out of watching them, but it was something of a relief to see my nephew laughing and joking around for what felt like the first time in a year. When I glanced back to Niall, he was giving me a curious look.

"What?" I asked, and stabbed a bite of his curried rice.

"He looks like you." Niall gave a surreptitious nod toward William.

I laughed. "He's my twin brother's kid. Makes sense."

"You're a good aunt." Niall dug through a pile of rice and took a bite, grains tumbling from his mouth to the plate as he tried not to let them.

I handed him a napkin. "Thanks. He's a great kid. And since he's the closest I'll probably ever get to one of my own..."

"You think so? How come? You don't want any kids?" Niall wiped his mouth clean, which drew my attention to his lips and made me want to kiss him.

I restrained myself. "I don't really think I'd be the greatest mom. You have to be pretty unselfish to have a kid, I think. If you want to be a good parent."

"You don't think you're unselfish?"

I shrugged. "No. I don't think I'm unselfish."

"Do you think you're more selfish than normal?" Niall pushed his plate toward me with a raised brow, inviting me to sneak another bite.

I didn't, though I liked that he'd offered. "Maybe."

I looked up to see him looking thoughtful. Under his scrutiny, I felt warm and flushed, watched and somehow weighed. I'd looked at men that way, I realized, but I couldn't ever remember anyone ever taking the time to study me with such intent.

"I don't think you are," Niall said. "You've been pretty generous, in my experience."

Before I could answer that, William's friends collectively got up to leave, and he crossed to our table.

"Their moms are here," he explained.

"We should get you home. It's getting late, and I have to work in the morning."

It pleased me and made me proud that I didn't have to remind William to thank Niall for the food. The three of us went out to the parking lot together, but Niall had parked in a different section of the lot. William asked for my keys so he could go on ahead and get in the car while we said our goodbyes.

"The kid's smart," Niall said, watching William head for my car. "Considerate enough to give us time to smooch."

"He just doesn't want to see it."

Niall pulled me into his arms. "Has he had to watch you kissing lots of men?"

"No." I let him tug me closer. "I haven't had a boyfriend around him in…well, ever, I guess."

"No?" Niall looked surprised.

I shook my head. "Nope."

"So how come you invited me along tonight?"

"I wanted to see you," I told him. "And I didn't think it was a big deal."

Niall squinched an eye closed to look at me. "Huh. Not sure if I like that or not. I'm not a big deal or not a boyfriend."

I'd been leaning to kiss him, but now stopped. I'd asked him this before, and come to think of it, he hadn't exactly answered. "Do you *want* to be a boyfriend?"

"I *am* kind of a big deal," he said.

I laughed a little uncertainly. "Niall."

He kissed me hard enough to make me feel it, but briefly enough that we weren't making a spectacle of ourselves. His hands settled naturally on my hips. I looked toward my car, but William must already have gotten in, because I didn't see him. I looked back at Niall.

"*Boyfriend* is…a word."

He smiled. "Yeah. It's just a word."

I tried to take a step back, but he didn't let me go. I put my hands over his to get him to release his grip. He did, then, but linked his fingers with mine to trap me.

"Okay," he said. "Just thought I'd toss it out there. See what you'd say. I mean, some girls, you take them out once, and they're picking out china patterns and talking about the catering menu."

"Girls like the ones who broke your heart?" I kissed him, and this time I was the one making it fierce but brief. I couldn't stop myself from nipping his lower lip lightly as I pulled away. Not enough to hurt him, but enough to…what? I didn't know. Show him who was boss? Make him forget there'd ever been a woman before me? This conversation had unexpectedly disgruntled me.

"Anyway," he continued, rubbing his thumb along his lower lip while his eyes gleamed and didn't leave mine. "You're the girl who takes lovers instead of boyfriends, isn't that right?"

He was poking at me, teasing, and unexpected heat rushed through me. My nipples tightened. The seam of my jeans rubbed me with a delicious pressure, and my breath caught.

"Yes. That's what I told you."

No music, no steps. We weren't even moving, but this was a dance all the same. Or maybe it was more like a sword fight. Thrust and parry. Dodge and weave.

"Thanks for asking me to the movies," Niall said and took a step back. Then another. He put his hands in his pockets and gave me a slow, sly smile that made me want to chase after him and push him up against the wall and have my way with him. "It was fun."

"Thanks for coming. And for treating William and his friends."

"I'll call you," Niall said then pivoted and stalked away without looking back.

I watched him, though, waiting to see if he'd turn at least once. He didn't, which was the worst and best thing he could've done, whether he knew it or not. Because I wanted him to look back at me, of course. Wanted him to want me enough to look even if he didn't want to. But I also wanted him to be the sort of man who didn't have to.

What the fuck was happening to me?

"Is he your boyfriend?"

The first words out of William's mouth when I got in the car stumped me. I put the key into the ignition and started the engine before I twisted in my seat to answer him. "No. Why?"

"He's cool." William shrugged. "He works with Dad."

"I know." I drove for a bit before saying, "What made you ask me if he was my boyfriend?"

William shrugged, looking totally uninterested. "I don't know. I heard my mom saying she thought you needed to spend more time on your own boyfriend than worrying about what everyone else was doing."

The way he said it, so carefully without looking at me, told me a lot. But Susan was his mother, and I could be the favorite aunt from here until the end of time without ever trumping that. Still, it was hard not to sneer about it.

"Who'd she say that to? Your dad?"

"No. Someone on the phone," William said. "I shouldn't have told you."

I sighed, making the turn onto his street. "Probably not, kid. But it's okay. Your mom has a right to her opinion."

"I don't think you butt in, Auntie," William told me. "Grandma and Aunt Jill do, but you don't. It made me mad that she'd say that."

A rush of love for him pricked tears into my eyes. "Thanks, kid. But your mom still has a right to feel however she feels."

And had her own shit to shovel, I did not add, though the more I thought about it, the angrier I got. When we got to William's house, I told him I needed to come in and use the bathroom. I did, then greeted my brother, who'd planted himself in his recliner in front of the TV, beer in hand. A pile of about ten pairs of dirty socks were next to him.

"You're a pig," I said flatly. "What the hell is wrong with you?"

Evan gave me a bleary, offended glare. "What the hell is wrong with *you*?"

I kicked a foot in the direction of the socks. "You're still doing that."

He looked over the arm of his chair then at me without a blink. "What?"

"Your fucking socks, man. Gross." I shook my head. "It was gross when we lived together, and it's still gross now."

Evan snorted. "Why should you care?"

I don't, I wanted to say, *but your wife clearly does, and you're pissing her off enough that she's cheating on you with some guy who looks like Ricardo Montalban in* Escape From the Planet of the Apes. I clamped my mouth shut, thinking of William upstairs. Of my own parents screaming. Evan and I were fifteen when they split, though their problems had started long before that. I didn't believe my brother would fuck off into the world without a second glance at his son, but that didn't mean I was going to be the one to bring his world crashing down.

I found Susan on the front porch. She startled when I came through the door, turning, her face twisted in guilt of a different kind. She had a lit cigarette in her hand.

"You scared me," she said.

"Sorry. I didn't want to come out through the garage and not be able to close the door behind me." I hesitated, looking her over. "You took it back up, huh?"

"Some things you quit because you want to," my sister-in-law said kind of sourly. "Some things you give up because everyone tells you it's bad for you, but eventually, you know you'll go back to it. If it's something you love."

I wasn't making a judgment about smoking. I'd been known to light up now and then, usually when I was drinking. For as long as I'd known Susan, though, she'd been the sort to look down at people with vices, no matter what they were. Smoking, drinking too much, overeating. Cheating would've been on that list, too, I supposed, though it was funny how easy it was to change your mind about something you discovered was easier to get into than you might've thought. We stared at each other for a few seconds while her cigarette burned, and she didn't even take a puff.

"Tastes like shit," she said after another awkward moment. "I wanted to love it the way I used to, but I guess I just don't."

I wanted to ask her if she was talking about the smokes or my brother, but wisely refrained. "It must be a relief that the Bar Mitzvah's over."

"Yeah. Totally." She ashed into a small glass bowl and then took a long drag. She didn't cough it out, but she definitely didn't look as though she were loving it. She offered me the pack, but I shook my head.

"Your mother called me, by the way. Left a message telling me to call her back."

"Ugh, sorry. Did you?"

William had inherited his distinctive laugh from his mother. She shook her head. "Nope."

"You'll probably have to, at some point."

She looked at me. "Why? Really, Elise, why do I have to?"

"Because…she's your mother-in-law." I couldn't even make myself sound convincing.

"Life's too short to put up with people who treat you like shit, you know that? In all the time you've known me, has your mother ever been anything other than some degree of shitty to me?" Susan took another drag. She seemed to be getting the hang of it again anyway.

What she said was true, but still, as I'd thought earlier about William having to take sides, my mother was my mother. "It's how she is."

"Sorry, but I don't think the length of time someone behaves badly is an excuse to continue to allow it. I don't care if it's how she's always been."

"I didn't say it was how she'd always been," I said sharply. "I said it's how she *is*. If you want to know, she didn't really start being such a bitch until my father left her."

Susan didn't say anything for a moment. "That's not what your father says."

"Since when are you and my dad best friends?" I frowned.

"We're not. I wanted to invite him to the Bar Mitzvah, but your mother started flipping tables over it, so I had to talk to him to explain to him why we couldn't have him there to celebrate." Susan stubbed out her cigarette and pulled out another, tucked it between her lips, but didn't light it right away. "It was stupid. Your dad loves William, even if he and your mother can't stand each other."

"He hasn't exactly been the best dad to us, either. What did Evan say about it?" I asked, genuinely curious. I hadn't spoken to my dad in about a year. When he didn't show up, I assumed it was because, as my mother had said, he couldn't be bothered.

"He said it wasn't worth getting your mother all worked up." Susan fought with her lighter, which refused to give a good flame, then tossed it down with a sigh of disgust. "God forbid."

"But you had a nice long talk with my dad about her." It was stupid, getting agitated about defending my mother, who absolutely was a pain in the ass.

Susan gave me an exasperated and somehow defiant look. "Your mother likes to paint herself as quite the martyr, Elise. Don't act like that's a surprise."

"No. I can't say that. But you barely know my dad. You don't know what it was like when they were splitting up. He left us," I told her harshly, hating the way the words snagged and tore at my throat. It had been years, and I hated that the pain could still punch me in the guts. "I don't really care what happened between the two of them, but he left us, the kids, just up and fucking abandoned us like we meant nothing. Went off to Florida, miles and miles away. We didn't know where he was for the first six months." Shaking, I lowered my voice. "I don't care how much of a bitch he says my mother was. He. Left. Us."

"Elise." Susan shook her head and sounded sad. "You don't know…"

"Just stop, okay? I don't want to hear it from you. I know my mom hasn't been good to you. I'm sorry that you have to put up with it. I'm sorry my brother doesn't fucking stand up for you the way he should and that he leaves his socks all over the place, too, but for fuck's sake, Susan…he's my brother. And William, I love that kid." Breathing hard, I stared at her, waiting for her to say something even though I hadn't asked a question. After a second or so, I tossed up my hands. "You have a family! Jesus. Don't throw it away the way my dad did."

"You mean the way your mother did," Susan said quietly, in a voice like the scratch of fingernails on sandpaper.

I didn't say anything. She picked up her lighter. Another try and the flame caught, and she held it to the end of her cigarette. She looked up at me with the smoke filtering through her nostrils.

"She had an affair," Susan said. "She told your dad to get out so she could move in some other guy. I don't know what happened after that, but apparently it didn't work out."

"No," I said around the taste of ashes in my mouth, my lips so numb I was surprised they could form words at all. "I guess it didn't."

32

I immediately knew the man Susan had been talking about. Sam Peters. Tall, sandy haired, big smile. He always had gum in his pocket, maybe to cover up the fact his breath was perpetually bad. He had square white teeth I realized now must've been dentures, hence the stench. He had a tattoo on his biceps of a little red devil, though over the years it had faded into a pale blob. You could see the tattoo because he favored shirts with the sleeves torn off, threads dangling. He was the guy who fixed my parents' cars.

The summer before my father left, he'd traveled a lot on business. At the time I hadn't thought much of it—parents did things, kids accepted them without question. My mother told us our dad was looking for a new job, but until he got one, he had to spend a lot of his time on the road. I'd heard them arguing about money a few times as the school year ended, so the idea that he needed to find a new job wasn't entirely out of line, especially since my mom's car had been in the shop.

A lot.

Sick with the memories of it now, the smell of oil and exhaust overlaid by the sweetly minty gum Sam always offered me, I sat at my kitchen table flipping through an old photo album from that year. Looking for proof. I didn't want it to be true, but there was no denying that the moment Susan told me, I'd known it had to be.

And there it was. A picture of me and Evan standing in front of my mom's slate-gray Volvo station wagon, both of us in matching denim shorts and white T-shirts. Normally I'd have chuckled at the sight of our mutually questionable fashion sense, but now all I could do was stare into the background of the photo. Behind the car, into the garage, in the shadows, where a hint of a familiar pattern blended enough that it was easy to pass over unless you were really looking hard. My mother's skirt, one she'd worn to tatters that summer. It was a wrap skirt, tied at the hip, in a bright floral, and she'd always worn it with a white peasant blouse. At least until one day I'd found it smeared with grease in the pile of things to be sent to the thrift store. I hadn't thought about it at the time, but those smears could've been made by dirty hands.

I remembered muffled shouting behind closed doors. Trips to the grocery store with my mother, who'd ticked off items on her list with increasing vehemence and made me put back the sugary cereal I wanted because it was "too expensive." I thought of the scent of minty gum and cigarettes clinging to her when I hugged her before I went to bed, and how I'd known that my mother smelled of Wind Song perfume and fabric softener, how unsettled I'd been by this strangeness, but how I'd also put it out of my mind because Alicia had called to tell me that David Birnbaum had a crush on me.

My father had moved out just before school started for my and Evan's sophomore year. No explanation, no forwarding address for six months. I'd listened to my mother crying in her bedroom, her shrieks cycling up and up. The crash of broken glass. The late-night sound of the telephone and silence if I answered it before she did. I'd always thought it was my father, too ashamed to say hello to the daughter he'd seemingly left behind without a second thought, but now I thought it must've been Sam Peters.

I was still sitting at my table when Niall knocked at the front door. With my head in my hands, I considered simply texting him that I'd gone to bed sick, but there was something beautiful and terrible about having someone in your life who was more than a fuck buddy. I could tell him all about this upheaval, and he would comfort me. The kicker was, if I told him all about what I'd learned, then I might have to *let* him comfort me.

"Hey..." He stopped at the sight of my face. "What's wrong?"

There was still a silly few seconds when I thought I would lie and pretend nothing was wrong, but then without another word, Niall took me in his arms. He kicked the door shut behind us, and he held me without speaking. His lips to my temple. His breath warm on my cheek. His hands smoothed up and down my back, and I melted into him. Clung to him, in fact, hard and desperate and on the verge of tears.

Something crinkled between us.

I ignored it at first, but when he pulled me closer, the distinct sound of rustling paper pushed me away from him. "What's that?"

"It's... I brought something for you. But it can wait." Niall brushed his fingertips across my forehead, smoothing my hair off my face.

"You brought me something? Honestly, I could use a present." I poked the front of his shirt, trying to find the source of the noise. I found it in his breast pocket. A piece of paper, folded into quarters. I looked up at him, confused.

Niall looked sheepish and pulled it out to hand it to me, though he held it just out of reach. "It can wait, Elise. Why don't you tell me what's going on first?"

I shook my head. "It's just…some family stuff."

"Oh." He frowned. "Everything ok?"

"Yeah. I guess so. I mean, no. I don't know."

He hesitated. "Maybe I shouldn't say anything, but…is it Evan and Susan?"

"What makes you say that?" I reached again for the paper, but he pulled it again out of my grasp.

"Just some things he's said at work lately. Nothing specific. It's not really any of my business…ah, sneaky."

I'd managed to snag the paper and take a few steps away so he couldn't grab it back. "Ha!"

"There's a smile anyway," he said.

I unfolded the paper. Printed in gray ink, at first the tabulated contents meant nothing to me, but I got it after studying it for a few seconds. I looked at him, unsure what to say except, "Wow."

"I didn't want to tell you until I had all the results," Niall said. "But you can see it all right there. I'm safe as houses."

I blinked and looked over the test results again. Then at him. "You did this for me?"

"Well…I guess I did it for me," he said, reaching into his pocket and pulling out a small plastic shopping bag wrapped around a box of condoms. "But I also brought these. Just in case."

Upstairs, I let him take me to bed. Kissing, kissing, kissing until I couldn't breathe. Niall laid me back on my bed, his weight covering me but never too heavy. Propped on his elbows, he again smoothed my hair from my face, his eyes searching mine. I wanted to ask him what he was thinking, but I didn't have time before he kissed me again.

Long, deep thrusts of his tongue had me gasping. I rolled my hips against him. He ground against me, then moved to kneel over me. He looked down at me and swiped his already glistening mouth with his tongue so that I groaned.

"Touch me," I whispered, arching my back so my breasts, naked beneath my thin T-shirt, could tempt him.

He ran his hands up my sides then cupped my breasts for only a moment before moving back to the hem of my shirt and sliding beneath. At the touch of his skin on mine, I shuddered. He groaned. He pushed my shirt up to bare me to him, and I helped by tugging it the rest of the way over my head.

"You have such amazing tits…breasts," he corrected. "Is it cool to say tits?"

I cupped them, thumbing my nipples as I gave him a look. "What do you think?"

"I think," he said, kissing me again, "I want to slide my cock between your amazing tits. How about that?"

I laughed and gasped and moaned a little, too. I put my hands on his chest, digging my nails in a little bit. "Ffffff…"

"Go on. Say it. You know you want to."

"Fuck," I finished, breathless. "Say it again."

Niall shook his head and pulled away before I could capture his mouth with mine. "I changed my mind."

"What? No!" I nudged his thigh with my foot. "That's not fair."

"I've waited too long to be inside you," he said matter-of-factly, though his gaze burned me. "I want to make you come with my cock deep inside you and my mouth on those luscious tits, instead. Is that better?"

"Much." I fell back on the bed and toyed with the zipper on my jeans. Niall was idly stroking himself through his khakis.

He stopped long enough to unbutton his shirt and toss it onto the floor. Idly, he ran a hand across his chest, fingers tapping on his belly. He stretched out over me to kiss me again. Side by side, we lingered in the kissing, joking gone. Hungry

for each other, but not urgent. Slowly, he undressed me, following with his mouth every bit of skin his fingers revealed.
Then himself, and I lay back to watch him in, for me, unac-
customed acquiescence.

I liked watching Niall get naked for me. I didn't have to
tell him which way to turn to show me his body. He moved
exactly the way I'd have asked him to, if I'd been command-
ing. Right now, it was a pleasure, simply watching. When he
moved over me again, his cock thick and hot on my belly, I
put my arms around him and held him close, and he let me
without trying to force us along any faster.

Niall kissed me slowly. His hands moved over me, finding
the places I liked best to be touched. A few times I moved his
fingers to the left or right, or shifted so he could get to me a
little better, but mostly I just reveled in being so completely
and utterly…known.

Because he learned me, you see, inch by inch. Moan by
sigh by gasp and groan, Niall paid attention to every noise
that slipped from my lips, every shift and shudder of my body.
Slower, faster, a little harder, sometimes softer, he taught himself the way my body worked, and I barely had to correct him.

Trembling, I arched when he at last slipped his fingers up
my inner thigh to press inside me. I was so wet I was almost
embarrassed at how easily and deeply his fingers went. Almost.

His thumb pressed my clit as his fingers moved, and in moments I was moving beneath him. Then grumbling when he
stopped. He laughed into my mouth.

"I told you it would happen when it happened."

"It hasn't happened yet," I murmured, circling my fingers
on his wrist and guiding him back between my legs. "So get
back to it. Please."

"So polite," Niall breathed. "How could a guy say no to that?"

He was kissing me when he pushed inside me. We both sighed. I tensed a little, unable to stop myself.

"You feel so good," I whispered.

He nuzzled my throat, not moving. "It's been a long time since I did this without something. Fuck, Elise, you're so wet."

I rocked my hips a little to urge him deeper. "Fuck me."

"You're going to kill me," he said, his words stuttering when I moved again.

"Hush," I told him, and he did.

Slow, smooth thrusts built as Niall perfectly found the right rhythm. It had been quite some time since I'd had a man bareback inside me, and it was as much a turn-on for me as it seemed to be for him. We moved together the same way we'd done on the dance floor, as though in some crazy factory somewhere the pair of us had been built from matching pieces. We fit. We just…fit.

I don't come from the missionary position; most of the time I refuse to even fuck that way. I like to be on top, or taken from behind, or standing, even side by side, but I've never liked a man's full weight on top of me as he bangs away, focusing on getting off while I struggle to catch a breath. It wasn't like that with Niall, though, and though I wouldn't have expected it, every thrust pressed his pelvis deliciously just right against my clit until all I could do was lift my hips to meet each one.

My nails raked his back. Niall bit into the curve of my neck and shoulder. I cried out his name, low then louder, and grabbed a double handful of his ass. He'd called my tits amazing, but the same could definitely be said for that butt. Firm, smooth, muscled. To die for, as the saying went.

"I'm gonna come," he muttered in my ear. "Come with me…"

"I'm there," I told him, tipping over. "Fuck me a little harder, baby, I'm there with you."

Firefuckingworks. The kind that burst and burst again, and when you thought they were finished, another cluster of crackling, sparkling flames exploded. That was how I came with Niall the first time we made love. Just like the Fourth of July.

He shuddered against me and went still. Now, especially, was the time when I most often felt trapped, but I didn't even have time to feel crushed or squished, because he rolled off me. Heat spilled from me, but I was too lazy in that moment to care. Sheets could be washed. I wasn't fucking moving.

Niall turned onto his back, one arm behind his head, the other gesturing for me to cuddle next to him. My body curved to his, and though I knew at some point my arm would cramp or fall asleep, for the moment I was content to press my face to his sweaty, fragrant chest and breathe him in deep. He turned his face to kiss my forehead.

We didn't say anything for a while, both of us breathing in sync. I ran a hand down his chest and over his belly, toying with the line of dark hair below his navel. After a bit, I propped myself on my elbow to look him over. I'd only seen pieces of him before. Now with him fully naked and sated, I wanted to see everything about him. Every line and bump and freckle, mole and scar. I kissed the small brown spot next to his belly button, and he laughed.

I looked up at him for a second before settling back with my cheek on his belly. His swimmer's body, nice and lean, wasn't soft enough to make a good pillow, but I loved the soft tickle of his hair on my skin. I cupped his balls, weighing them and the soft length of his cock, and he jumped.

"Sorry," I murmured. "Didn't mean to startle you."

"It's okay." His hand stroked over my hair, tangling for a second before he worked his fingers free of the knot.

"So pretty," I said.

He laughed awkwardly. "What. My dick?"

"Yep." I looked up at him again with a grin. "Blue ribbon winner, right here."

He didn't laugh again, though I'd been trying to make him. "Thanks."

I pushed up on my elbow again. "I'm teasing you. I mean, it's gorgeous, I'm not teasing about that…"

He shook his head slightly, and I stopped. I settled for kissing his hip bone and moving up to snuggle back against him. I didn't want there to be any kind of weirdness with him.

"Do you want me to go?" he asked after another few minutes when my eyes had started drifting closed.

That woke me up. "No. Do you want to go?"

"No. I brought a bag. It's out in the car." He hesitated. "I don't feel like getting up to get it right now."

"No, stay here with me in bed, just a little longer anyway. Then we can get up and shower, and you can get your bag if you want, but right now, I want to be naked and sticky with you."

"I can honestly say nobody has ever said that to me before." He snorted softly.

I burrowed my face again into the salty-sweet goodness of his skin. "I love the way you smell right now. All fucked out."

"That's…damn," he said. "I'm getting hard again."

I laughed and rolled onto my back, flopping on the pillows. "Good. I want you hard all the time."

Niall turned on his side to pull me closer, my hip nudging his groin. "That's going to make it a little awkward at the grocery store and stuff."

"So I'll keep you here in my bed all the time." God, I was fuckdrunk. Giggling and slurring like I'd downed a couple shots of Fireball whiskey. I stretched, bones crackling down my spine. "Constantly hard so you can fuck me whenever I want."

He was quiet for a second. "That's what you want, huh?"

"Sure." I turned my face to his. "Don't worry, the gig comes with pizza and beer. Got to keep your strength up if you're going to be my personal sex slave."

It was the second time Niall didn't laugh. Instead, he reached to brush the hair from my face. Then he kissed my shoulder, hiding his face. I let my hand rest on his head, wondering where I'd gone wrong. Too far? Too much? Too soon?

We were both quiet for a few minutes after that, and though I'd meant it when I said I liked being naked and sticky with him, it was getting to be time to clean up. I was just about to say so, when Niall pulled me closer to spoon against him. I hadn't been expecting that, but I did it, nestling my ass against him. He pushed my hair to the side and kissed the back of my neck.

"Are you feeling better?" he asked.

I had, for a time, forgotten I'd been upset. I frowned for a second, but the discovery of my mother's infidelity didn't sting me at the moment. It wasn't about me and never had been, really. It explained a lot, actually, though no matter what my mother's betrayal had done to their marriage, or to my father, I still couldn't find it in me to forgive him for fleeing to Florida and leaving us behind.

"Yes."

"Good."

"Susan told me today that my mother cheated on my dad," I blurted. "She said my dad had told her that. Another time she also told me a bunch of stuff about my sister that I never knew. It made me feel like I don't know what's going on anymore. Like I'm standing on shifting sands."

"Shit," Niall said, but kept me spooned close. "Wow."

I tucked his hand beneath my chin. "Yeah. Total fuckery. I wish I didn't know, I guess. It doesn't change anything, really, and it's just…gross."

"Did Susan say anything else?" Niall paused. "Shit, never mind, not my business."

I weighed the burden of telling him what I knew, silent at first. I kissed his knuckles. Finally, I said in a low voice, "Susan's having an affair. I haven't told my brother because I don't want to be the one to blow up their family. I don't want to do that to William…I can't. And I don't want to do it to Evan, either."

"Do you think by not telling him, it will go away?"

I sat up, drawing my knees close to my chest. "No. She should be the one, that's all. And shit, I don't know, Niall, maybe I hoped she'll get her act together? Something? And you know, what if I do tell him, and they reconcile, then I'm the asshole who messed with their marriage—"

"She's the one doing that, not you."

I looked at him. "You know what people do when they have to face something uncomfortable? They blame the thing that makes them feel bad, even if it's not that thing's fault. I'd be the thing that made them feel bad, Niall. Let's say they figure out a way to work through it. They'd always know that I know, and it would be just one of those…things."

"Yeah. I guess you're right. Except I think he knows. Or suspects anyway." Niall frowned. "Sorry, it's a tough situation, for everyone."

"The one I care most about is William," I said flatly. "I love my brother, but I have to say, he's brought some of this on himself. Not saying he deserves it," I added quickly. "I love him pretty much unconditionally, but I don't think I'd want to be married to him."

"Well, no," Niall said, deadpan. "That's a little too *Flowers in the Attic*, don't you think?"

"Ew, gross!" I cried and leaped to pummel him.

He held me off easily enough, gripping my wrists with one

hand while the other pulled me onto his lap. I wasn't used to feeling so…well, small, I guess. Not delicate or weak. Cuddled and protected, though. Soft.

It was what I'd told him I wanted, but faced with actually getting what I'd asked for, my insides froze. I untangled myself from him firmly but gently. "I'm going to take a shower."

"Not yet. One more minute?" Niall asked.

I let him pull me close for a kiss. Then another. I laughed, pulling away when he went for a third. "Hey, now!"

"You know what," he said. "Let's go away next weekend together. We'll do it up right. Nice hotel, big bed. Clean sheets."

I nodded, solemn, and gave my own bed a raised eyebrow. "Oh, yes, definitely we need clean sheets. And what about a great view? Gotta have a great view."

"Oh, yeah, tell me about this view."

"Tell me about them rabbits, George." It just came out, and as soon as it did, I bit my tongue.

Niall frowned. "Huh?"

"It's from a book. *Of Mice and Men*. He always used to spin these stories for me, see, like about how we were going to do all these things and go to all these places. Usually when we were in bed. Once he told me…" I hesitated, not wanting to remember, not wanting to say it out loud, because at the time it had been wonderful, and now it only caused me pain. But Niall had said he wanted to know the things I didn't like, so he didn't do them.

"Tell me."

I took a breath. "He told me that if he won the lottery, he was going to build me a castle."

"Huh." Niall didn't say anything after that.

"Anyway, in *Of Mice and Men*, Lenny always asks George to tell him about—"

"The rabbits," Niall interrupted. "I get it. Like in the old

Bugs Bunny cartoon. 'I'll love him and squeeze him and call him George.'"

"Yes." I touched the rabbit on my wrist. "So I called him George. It was a thing my friend Alicia and I did. Give the boys we loved nicknames."

Niall made a soft noise. "Do I have one?"

"No. You're just you."

"Huh," he said again.

I kissed him, pushing away all thoughts of anyone else. "I think a trip sounds like an amazing idea. Where do you want to go?"

He looked far away for a moment before he came back to me. "How about I surprise you?"

I thought on that. I wasn't a fan of surprises, in general. Not parties, not quizzes. Once in the eighth grade Evan had jumped out of the closet to "surprise" me, and he'd ended up with a broken nose. But I did like being known, and the best way to find out if someone really knew you was to see what they chose for you. So far, Niall had done an excellent job picking out things I'd like.

"Okay," I said. "Surprise me."

He slept with me that night, in my bed, spooned up behind me with his breath on the back of my neck. When I wriggled against him, he got hard, and we giggled about it, though the giggles turned to sighs when his hand went to my belly to press me back against him.

I had no trouble falling asleep.

His murmured voice woke me, I wasn't sure at what time, only that I'd been dreaming. "What did he do to you that hurt you so bad? That other guy?"

"I loved him too much," I said, still half-asleep. "And he didn't love me enough."

33

Niall asked me to meet him at Baltimore's Inner Harbor. I hadn't been there since I was a kid. The aquarium was much the same as I remembered it, minus the sea lions that used to sun themselves on the rocks outside.

"Too many people threw coins and stuff into the enclosure." Niall leaned on the railing. "They'd eat stuff and get sick and die."

I frowned. "That's terrible."

"Yeah, people suck." He turned away from the empty concrete display and let the railing press against his back, his elbows propped on it. "I thought we'd go tour the submarine next. If you want."

"That sounds fun." I kissed him. We did that for a while. "This is fun, too."

He brushed my hair, tossed by the breeze off the water, out of my eyes. It had become one of his favorite gestures, and surprisingly, it hadn't started working on my nerves. "You make everything fun."

"I do?" I blushed a little, pleased.

"Yeah. I mean, whatever I'm up for, you're like, 'yeah. Let's do this.'" He paused. "I don't know, I'm surprised."

"Why?" Walking, I took his hand and swung it gently between us. He glanced at me with a raised brow. "Oh. That." With a sigh, I turned to face him and took both his hands in mine. "Niall. I don't have to be in charge all the time. I like being taken care of, actually. If I didn't want to do something you'd planned, I'd tell you. But so far, I like it all."

"Good." He grinned. "Let's do the Ripley's Museum, too."

My answer had seemed to set him at ease, but the conversation stayed with me all day. It was true that everything he'd laid out for us was fun and all stuff I'd have wanted to do anyway, even if I hadn't known about it before. And I did like that he'd taken care of all the details to make the whole day magic, so that I didn't really have to think or do anything but enjoy it all.

"It's because you picked them all for me," I said abruptly while we waited for our drinks to come at dinner. He'd picked the restaurant because it had vegetarian options in case I didn't want to eat shellfish. Which I did not, but hadn't told him. I'd said I didn't eat pig, but had never mentioned crustaceans. He'd been doing a little homework, and it squeezed my heart until I thought it was going to pop.

"Hmm?" He looked up from the basket of bread sticks in the center of the table.

"The day. The sightseeing, the restaurant." I drew in a light breath. "It's not that I like you taking over and choosing for me. I mean, I would actually hate that."

Niall broke the bread stick in half and offered one side to me. "I don't get it."

"I had a lover once—hear me out," I said at the way his expression twisted. "I had a lover who really just liked to boss me around. He'd buy me clothes and tell me to wear them, and it was supposed to be sexy except he'd get the sizes wrong or choose a color I hated, and he'd get really pissed off if I didn't want to do it. He always picked where we went out to eat."

"I picked out where we went to eat today."

"Yes, but…everything you planned for today, everything you ever plan for us, ever, you do because you think I'm going to really like it. Not because it's only what you want or like. You try to pick things because you think I'm going to like them, and that makes me…" I shook my head and leaned forward a little. "It makes me insane, Niall. In a good way. A really good way."

He smiled then, slowly. His eyes blazed. His foot nudged mine.

"Good," he said, and then the drinks came.

He took me dancing, too. The Power Plant Live had enough bars and clubs to keep anyone occupied for an evening. We hadn't been dancing since the night in the bar after William's Bar Mitzvah, the first time he'd ever pulled me close. He'd made me his that night, not that either one of us had known it at the time. I knew it now, though, and I wanted him to know it, too.

I had never been the first to say it. Love. No matter how I'd ever felt about anyone, I'd never been the first to admit it, until tonight.

"I love you," I said into his ear as we danced. "And I want you. Now."

The music was so loud it was easy to pretend he hadn't heard me, so I didn't have to be embarrassed when he didn't say it back. And he didn't, not with words, and maybe I imagined the look in his eyes right before he kissed me so hard I couldn't breathe. It didn't matter. I felt it, and I said it, and I did not regret it.

"Let's get out of here," Niall said.

In the hotel elevator, we stood apart from one another, like that would keep anyone from knowing that the second our room door closed behind us, we were going to fall upon each other like wolves on a wounded deer. I could see him in the mirror, just as I could see myself, and there was no hiding the way we strained toward each other without moving an inch. Hell, I'm sure the other people with us could smell it on us. Desire. Yearning.

He didn't touch me even when the elevator opened and we walked down the long, long hall as leisurely as if we were strolling along the beach. Like we didn't want to run. We chatted about dinner and the club, about stupid things I wouldn't remember twenty minutes later. Our voices rose and fell, and the words came out, but the steady beat, beat, beat of "fuck me, fuck me, fuck me" was all I could really hear.

He opened the door with his key and let me go through first. I was shaking by the time I got to the bed. My back still to him. At the click of the door, the slide of the lock, I had to close my eyes and concentrate on breathing so I wouldn't feel faint. The wine from dinner, the cocktails after, I could blame those for the way the world tipped, but the truth was it had nothing to do with alcohol. I'd danced all that away.

I was drunk on Niall and anticipation, and all I could do was shiver while I waited for him to touch me.

Oh, finally, to touch me.

Of course he'd been touching me all night. A hand on the small of my back as we crossed the street. Fingers linking across the table. His front against my back when we danced.

With my eyes closed, every sound magnified. The slap of his key on the dresser. The shuffle of his shoes on the carpet.

And then, at last, Niall put his hands on me. He moved up behind me, gripping my hips to pull my ass against his crotch. His mouth found the back of my neck. His teeth, the slope of my shoulder. He bit as he pulled me back against him, and

I arched and gasped. My nipples got immediately hard. One of his hands slid across my belly and between my legs, then down to curl his fingers in the hem of my dress.

"Yes," I said as he inched it upward.

Niall's breath heated my ear as he slipped his fingers inside my panties. He dipped low, sliding inside me for a second before moving up again to find my clit. He pinched it gently between his thumb and forefinger. My head fell back against his shoulder. My hand went to the back of his head.

"I'm going to fuck you," he said into my ear, "until you can't stand."

I was already having trouble. Weak knees. His fingers jerked my clit in a steady, relentless pattern, and when he bit down on my bare shoulder again, I cried out.

I turned. We found each other's mouths. Kissing, hungry, demanding. Teeth clashing. His hand dug into my hair at the base of my skull, his fingers working deep into the updo. He pulled, hard enough to tip my head back so he could get to my throat with his lips and teeth.

"I want you," I told him. "I want you, I want you, I want you."

He paused then, for a second or so, looking into my eyes. Slowly, deliberately, he returned his hand between my legs. Slid his fingers inside me, then out, each stroke hitting me just right.

My fingers dug hard into his shoulders. I widened my stance a little. Letting him in. I wasn't going to come this way—the position slightly too awkward. But oh, it was going to be close.

He kissed me again as he eased his hand out of my panties. Pushing me gently, Niall backed me toward the bed. With my fists curled in the front of his shirt, I turned us both as we got there. I meant to push him onto it, to climb on top of him and devour him with more hungry kisses, but he stopped me.

We didn't wrestle. Nothing that obvious. But he did give his head one small shake as he urged me onto my back. I ended up propped on my elbows, one knee bent so that my dress showed off my bare thighs. Niall at the foot of the bed, one hand on my calf. His eyes gleamed as I trailed a fingertip up my leg and along the lace of my panties.

"I want to watch you make yourself come," he said.

It wasn't what I was expecting. "You do?"

He nodded. A small smile tilted the corner of his mouth and faded so fast I almost missed it. "Yeah. I do."

I scooted back on the bed to arrange the pillows in a pile high enough to prop me up. I let my thighs fall open, my dress still shadowing my panties. "Like this?"

"Yes." He'd gone solemn and grim-mouthed. "I want to see your pussy."

I drew in a breath. I ran my hands up the insides of my thighs, pushing my dress up and out of the way. In the summer's last gasp of late September, the heat had been too much for stockings and garters. He didn't seem to miss them. I watched his face, his eyes going dark. His hand went to the bulge in his jeans, rubbing. When I stroked a finger over the lace of my panties, his fingers curled.

"Niall."

He looked at me.

I slid my fingers into the front of my panties. He licked his bottom lip then caught it in his teeth. His gaze speared and held me. I couldn't have looked away if I'd wanted to, and part of me did. Part of me wanted to close my eyes, to be made blind. To be made a little helpless.

I lifted my ass from the bed to push my panties down my thighs. Over my knees. It's hard to be graceful when you're on your back, but I managed to somehow wriggle out of the lace and lie back again. Legs closed, coy though not shy. The hem of my dress had fallen down again, shielding me from his hungry gaze.

We'd already been naked together. He'd already made me come. But this was different, the way he commanded me. I liked it the way I'd liked the restaurant he'd chosen and where he'd taken me to dance. Because he knew what I wanted without my having to tell him.

When I again slowly tugged my dress up to expose my nakedness to him, Niall unbuckled his belt. Then his button and zipper. I focused greedily on the bulge in his briefs and oh, God, oh, fuck yes, the head of his cock peeking out. He pushed his jeans down low enough to free himself and took himself in his fist.

"Make yourself come," Niall ordered.

I was happy to oblige. I was already wet and slick, my cunt tight around my first and middle fingers as I dipped them inside. I circled the tight, hard knot of my clit with slippery fingertips and let my knees fall apart to give him a clear view.

His guttural groan was the best response. Niall stroked himself, keeping his fist curled around the shaft. His hips pumped forward.

"I want you inside me," I said.

He smiled. "Not yet."

I laughed hoarsely, but I didn't argue. This felt too fucking good. My back arched a little as I stroked faster. I fucked my fingers inside again for a few seconds then back to my clit. I was already shaking. Breathing hard.

Sometimes, the best way to keep control is deciding to give it up to someone else.

"You gonna come for me?" Niall murmured. "C'mon, girl. I want to see you."

I was getting closer. Words more difficult to say, catching on a moan. I said his name, I think, or maybe just groaned.

The muscles in my belly and thighs were tight. I couldn't stop my hips from rolling, or my free hand from fisting in the sheets. He wanted me to come; I wanted to make him lose his mind.

"I'm close," I managed to say. The first waves of orgasm were building, building. Just a little more, and I would be swept away.

Niall muttered something I couldn't hear. I shifted, teasing myself a little to draw out the pleasure. I wanted us to finish together.

"So close," I said, looking into his eyes. Wanting to urge him toward me, wanting him inside me, but giving him this, what he'd asked for. To see me. "Jerk that cock for me, baby. Make yourself come for me."

His stroking hand slowed then stopped. His mouth twisted. He shook his head.

Thinking he needed a little encouragement, wanting to give him time to catch up, I slowed my fingers. "I want you to fucking make yourself come for me. C'mon, I'm so close, baby, I want you with me. Come all over me. Cover me with it."

"I don't want to do that."

Caught up in my own pleasure, I was sure I'd misheard him. Or misunderstood. "I want you to—"

"I said no." Niall shook his head again and, incredibly, pulled his pants up.

Once, when I was fifteen, I'd been riding in a car driven by one of my good friends. She hadn't been paying attention and had rear-ended a car that had suddenly come to a stop in front of us. I hadn't been wearing my seat belt, stupid of course, and though I'd tried to shield myself from the impact, I'd hit the dashboard with my neck and shoulder. It wasn't the windshield, I could count myself lucky for that, but the feeling of moving and all at once hitting something hard enough to make stars dance in my vision…I'd never forgotten it.

We'd been moving, but suddenly we had stopped.

I sat up. "What?"

"I don't want to do that." Niall said. He zipped up, buttoned up, buckled his belt. Stepped back from the bed.

Everything inside me turned cold, and I became very small.

I let my dress cover me. Being naked is being vulnerable, and I was glad I'd only pulled it up, not taken it off. I tucked my knees to the side.

Pushing his hand up my thigh, having him pull away. Telling him to keep his mouth on me and him moving to use his hand, instead. A dozen little things here or there that he'd fought me on and I'd let pass because it hadn't mattered so much at the time. But now, this.

And it mattered to me very, very much.

We stared at each other, saying nothing. I couldn't tell my own expression, though I was trying desperately for casually neutral so I could keep myself from bursting into startled, embarrassed tears. Niall looked distant before he wouldn't look at me at all. He took the remote from the dresser and clicked on the TV then sat on the edge of the bed.

"I guess we're…finished?" I asked around the lump in my throat.

"Yeah. Sure. I'm tired anyway. Drank too much, too."

I didn't know what to say. How to move, where to go. If I should touch him, or even if I wanted to. I breathed in, counting slowly, and then got up and went into the bathroom. I ran the water in the sink and put my hands on it, bracing myself physically against the countertop.

Breathe, breathe, breathe, I told myself. *Breathe, Elise.*

I'd been with men I did not allow to come. Tease and denial had been part of our play, mutually agreed upon and enjoyed.

I'd been with men who'd had trouble reaching orgasm—
Esteban sometimes did not finish, and I'd learned early on not
to take it personally but to trust him when he told me his climax was not the only end point to our play. But I'd never been
with a man who flat-out refused to come, especially not when
he'd been urging me on to come myself, while he jacked off.

I'd never had a man refuse me anything, really, when it
came to sex.

Ever efficient, I'd unpacked my bag shortly after we'd
checked in. I had my toiletries bag in the bathroom already,
along with the pajamas I hadn't intended to need. Splashing my
face with cold water, I tried to convince myself that whatever
had happened in the bedroom wasn't personal. He was tired,
a little drunk, we'd veered off course in the way you sometimes do when you're not on the same page. It wasn't meant
to hurt me. But it sure felt like shit, no matter how I played it
out, and no matter what I did, I couldn't rinse the sour, bitter
taste of dismay from my mouth. I took a shower, and couldn't
wash away the feeling of somehow being dirty, either.

I wanted to face him again with my full face on, painted
like a warrior, but instead I came out of the bathroom freshly
scrubbed, my hair towel-dried and still damp. My pajamas
were cute, a tank top and silky boxers, but I went without a
word to my suitcase to pull out an oversize T-shirt to put on
top. Niall hadn't changed, but he'd pushed himself back onto
the pillows, on top of the covers, to watch TV.

Face impassive, he didn't say anything when I took up my
book, which, like my pajamas I hadn't intended to need. I got
into bed on the wrong side, but didn't ask him if we could
switch. I tried to concentrate on the book, but the words
swam, blurring. After a few minutes, Niall got up and went
into the bathroom. He was in there longer than I had been.

The room had gone chilly from the air-conditioning, and

I shivered from it. Anxious that my stomach was going to get upset enough to make me truly ill, I swallowed hard. Then again. I turned off the light, put my book on the bedside stand and curled into myself so I could count backward from a hundred. But my tried-and-true method of putting myself to sleep didn't work. I was still awake when he came out.

He turned off the light first. I heard shuffling near his suitcase. The bed dipped when he got into it. I waited for him to touch me...but he did not.

"Are you upset?" Niall asked finally, his voice quiet as the shadows.

I didn't turn to face him. "Yes. I am."

"Why?"

Blinking rapidly, I tried to find an answer that would come out calm and in control. What I managed, instead, was a low rasp. "*Why? What do you mean, why?*"

"Just what I said. Why?"

I was glad now that he hadn't curled up behind me. I couldn't have borne his touch now. I punched my pillow and eased to the edge of the bed, as far from him as possible. "That was pretty much the ultimate rejection, wasn't it?"

He laughed.

The motherfucker laughed.

It wasn't an easy laugh, and it lacked humor, and I could tell he'd forced it, but even so it was not the response I wanted. Niall sat up. I could see his shadow and from the corner of my eye, the outline of him, but fortunately for him, he kept his hands to himself.

"Don't be like that," he told me.

The only thing that kept me from leaping from the bed in a white-hot rage at that point was that I was genuinely too stunned to move. I couldn't even speak. Behind me, Niall lay back down, close enough that his shoulder would've brushed mine if I turned onto my back. I didn't. I didn't move, didn't say a word, because to do anything in that moment would've made me lose it. All of it, everything, I'd have screamed and raged and possibly thrown things; I would've wept for sure, great gushing buckets of the tears trying to stab me in the throat and eyes even now. I would've lost control, and I refused to give him that.

"Good night," Niall said.

I did not answer him.

34

I did not sleep.

Beside me, the soft in-out huff of Niall's breathing told me he did, or at least did a good job of pretending. Morning light started peeking around the blackout curtain in only a few hours, but I'd never been so glad for a reason to get out of bed. Though I'd showered so recently that my hair was still wet, I took another, this time forcing myself to endure a lukewarm spray to keep myself from dissolving into dismay.

I blew my hair dry, not caring if it woke him. I did my makeup. And finally, I dressed in the clothes I'd brought along to travel in.

He was up when I came back into the bedroom, the TV on but the volume so low there was no way he could really hear it. He'd propped himself on the pillows, an arm beneath his head. He looked rumpled and gorgeous, and I kind of hated him for making me want to slip back beneath the covers with him and be naked all day long.

"You're up early," he said.

I tucked my toiletries into my suitcase and made sure my dirty laundry was separated from the clothes I hadn't yet worn. I slipped on a pair of flats and settled my fuck-me pumps alongside my cosmetics bag. When I turned to get my book from the bedside stand, Niall was watching me.

"What's going on?"

"I'm going to head home early." My chin went up. I heard the steel in my voice. I knew the look on my face.

Other men would've known better than to try and charm me in that moment, but I'd already figured out that Niall wasn't other men. "Don't be like that. C'mere."

He sat up and crooked a finger at me. Actually gestured to me like I was some woebegone, delicate little flower who needed to somehow be comforted. Or wooed. Fuck that. Fuck being soft. What had that gotten me but rejection, humiliation and pain?

I didn't move. I put my book away and closed my suitcase. I visually checked the room for anything I might have left behind then found my purse on the chair and put it over my shoulder.

"Elise," Niall said like a warning. "Don't do this."

"I think it's best if I leave."

Niall got out of bed to stand in front of me. I could've pushed past him, but that would've meant touching him. And frankly, I didn't need to be that aggressive to get what I wanted. I knew that well enough. I didn't move.

"C'mon," he said with another of those half laughs that sounded nothing like his usual good humor. "What's going on? I thought we were going to have a great weekend together."

"So did I."

A shadow crossed his expression, but he was still pretending last night hadn't happened. "We still could. I have dinner reservations for tonight. I thought we were going to the art museum…don't let last night upset you so much."

"Don't tell me how to feel, please." My words were clipped, precise, but polite. Cold, though. Really fucking cold.

He frowned. "Why don't you go ahead and tell me how you feel, then. Since I can't figure it out."

"I'm upset about what happened last night," I said carefully. "About you choosing not to finish."

Niall's gaze darkened. His mouth thinned. He was pissed off, now, but I didn't care.

"You told me to come for you," Niall said flatly. "My orgasm is my decision."

I gaped, jaw dropping. "What the hell does that mean?"

"Look, I know you've had bunches of guys who get off being bossed around by you, but in case you haven't figured it out, that's not me. It's never going to be me."

My fingers curled on the strap of my bag, but I wanted to make them a fist. "I wasn't bossing you around. I was...we were both talking. I thought it was something we were both doing with each other, Niall."

"It felt like you were trying to get me to do what *you* wanted me to do," he said. "Not what *I* wanted to do."

I reeled at this, not sure what to say or how to say it. All I could do was shake my head, helpless to find words even to defend myself. "I thought you'd want to!"

"I don't get off on being ordered around!"

"I wasn't ordering you," I cried, resenting his accusation even as I tried replaying the night before in my head to see if I'd come on too strong. Too dominant.

"It sounded like you were," Niall snapped.

I recoiled, physically and emotionally. I shook my head again, grasping for control and finding it only by biting my tongue hard enough to make a star or two dance across my vision. I rubbed the soreness against the back of my teeth.

"I thought we were doing something together," I told him

in the same flat tone he'd used with me earlier. "You were telling me to do things, and I was telling you to do things… and you made me feel like I was less than…porn."

It was his turn to take a step back. "The fuck does that mean?"

"It means that you made me feel like it was something you were orchestrating all for yourself, like you were watching porn or something. Except that I'm pretty sure when you do watch porn," I added with a sneer, "you actually get off."

Niall's lip curled. "You're the one who was making it like porn, asking me to come all over your tits. Maybe that's the sort of thing you did with all your lovers, but I'm not that guy. I don't get off on being bossed around."

I went hot. I went cold. Like a fever, an illness, I started to shake. "You were the one bossing," I whispered. "And I was letting you."

"I guess you don't like it when you're on the other side of things."

I'd bitten my tongue plenty of times to keep myself from saying cruel words aloud, but at this I found myself utterly speechless. I bent to lift my suitcase, focusing on that one thing, that action, to keep myself from screaming or bursting into tears or needing to sit because my legs had started to shake. I wanted to puke. Mostly, I just wanted to get out of there.

I suddenly resented all the times I hadn't pushed, hadn't demanded or commanded or insisted on getting my way. All for what? For the sake of love.

He tried again to smile. "C'mon, Elise. Don't go."

I didn't look at him. When he took a step toward me, I didn't step back. I turned my face away, though. I could not look at him. I didn't want to.

When he stepped aside, I pushed past him without touching him. My suitcase bumped his leg, but I didn't apologize. If I opened my mouth, I wasn't sure what would spill out, but I knew it wouldn't be good. And still, now, as angry and hurt and dismayed as I was, I didn't want to break open in front of him. I didn't want to be hurtful.

So instead, I swallowed everything, and I left without looking behind me.

No games. That's what I had said, and if I expected Niall not to play them, I couldn't, either. So, although I didn't want to, I texted him as soon as I got home.

We should talk.

He did not answer.

I waited an hour and texted again. Please call me. And again, Niall didn't reply. I waited for the rest of the day, trying to lose myself in laundry and bill paying, all the things I would not have been doing if I were still in Baltimore, holding his hand while we looked at weird art. When night fell, he still had not replied.

I didn't text him again.

35

One week. Not a word. Then another week as deathly cold and silent as the first. Niall's silence seemed as clear an answer to me as if he'd told me to my face he never wanted to see me again.

I don't make good decisions when I'm upset. Hell, I don't make good decisions when I'm happy. As far as shitty choices went, I was in no frame of mind to figure out if trusting Niall had been one more in a long string of them, worse than a tattoo could ever be. All I knew was that I was hurting, and the last person who'd done anything to make me feel better in any way had been Esteban. So I made another stupid decision, and I called him. I'd never called him before. He'd only ever called me. He answered, sounding distant and wary, but he answered.

"I need you," I said.

He sighed. *"Querida…"*

I wasn't crying, but close to it. I closed my eyes. My fingers gripped the phone, and I pressed it hard enough to my ear to hurt. And because I knew him well enough to know what buttons to press and how hard to press them, I pushed them. Hard.

"Esteban," I whispered. *"Por favor."*

★ ★ ★

Esteban met me, as I knew he would. I was the one who got there first, waiting for him, and when he came inside, I didn't make him get on his knees. I didn't toss down a bag of toys. I simply took his hand and led him to the bed, where I pushed him gently until he sat. Then I straddled his lap and took his face in my hands, and I kissed him on the mouth.

"What do you want," he asked against my mouth. "What do you need?"

"I don't know anymore," I whispered.

Esteban pulled away to look at me, his dark eyes clouded with concern. He stroked a thumb under each of my eyes then tucked it into his mouth. I licked my lips and tasted salt. Then he nodded.

He rolled me over and moved me up the bed like I weighed nothing. He kissed my eyes. My cheeks. My jaw, my throat, my chin. He unbuttoned my blouse and caressed my breasts, bare beneath, cupping them in his hands. He sucked gently at each nipple until they stood up, tight and red, then flicked them with his tongue until I writhed.

He undressed me and covered every inch of me with kisses. He moved between my legs and parted me, opening me to his mouth and tongue, the press of his teeth shielded by his lips. Esteban knew my body. He didn't need my commands. His worship went on and on until I came, gasping, and then he left me only long enough to put on a condom before he was on top of me again.

He pushed inside me with a low grunt. He bent his face to the side of my neck. At first he fucked me slowly, and then he moved faster, harder. He came with a shudder and a low shout and fell on top of me.

He rolled off me a moment or so later and lay staring up at the ceiling with his hands folded on his chest. I lay in a similar position next to him. I listened to his breathing slow. I still tasted salt. Tears, sweat, it didn't matter.

"We've never done it like that before," Esteban said. "Me on top."

I didn't move. "You didn't like it."

He turned his head to look at me. "I always like it with you."

"Then why—" I stopped myself with a shake of my head and turned away from him on my side. I didn't want to ask. As always with him, I didn't want to know.

He spooned me from behind, his lips pressed to my shoulder. "I missed you."

"Then you shouldn't have gone away." It came out harder than I meant it to.

He sighed. "I'm sorry. I had to. I thought it would be easier if I did it that way. Because I knew if I told you, I would not be able to do it."

I covered my face with my hands, weeping in silence. Quaking with it, while he held me. The thing was, I couldn't tell if I was crying because of Esteban, or Niall, or that other one whose real name I never said. For all three, I guessed. And for myself, who kept making the wrong choices over and over again. Like hurt was all I was ever destined to have.

We lay there until his phone blared, startling us both. He didn't answer it or even look to see who was calling, but I felt the tension in his muscles. I sat up and excused myself to the restroom, where though I ran the water, I still heard him murmuring into the phone. When I came out, he'd dressed and was sitting on the edge of the bed.

"I know," I said. "You have to go."

"Come. Sit." He patted the edge of the bed.

I did. He took my hand. Our fingers linked. We sat like that for the time it took the numbers to change on the clock.

"I can't see you anymore," Esteban said. "I thought it would be easier not to say it to your face, but it was not. I'm sorry I didn't do a better job of it. And I'm sorry about whatever happened to you that made you so sad."

"Thank you for telling me and not making me have to guess it. Again," I added, just to watch him wince. But then I kissed him. "It was the agreement. Thank you for telling me."

"I was bad at it before. I'm sorry."

I leaned my shoulder into his then put my head on it. "I'm going to miss you."

Esteban made a small noise, and when I looked at him, he'd covered his eyes. All I could see was the downward curve of his mouth. When he reached for me, I held him. Tight.

"You've been so dear to me," I told him. "I cherish you, Esteban. I'm sorry I never said it before. I know you wanted to hear it. I'm sorry I never gave you that."

"You gave me much," he said.

I smiled, still tasting tears. "You gave me much, too."

He leaned to kiss me, but at the last moment, I turned my face. Not out of spite, but because I could not bear it. That our last kiss should taste of tears. He kissed my cheek instead, and the corners of my eyes. I wanted to hold on to him harder before he left, but I didn't.

I let him go.

36

Niall was waiting in my driveway when I got home.

I hadn't showered. I wore the stink of sex on me like a cloak; my hair was mussed. I was sure my lips were swollen. But so were my eyes, because I'd cried the entire way home. I pulled in beside him and thought, oh, fuck.

I got out of the car. So did he. I waited for him to speak, and when he didn't, I headed for my front door.

"So," he said from behind me on the porch.

I turned. "What do you want?"

"I want to talk to you."

I stared at him without speaking. I wasn't sure what I had to say. Oh, I had plenty of words, but none seemed willing to force themselves out of my mouth. I wanted to fall into his arms and kiss him, but I didn't move.

"We can talk out here," I said.

"What, like strangers? Like I'm trying to sell you a vacuum cleaner?"

I crossed my arms. "You have something to say to me? You'd better start talking, because in about a minute I'm going to go inside and ignore you the way you were ignoring me for two weeks."

"Is that what this is about?"

"No," I told him. "This is also about what happened in Baltimore, and how you acted there, not just the fact you haven't answered a single fucking text in two weeks. You just disappeared, Niall."

I started crying then. He moved toward me, but I blocked his embrace with my shoulder. "Don't touch me."

"Can we not do this on your front porch, please?"

I swiped at my face. "You don't want the neighbors to see?"

"I don't think *you* want the neighbors to see," he said under his breath, looking over his shoulder then back at me. Everything in his expression screamed misery.

I wanted him to be miserable. I also wanted him to be wrong about me, though he wasn't. I unlocked my door and went inside without inviting him in. He was already in anyway, in every way that counted.

"Where were you?"

"Out." I tossed my bag onto the chair and went into the powder room to rinse my mouth and smooth my hair. I turned my face from side to side, trying to see if he would know I'd been with Esteban. Not sure I cared.

Niall was waiting for me in the kitchen. He'd helped himself to a glass of water and set one out for me. I sat, but didn't pick up the water. He was wrong this time, I thought meanly. I wasn't thirsty.

It didn't make me feel any better.

"I just don't understand why you got so upset," Niall began, and I stopped him with a look.

"I don't understand why you don't understand."

He looked mad then sad. "I'm sorry. Okay? I'm really sorry. I'm trying to apologize."

"You made me feel like shit. About us. About me," I said. "You don't understand why?"

"No. Not really. But I'm sorry I did."

I shook my head. "How can you be sorry if you don't really think you did something wrong?"

"I can be sorry I hurt you," Niall said.

I started to cry again. No sobs. Just tears leaking hotly down my cheeks, myself incapable of holding them back. I sat in front of him and let him see me weep, not caring if I looked ugly, if he saw me breaking, if he saw by watching how much he'd made me come undone.

Because that was love, at least the only kind it seemed I'd ever have.

Niall reached for my hand, and I let him take it. "Let me make it up to you. Please?"

"How are you going to do that?"

"Dinner? Flowers? You name it," he told me. "Whatever you want, whatever you like."

"Would you let me tie you up? Blindfold you? Would you get on your knees for me, Niall, or let me dress you in lingerie or fuck you in the ass?" I took my hand from his and got up. My chair screeched on the linoleum. "Would you come for me, if I ask you to?"

"I don't... Elise." He shook his head, looking pained, lip a little curled.

"Because I like those things. A lot. I like to have a man on his knees for me, worshipping me, doing whatever I tell him to do. I like lingerie on men. Hard cocks in lace panties damp with precome, because he's so fucking hard for me that not only would he come for me if I told him to, I wouldn't have to fucking touch him." The words tumbled out of me, cold and hard and somehow emotionless. I heard myself saying them, still felt the scald of tears on my face, but inside I felt...nothing. I'd gone numb.

Niall recoiled. "You want to know why I wouldn't do it?

Why I wouldn't just come for you on command, like I was your lapdog?"

"Yes. I want to know why my asking you to give me something you seemed really eager to give me was such a huge, enormous deal. Tell me."

"Because all I could think about was how many other guys you'd probably done the same thing with. Your lovers, whatever the hell you called them. All I could think about were those pictures of you, and how beautiful you looked in them, and how content, and how I was never going to be able to do any of that stuff for you. I was never going to be that guy, and I was never going to like that sort of thing, and how you were going to keep asking me to push my boundaries, and I didn't want to do it. Okay? I didn't want to try and measure up to something I just don't have in me. I'm never going to make you happy, Elise. Not like that. If that's what you need, I just can't."

"So then why bother?" I asked him. "Why fucking bother with the dinner and the flowers and all that other bullshit? If you really think you'll never make me happy?"

He didn't say anything, but that was exactly what I expected him to say.

"You want to know why you'll never make me happy?" I didn't want to look at his face, but I made myself stare him right in the eye. "Because you don't know me."

"I know you," he said, but I cut him off with a shake of my head.

"You can't possibly. If you'd ever listened to me, all along, you'd know. But I don't think you've listened, Niall, because it's obvious you believe there's only one way for me to be, and it's something you don't want. Did it ever occur to you that there's more to me than any one thing?"

Again, nothing.

"You're so caught up in what you think I want that you have no idea who I am," I told him. "But what you don't seem to understand is that I love you, Niall."

In Baltimore I'd told him I loved him, and he had not said it back. I'd taken a chance and said it again, and if that made me desperate and pathetic, well…if you can't make yourself a fool for love, you don't deserve to have it. I waited for him to answer me.

He stood. "I'll just go."

I'd jumped, but Niall did not catch me.

37

I told myself it was for the best. I'd already gone down the road with someone who would not give me what I wanted, and it had left me shattered. Better to end things now, I thought, before I got in too deep.

"I don't want to talk about it," I told Evan, who'd only given me a look and hadn't said anything at all about it. "Things end. It's just what happens sometimes."

"Shit, you got that right," he said bitterly and dumped sugar in his coffee with such vehemence a bunch of it scattered across the table.

I added cream to mine, waiting patiently for the sugar he was abusing. "What's going on?"

"I told her to get the fuck out," my brother said quietly and far more calmly in tone than his words suggested he felt.

"Oh." I stirred my coffee.

"She said you knew."

My heart sank. "I'm sorry. I thought it was her place to tell you."

"Yeah. I'm not...well, I am sort of pissed at you. I feel like an asshole. How long?" He sat back in the diner booth, his hair standing on end from where he'd run a hand through it over and over.

"I don't know. And I didn't know for a long time, Evan. I promise. I mean, I thought she was acting weird—"

"Yeah, right? Shit." He shook his head. "I thought it was just stress about the Bar Mitzvah."

"That might've been part of it. Did she say that?"

My brother hunched forward, both hands wrapped around his mug. "She said a lot of things. It doesn't really matter. She's in love with the other guy."

"I'm sorry."

"We got married too young. Had a kid. I'd never have married her if not for William, you know. We weren't really all that good together. I just thought it was the right thing to do. And then after a while it's so much easier to be with someone than it is to even think about trying to start all over. At least, that's what I thought. I guess she didn't."

"How's William?"

"He's okay, actually. He joined the cross-country team and got a part in the school play. Keeps him busy after school pretty much every day. And maybe it'll be good for him, get his mind off it. Gives Susan time to look for a place. We'll have to refinance, get a home equity loan so I can buy her out. It's going to fuck us financially."

I winced. "Ouch. I'm sorry."

"Hey. Better now than in ten years. Or twenty. I'm trying to look at it practically." My brother cut a square of his chicken parmesan and chewed.

I poked at my cheese omelet, but didn't feel like eating it. "What did Mom say about it? Jill?"

"Jill was a dick about it, of course. Mom was more understanding. She said Susan was a good mother and she'd be sure to do the best thing for William, and that's all that mattered. I didn't tell either one of them about the other guy, though."

"Probably better not to. How are you about that?"

Evan scowled. "Well. I don't like it, that's for sure. But let's face it. Another guy wasn't the real problem. Happy people don't cheat. She wasn't happy. I wasn't happy. Maybe we both have a chance to you know, get happy."

"You're a lot more understanding about it than I would be."

He laughed. "I punched a hole in the wall in the den when I found out."

"No way!" I gaped.

He nodded. Then looked sad. "It nearly fucking broke my hand. Didn't make me feel any better, and it cost me a hundred and some change to fix it."

"Moral lesson, don't punch a wall. Got it." I gave him a sympathetic smile. "You sure you're not mad at me for not telling?"

"Would it have made it any better?"

"I don't know. You might've found out a little sooner."

"She'd have lied about it. She flat-out told me so. Then it would've been ugly between you and me. Nah, it's okay. Susan told me what you said to her, about how she needed to get her act together. She said it was why she came clean." Evan cut another piece of chicken and chewed slowly. When he opened his mouth to show me the disgusting mess inside his mouth, I knew he was going to be okay.

"You're such a pig."

Evan grinned. "Love you, sis. It's going to be okay. One way or another."

I nodded, hating the tears threatening again and forcing them away. "Yep. One way or another, everything always is."

38

It had been a long-standing summer tradition for me to take William to as many street fairs and carnivals as we could find over the summer, but so far we hadn't managed to get to even one. When I heard about this fall's Fireman's Carnival in Mechanicsburg, I knew I had to take him.

I'd asked him if he wanted to invite any friends along, but he hadn't, so it was the two of us stuffing our faces with funnel cakes and curly fries. I bought him an all-day ride bracelet, but I refused to go on the creaking, twirling monstrosity that looked like it was held together with an old carny's beard hairs and some spit.

"I'll go in the haunted house, if you want. Or that Crazy Maze. But that vomitron? Nope. Text me when you're done. I'll come get you."

It didn't take him much more convincing than that before he was off and waiting in line. I fended off the game operators trying to get me to try my hand at popping balloons or squirting streams of water into scary clown mouths for a chance to win shoddy stuffed animals or square mirrors painted with skewed designs of bands kids at the carnival probably didn't even know. As much as I might've had a hankering for a red-

and-white AC/DC mirror, though, I shook my head and kept walking. After an oversize limeade, I needed the bathroom in the worst way. Thanking the goddesses of tiny bladders, I found the restroom in the back of the fairground's main building, not far from where I'd left William.

The line for the women's room was long but moved fast, and I came out a different door than I'd used to go in. Conveniently located near the milk shake stand, I noticed, and knew I should pass it up the same way I knew I was going to indulge in a chocolate treat because fuck calories. Chocolate.

The milk shake stand was near the kiddie ride area, set away from the bigger rides William had been going on. A tiny train on a bumpy track. A mini carousel. Lots of things that go around in a circle and make noise if you push the buttons in the elephant or car or airplane or whatever it is your kid decided to ride in. William had loved rides like that, and I had a nostalgic pang for the days when ten bucks had been enough to keep him occupied for as long as we could stand to stay at a carnival.

I didn't notice Esteban right away. Why would I? Out of the context of our usual meetings, he didn't look at all the same. He wore khaki shorts and a polo shirt and sandals, with a backpack slung over his shoulder. He looked every inch the suburban dad.

Because, I realized, that's exactly what he was.

He had a little girl by one hand, and there was no doubting she belonged to him. Her curly black pigtails, her tiny round face, her chubby little feet in plastic sandals all killed me with the cuteness. He was bent to listen to something she was saying as she pointed toward one of the rides. He didn't see me.

The woman next to him did, though. She wore a flowing maxi dress that couldn't hide the softness of her belly or size of her boobs. The baby in her arms was the obvious reason for both as well as the tiredness around her eyes, but she was laughing at the baby trying to pull down her elastic top. She was beautiful. She caught me looking and smiled. She had no idea who I was, for which I was supremely grateful.

I didn't want him to see me. I would lose my place in line if I ducked away now, but the milk shake no longer appealed to me. To get through the crowd I would have to push past him and his family, though. To go the other way meant elbowing my way through a pack of shoving preteens. And, as is the way with most things, while I hesitated, it became too late to do anything.

His gaze caught mine. We stood and stared, no more than an arm's length apart. I froze, desperately trying to keep a neutral face. Give nothing away.

Esteban smiled at me. Tiny, secret, brief as a blink, but it was there. Then he was bending again, this time to pick up his daughter and carry her toward the carousel. He didn't look back but that was all right. He'd shown me he still knew me, and that was enough.

39

The brown paper bag hit my desk with a soft thump. I looked up. Alex held two oversize paper cups with steam curling from the holes in the lids.

"I added Baileys Mint," he said.

I sat back in my chair. "It's ten in the morning."

"And?" Alex took the chair across from my desk and thumped my coffee down in front of me. "You look like you could use it."

"I have work to do, Alex."

He grinned. "I could fire you. Then you'd have no work to do, and you could sit here and drink boozed-up coffee with me and eat those pastries and tell me all about what the hell crawled up your ass and died."

"You can't fire me," I said as I opened the paper bag and peeked inside, "and fuck you."

"So hostile." He pretended to look upset, but then propped his feet on the desk and rocked back. He lifted the coffee. "Here's to you and me, may we never disagree. And if we do, fuck you, here's to me."

I laughed.

It had been days since I'd done so much as crack a smile,

so the laughter croaked out of me like a rusty robot grinding its gears. It sounded quite a bit like sobbing. It sounded a little like screaming, too.

Alex watched me in silence for a moment before putting his feet down and coming around the desk to put his arms around me. I didn't want him to hug me. Yet I found myself with my face pressed to his warm, broad chest, the subtle scent of his cologne surrounding me, and the steady beat of his heart against my cheek soothing me despite my unwillingness to be comforted.

I didn't cry, not with tears. I did silence myself, though, the sharp, ragged edges of my sobbing laughter easing into nothing. He let go of me after a minute or so and stepped back to look at me.

"Drink the coffee," he said. "Eat a pastry. And tell me what's going on."

I hadn't laughed in a few days; I hadn't eaten more than a few saltines or pretzels in a bit longer than that. After leaving the carnival I'd told myself it was bad carnival food, but I knew it was really just my heart twisting up my stomach. My stomach churned at the thought of food, but as soon as I caught a whiff of the sweet, caramel-topped pastry, my mouth watered. Just like my head and heart, my body was at war with itself. I pulled out the pastries and set them out on the paper napkins also in the bag. I pushed one toward Alex, who'd taken his seat again. I felt him staring at me, but didn't look at him until I'd pulled my pastry apart into small pieces and taken a sip of the minty, boozy coffee.

"I don't want to talk about it," I said.

"Too bad."

I frowned and nibbled on sugary goodness. Flavor exploded in my mouth, and my stomach settled at once. I tried not to gobble the rest of it. Discipline. Self-control. My old friends.

"It's personal," I said.

Alex snorted. "Yeah? And?"

"And this is where I work. You're my partner." I sipped more coffee, letting the warmth roll through me.

"I thought I was also your friend." He tipped his cup in my direction. He waited. Alex could be very patient when he wanted to be.

"I broke up with my… He was… Well… Whatever he was, we broke up."

"Your boyfriend?"

"He wasn't my *boyfriend*," I said sourly.

Alex laughed. I should've been pissed off that he was making fun of me, but I couldn't really blame him. It was stupid. Everything about my relationship with Niall had been stupid.

"Your lovah?"

"I broke up with him, too."

Alex's laughter faded. "Shit."

I shrugged. "It happens."

"No wonder you've been looking like that." He shook his head. "Shit, Elise. I'm sorry."

"It happens," I repeated. The booze had started to make me a little swimmy. So had the sugar.

Alex reached for his pastry and took a big bite. He chewed solemnly and swallowed, then drank some coffee. "It was the guy who came to see the acrobats with us, right? The one who works with your brother. The guy who took you to Baltimore."

I paused to give him a look. "Stalker?"

"You talk on the phone in a very loud voice," Alex told me. "What, can I help overhearing?"

I toyed with the crumbs of my pastry then licked a finger. "Yeah. That guy. He wasn't my boyfriend."

"Why not?"

"I didn't want a boyfriend? He didn't want a girlfriend? Why is anyone anything to anyone these days?" I curled my lip.

Alex frowned, his brow furrowed. "Yeah. Well. I know what you mean."

"Says the happily married man."

He laughed shortly. "Who was an asshole bachelor forever before that."

I'd met Alex through his wife, so I'd never known either of them before they were married. In truth, I had no idea how long they'd been together, only that they were one of the best-matched couples I'd ever met. Not because they were "perfect"—but somehow, they were perfect for each other.

"He was a mistake. I knew better."

"Don't we always?" Alex asked.

"And we still do it. Always. Why?" I took another slow swig of my cooling coffee. "Why are people so stupid when it comes to this stuff?"

"Because the heart wants what the heart wants. Sometimes, so do other parts. I read that in a book once." Alex grinned, but only a little, and without a whole lot of humor.

I groaned and let myself rock back in the chair. I closed my eyes, not wanting to think of Niall, but his face flashed into my head anyway. I thought of Esteban, too, though I had an easier time pushing away his face. And finally, predictably, another man's face forced its way out of memory. I opened my eyes to look at Alex.

"I should have known it wouldn't work out, long-term."

"How could you know that in advance? That's what people say when they're too afraid to try it."

"That's a hell of a thing to say to me, when you've plied me with pastry and boozy coffee," I snapped. "Either you're understanding and sympathetic or you're not. Quit trying to swing both ways."

At that, he burst into guffaws. Loud, genuine laughter. Taken aback, I narrowed my eyes. Alex rocked back in his chair, actually slapping his knee.

"What?"

He swallowed his chortles and propped his feet back on the desk. "You have no idea."

I put my cup on the desk and turned it around and around in my hands. "So, tell me."

"It's not my day for telling stories. It's yours. Okay, so, you met this guy. You knew right away it wasn't going to work out, but you fucked him anyway. And then you broke up. Am I getting it right so far?"

"Yes."

Alex gave me a sympathetic look that was as sincere as his laughter had been a moment ago. "So…why the broken heart?"

"It's not… I'm not…" I stopped myself, appalled at the way my throat closed. At how bitter the words tasted. At how close to tears I was. Again.

"Elise," Alex said gently, "I didn't have to overhear you talking to him on the phone to figure out that you've been head over heels for this guy for the past couple months. It was in everything you said or did. You kind of had it all over you."

"Like a rash," I said bitterly.

"I'd have called it a glow. But sure. A rash. A glow. Whatever it was, you walked like you were floating." Alex took another long sip of coffee, watching me over the top of his cup. "You were happy."

Tears threatened to throttle me, but I forced them back. I would not cry over this. I would not cry in this office. Not in front of Alex. I would not let myself lose control.

I. Would. Not.

I shook my head. "He knew me before I knew him. I mean, about…"

I hesitated. I liked Alex a lot. We worked great together. He'd seen my pictures.

"He didn't like what I like," I finished. "And he made it into a really big deal."

"Dumbass," Alex said promptly.

It urged a small laugh from me that helped to quash the threatening tears. "Like I said, it happens."

"Tell me what happened." Alex shifted in his chair. "I know I'm not your best girlfriend but trust me, I can pretend."

I laughed again, giving him the eye. "Weirdo."

"From one deviant to another," he said, "lay it on me. Confession is good for the soul or something like that. And it's eating you up inside, Elise. I can tell."

"You're awfully observant." I bit the inside of my cheek lightly, rubbing at the sore spot already there with my tongue.

"I hate that he's making you sad." Alex frowned. "I'd like to punch him in the junk."

This surprised me. "You would?"

"Fuck, yes." He looked surprised, too. "Why wouldn't I?"

This pricked tears into my eyes for a very different reason. "He's not making me sad. It is what it is."

Alex said nothing. He waited. And the longer he stayed quiet, the more compelled I felt to unburden myself.

"He made me laugh," I said.

Alex nodded. "Heavy. He also made you cry."

I shook my head again. "No. I just won't anymore. It's not worth it. I was that girl once, that one who let a man carve her up and toss her out to feed the sharks. I won't do it again. Not for anyone."

Alex shrugged. "We all go through it. Sometimes we're

the ones crying, sometimes we're the ones who made someone else cry. Love hurts. That's how it works, even when it
does work."

"I didn't love him," I lied aloud, trying to make myself
believe it.

Alex said nothing.

"Fuck my life," I whispered. We both said nothing until
finally, I sighed and downed the last of my coffee. "When we
were together, I thought that maybe it could work."

"Sure," he said as though that made sense.

I shrugged. "We had fun. And it got complicated, that's
all. The way things do. And I let myself be an idiot. I just
didn't think..."

Alex waited. I hadn't wanted a hug. I refused to cry. I didn't
want to spill myself out to him this way, but I could not hold it
back. My words ground out of me, rusty and raspy and harsh,
tasting of the grief I was trying so hard not to let myself feel.

"I didn't think I would care so much," I said. "I didn't think
he would matter to me."

"You can't choose who you love." Alex took his feet off the
desk and put them flat on the floor. His cup on the desk. His
elbows on his knees, he leaned forward with his hands linked
in front of him. He didn't look at me for a few seconds, and
when he did, his gaze glittered.

"He didn't love me. I thought he knew me, but he didn't,"
I added bitterly. "He had this idea of me, but it was a fantasy. Not real. But I was the one who let him in. I let him get
close. I knew I shouldn't, but I did, so in the end, who's the
dumbass? Me."

Alex frowned, and I kept talking.

"There was no point in being with him, not when I knew
that in the end, he was never going to let me be who I am.
Oh, sure, he said he was fascinated. Intrigued. But when it

came right down to it, he was never going to give me what I need and want and like." I drew in a breath then swallowed hard. "Even if what I want and need and like doesn't have to be the same thing all the time."

"Sometimes I like peanut butter on a sandwich. Sometimes I like a grilled cheese." Alex shrugged. "So long as when I'm hungry I get a fucking sandwich, I usually don't care. Unless it's liverwurst or some shit like that. Then forget it, I'll starve."

My mouth twisted into what might've passed for a smile, if you tried very hard to pretend. "Yes. That. Exactly that. But I'm the asshole who let it hurt so much."

Alex sighed, linking his fingers tighter. "That's rough."

"It's life," I said coldly. "I'll get over it. I did the first time."

He looked at me, his mouth twisting. "Sounds like you didn't."

My mouth opened in protest, but I had none that wouldn't be a lie. I gripped the desk, my fingernails scratching at the polished wood. A small, broken sound escaped me, no calling it back.

"You have a story," Alex said. Before I knew it, I was telling it to him.

Sometimes love takes you by the hand and leads you to run through fields of flowers while butterflies weave you a dress out of rainbows. Other times, love takes you by the throat and chokes you until all you see is the bright, sharp trail of shooting stars right before everything turns to black. The problem is, you can never tell in advance which way the story ends, not until you're too far into it, and you have no choice but to keep turning the pages.

Four years ago, I met him.

I didn't think there was anything special about it at the time. I turned around in a dance club when he jostled me as he tried to get past me toward the bar. I made a smart-ass comment. He gave one back and offered to buy me a drink. We danced, fast at first, and then at the end of the night, slow.

He pulled me in closer than I'd have let anyone else. My face found the curve of his neck, and I breathed him in. His hands settled on my hips. The song ended, but we kept dancing even when the "fuck you, time to go home" lights came on.

He asked for my number.

I gave it to him.

He called while I was still in the cab on the way back to the house we'd rented, not beachfront but one block back. My friends, shouting with laughter, cried out obscenities when I tried to talk to him. They hooted and hollered. By the time we got to the house, I'd already decided I was going back out to meet him again.

We walked on the sand, his hand in mine, dodging the late-night beach patrol who'd have thrown us off if we hadn't ducked into the shadows, standing still. Pressed against him, barely daring to breathe while we waited for the patrol to find us, I shivered in the chilly late-June sea air, and he warmed me. First with his hands. Later, his mouth, sweet and cautious when he kissed me. He could've done it harder. I wouldn't have minded.

It was the last day of my vacation but the first of his. I didn't expect to hear from him again, much less while he was enjoying the sun and sand and the possibilities of dozens of other girls at dance clubs who'd let him take them for late-night walks on the sand. But he called me every day. Texted me, too. He sent me pictures of himself on the beach, at the bar, grilling burgers with his buddies. And by the next Friday, he was urging me to come down and spend the weekend with him—because he wasn't renting a house, he owned it, and though he did have to go back to work on Monday, he could stay those two extra days.

Did I cancel all my plans to spend the weekend with a man I just met?

You bet your ass I did. And it was glorious. He grilled me steaks and asparagus on his deck, plied me with expensive wine, made love to me and then slept beside me with the sounds of the ocean rocking us into dreamland. He made sure I wore sunscreen so I didn't burn. He made sure to send back the salad I ordered that came with bacon bits on it that I'd requested not be there. I left late Sunday night, already missing him.

That was our summer. Weekends at his place by the ocean, and though the three-hour drive put too many miles on my car and got boring as shit really fast, I didn't care. During the week, we talked every night and texted throughout the day. With another nearly three-hour drive between us when he was at home in DC, getting together during the week was out of the question. We had to make do with technology. As summer heat became autumn chill, he shut down the beach house, and I spent my Friday and Sunday nights traveling to Washington, instead.

I knew I was in love with him the first time he let me tie his hands.

It started off silly. We'd been watching a movie, the typical sort of porny femdom type scene played for laughs as the black-vinyl-clad woman whipped a fat, sputtering businessman who vowed to empty his bank account for her. My chilly bare toes were tucked beneath his thighs on his oversize leather couch, because even though winter was sniffing around us, I was determined to hold on to summer as long as I could. He had a beer. I had a glass of wine. We'd stuffed ourselves on homemade lasagna I'd put together from my mom's recipe, one of the few things I could proudly say she'd taught me to manage in the kitchen. When the woman on the screen planted her stiletto heel in the small of the businessman's back and snarled, "And I want the stock options, too, you worm!" I coughed out spurious laughter.

"Why's it always got to be like that?" I said. "All degradation and humiliation. They never, ever show how beautiful it should be."

His fingers curled under my calf, and he looked at me with shining eyes. "How beautiful what should be?"

"A man on his knees." I leaned close to kiss him. The wine had made me sleepy and sexy and warm. So did he. "Worshipping a woman, adoring her. That's beautiful."

He slid from the couch and got on his knees in front of me, between my legs. His hands on my thighs below the hem of the summer-weight dress I was still so stubbornly wearing despite my goose bumps. He pressed a kiss to my bare knee, and the shudder that rippled up and down my spine had nothing to do with the temperature.

I put my hand lightly on his hair. He turned his face to press his cheek to my flesh and gave me a wicked, tempting grin. My fingers tightened in his hair, testing him. When his eyes fluttered closed and his mouth thinned, I might have taken that for distaste, except for the soft moan that slipped out of him.

We'd fucked a hundred times by that point. Backward, frontward, side by side. We'd never talked specifically about how I liked to pin his wrists above his head when I was on top, or how he so often urged me to straddle his face while he stroked himself.

On the television screen, the dominatrix had cuffed the businessman's hands while she wielded a flogger with a multitude of leather straps. The movie was still playing the scene for shits and giggles, semi-mocking the entire exchange. It wasn't very sexy to me at all, nowhere near as arousing as the man on his knees in front of me.

"Would you let me tie you up?" I breathed into his ear, leaning forward to take his chin in my hand. I nuzzled his cheek and found his waiting, eager mouth.

"Yes. If you wanted to."

I stood, drunker than I ought to have been. Not from the wine. From possibility. I took him by the hand and led him upstairs. I didn't look at him along the way. My heart pounded in my ears loud enough to block out everything else. I was dreaming, wasn't I?

But it was better than a dream.

I'd played around with control in high school without knowing it, only that I liked it best when my boyfriend was underneath me when we dry humped our way to mutual orgasms. In college and thereafter I'd tried to find my pace, led by the sorts of movies George and I had been watching. Porn, too. I demanded things of the guys I dated. I was bossy. A bitch, even when I didn't want to be, because that was how I thought it was supposed to work. But although the idea of some of what I watched excited me, humiliating the men I was supposed to love—or at least like enough to fuck—left me cold. I liked the clothes a dominatrix wore, high heels and lingerie. But I didn't care for being a dominatrix if it meant hurting someone else in order for them to give me what I wanted, and that was the only way I'd ever seen women on top behaving.

In his bedroom, I said, "Take off your clothes."

He pulled his polo shirt off over his head and tossed it to the side. I loved his body. He'd been an athlete in high school and college, and it showed. Smooth skin that didn't tan, against which my own olive coloring looked even darker. He undid his braided leather belt and pushed his khakis over his hips, down his thighs. He was self-conscious about his legs, complaining that no matter how much he worked out, he couldn't bulk up his thighs. But I loved his legs like I did the rest of him, lean and strong and sleek.

He wore dark blue boxer briefs, but hesitated with his thumbs in the waistband. "Elise."

"Those, too."

Then he was naked in front of me, his cock already stirring as I watched him without so much as lifting the hem of my skirt. We stared at each other for what seemed like forever before I deliberately and obviously let my gaze roam over the rest of him. Assessing. Judging.

Owning.

He was fully erect by the time I looked into his eyes again. His breathing, short pants. His fingers had curled into fists.

I'd waited for him to refuse me somewhere along the way, or to move or somehow to take control the way so many men did, even those who seemed to like it when I took charge. But he didn't. He gave me what I wanted, and it turned him on as much as it did me.

Later, I would learn how to choose rope that wouldn't rub his flesh raw, how to tie knots and decorate him in silken cord. But that first time, all I had was the necktie I grabbed from the rack inside his closet door. I'd never seen him wear one—our time together had so far always been casual dress. I snapped the fabric between my fists, making it taut.

I didn't have to ask him to go to his knees. Or to put his hands behind his back, crossed at the wrists. He did those things with only a look from me, and at first, I couldn't move. I was afraid to. My knees had gone so weak, I thought I might fall.

I tied him sloppily, without finesse. At first too tight, so that the edges of his tie cut into his skin. Then too loose, so that he could have easily gotten free, if he tugged. He didn't. He let me take my time. He let me bind him. And when I urged him forward on his knees to eat my pussy as I lay back on the edge of his bed, he did that, too.

I came three times with him tied up in front of me. I came a fourth with him inside me, his hands no longer bound but moving over my body. He fucked me so hard something rubbed raw inside me, bringing blood, but no regrets.

"How many times have you done that?" I asked him when it was over, in the dark and quiet as he spooned me.

"Never."

My heart lifted even as my head told me he had to be lying. "Oh, c'mon."

"No." He nuzzled the back of my neck and pulled me closer. "You were the first."

"He was not the first," I told Alex. "Not the first man I'd ever loved or the first to let me play around with being on top. But he was the first I'd ever gone that far with in terms of domination, the first I'd ever felt fully like myself with. The first relationship I didn't doubt myself in. With George, I was always beautiful and always strong, at least until the end, when it all fell apart."

"Why'd you break up?"

"That," I said, "is the question, isn't it?"

Alex looked thoughtful. "You were crazy in love with him."

"Yes. Too much."

"Did he love you?"

I let out a low, strangled laugh. "Ultimately, not enough. So does it matter if he loved me a little, or at all? I don't know."

"Shit." Alex leaned back in his chair and ran both hands

through his dark hair, standing it on end though it usually fell haphazardly into his eyes. "What happened?"

"We were together for just over a year. The sex was fantastic. We got along great. I'd had a bunch of short relationships that hadn't been very deep or meaningful, but with George I fell hard. He was smart and funny, he had a good job, he had his shit together. I imagined myself baking him pies and making babies, doing it all up June Cleaver style, except instead of a white picket fence and an apron, I'd have a leather flogger and a headboard with permanent eyebolts in it."

Alex snorted soft laughter, but that was all right. I'd been making light, though I felt anything but.

I shrugged. "He had this way of looking at me…he didn't need to say a word. He'd just stare. Like he thought I was amazing and wonderful. I thought…" I paused, hating the way my voice rasped. "I thought I made him happy, you know?"

"I understand. Totally."

Looking at him, I thought he did. "I let myself get lost in him, though. Addicted, I guess. Part of it was the sex. That power, the control. It was heady stuff I'd dreamed about for a long time but hadn't really had, not in that way. He made me cockdrunk, but it was more than that. I *was* crazy in love with him, like you said, the key word being *crazy*. Loved, loved, loved, crazy mad insane with it, to the point where as much as I might have exerted control in the bedroom, I was totally out of control in the relationship. He was the one who was in control because he just…didn't feel the same way."

"Uh-oh."

"We had this intense sexual connection, but for me it wasn't always about trussing him up like a turkey or any of that other stuff. I mean, sure, I liked it, but it's never been all about constantly topping someone for me. I know there are people who can't get off without a script and a scene and all that, but it doesn't have to be like that every time for me. There's more to life than handcuffs and paddles." I paused. "My switch gets flipped for all kinds of things, like the way he always opened the car door for me or got the things down from the high shelf. How he stocked his fridge with the kind of cheese I liked, even though I'd never mentioned it. He just knew. Myriad tiny things all making up the whole. It's always been about that, for me."

"Who doesn't like to feel they're understood?" Alex asked quietly. "I get it."

"So we had this time, you know, this bright and shining time when he made me feel like I was the best thing that had ever happened to him. I didn't doubt ever, not for a second, that George thought I was beautiful and amazing and wonderful." I paused again, hating the sting. "And then one day, I wasn't so wonderful anymore. He stopped doing all the little things. Then he stopped answering my messages. He stopped reaching out first. He started to cancel plans."

"All bad signs."

I laughed bitterly. "He stopped making me important. And I can forgive a lot of things, but not that. When I asked him where things were going with us—"

Alex winced. "The conversation every man dreads."

I laughed. "You think women like it any better?"

"I guess not."

"I had to ask. I didn't want to. But I had to know what he felt about me. What he wanted. I told him I loved him and wanted to be with him, and I was willing to do whatever it took to make it work for us. He gave me the romantic equivalent of a pat on the head and a chuck under the chin. He said he loved me in his own way, but that being with me was like eating ice cream every day. You decide you like a new flavor, right? And you glut yourself on it. You eat it every day. You think you'll never get tired of eating it. It's your favorite flavor. You can't get enough, until one day, you wake up and you decide you're sick of that flavor."

"Ugh," Alex said, but nodded. "He wanted a new flavor?"

"Yes. I guess he decided he really wanted to try vanilla."

"Wow."

I nodded. "Right? He said he'd never been able to make anything work out, that he was always looking ahead for the next best thing."

"After a year, he said this to you?" Alex looked disgusted.

I laughed, not because it was funny but because it was all I could do. "Yes. After a year, he said that to me."

"He was stupid, you know. You were the best thing that ever happened to him."

"Thanks." I shrugged. "Didn't feel like that, though. It felt like shit. It felt like he was telling me that everything we'd done wasn't what he really wanted. It made me feel like he'd never truly understood me at all—that I'd been alone in this thing the whole time."

"What do men do when they fear women?" Alex asked after a second. "They make them doubt."

"He said he needed some time, but that we could just stay in each other's lives while we dated other people. As if I could've handled that. And that maybe, after some time, if neither of us had found someone we liked better, we might get back together."

"Oh. Wow. The fucker. Jesus, Elise."

I drew in a breath, hating the sick feeling in my stomach. "He said we'd keep in touch. I told him he could go fuck himself with broken glass. He said good-night. I said goodbye."

"Good for you!"

I laughed again, embarrassed this time, but hell, I'd owned up to everything else, I might as well finish the story with the truth. "I regretted saying it immediately. That's the thing about crazy. It tends to stick."

"So does shit when you throw it at the wall," Alex said.

This time, my laugh was not bitter or embarrassed. A full-fledged guffaw burst out of me, hard enough to hurt. "You have such a way with words."

He grinned and buffed his nails on his shirt. "Thanks."

"He told me there was a chance, Alex. There was a maybe. And I...God. I'm such an idiot. I took that maybe, and I held it close to my heart, and I kept it there for the past three, no, almost four now, years. Because as long as there was a maybe, it wasn't a no."

"Have you talked to him since?"

"I used to talk to him all the time." I frowned, not proud. "I've apologized. I've asked him to reconsider. I've asked him to tell me he hates me. I've asked him to tell me he doesn't. He never answered me. He never told me to stop. He didn't block or delete me. I know because the messages went through and because I still see him in my contacts list. He read the messages, but never answered. He just kept letting me hold on to that maybe."

"That's fucked up."

I almost gagged on the thought of it. "Yeah. Stupid. Pathetic. Embarrassing, God, so fucking embarrassing. It was like a sickness with me. And I knew it, but I didn't care. Because there was that tiny, teensy-weensy spark of hope. At least I told myself there was."

Alex frowned. He looked embarrassed then, himself. Then determined. "Look. I'm going to be blunt. Can I be blunt?"

"If I say no, will you say it anyway?"

"He put you on his *C* list," Alex said.

I blinked. I swallowed a sour taste. "Ugh."

"Look, I'm not proud to say this, but...I've been that guy.

That asshole guy who keeps people around just in case." He looked ashamed. "Sometimes you had to work a little harder than others to keep someone on the string, but sometimes all it took was letting them know you were reading their messages and just not answering to keep them around in case you wanted them, when you didn't have something better."

I put my face in my hands. "Oh, I think I'm going to puke."

"Don't," he said. "If you puke, I'll puke. It'll be like the pie-eating scene in *Stand By Me*."

I peeked at him through my fingers. "So that's my story. I've held on to a man who dumped me, hoping one day he'd come back around and we could have what we had when it was good. I fucked my way through half a dozen men since then and wouldn't let any of them in, just in case one day George answered me. I met my lover, who was totally into letting me tie him up and do all manner of kinky things to him, and it was really great, until I found out he's married with two kids, one an infant that can't be more than a couple months old, and the last time I saw him was only weeks ago."

Alex choked on his last sip of coffee.

"Yeah," I said. "Fuckery. I didn't know. I thought we had rules because I didn't want it to be more than sex with him. I didn't want to get caught up in a relationship or fall in love or anything like that. I should have guessed it, though, that he had his own reasons for the rules. I should've known. I guess I didn't want to know. That doesn't make it any better."

"Knowing definitely is worse than not knowing," Alex said. "Don't beat yourself up about something he kept from you."

"He broke it off. And now that I do know, I could never go back to the way things were. But I miss him. God." I shuddered with unhumorous laughter. "I miss what we did anyway."

"And Niall," Alex added. "What about him?"

I squared my shoulders. "He embarrassed me, Alex. He made me ashamed of myself. Of what I like to do. Of what we'd done together, which was honestly nothing compared to what I've done with other men. That's worse than making me feel unimportant or making me doubt myself. I can't forgive him for it."

"Has he asked you to?"

I hesitated, thinking of Niall's pleading gaze. "He said he was sorry for getting bent out of shape during an argument we had. And for hurting me."

"It takes a lot to apologize, Elise."

I was silent for a few seconds. "I know. But it didn't matter. The damage had been done. I went through this already. I'm not doing it again."

Alex groaned and scrubbed at his face. Then he set all four legs of the chair on the ground with a solid thump. "Let me tell you a story."

40

Alex

Her name is Anne. She's my best friend Jamie's wife. And one summer, because Jamie asked me to seduce her, I did. He said she wanted it, that it had been her fantasy. I thought he was being an open-minded and caring husband, giving her what she wanted. Later I found out she had no idea he'd set it up, but by then it was too late. She'd fallen into it as hard as I had, and we'd all gotten lost in it. They made me a guest in their home, and I came in like a fucking tornado and almost ripped it all apart.

There's a problem with taking something you know you're not meant to have, especially when it's given to you all wrapped up with pretty ribbons and paper. When it's a gift, you should be grateful for it in a way you don't have to be if you stole it. Jamie gave me his wife, and I took her, but I wasn't grateful for her until it was too late.

I loved Anne, and I could tell you I loved her like I never loved any other woman, but all that means is that everyone you love, you love differently. More, less, sane or not, every time you fall in love it's never the same. What I can say is that I fell for her, hard, but I hurt her because I couldn't bring myself to tell her that. Because I was scared, or arrogant, or because

I thought she would never leave her husband to be with me. Or maybe I thought she would, and I knew I could never be the man she deserved. I don't know. I ran away at the end of that summer so she couldn't tell me, and I didn't have to know.

Then when Jamie invited me to come to Cleveland to see one of our favorite bands in concert at some little club I'd never heard of, I said yes. It had been about six months since I'd left Sandusky. Since the last time I'd seen Anne, though, Jamie and I had stayed in touch. He told me Anne was going to be at the concert. I didn't think to ask him if he told her I would be there, too.

The moment she saw me it was obvious she hadn't expected me. When I came around the corner, Jamie and I hugged it out, but when I moved to hug Anne, the look on her face fucking killed me. Her eyes lit up then skated away from mine like she couldn't stand the sight of me. She wouldn't look at me, even though all I could do was drink in the sight of her.

When we crossed the street toward the concert hall, I automatically reached for her arm to make sure she didn't stumble. She didn't yank it away; she didn't make a scene. But she pulled away and gave me a disgusted look.

"Hey," I said, stupid and trying to make nice. "It's all good. We're good."

She didn't answer me.

We got to the concert, and Jamie was buying shots, and at some point, there in the crowd, I found myself next to her. Shit. I say *found myself* like it was an accident, but I put myself there. I'd told myself it would all be okay, that I wouldn't need to touch her, but that close, there was no way I couldn't reach for her.

I moved up behind her and slid a hand into the thickness of her hair. I meant to cup the back of her neck, but instead I wrapped my fingers in her hair and tugged her back against me. She molded herself to me. I can't say what we did was dancing, not with so many people pressed up against us or her husband two feet away, bouncing and throwing up the devil horns to whatever song the band was playing. But we moved together for a minute or so, and all I could do was soak her in.

Until she turned, that look of disgust back on her face. She put her fingertips on my chest, over my heart, and shoved. It hurt. Not just the physical touch, her fingers digging into the meat of me, but the way she did it so vehemently. She was pissed, but worse, I saw the flash of tears in her eyes. All I wanted was to touch her again, even if it could only be for a minute or two, and instead I'd hurt her. Again.

Jamie had booked us rooms at the same hotel, since the drive from Cleveland to Sandusky at two in the morning after a night of drinking and carousing wouldn't have been smart. Twenty minutes after we parted ways at the elevator, she knocked on my door. I let her in. Of course I did. Some stupid part of me hoped that she was there to fuck or forgive me. I'd have taken either.

She wasn't.

"Why are you here?" she demanded.

Words came out, but like a dumbass, they weren't what I really meant to say. "I thought it would be fun."

I might as well have slapped her in the face, the way she flinched. Anne looked away from me. I'd never felt so small.

"You are so selfish," she said. I wanted to protest, but I knew she was right. "You knew how I feel about you, and you show up to a fucking concert? Like nothing happened? Like you didn't fucking break my heart into a million pieces, and what, you just think you can come along and put your hands all over me and make me want you again?"

"Anne…"

But she wasn't having any of it. When she looked at me, I

realized it was better when she wouldn't, because seeing what I'd done to her was like watching her set herself on fire. I couldn't stop it; all I could do was watch her burn.

"I've tried to hate you, and there are times when I almost make it, Alex. And then I am reminded that I love you, and everything hurts all over again, and all I can do is hate myself for ever thinking that maybe you had one shred of feeling for me." She held up a hand to stop me from speaking, though all I'd managed was a noise. "But obviously, you think nothing of me. You care nothing for me. If you did, if you had the tiniest crumb of love for me, you would never have been so simply, casually selfish. But that's what I guess I should expect from you, isn't it? It's all you've ever been. It's all you will ever be."

I don't know if I reached for her then, or she meant to hit me, maybe, but then she was in my arms, and I was kissing her. If you've ever kissed someone like you wanted to punch them in the face with your lips, that's pretty much how that went. I pulled away bruised and stinging. I'm pretty sure she bit me. I tasted blood and her tears, and it didn't matter if Anne couldn't bring herself to hate me. I hated myself plenty.

"I'm sorry," I said. It wasn't enough. It couldn't ever be enough, but I said it. "I'm sorry, Anne, I'm really sorry."

She let me hold her. She didn't relax against me at first. It was like hugging a board or a rod of iron. But she pressed her face to the side of my neck after a minute, and her arms went around me.

She whispered in my ear, "I hate you."

We looked at each other. I wanted to kiss her again, but maybe for the first time, I was man enough not to give in to taking what I wanted and fuck the consequences. She studied me, and I had no idea what she was thinking. I probably never had.

"Are you here to ask me to run away with you, Alex?"

I could have said yes, and meant it, at least in that moment. I could've told her *maybe*, to keep her hoping and waiting for me until I figured out how to be what she needed me to be, and that's what I wanted to come out of my mouth right then, believe me. Because I couldn't say yes, but I didn't want to give her up in case I never had a chance at anything so great again.

Instead, I gave her the truth that would last a lot longer than a minute. "No."

"I love you, Alex. But I love my husband, too. And you're his best friend, and I know you love him, and he loves you, and all of this is a huge fucking disastrous mess, but when you love someone, you want them to be happy. I want James to be happy. *I* want to be happy. I want you to be happy, too. But I don't want you to ever again touch me the way you did tonight." She drew in a long, shaky breath. "How does that make you feel?"

"Like shit," I said honestly.

"Good. I hope it breaks you. I hope the thought of never touching me again makes you want to die," Anne said.

Then she stepped away from me, though she let our fingers link and linger until I could no longer hold on to her, and I had to let her go.

41

"And I did," Alex said. "I let her go. Because I did love her, and I did want her to be happy."

I wasn't sure what to say, so I didn't say much of anything. He'd gotten up to pace while he talked, and now his hair was a rumpled mess from running his hands through it. His voice had cracked and broken several times during the story, and when he looked at me now, it was with red-rimmed eyes.

I tried hard to parse what he'd been trying to tell me. "Are you trying to tell me that George loved me enough to let me go?"

"I'm trying to say that *maybe* is a selfish fucking thing to do to someone. Sometimes, just because you love someone, that doesn't mean you're supposed to end up together. You learn more from the things that end," Alex said. "I don't know what that guy thought or felt. But when you really love someone, you want them to be happy, even if it's not with you. You deserve better than maybe."

"I know." I swallowed hard against a fresh lump in my throat. "It was a good reason not to try with anyone else, though."

"It was a reason. Not a good one." He looked fierce.

I held up my hands. "I know. I know. Believe me, I feel like an idiot enough."

"You don't have to give Niall another chance," Alex continued. "I don't know the guy. He could be a douchebag. But he apologized to you. Did you believe he meant it?"

I hesitated but nodded. "Yeah. I do. He apologized and asked me what he could do to make it up to me, yes, but then he said he thought he could never make me happy, because he's not into the submissive stuff."

"That's what he thinks. What do you think?"

"I think," I said quietly, "that I was happy when I was with him. And that I don't need cuffs and toys to be fulfilled. And I think it doesn't matter, because you can't make someone love you if they don't. I kept thinking that we were going to work things out, that maybe...shit. I've spent years clinging to a *maybe*, Alex. I'm not going to do it again."

"So you're just going to let him go?"

I hesitated. "Yes. What should I do, chase him? Beg? I don't do that. A fancy dinner and some flowers isn't going to make anything up to me. A dozen orgasms won't."

Alex grinned. "Yeah, but at least you'll have a full stomach and a satisfied—"

"Don't!" I held up a hand to fend him off.

"At least think about it. It's clearly making you miserable not to talk to him."

I nodded, solemn. "I will."

"And that other asshole," Alex added, cracking his knuckles. "Just tell me where to go to kick his ass."

"You're not going to kick anyone's ass!"

He grinned. "Maybe not myself. But I got a guy. You want me to get my guy?"

At that, I laughed. Then some more, until finally it sounded real. Alex left me alone in my office, where I logged in to my IM account and studied my contacts list, and the little rabbit there, for a very long time.

42

So you reach this moment where finally, finally, it all shifts, you find a way to open up your hands and let go. When what used to matter stops breaking you so fucking hard; when you accept that empty place in your heart will always be there because only one person can fill it, and you get up anyway because goddamn it, one person who does not love you enough should never make you incapable of moving forward.

I knew what I should feel and think. I should stop being stupid, holding on to what didn't serve me. No more maybes. No more clinging to the past. I had a small square of paper I'd printed out from the internet tacked up onto the bulletin board in my kitchen, one of those dumb forwards people pass around on Connex or emails.

In the end, only three things matter. How much you loved, how gently you lived and how gracefully you let go of that which is not meant for you.

I'd printed it out because of George. Because of how non-graceful I'd been about letting go of someone who was so clearly not and had never been meant for me. It had been meant as a reminder, the way the ink imbedded in the most tender part of my arm had been meant to remind me.

But maybe, at last, I thought, it was time to stop remembering. Maybe it was time to forget.

"You sure about this?" The shop where I'd had the first tattoo done was still there, but the artist placing the template over the piece on the inside of my wrist was new. He looked up at me through oddly delicate reading glasses totally incongruous with his shaved head and biker mustache. "This piece is still pretty sweet."

He meant the rabbit, of course. I nodded. I'd picked out something from the book and had him customize it—it was not unique, but that was okay. I wanted something I wouldn't necessarily want to look at every day, something bland. Something I would have to work to remember.

"Yeah. I'm sure." I lay back in the chair with my arm on the padded rest and closed my eyes.

The burn of the needle in my skin transported me. The pain, clean and somehow sweet, and all of it over too soon. I wanted it to go on and on forever, but nothing ever does.

"Hey," the guy said gently. "You okay? You're not going to faint or anything, are you? I have smelling salts."

I opened my eyes. "No. I'm okay."

I'd been weeping, and swiped at my eyes to clear them. I should've been more embarrassed. I looked at the spot on the inside of my arm where once I'd carried all I had left of him. The rabbit was gone, covered over by a red rose.

"What do you think?" the guy asked.

"It's great." I flexed, waiting for more pain, but it had faded for the moment.

My mother had thrown a fit about my getting the tattoo in the first place, warning me I would regret it, but I never had. That small rabbit had become as much a part of me as the color of my eyes or curve of my smile.

And now, it was gone.

43

"This is nice," my mother said and beamed at me from across the table. She'd put on her reading glasses to look at the menu, but she would order the same things she always did.

Then again, so would I. Breakfast, anytime. I wasn't even hungry. The toast would be like sawdust in my mouth. I'd eat it anyway so she didn't scold.

"So," my mother said when the silence between us had stretched on too long for her to be comfortable with it, which was about three and a half minutes. "What's happening with the guy?"

I gestured to the waitress and held up my iced tea. I'd considered asking for it to be redone, lime instead of lemon, but instead I asked for water. I didn't have the energy to bother. I looked at my mother. "Nothing is happening with the guy."

"He was so nice."

I frowned. "I guess that was the problem, huh? Too nice for me."

"Bite your tongue," my mother said. "You deserve a nice man, Elise Genevieve. Don't you dare try to tell me you don't."

I stared at her, remembering the woman who'd taught me to dance and not the one who judged my art. That was the mother I wanted. It made me sad.

"I just want to see you happy. Your sister, she won't ever be happy. It's my fault. For the longest time I thought she'd be my only one, you know, and until you two came along, she was. I should've made it easier for her. She felt replaced. She was high strung as a baby, colicky. The two of you came along and you were such...joys," my mom said almost in wonder, as though she could hardly believe it. "Such a pleasure, both of you. Never a tantrum between you. I shouldn't have played favorites."

If either my brother or I had ever been my mother's favorite, that was news to me.

My mother lifted her chin. "Jill felt displaced. Left out. She was so much older than the two of you. You and Evan had each other. You never seemed to need your sister. It affected her."

My memories of Jill had always involved screaming, the taking of toys. When we were older, Jill had bitched and moaned until she got her way, and my mother had almost always sided with her. Out of guilt?

"Ma, you can't blame yourself because you had two more kids. Jill's an adult. She really needs to get her shit together."

My mother nodded but looked sad. "She took your father's leaving a lot harder than you and your brother did."

"She was twenty-two years old. She didn't even live at home!"

"She was distraught and made bad choices," my mother continued as though I hadn't said a word. She leaned forward to lower her voice. "Not like a tattoo or anything like that, thank God."

I sighed. The rose was still tender. My mother shrugged. We stared each other down.

"Mom. Susan told me..."

"I know what Susan told you," my mother said. To my surprise, she didn't sniff disdainfully. She only shrugged then gave me a long, steady look. "Sometimes you have to be selfish, if you want to be happy."

I didn't know what to say to that, but I didn't have to say anything, because my mother kept talking.

"Susan has to do what makes her happy," my mother said after a minute. "Better that than making everyone around her miserable."

"Is that what you did?" I blurted and immediately wished I hadn't.

My mother didn't look surprised. She nodded. She wrapped her straw paper around and around her fingers until it broke.

"I tried," she said finally.

I didn't like it when my mom had grilled me about my private life; it seemed wrong and invasive to do so to her. What had happened between her and my dad was their business, and old news. Knowing the details of it wouldn't change anything that had happened since.

My mother reached to take my hand, just for a second, before letting it go. "You were happy with him, Elise."

"I was…at least, I tried to be." I managed a smile. "Things don't always work out."

My mother gave me a look. "So, keep trying."

"That's your advice?"

"Yes. That's my advice. I didn't, and look where it got me." My mother linked her fingers together, her hands in front of her on the table, but her gaze was steady and unapologetic. "It doesn't get your sister anywhere, either, does it?"

"Being unhappy isn't a good excuse for being a jerk to everyone, Ma."

My mother nodded. "Exactly. Or for being a jerk to a nice man who's clearly over the moon for you."

"So it's my fault? You don't even know what happened!"

"I'm just saying." My mother spread her fingers apart and

gave me a look of wide-eyed innocence. "When a chance to be happy slaps you in the face—"

"I know, I know. You don't turn it down."

"You can want what you want," my mother said with one lifted, lecturing finger that somehow didn't annoy me the way it usually did. "But you get nothing if you give up on it."

That wasn't how the saying had gone when I was a kid, but it made a lot of sense. I grabbed my mother's hand and squeezed. Maybe someday she'd tell me about the summer before my dad left. Maybe she wouldn't. It didn't matter—for the moment, she was the mother I'd always wanted, and what she'd said made a lot of sense.

44

You learn more from the things that end. You get what you work for. My mother and Alex had both been dead right when it came down to matters of the heart. I'd learned so much from everything that had ended. Esteban. Niall.

George.

I had one more message to send him, this time in the light of day instead of 3:00 a.m. No words. Just a picture of the inside of my wrist.

He would know what it meant, I told myself as I tried to angle it just right so that he'd be able to see that the rose was now covering up the other piece, that it wasn't some weird, random picture of some other tattoo I'd had done. It could've been anyone's arm, actually. But I knew he would know it was mine.

All the other times I'd sent messages off into the ether, knowing he would read and not answer them, that I was being the worst sort of fool, I'd always regretted it immediately. Never enough to keep from doing it again and again, but that's the thing about being an idiot in love. It feels terrible, but not doing it feels worse.

This time, the second I hit Send and the little message bubble popped up with my picture inside it, all I felt was relief. Light. I felt unburdened.

I finally, after so long, felt free.

The small *D* next to the message turned to an *R*. In the past I would've held my breath, imagining him all those miles away with his phone in his hand. Getting the message notification. Opening the app, reading the message. Then deleting it, unanswered.

This time, I was moving to swipe the conversation into oblivion, then close out of my account entirely. Delete the app itself. I was done with him and this, all of it. Finally letting go.

And of course, that's when he answered me.

Hey, how are you? Hope things are well.

I stared at it. My hands shook. I drew in a breath and then another, feeling a little faint and sick to my stomach. I waited to feel something other than roiling nausea—hope? Excitement? Joy? Relief? But all I felt was…nothing.

On his phone, the *D* next to his message to me would have become an *R*. He would know I read his reply. It went both ways. And maybe he was waiting, holding his breath, imagining me on the other side of our tenuous connection, wondering what I would say to him. Maybe he was doing a lot of things I would never know.

I did not type an answer.

I logged out of my account.

And then I deleted that app from my phone and called Niall, instead.

He didn't have to see me. Niall. He could've said no when I asked him. But he didn't, so there I was on his living room couch, uncertain what was going to happen but desperately willing to find out.

Niall came out of the kitchen with a glass of iced tea that he set on the coffee table in front of me without a word. I hadn't thought I wanted anything to drink until he put the glass there. The question was, did I want it because he'd given it to me, or did he give it to me because he knew I'd want it?

Did it matter?

"So," he said just as I opened my mouth to speak, not that I was at all sure of what I meant to say. He stopped, waiting for me to go on, but I shook my head. "So."

"Yeah."

I drank some iced tea, perfect the way I liked it, and put the glass back. I wiped my damp fingers on the hem of my dress.

Niall sighed and settled onto the armchair across from me, leaning forward to prop his elbows on his knees. His fingers linked. He looked over at me through the fringe of his too-long bangs.

"So," he said a third time. "Elise. I'm so fucking sorry."

"You don't have to apologize, Niall. I'm sorry."

We stared at each other. In two seconds I could've been across the room and in his arms, but I didn't move. And that was stupid, I thought. Cutting off my nose to spite my face. Stupid and proud and—

Niall was suddenly at my feet. Kneeling there, reaching for my hands. I was so taken aback I didn't know what to do, only that my heart was pounding, and I was a little short of breath.

"I miss you too fucking much," he said, pulling me closer. "Tell me you don't hate me."

I'd never thought he'd go to my knees for me. I could barely speak. "I don't hate you."

"Tell me," he said, kissing me, "that you want me."

"I want you, Niall." Could it really be so easy? Could someone who'd almost slipped through my fingers be within my grasp again—just like that?

Maybe that's the thing about real love…it comes easier than the kind you have to break yourself for.

Maybe Niall and I wouldn't have to break ourselves for each other. That was a maybe I could handle.

I took his face in my hands as his arms went around my waist. Our mouths met, ravenous and devouring.

He moved onto the couch. We were tangled, arms and legs. Rolling, him beneath and me on top. He ran his hands up to my hips and tugged at my panties; when they didn't come off fast enough, he tore them. He worked open his belt and zipper and was inside me a half a minute after that.

I cried his name as he thrust inside me. I tore at his shirt, one button pinging off the coffee table. I got my hands all over his chest, my nails leaving faint pink marks. I couldn't stop myself from pinching his nipples, though only for a second before I put my hands flat on his chest, instead.

His teeth raked my throat. His fingers wound in my hair, tangling and pulling and keeping me from moving. His lips moved on my skin. "Fuck me."

I rolled my hips, taking him in deep. I did as he asked, hard and harder. The slap of our flesh sent me higher and higher, and so did the way he said my name over and over, urging me on. When he slid his other hand between us so that his knuckles rubbed my clit with every thrust, I couldn't hold back anymore. I came with a low shout.

Niall bucked. I felt him throb inside me and let out a surprised cry—I'd heard of that happening, but had never actually *felt* a man come inside me. I rocked on him, grinding down, so close to another orgasm that all it took was the shift of his hand against me to send me over.

We slowed. He was still hard inside me when I stopped moving. Breathing hard, I turned my head a little until he released my hair and I could sit up. I traced the marks I'd left on his skin with my nails. I leaned to kiss his mouth. Niall put his arms around me, and I rolled to his side where I found a way to fit between him and the back of the couch with one leg thrown over his and my skirt tucked tight between my legs to keep from making a mess. I was too worn out to worry about it more than that.

I ran my hand over his chest to settle on his belly and kissed his shoulder. We were quiet. When I heard the pattern of his breathing shift into the steady drone of sleep, I hugged him, hard.

He stroked my hair. "I love you."

I pushed upward to look at his face. "I thought you were asleep."

"No. Almost. I could be." He blinked and yawned and shifted so we were a little less cramped.

I sat up, still tangled up with him. "Niall."

"Elise," he said with a small smile.

"We really should talk."

He groaned, but good-naturedly. We untangled ourselves and managed to get off the couch without breaking anything. I went to the bathroom to sponge off my skirt and came out to find him in the kitchen, puttering around with plates and toast and butter and hot water on for tea.

He turned when I came in. "Hungry?"

"Starving."

He put his arms around me and held me tight. We stayed that way, slightly rocking, until the kettle started whistling. I took plates from the cupboard while Niall filled the mugs with hot water and tea bags. We both took seats at the table, though he got up after a second and went to the cupboard to bring something back that he slid toward me.

"Cinnamon sugar," he said.

I started to cry.

"Hey, hey!" He protested, moving around to sit next to me and take my hand. "No crying. It's your favorite, you told me so yourself."

"That's why I'm crying! Because you remembered!"

Niall laughed and kissed me then wiped away my tears with his thumbs. He cupped my face with both his hands. "Of course I did."

I didn't tell him that there was no *of course* about it. I kissed him, instead. "I love you."

"I love you, too," Niall said, "even if you're a weirdo about cinnamon sugar."

"And other things?"

He smiled again. "Yeah. And other things."

We drank tea and ate our perfect cinnamon-sugared toast and yawned our way upstairs to brush our teeth and flop into his bed. I fell asleep almost instantly. When I woke, the sun was bright, and the bed was empty.

I followed the scent of coffee. He'd made pancakes. I paused in the doorway wearing the T-shirt I'd borrowed from him the night before, self-conscious about my hair and smudged eyeliner and the fact I'd told him that I loved him, even though he'd said it first this time. I took a seat in front of the platter of pancakes, and he sat across from me.

"I've been making a list for you," Niall said formally.

Both my eyebrows went up. I was no stranger to making lists, but I hadn't often been the recipient of one. "Okay."

He cleared his throat and pushed the legal pad toward me. On it were two columns written in his tightly angled handwriting. "Yes" and "No."

There was *yes* to blindfolding and hand tying. *No* in capital letters with an extra *no* added to it in the front and back to "butt stuff." I had to clap a hand over my mouth to stop myself from bursting into laughter. Beneath "Yes" he'd added "clothes" with a small asterisk, which marked a footnote at the bottom of the page and the words "for you."

That was it; I had to guffaw. "Niall. Oh, my God."

"I figured I needed to be up front with you," he said, still sort of stiffly. He'd poured us both coffee, but he hadn't eaten very much. "Read the rest of the list."

"Yes to toys that are not meant for the back door. Yes to calling me Mistress—" I paused, still reading. "I don't care to be called Mistress, but thank you. Yes to being made to clean the bathroom?"

He shrugged. "I hate a nasty bathroom anyway."

"Well, I'm on board with you taking it over, but not like a sex thing," I said carefully. "Unless that's your…thing?"

"I don't have a thing. I just thought if it was your thing…"

"It's not my thing," I said, and looked at his list again. "No to anything in public like wearing a collar or being ordered around like a dog. No to anything that hurts too much, like clothespins on the balls— For fuck's sake!"

"I don't think I'd like it," he told me.

That was it, I had to touch him. I pushed out of my chair and settled onto his lap with the list still in my hand. "I don't want to put clothespins on your balls, Niall."

I kissed him for that look of blatant relief. And for lots of other reasons. Mostly because of love, pure and unadulterated and overwhelming.

His arms went around me. He had to tip his face up for my kiss because of the way I'd straddled him. "This…this is okay, though. You on top."

"I like to be on top, baby." I nuzzled his throat for a second before looking into his eyes. "Thank you very much for this list. You have no idea what this means to me. And I also think you've been watching way too much porn. I mean, I don't have a problem with porn or watching it, in general, but I think maybe you've been looking at some stuff that's a little too scary."

"I did a category search," he admitted. "I couldn't get through a lot of it. I'm sorry."

"Don't be sorry. God," I said. "The fact you even tried at all makes me want to kiss you all over. It's really special, Niall. But what did I tell you about porn before?"

"That what you like and do isn't the way it is in porn?"

"I shouldn't be surprised you remembered that, but the fact you did makes me love you so much right now I can't even stand it." I held back a sniffle.

He squeezed me hard again. "Don't you cry!"

"I won't. Okay, maybe a little." I buried my face against the side of his neck and breathed away the tears. His hands soothed up and down my back. I snuggled closer. I thought about what Alex had told me, about the reasons why we fall in love. "Niall, listen…it's not about the things we do or don't do. It's about how you make me feel."

He shifted my weight a little, but kept holding me close. "How do I make you feel?"

"Taken care of." I didn't even have to think about the answer; the words came out at once. "Understood."

"I like to take care of you, Elise."

I leaned back to look into his eyes. "You make me feel known, Niall. Inside and out. Hey, hey, don't you cry now."

"If you get to," he said sternly, eyes glittering, "I get to."

But neither of us dissolved into tears. We both smiled. I brushed his hair out of his eyes and let my fingertips trace his eyebrows. I marveled at how beautiful his face had become to me. I leaned close; I breathed him in.

"I love you," I whispered again so I could taste the words. Sweet like honey. Rich like wine.

We kissed for a while until both of us were breathing fast, and he was hard. It took a small change of position, a little rearranging, and I was straddling him. The chair creaked as I rocked on him. I tightened my thighs against his hips when he tried to move.

Niall kissed the curve of my collarbone above my scooped

neckline, then gathered me close with his head pillowed on my chest for a few seconds before he looked up at me. "I don't know if I can be what you want."

"You're exactly what I want. Better than that, Niall, you're what I need." I shook my head. "I told you, it's not about the toys or the games. Why don't you believe me?"

"Because I don't think if you like something that much you should have to give it up," he said seriously. "And I think that if I don't give it to you, you'll want to find it from someone else."

It was a fair concern. "I don't get off on making someone do something they don't want to do. So, sure, would I like to push your boundaries and explore some territory you've never tried? Well, wouldn't you want to do that with me, if there was something you liked and I hadn't done?"

"I don't think there's anything I'd like that you haven't done," Niall said.

"And that bothers you."

He shifted me again, one hand gripping my knee. "Yeah. Of course it does."

"I can't change it."

"I know," he said.

"For me, what it all comes down to is really pretty simple. I like to be taken care of. Even better when I don't have to explain or repeat myself. The rest is only icing, Niall." I ran my finger over his lips until he opened his mouth, and then I kissed him.

"The icing is the best part," he said into my kiss.

I smiled. "Eat too much, and it will make you sick."

"But you've had that kind of relationship. Guys who did those things. That guy who broke your heart. He did that stuff, right? And the other one, the one you were with when we met." Niall frowned. "Hard to convince me that after having that, you'll settle for plain, old-fashioned sex."

"You made me a list," I reminded him. "You're willing to try some new things. What more could I possibly want?"

"Everything," Niall said.

I took his face in my hands until he looked into my eyes. "Listen to me, because I'm not going to repeat myself again. Four years ago I was crazy mad in love with a guy I loved too much. Three months ago, I was with a man I didn't love enough. But you, Niall…you, I love just right. I love being with you. Not just fucking you, but being with you. When I'm with you, I feel complete. Now stop your arguing and fretting and accept the fact that me and you, baby, we're like salt and pepper. Wherever we go, we're gonna be together."

"I do kind of like it when you talk to me like that," he said with a grin and a waggle of his brows. "All stern, like a pissed-off librarian."

I laughed. "Tell me you love me."

"I love you."

"Now make love to me," I told him.

Niall grinned and nodded, heat flaring in his gaze, and as with everything else he'd ever given me, his answer was just right. "Yes, ma'am."

★ ★ ★ ★ ★

If you enjoyed the character of Alex Kennedy, be sure to check out other stories from Megan Hart featuring this fan-favorite character:

TEMPTED
EVERYTHING CHANGES
NAKED

Available now.

author song list

I could write without music, but I'm so glad I don't have to. Below is a partial list of the songs I listened to while writing *Vanilla*. Please support the artists by buying their music.

"In My Veins" —Andrew Belle (featuring Erin McCarley)

"One Heart Missing" —Grace Potter and the Nocturnals

"Stars" —Grace Potter and the Nocturnals

"Wasting All These Tears" —Cassadee Pope

"Near to You" —A Fine Frenzy

"Use Somebody" —Laura Jansen

"Maybe" —Lily Kershaw

"Over You" —Ingrid Michaelson (featuring A Great Big World)

"Nicotine" —Panic! at the Disco

"1000 Times" —Sara Bareilles

"Silence & Scars" —Pop Evil

"Cry to Me" —Solomon Burke

"All of Me" —John Legend

"Maybe" —Ingrid Michaelson